# *Treasure of* DARKNESS

## S.W. HUBBARD

# DEDICATION

For the volunteers, staff, and guests of The
Community Soup Kitchen of Morristown
You inspire me.

# ACKNOWLEDGEMENTS

Many thanks to my fabulous editor, Ramona DeFelice Long, for her guidance and sharp eye. Thanks also to my fellow authors Pamela Hegarty, Roberta Isleib (aka Lucy Burdette) and Sandra Parshall for their support and encouragement.

As always, greatest thanks go to my husband, Kevin, patron of the arts extraordinaire.

# CHAPTER 1

Mr. Wainwright seems deader now than he did eight hours ago.

This morning, 79 Sycamore Avenue was brimming with every comfort of home: two Oriental carpets, a deep red leather Chesterfield sofa, a fifteen-piece set of Calphalon pots and pans, an antique armoire, twenty-seven Madame Alexander dolls, a baseball signed by Cal Ripken, and service for twelve of Royal Doulton "Harlow", one salad plate missing.

Now, as the winter sunlight fades, only hints of the lives lived here remain. Four worn spots on the hardwood floor mark where a favorite armchair stood next to a southern window—a nice place to read. A ghostly outline of the china cabinet on the flowered wallpaper is all that's left of countless Christmas dinners and Sunday brunches and baby showers hosted in the dining room. Little pencil marks mar the trim around the pantry door—measurement of a grandchild's growth.

There's no point getting morose about what I've done. This is why the Wainwright children hired me: to get rid of the things they grew up with but didn't love enough to keep. Another Man's Treasure Estate Sales—we do the dirty work families don't have the energy or the courage to do themselves.

I stand contemplating the empty living room. The only stick of furniture left in the house is a massive armoire. Ty staggers down the steps carrying an overloaded box.

"This is everything from upstairs, Audrey. We only got two boxes for the dump."

Not surprising. At a sale with so much good stuff, even the bad stuff sells. Somehow the unfashionably wide ties and scratched LP records here are more desirable than those at a trailer park tag sale.

I rush to open the front door for my assistant and he drops the box on the porch next to another with DUMP scrawled on the side. "That's it. Sweep up. Load the van. I got Ramon coming to help me with that armoire. We're ready to rock. Where's Jill?"

"Working on the pantry."

"Damn. I forgot the pantry. C'mon—let's get that shit hauled out."

We head back to the kitchen and find Jill on a step-ladder clearing the pantry from the top down.

"Want some oatmeal, Ty?" She sticks an open Quaker container under his nose.

"Aiyee!" Ty leaps back. "Worms! I hate them mothers."

Old people's houses are full of entomological wonders: pantry moths, hornets' nests, occupied spider webs, centipedes. Jill peers into the container. "Cool—the whole package is just pulsating with larva. Imagine living in your favorite food. I'd live in a Red Mango fro-yo. How about you, Audrey?"

Before I can answer, Ty tosses a garbage bag at her. He doesn't share Jill's passion for the insect world. "Throw that shit away or I ain't helping with the pantry. What about roaches? You know how I feel about them."

"Haven't seen any," Jill says. "The kitchen's pretty clean. It's just this top shelf that's full of old dusty stuff." She squints at the top of a can. "This pumpkin expired in 2005."

"Mrs. Wainwright must've died before she got a chance to bake the Thanksgiving pies," I say. "Their daughter told me the mother died a few years ago, and the father's been living here alone ever since."

"I guess he never purged any of his wife's baking supplies." Jill finishes tossing packages of hardened baking soda and desiccated raisins in the garbage bag and hops off the ladder to start checking cans from a lower shelf. "The expiration dates on these are all next year. All this soup and tuna and canned peaches must've been what the old guy was living on. These two shelves of cans can all be donated to the soup kitchen."

Ty whips out another garbage bag. "Aw, c'mon. Can't we just toss all this crap? I don't feel like goin' clear to the other side a town just to drop off some old cans."

"No! This is good food." Jill starts stacking cans neatly in boxes. "I just got an email from the soup kitchen yesterday saying support always drops off after the holidays, but they need food all year round. They're feeding two hundred people a day."

Jill has been volunteering there lately and is always on the lookout for donations.

Ty turns pleading eyes on me. "Can't we toss it, Audge? It'd save so much time."

"No-o-o—" Jill starts howling.

"I didn't ask you." Ty snaps open a trash bag. "After the dump, me and Ramon still have to go deliver that armoire. I'll never get outta here. I got plans."

"You volunteered to do the delivery. And you're getting paid extra for it. Do you know that the average person who eats at the soup kitchen experiences food insecurity—"

Ty turns on her. "Don't you lecture me on what it means to be poor. You think I never seen an empty refrigerator? You think I never went to bed hungry?"

We're all silent. Ty leans over and picks up the two stacked boxes. "I'll take the cans."

Although Ty has worked for me for over a year,

these awkward moments still crop up. Jill and I sometimes gloss over the details of Ty's childhood: the mom who died young, the dad in prison, the grandmother struggling to keep the family clothed and fed. Ty's cheerful strength in the present allows us to forget about his past. But Ty never forgets.

Ahead of me, I hear Ty's raised voice. "Hey! Whatchu doin' out here? Don't be makin' a mess for me to clean up."

I arrive on the front porch to find Ty looming over a much smaller man. Junk from one of the boxes destined for the dump is strewn all over the porch steps.

Stepping around Ty, I see the culprit: a skinny man with a stringy gray ponytail and a frayed backpack that crushes his bony shoulders. Harold.

Harold is a regular, a customer who's been at every single one of my sales since I started the business ten years ago. Well, every single sale within cycling distance of Palmyrton. Harold is usually first or second in line when we open a sale, arriving and departing on a rickety bicycle. He was here this morning, and after several hours of browsing, purchased a Big Ben alarm clock, an illustrated guide to the castles of the Loire Valley, and a lemon zester. He paid with seven worn and creased one-dollar bills pulled from a bulging wallet held together with duct tape and rubber bands. Jill has noticed this about Harold: he always pays with exact change. It's as if the man has never possessed crisp twenties from the bank that need to be broken, only an endless supply of frayed and creased ones, fives, and tens.

"What do you think you're doing, Harold? Now I gotta repack this box." Ty kicks the box labeled DUMP out of Harold's reach. "I don't have time for this foolishness. I got plans tonight, man."

Although Ty is twice his size and a third his age, Harold is undeterred. He scuttles after the box, diving into its depths.

"What are you after? There's nothing in there but broken up junk." Ty turns pleading eyes on me. "Make him stop, Audge."

"Harold, the sale is over. We're cleaning up here." I step toward him and try to tug the box away. For someone so frail looking, his grip is surprisingly tenacious.

"I need this." Harold's reply is muffled as his entire upper body is now inside the box. He finally emerges holding a long metal object about three feet long and six inches in diameter. We'd found it on Mr. Wainwright's basement tool bench. Although I'm pretty good at tool ID, I had no idea what this might be. Or if it was anything at all. But I've sold unidentified objects before, so I figured there was no harm in slapping a five-dollar price tag on it and seeing what would happen. No one bit, so now it's going to the dump.

"What is that thing anyway?"

"It's the column of a washing machine agitator."

Harold declares this with great confidence. I suppose it might be that, but I don't see any conclusive evidence.

"I can use this in case my washing machine breaks."

Ty squints his eyes. "But how do you know it will fit? And if your washer's not even broken, why...."

Harold tucks the thing under his arm. "I wanted to buy it earlier, but five dollars was too much."

"Well, you can have it for free now, but first you gotta help me pick up all this stuff you dumped outta the box."

The words have barely left his lips and I know I know Ty's made a terrible mistake. As quickly as he tosses the junk back in the box, Harold dives in to reclaim it.

"This lamp is useful." Harold holds it aloft.

Ty tries to yank it away. "No, it's busted—we

already tried it out."

"I could fix it," Harold says.

I see his eyes dart frantically back and forth and he takes a step closer to the other loaded box.

"No!" Ty and I shout in unison.

"Look, Harold, you can't carry any more stuff on your bicycle," I say in my most reasonable voice. The bike is propped against the porch railing, its basket weighed down with books, garden shears and a fierce looking statue—Montezuma, Tecumsuh? Harold has clearly made the rounds of other sales. Bulging saddlebags cover the rear wheel. It's a miracle the tires stay inflated.

Harold clutches his two newest finds to his chest like a father reunited with his lost children at the end of a war. "I can come back. Just leave the boxes on the porch for me."

"No way." Ty steps towards the packed box. "When we leave here, the place will be empty."

Harold pitches himself over the box. "There are useful things in here. It can't go to the dump."

"Audrey, where are the brooms?" Jill appears in the doorway. Her mascara has reached end-of-the-day smudginess and she looks like a perplexed raccoon. "What's going on? Hi, Harold."

Ty starts to explain. Harold interrupts. I try shouting over both of them. Somehow, Jill figures it out. She sits down cross-legged next to Harold and the box. "We're not taking this box to the dump, Harold." She speaks in the soothing sing-song I use on my dog Ethel during thunderstorms. "We're giving it to our friend, Sister Alice, the nun who helps people in Newark. Remember I told you about her?"

Harold nods. His hands are trembling but he listens intently.

Jill pulls a marker from her back pocket and scratches out DUMP. She starts printing S-I-S "Ty just mislabeled this box. Isn't that right, Ty?"

Ty scowls, but clearly Jill's ploy is the quickest way to free us from Harold. "Yeah, right. I musta had my wires crossed....or somethin'."

Gently, Jill lays her hand on Harold's. "Sister Alice could really use this lamp, Harold. She's helping a family who lost everything in a fire."

Slowly, Harold's pinscher grasp loosens. "You're sure both boxes are going to Sister Alice? Because there are some useful things in there."

"Absolutely. Right, Audrey?"

"Definitely. And you can keep the washing machine part."

Harold allows Jill to take the lamp and limps off the porch with the presumptive washing machine thingie. Resting it across the bike's basket, he wobbles away, the unbalanced bike sometimes swerving into oncoming traffic. We can hear horns blowing even after he's disappeared around the corner.

"Nice save, Jill!" I squeeze her shoulder and hand her a broom.

Ty shakes his head, grabs the dump boxes, and starts loading the van. As he returns for the boxes destined for the soup kitchen, a short, dark-haired man approaches the van. "Ramon!" Ty shouts. "Perfect timing, man. Come on in the house. I'll show you what we got."

Ramon nods shyly to Jill and me as he passes. He speaks very little English. He's one of the many Central American men who stand in front of the hardware store in town hoping that contractors will hire them for a day's work spreading mulch or hauling bricks. Whenever Ty needs an extra set of strong arms, he swings by there for help. He's used different men, but Ramon is his favorite because he's so hard-working, and they've figured out their own Spanglish communication.

Before long, they emerge carrying the unwieldy armoire.

"*Cuidado* on the steps, man," Ty advises.

Although Ramon is much shorter than Ty, his arms and shoulders are powerful and he holds his end up with no problem. I watch until they have the furniture safely in the van, then wave them off.

"When I get back, y'all better be ready to move," Ty calls out the window as he drives off.

"Ty's meeting Marcus in the city. They've got some big night planned," Jill tells me as we return to the kitchen to finish sweeping.

"Ah, to be young!"

"Oh, Audrey—thirty-three isn't old. You should go clubbing in the city." Jill twirls with her broom. "Meet some new people."

"I'm not the clubbing type." But Jill is right. I'm in a rut. I do need to meet some new people. "My friend Maura gets back from England soon. She'll drag me out to parties. Maybe I'll at least make it as far as Hoboken."

"Hoboken has too many frat boys. You'd do better in Williamsburg. It's arty."

"Been there, done that. I've sworn off depressed poets and starving musicians. What neighborhood do I go to for smart and well-adjusted?"

"Camelot."

"Narnia."

"Neverland."

Our laughter is interrupted by footsteps pounding down the hall. Seconds later, a woman skids into the kitchen.

"Oh, thank God you're still here!"

It's Martha, Mr. Wainwright's daughter, the one who hired me to organize the sale. Blonde hair disheveled, chest heaving, she brushes past me and flings open the pantry door.

She shrieks as if I'd just tossed her baby off a bridge. Eyes blazing, she turns on me. "Where are they?"

"Wha—?"

"The cans. Where are they?"

"Ty just took them to the soup kitchen. You said you wanted to donate—"

"Not any more. Call him! Get them back!"

I'm really not in the mood for this. Martha Wainwright had seemed like such a nice, reasonable client. Of course she wanted to donate anything useful that didn't sell. No, she didn't need to approve the donations. Now here she is going batshit on me.

"What's the problem?"

She reaches inside her large purse and pulls out a can of Progresso Minestrone. The pop top has been pulled. She thrusts it toward me.

Inside is a tightly coiled wad of cash.

# CHAPTER 2

"Wait...how in the world...?"

"My dad just barely popped the top, emptied the can, slipped the money in and soldered it shut. It looked like an unopened can," Martha explains. "My brother Bob took some cans from the pantry when we were here on Monday. Today, he decided to have minestrone for lunch and found this. Now you see – I have to get all the cans back."

Old people hide money all the time, but I must say, soldering open cans shut again demonstrates exceptional persistence. I guess that explains the professional grade soldering iron we found on the tool bench.

I call Ty but he doesn't answer. "He's delivering some heavy furniture. He's probably carrying it in right now and can't pick up. He'll call right back when he sees the missed call."

"Call the soup kitchen where he took them," Martha demands.

"I think they're closed by now, but I'll try," Jill says. We watch as she shakes her head. "I'm getting the voicemail. They won't be open until tomorrow."

Martha kicks the pantry door and the dustpan hanging on the inside crashes to the floor. "I have to get those cans back."

I'm getting a little annoyed now. So the old man hid some money in a can. Who's to say any of the others were loaded?

Jill speaks as if reading my thoughts. "He might've made one secret hiding place just to safely keep a little cash around the house."

Martha waves the can at her, her voice escalating like an American Idol contestant destined for elimination. "These are hundred dollar bills. One hundred of them."

I can see Jill struggling with the math and I help her out. "Ten thousand dollars. Not household petty cash. But how can you be sure all the cans held money?"

"The beef vegetable that my brother took had another ten thousand, but not the pineapple. There must've been something about those Progresso cans that made them easy to close up again. How many soup cans were in the pantry?"

Jill and I exchange glances. "Fifteen?" Jill finally offers.

"One hundred and fifty thousand dollars!" Martha is spinning around the empty kitchen of her childhood, a dervish of despair. All I can think is that it's a good thing we sold the set of carving knives that used to sit on the counter.

"What was your father's financial position?" I ask. "Could he really have had $150,000 in cash that you and your brother weren't aware of?"

"My father had a long history of claiming to be broke, then producing money when it suited his purposes. This little scheme is just what I'd expect from him." Martha grabs my arm. "Why hasn't your man called back? I have to *do* something. Where is this soup kitchen place? I'll get the police and make them open it up."

I have no idea if the police will be sympathetic to her plight, but I'm not about to argue. Worst case scenario, she'll have to wait until tomorrow morning. Really, the cans are just as safe in the locked soup kitchen pantry as they are here. "152 Patriot Street. The entrance is in the back of the Episcopal church."

Martha grabs her five-figure minestrone and storms out the door.

"You still messin' around in here? I thought you'd be done by now."

"Ty! You're back already?"

"You'll never believe what happened," Jill begins.

"Tell me in the van. I'm ahead of schedule and I want to stay that way."

I glance at the clock on the stove. Ty has delivered the armoire, dropped off the cans, and gone to the dump in an impossibly brief time. An uneasy feeling rises. "How did you make such good time? Traffic was light?"

"Hell, no. Traffic was all messed up downtown. Big accident in the Green. You know how all the streets around the soup kitchen are one-way? I coulda been stuck there for an hour tryin' to drive up to the soup kitchen. So I gave Ramon an extra ten bucks and dropped him on the corner of Pine so he could walk them over to Patriot."

"No!" Jill's eyes widen and her hand comes up to her mouth.

"What's the big deal? It's only two blocks. Ramon's strong."

"Ty, did he understand that he had to take them to the soup kitchen?" Ramon's English is pretty sketchy and he frequently smiles and nods even when he has no idea what we've just said.

Ty shrugs. "He eats there all the time, so I know he knows where it is. I asked him would he drop them off and he said, 'I take them'."

This is not the reassurance I'm seeking. " 'I take them'? Did he mean 'I take them there' or 'I take them myself'?" My normal alto is ascending into soprano range.

Ty scowls at Jill and me in turn. "What difference does it make? You wanted to give the food to poor people. Shit, ain't nobody poorer than Ramon. Dude don't even have his own bed."

Jill has her shoulders hunched up around her ears. I'm taking deep breaths.

Ty's eyebrows draw down. He knows Jill's "braced for trouble" expression. He knows my "I'm counting to ten" expression. What he can't figure out is what he did to provoke them. "What's the big deal? We talkin' about a few cans of soup goin' to Ramon and his friends."

My sweaty palms slip against the kitchen counter. "No, Ty. We're talking about $150,000 donation to the Honduran immigrant community."

I have tuned out the high-pitched hum of Jill explaining our predicament to Ty. All I register is Ty's occasional, "Well, how the hell was I supposed to know?"

Remain calm. It's important to remain calm. Maybe Ramon actually delivered the boxes and they're at the soup kitchen right now. If that's the case, we don't have a problem. When Martha Wainwright signed her contract with Another Man's Treasure, she chose the option that all unsold usable items should be donated to a registered charity from which she would receive a receipt for her tax purposes. Even if the soup kitchen immediately gave the cans to their hungry guests, AMT is in the clear.

On the other hand, maybe Ramon and ten of his undocumented friends are ready to pop open a Progresso feast in the apartment they all share. And when they see what's in the cans, hop a plane for Managua, never to be seen again. In that case, not only is Martha's money gone, but I'm on the hook for violating the terms of our contract. I feel a tremor emanating from my gut to my fingertips. It's my fault for never explaining to Ty that giving usable unsold items to any random poor person is not the same as giving them to a registered charity.

Suddenly I'm aware of silence. Clearly, Ty and Jill think I should do something to stop this nervous breakdown in progress. *I* think I should do something. But what?

"Um...should we call the police?" Jill suggests.

"No way!" Ty springs up from his slouch against the wall. "I'm not snitchin' on Ramon."

"It wouldn't be snitching. He didn't commit a crime. We just need help getting the cans back," I explain.

"The man is il-*le*-gal. He hates the cops worse than I do. They're just looking for an excuse to ship his ass back to South America."

"Central," Jill corrects.

Ty turns on Jill, looming over her. "Why you always got to do that? Why you always have to find some little way to show you're smarter than me? You *think* you're smarter."

"I was just saying. You don't always have to be so touchy."

"I'm not—"

"Guys, please! Not now. We need to figure this out." I close my eyes to impose calm logic on my seething brain. "Ty, where does Ramon live?"

"I don't know his address. When I need him, I look for him by the hardware store."

"The men aren't there at night. Where does he eat? Where does he sleep? You said he didn't have his own bed. What did you mean by that?"

"All I know is a bunch of the Spanish guys live together in one house. I only understand half of what he tells me. There's *diez hombres* and only *seis camas*. *Camas* are beds. So they gotta share. When one's awake, the other sleeps. But I don't know where the house is."

"Does he have a phone?"

"Sometimes. Verizon always shuttin' it down when

he can't pay his bill. Right now, he's got no service."

"Maybe Detective Coughlin could help," Jill offers.

Ty freezes. So do I. Tension radiates between us like static electricity.

"I'm outta here." Ty pivots and heads for the door.

I don't try to stop him. He doesn't like Sean Coughlin. Doesn't want to encounter him. Doesn't want to be on the other end of Coughlin's penetrating stare. Doesn't want to fall under suspicion again. Can't say I blame him. I'm not sure I want to see Sean Coughlin either. Not quite two months have passed since I told him I wasn't ready yet. Ready for what, I'm not sure. There have been times when I've thought of him, I admit that. Christmas Day...New Year's Eve...every long and lonely Sunday. But I haven't called. Haven't even come close.

"Get back here, Ty," Jill says. "You can't abandon Audrey now. It's time to get over all that."

All that: murder, attempted murder, drug dealing. Yes, "all that" has resulted in my having one of Palmyrton's finest on my speed dial. But "all that" is over now. I've been given my fifteen minutes of grieving. Time to move on. Slowly I pull out my phone, scroll through my contacts, and stare at the name Sean Coughlin.

A slammed front door is the last we hear of Ty. Jill is watching me. "Call him."

I lift my finger and drop it on the screen. The deed is done.

"Coughlin," the phone barks in my ear. Before I can answer, the voice continues, suddenly softer. "Oh! Audrey! Hey...just hang on a minute, okay?" There's noise and voices in the background, dimming from loud to negligible. Then Sean speaks again. "Hi. How are you?"

Oh, I don't like this. I don't like the two-syllable way he says hi. I don't like the emphasis on "are". I fight the urge to press END.

"Hi...Sean." His first name trips me up. I'm still more used to calling him Coughlin. "I'm fine. Uh, so the reason I'm calling is...I'm finishing up a sale, and we have a kind of an odd problem here..."

"Where are you?" The voice is now law enforcement high alert. "I'll be right there."

"Relax, Sean. It's nothing dangerous." I explain the situation and trail off with, "We're not sure if he took them to the soup kitchen or not. Any idea what we can do to get the cans back?"

"Sit tight. I have some contacts. I'll handle this." He hangs up.

*I'll handle this.* How is it that I find Sean's remark simultaneously reassuring and irritating? Always in charge, that's Sean Coughlin.

Twenty minutes later, Sean arrives at the Wainwrights' house. As soon as he walks in, the kitchen shrinks. I haven't seen him since right before Thanksgiving, and I've forgotten how big he is.

He smiles at me without quite meeting my eyes. "How've you been?"

"Fine, up until an hour ago." I know I should make some polite chit-chat, but I'm too tense. "Were you able to find out anything from the soup kitchen?"

"I talked to the maintenance man. He was there until six cleaning, then locked up. No donations came in."

Jill and I moan in unison. "That means we have to find Ramon," I say.

"I know where to look," Sean says. "You two come with me to ID him."

I toss Jill my keys. "Drive my car to your house, Jill. I'll walk over and get it in the morning. There's no need for your night to be ruined too."

"Oh, Audrey—"

Even though I really don't want to be alone with Sean, I insist that Jill leave. After all, if Ty isn't coming, what's the point of having Jill along? She doesn't know Ramon any better than I do. I follow Sean out to an unmarked police car parked in the Wainwrights' driveway. He opens the passenger door for me as if he's taking me to a country club dance, not a tour of Palmyrton's sketchiest neighborhood. The driver's seat is pushed back as far as it will go to accommodate Sean's large frame, and he drives sprawled back against the headrest, only one hand on the wheel. I have to twist in my seat to see his face slightly behind me.

"The immigrant community is centered in The Bottoms, the neighborhood along the Whippany River. You know it?"

"Of course I've driven through. But there's not much call for estate sales there."

Sean snorts. "Yeah, someone dies in The Bottoms, the neighbors come and steal all his stuff."

It's cracks like that that bother me about Sean. I think he's too cynical. He thinks I'm naïve and painfully politically correct. How can we ever get past that?

Sean notices that I didn't laugh at his joke. "Relax, Audrey. Most of the folks who live in the neighborhood are hard workers. They came here looking for a better life for their families. I know that. Hell, that's why my grandfather came here from Ireland. But a lot of the guys come without their wives and kids. They're lonely at night and they drink too much and they're crammed into apartments too small to hold them all. So they hang out on the corners and trouble follows. That's why I didn't want you coming over here by yourself."

See, just when I'm ready to dismiss him as a jerk he says something that comes within spitting distance of sensitivity, and I'm forced to reconsider. "Ramon is a nice guy, but yeah—I wouldn't want to roam around looking for him by myself."

We've left the stylish restaurants and stores of downtown Palmyrton and passed through the

Brighton Park neighborhood of quaint older homes
surrounding the duck pond and playground. Now
Findlay Avenue descends a long hill and the stores
have signs in English and Spanish. *Comidas
Salvadorenos. Pollo Pucalor. Sonia's House of Beauty.*
We leave the main commercial strip and turn onto a
more residential street. Some of the houses are
painted in brighter colors than you'd find on the street
where I grew up. Some haven't been painted in years.
Despite the freezing temperature, a dark-haired
woman pushes a dozing baby in a stroller. His little
head bobs every time she hits a rut in the uneven
sidewalk. How would I even begin to find Ramon here?

Sean glances at me from the corner of his eye.
"You're tough, but there's no need to take chances. I
know some guys. They'll talk to me."

"Okay. But please—don't threaten anyone. Poor
Ramon didn't do anything wrong. I'm not mad that he
kept the soup."

There's a movement in Sean's face that might be a
smile or might be a grimace. "You may find this hard
to believe, Audrey, but I don't conduct all
investigations by knocking heads together."

So now I've succeeded in insulting someone who's
doing me a favor. A really big favor. "I didn't mean—"

But before I can finish, Sean has abruptly pulled the
car over to the curb. Two Hispanic men are walking
down the street. They smile when he gets out of the
car and exchange high fives. They're wearing thick
hooded sweatshirts and work gloves, just like the guys
who hang with Ramon in front of the hardware store.
After some chit-chat, I can tell Sean is asking them
something, and I roll down my window a bit to listen.
The two men talk to each other in rapid-fire Spanish
then the older of the two faces Sean and continues
nattering along. Sean nods and asks another question
in Spanish that's slower and less musical, but
obviously effective since the men start pointing and

gesturing as they give directions. I allow myself a glimmer of optimism.

"You speak Spanish? I'm impressed," I say when Sean gets back in the car.

"I understand Spanish. I speak Spanglish. And I can't discuss anything that's going to happen tomorrow because I can't conjugate verbs in the future tense."

"You seem to make yourself understood. They told you where Ramon lives?"

"Two family house with a yellow door on Cherry Street."

This news ignites both excitement and anxiety. If we really find Ramon, will Sean be able to get the cans back with no conflict? Then I remember what Ty said. Ramon is here illegally. He lives in fear of being deported. Even if he's opened the cans, he's in no position to argue with Sean and me.

Sean drives the few short blocks to Cherry Street and finds the house with the yellow door. It's not a cheerful yellow. More like a "this is the only paint we've got, so yellow it is" sort of color. The steps leading to the door slope strongly to the right, and a broken bottle glistens in the light leaking from behind a sheet pinned to the front window. Despite the cold, three guys sit on overturned milk crates on the small front porch watching our arrival.

I can tell from the look on Sean's face that he's not sure what to do with me. Is it more dangerous to leave me alone in the car or worse to bring me inside a house full of single men who might be really pissed about losing that money? I make the decision for him by jumping out of the car. Hopefully my presence will keep poor Ramon from panicking. When we get to the porch, Sean says, "*Buscaramos* Ramon."

The three young men stare at us for several long moments. Then the oldest of them shrugs and nods toward the door. It's unlocked, and Sean pushes it open. He holds my elbow as we enter.

The front hall is narrow and dark with no carpet on the battered wood floor. The air smells of fried food and sweat and mildew. Straight ahead I can barely see into a kitchen with a sink overflowing with dishes. To our right is what should be the living room, but it's filled with four beds, all occupied by sleeping men. One snores loudly.

"Let's go in the kitchen," I whisper. "Maybe the soup is in there."

My heart swells with anticipation. I imagine what I want to happen. The boxes will be right there. We can take them and be on our way. I'll send Ty over tomorrow with a load of real groceries and Ramon will never know what he missed.

But that's not what unfolds. The kitchen is tiny with just a sink, fridge and stove. There aren't even any cabinets, just a rickety set of metal shelves, which hold some grimy pots and dishes and a bag of rice. There's no place to store—or hide—anything in here.

We can see into the dining room—a card table, four folding chairs and two more occupied beds.

Sean strides into the dining room, and I trail behind. This feels so invasive. Even though the guy on the porch told us we could go in, I feel like we're burglars.

"You see your man?"

A light fixture dangles from the ceiling as if someone pulled on the chain once too often. The dim light illuminates two mops of dark hair, two brown-skinned faces, two bodies covered by ratty blankets. How can I tell?

Sean pulls out a small flashlight and shines its bright beam on each face. Amazingly, they don't wake. They must be too exhausted from a day of cleaning gutters or hauling shingles up a ladder. I shake my head, and we continue into the living room.

The snoring man's mouth is wide open, revealing

several missing teeth. Definitely not Ramon. I approach a man who's sleeping on his side, curled into a ball with a faded blue and yellow quilt pulled up to his eyes. This might be Ramon, if only I could see his face better. I lean over him as Sean shines the light on his face. Our heads are about a foot apart when his eyes open. I'm startled, but he's terrified. The man pulls back, struggling out of the quilt to escape. He lets out a strangled cry in Spanish, maybe a curse, maybe a prayer. Has he been awakened like this before, back in his homeland, by a soldier or a drug lord?

"I'm sorry," I cry. "It's okay."

Now all the men are awake, and Sean is showing his badge and speaking in Spanish that's slower than theirs, but which they all seem to understand. *Buscaramos Ramon* are the only words I can pick out of the stream. Sean is shaking his head and making calming gestures with his hands, so I assume he's assuring them that no one is in trouble and no one is getting deported. I notice the guys keep glancing toward the snoring guy with the missing teeth. He's older than the others, with a lined face and hair that's streaked with gray.

"*Se llama* Ramon?" Sean asks him.

"*Si.*"

I feel the anticipation fizzle out of me as I meet Sean's eye.

I shake my head. "Let's go, Sean. We found *a* Ramon. We didn't find *the* Ramon."

# CHAPTER 3

Back in the car, I let my head slump against the window. What a freakin' mess! How can I explain what happened to Martha Wainwright? If the damn cans had contained soup, she would never have known or cared that Ty gave them to some poor illegal immigrant. Now his act—part laziness, part generosity—looks like grand larceny. I can't have my customers suspecting me of thievery—my entire business rests on my reputation for honesty.

Sean slides into the driver's seat. "Don't worry. Like I said, we'll keep looking tomorrow." He makes a motion to pat my hand, which is resting on my thigh, but pulls back and instead delivers an awkward brush to my shoulder.

He coughs. "Wanna grab some dinner?"

This is the moment I've been dreading. How can I say no when Sean has dropped everything to help me find Ramon? He has already mapped out a plan to be outside the hardware store—the one place we know Ramon hangs out–at 7:00 AM tomorrow morning to continue the search. But I know this dinner won't just be a friendly snack. It'll be the beginning of a thing. And a thing leads to expectations. And expectations lead to misunderstandings and disappointments and, and…. And I'm just not ready. Not after I laid my heart out for Cal and had it chopped to pieces. His deception and his affection and his sacrifice, all tangled together and never unknotted. So I have my excuse all ready.

"Gee, I'd love to. But I've got to get home to feed Ethel. No one else can do it. She's been very skittish since she got lost."

"I knew you were going to say that." Sean turns in the direction of my condo. "That's why I'm taking you to a dog-friendly place. Ethel can come with us. We'll just swing by your place and get her."

There are plenty of sidewalk cafes in Palmyrton where you can bring your dog when the weather is nice. But none of those are open in January. "What kind of place lets you bring a dog inside?"

"Blue Monday. You ever been there?"

"Isn't that the place whose neon sign you can see from the train if you're going into the city? I wouldn't even know how to drive there."

"Oh, it's off the beaten track, for sure. Willard Street—a dead end that backs up to the railroad tracks. Kind of a cop hangout. And the K-9 guys all bring their dogs."

"Isn't that against the health code or something?"

"Sure, but Code Enforcement hangs there too."

See, this is what bugs me about Sean Coughlin. He's always one jump ahead, anticipating everyone's next move. I guess that's what makes him a good cop. But I'm not some perp he's trying to outsmart, and I don't appreciate being backed into a corner.

"I don't know, Sean. I—"

I notice his hands tighten on the steering wheel. He's staring intently at the road, as if driving down a suburban residential street requires the same level of concentration as driving through Kabul. A little muscle under his right eye twitches madly. That happens when he's trying to control himself. It bothers me that I know this intimate detail.

So, now I feel bad. Why can't I summon my inner bitch and just blow him off? Thank you very much. I have other plans tonight. Catch up with you some other time. But no. I feel myself caving.

"Okay, sure. I guess it will do Ethel good to get out and socialize with some German Shepherds."

Immediately he starts steering with just one hand. The muscle stops twitching. "You'll thank me for this, Audrey. Once you have your first Blue Burger, you'll be hooked for life."

Hooked for life. This is definitely turning into a thing.

Unlike me, Ethel is quite elated at the prospect of dining out. When I grab her leash and ask if she wants to go for a ride in the car, she practically flattens me in her haste to get out the door. But when we reach the curb and she realizes the car is not our car and there's an unfamiliar man at the wheel, she skids to a halt and her hackles go up. She'll refuse to get in the car. I'm off the hook. Sean will understand that I can't traumatize my dog.

He gets out of the car and Ethel rears back. A low growl rumbles from somewhere deep inside her.

"Easy, Ethel," I warn. I want her to rescue me, but I don't want her to go so far as to snap at him.

Sean stays silent and extends his hand. I see Ethel's nostril twitch. She steps a little closer to get a better sniff. Slowly, her tail begins to rotate.

He crouches down and scratches behind her ears. Ethel leaps into his arms.

So much for doggie trauma. Clearly we're going out to dinner.

The Blue Monday began life, maybe around World War II, as a modest frame house. Over the years various additions, porches, and extensions have sprouted from the core, creating an architect's nightmare. To add insult to injury, the whole monstrosity is painted Smurf blue. Coughlin holds open the door for Ethel and me as if he's ushering us into The Four Seasons. We're greeted by a wall of sound: The Allman Brothers wailing from the juke box, scores of guys yelling at three TVs playing three different games, and an occasional bark.

Drawn by the scent of sizzling burger grease, Ethel forges into the crowd. People call out greetings to Sean and he works his way through the bar slapping shoulders and shaking hands. As my eyes adjust to the gloom, I realize there are a few women in here too. Is it my imagination that they're checking me out?

The leash goes slack in my hand as Ethel comes to a dead stop, nose-to-nose with a German Shepherd in a police vest. Ethel's adoption papers from the pound say she is a "shepherd mix" but when I see her next to a full-blooded shepherd, I realize how much smaller and sleeker she is, despite the similarity in color. The two dogs are on high alert until a beefy guy at the bar speaks one word: "Thor." Immediately the police dog turns his back on Ethel and lies down at his handler's feet. As an obedience school drop-out, Ethel wants to keep investigating, but I drag her to a booth in the corner. Before I even have my jacket off, a waitress drops off a paper plate of broken burgers under the table and two draft beers on top.

"Is that okay?" Coughlin asks. "Would you rather have wine or something?"

As if the Blue Monday has a list of Argentine Malbecs and Oregon Pinots. I raise my mug in a toast and take a big swig. Whatever it contains, I need it after all that's happened today.

Sean drinks too. Then we set our mugs on the table and look at each other. After all his efforts to get me to go out with him, Coughlin's got the same look on his face that Ethel had on the one occasion that she actually managed to catch a squirrel.

This is his show. I'm not the one shopping for a relationship, so I feel no need to help him out.

"So...how's your dad?" he finally manages.

"Getting better. His left hand is weak from the stroke and he still can't drive, so he's on leave from teaching at Rutgers. But he can walk all around town from his new apartment. He's started an after school chess club for the kids at the Rosa Parks Center."

"Parks is a good place. Sometimes I coach basketball there."

"That's nice."

I sit with my hands folded primly well away from Sean's huge mitts. I know I'm being difficult. I could ask him about his family, ask him about coaching basketball, volley the conversational ball back to him. But I don't. The best way to get him to give up on me is to make him realize we're just not right for each other. For one thing, he's just so damn big! Big hands. Big neck. Big biceps. Not my type at all. I struggle to keep to keep the image of Cal's long-fingered hands and lithe torso out of my mind's eye. For another thing, Sean and I have nothing in common. I'm a bleeding-heart, math-nerd only child obsessed with art and antiques. He's a law and order, weight-lifting sports nut related by blood or marriage to half of Palmer County. Where can we go with that?

The waitress sets down our bleu cheese burgers and I realize how truly ravenous I am. And Sean's right—this is an uncommonly good burger.

He points at me with a French fry. "Did you ever see the episode of *Antiques Roadshow* where the wife hauls the big, garish vase out to the curb and the husband drags it back and they're on TV fighting like Ali and Frazier?"

"And the thing's butt ugly, so you totally understand why the wife wants it gone..."

"And the husband keeps insisting it's his great grandmother's Victorian vase worth five hundred bucks 'cause he looked it up on eBay."

"And the dealer shakes his head."

"And you feel bad for the guy 'cause the wife is such a bitch..."

"And then the dealer says it's not Victorian, it's early Qing Dynasty. And it's worth two hundred grand!"

We burst into laughter.

"You watch *Antiques Roadshow?*" I ask.

Sean cocks an eyebrow. "What? You think the TVs of knucklehead cops don't get PBS?"

Busted! I slip Ethel a French fry to cover my embarrassment.

"I watch with my Great Aunt Moira every Sunday that I'm not working. She loves it." Sean doesn't hold a grudge. "You ever save something from the dump like that?"

"All the time." So I tell him about Mid-Century Modern coffee table that came out of a retired dentist's rec room covered with water rings and ended up auctioning for fifty-grand.

And then he tells me about Aunt Moira's collection of antique Waterford that he and his brothers nearly destroyed playing whiffle ball in the house.

Before I know it, the waitress is handing Sean the check saying table service has ended for the night and we'll have to move to the bar. It's 11:30.

I look under the table. Ethel is sound asleep. She staggers up and looks around blearily, as puzzled as I am to find herself still here.

"Guess we better get going," Sean says, waving off my attempt to split the check.

Out in the car, awkwardness descends again as I frantically calculate how to fend off the goodnight kiss and any expectation that he'll come in for the proverbial nightcap. Sean also seems to be lost in thought as he drives toward my condo. Probably planning his offensive.

After two blocks of silence, he speaks. "Look, Audrey...I gotta ask you this, but don't take it the wrong way, okay?"

Uh-oh. Here it comes.

"I'm going to go to the corner by the hardware store tomorrow morning to look for Ramon. But I need to know—is there any possibility that your man Griggs knew—"

I flip from anxiety to outrage. "No! Can't you get past this constant suspicion of Ty? You were wrong last fall when you suspected him of being involved when I was attacked. You're wrong now."

"You're twisting my words before they're even out of my mouth," The easy charm has disappeared from his voice. "Look, Audrey, it's my job to consider all the angles. Isn't it possible that Griggs discovered the cans didn't contain soup while you were working in the house? I mean, anyone would be tempted to keep a few under circumstances like that."

I take a deep breath. Coughlin has accused me of being blinded by emotion when I deal with Ty, and maybe sometimes I am. But this isn't one of those times. "I'm going to explain it to you one more time," I say in the tone I used to use when I tutored floundering UVA athletes in the intricacies of multiplying fractions. "Ty was not working in the kitchen at any point during the day. He managed the second floor during the sale. He only came into the kitchen at the end, to haul stuff out to the truck. I saw him toss the box into the back of the truck and drive off. He had no opportunity to examine those cans."

Sean's lips press into a hard line. "What about this client of yours? Is she legit? She came back to the house with money in a can. How do you know she's not setting you up?"

"Setting me up for what? If we had really given the cans to the soup kitchen, I wouldn't be obligated to get them back for her. She'd be on her own." I pull my phone from my pocket. "She called me four times while we were eating. She's positive there's more money in those other cans."

"Have you ever had a case like this before, with cash hidden in cans?"

"Not in cans, but we find money squirreled away all over houses all the time. I've explained to Jill and Ty how important it is that we always turn it over to the owners. A reputation for honesty is what sells my business. Ninety five percent of the time, the owners had no idea the cash was there and they're grateful and impressed that we handed it over."

"And the other five percent?"

"They're people who have intentionally set up a test to see if we'll clear the bar. They put a few bills in a Tupperware container or between the pages of a book just to catch us cheating."

Coughlin glances at me. "How can you be sure of that?"

"They have a funny look on their faces when I give it back. Almost like they're disappointed that they were wrong about human nature."

Coughlin glides up to stop sign and twists sideways to face me. "And have you ever used that test on your staff?"

"Yes. But I hide the cash much more artfully than my clients do. And Jill and Ty have passed every time. I trust them completely."

Coughlin pulls into traffic without a word. But the mood in the car has shifted a bit. Maybe I've finally proven I'm not the naïve chump he takes me for.

He parks in front of my condo. Recognizing home, Ethel launches herself into the front seat, stomping on my beer-swollen bladder and waving her tail in Coughlin's face. God bless her.

"Let me get this crazy mutt out of your way!" I spring the passenger door open and prepare to dash.

Coughlin's hand comes down on my shoulder. "I'll call you in morning after I check out the corner by the hardware." His index finger brushes a tiny patch of skin between my hairline and coat collar. "Dinner was fun."

I shiver. Because it's January, right? I follow Ethel out onto the sidewalk, then poke my head back into Coughlin's car.

"Thank you, Sean. For everything."

He waits at the curb until Ethel and I are safely inside. I hear a little farewell toot.

The dog sits at my feet with her head tilted and her ears pricked.

"Don't give me that look, Ethel. I don't know. I just don't know."

# CHAPTER 4

I wake up on Sunday morning to four emails from my dad: 7:12, 7:43, 7:49, 8:17. Only the first one has a subject line—breakfast. Shit. I forgot I promised I'd take him to the Athenian Diner. I hadn't planned on going out on Saturday night, so I thought I could get there early enough to suit him. I don't need to read the emails to know what they say: What time are you coming? Aren't you awake yet? Should I just eat at home? Never mind the diner, I've eaten.

My father knows that emails don't arouse a sleeping daughter, but he sends them anyway. If he really wanted to go to the diner, he could've called to wake me. But Dad has always hated the phone, and since his speech is still slightly slurred from the stroke, phone conversations are one long string of "Huh? What? Baton? Barcode? Oh, bacon!" So I can't really blame him for wanting to avoid that frustration. Still, he could manage, "Hello, wake up." But email is his medium, so email is what we use.

I email, "On my way. Be there in 10," then leap out of bed and into the closest pair of jeans. There's really no need to look good at the Athenian. Clear out on Route 10, it attracts a mixed crowd of early-bird old-timers and up-all-night twentysomethings, so I'm unlikely to run into anyone I know. Ethel whines by the door.

"Don't worry. You're coming too. Dad will complain

less if you're there." Then I remember. My car isn't
here. I have to walk over to Jill's house to get it. And
the events of yesterday come rushing back. The lost
soup cans. The strangely enjoyable dinner with Sean.
The four calls from my client that I still haven't
answered. I'm not sure which causes more turmoil in
my gut.

I retrieve my car and arrive even later than
promised at Dad's place. Turns out I don't need Ethel
to act as a guard dog. My father is unaccountably
chipper as he lets us into his apartment.

"Good morning, ladies!"

I listen closely for sarcasm but hear none.
Sometimes good morning is just good morning. He pets
Ethel, but doesn't touch me. I want to hug him, but
don't. You go first. No, you. Old habits die hard. The
events of the past few months upended our lives and
now we tip-toe around each other trying to figure out
how to behave in our new reality. The reality in which
both of us were wrong about my mother, and wrong
about each other.

"Sorry I'm late. My grandma died." This is as close
to joking around as we come. Years of teaching
undergrads has left my father impervious to all
excuses. He claims grandparental death is the number
one apologia offered up for missing exams, late
homework, and unwritten papers. Some kids'
grandparents die two or three times per semester.

"No problem." He walks ahead of me toward his
kitchen. "Want a cup of tea?"

"I thought you were anxious for breakfast."

"No point in getting to the diner too early. I want to
go to the mall afterwards and it doesn't open 'til 11:00
on Sunday."

"The mall!" Now I'm totally flummoxed. No one
hates shopping more than my dad. He hasn't set foot
in the Short Hills Mall since the birth of the Internet.
Amazon Prime membership was the best gift I've ever

given him.

"I need a birthday gift by tomorrow. No time for shipping."

Curiouser and curiouser. Who could possibly be on the receiving end of this generosity? All the birthday gifts I ostensibly received from him in my childhood were selected by my grandmother. When she died, my birthday gifts from Dad went with her. I want to ask Dad who in his life merits a birthday gift, but I don't trust my voice not to reveal a touch of envy.

An edgy silence settles over us. I still haven't gotten used to the crisp newness of every item in this apartment. Dad offers me the *Sunday New York Times* crossword, three-quarters completed in ink. I scan the blanks. "Seventeen down: 'Book that makes light of the missionary position' 'of Mormon.'" I toss it back.

"Humph." That one clue opens up a logjam and he busily fills in more squares. I watch his bowed gray head, his thin, veiny hands forming precise block capitals. "I have a friend at the Parks Center," he says, his eyes never leaving the newspaper. "Just found out about the birthday. I'd like to get her a little something."

Her? *Her?* So far as I know, in the thirty years since my mother's death, Dad has never had a date. "A lady friend! What's going on?"

His brow furrows and his lips compress. Still his eyes don't leave the paper. "Don't be ridiculous, Audrey. She's been kind to me. I just want to show her I appreciate it." His hand stops printing. "You know that can be hard for me."

*Tell me about it.*

"What's her name?"

"Natalie. Natalie Renfrew. She's a retired pediatrics nurse. Teaches a parenting class at the Center. And she teaches a knitting class for the kids. Kyle and Jamal take it, and they persuaded me to go along." He glances up from the crossword and nods towards his easy chair.

For the first time, I notice a tangle of gray yarn on the end table. I walk over and pick it up: the outline of half a mitten attached to two needles. My father has fallen for a woman who teaches parenting skills. The irony is too rich to stomach. And he's knitting?

"Whoa. Back up. You've taken up knitting because Kyle and Jamal are doing it?" Kyle is Ty's 10-year-old cousin and Jamal is his best friend. They were the charter members of Dad's chess club, and they made it cool for other kids to join. But chess is the limit of quiet indoor activity I can imagine for those two bike-crashing, hoops-shooting, skateboard-riding yahoos.

Dad puts his pen down and a smile touches his lips. "Natalie bet them lunch at Cluck U that they couldn't learn to knit. Greasy fried chicken is a powerful motivator. Then they bet me a Boston crème donut that I couldn't learn. Turns out knitting is very mathematical. You should try it. And it's been great therapy for me. Better than the stupid tricks that occupational therapist wants me to perform."

I study the neat rows of stitches reducing by twos to form the rounded top of the mitten. "So bet me."

"Dinner at the Green Pagoda."

"That would inspire Ethel to take up knitting, but not me. How about dinner at the Green Pagoda with you and Natalie? I want to meet this woman."

Dad actually blushes. "I, uh, haven't actually been out with her yet. It's awkward with my not being able to drive."

"It's the twenty-first century, Dad. You don't have to be her chauffeur. Just tell her to meet you there."

Dad makes a face and returns to the crossword puzzle. I glance at the clock on the wall in the kitchen. 9:45. It dawns on me that Coughlin must be at the corner by the hardware store by now. Could I have missed his call? I pull out my phone: no texts, no missed calls.

"Am I keeping you from something?" Dad asks.

"No. Not at all. I'm just expecting a call."

He fixes me with a penetrating stare above his reading glasses. I realize I might as well tell him about yesterday because when Sean does call, I won't be able to cover up what's going on. So I fill him in: cans, Ramon, dinner.

Dad listens without interruption. "I can see that these missing cans put you in an awkward position. I'm glad you called Sean to help you." He folds up the newspaper. "I see your bet and raise you. Dinner at the Green Pagoda with Natalie and me and Sean Coughlin. Final offer."

"Since when are you in the matchmaking business? And since when is a sports-loving, Irish Catholic cop your idea of a dream man for me? Wouldn't you prefer an actuary, a hedge fund manager?"

"I'd prefer someone who doesn't nearly get you killed. Like that Cal person."

I'd prefer someone who doesn't break my heart. Nobody seems the safest bet.

"I'm not looking to get involved, Dad."

"It's not good to spend so much time alone, Audrey. I've been much happier since I've been volunteering at the Parks Center. I've enjoyed getting to know Sean better. He's remarkably patient."

Patient? That's not the first adjective that springs to mind when I think of Sean Coughlin. And it seems Coughlin and my dad have been talking. So when Coughlin asked how my dad was last night, he already knew. "So you two have been chatting? What about?"

"The kids at the Center. His work. My work. I suspect he'd like to inquire about you, but he restrains himself."

Something about Dad and Sean's coziness brings out the pettiness in me. "You know Coughlin graduated from Montclair State. The school you always say uses a heart rate monitor to make its admissions decisions."

Dad and I lock eyes for a long moment. He is the first to look away. He walks to the big window overlooking downtown and speaks with his back to me. "People can change, Audrey. I've lived the past thirty years not believing that to be true. But the stroke, this business with your mother, my time at the Parks Center—they've changed me. I'd like to think I'm a little more open to...variety."

Variety. The man who read the *New York Times* for two hours in the same green wing chair while listening to Bach every evening of my childhood is now open to variety. All righty.

"Look, Dad, I came over here expecting to spend an hour eating greasy eggs with you. You're kinda blowin' me away here, if you know what I mean."

Just as Dad is about to answer, my phone rings. Coughlin.

He starts talking without a hello. "I'm at the hardware store. The guys on the corner said a tall black kid came twenty minutes ago looking for Ramon. They told him to check an apartment on Filmore. I just got a call from work that I have to take care of, so I can't go to Filmore right away. I'll be there in thirty. Call your man off, Audrey." The line goes dead.

Why is it necessary to bark out orders like that? My hands tremble as I dial Ty, whether from anger or excitement I don't know. Immediately, my call rolls to Ty's voicemail. He never turns his phone off or lets it run out of juice. So he's calling someone.

Or he declined my call.

Dad looks at me with his eyebrows raised. I text Ty "Call me NOW." A moment later, the phone rings.

"Audge, I found out from the guys on the corner where Ramon lives. I'm headed there now."

"No! Don't you go. Let Detective Coughlin handle it. He has the address."

"He's ahead of me?"

"No. He has something to take care of, then he's going over there."

"Audge, there's no time to mess around. Ramon might be headin' outta town with that cash. I gotta move!"

"No—if there's trouble, you'll get blamed."

"I can handle this. I gave Ramon the cans. I'm gettin' them back."

I know that tone in Ty's voice. This is a point of honor to him. Respect. Street cred. All the nonsense that means so much to men Ty's age. "Listen, I'm at my dad's place. That's only a few blocks from Filmore. I'll meet you there."

"I don't need you to protect me. I'm twice as big as Ramon."

"I don't want a fight. Wait for me there." And Ty knows that tone in my voice. I'm the boss. Listen or die.

I grab my coat. My phone rings again: Martha Wainwright. I'm not talking to her right now, but with any luck, I'll have good news for her soon. I text: *I have a lead on the cans. Talk soon.* Then I turn to Dad. "I'm afraid you'll have to eat Raisin Bran for breakfast, Dad. But I'll come back to take you to the mall, I promise."

"Audrey, this isn't wise. Stay here at let Sean handle it."

"I didn't ask for your advice. I know what I need to do."

# CHAPTER 5

True to his word, Ty is waiting on the corner of Filmore and Monroe Streets, pacing a groove into the sidewalk. He barely waits for my car to slow down before he yanks the passenger door open and folds his long body into the Civic.

"Guys said it's three blocks down, last house on the right." Ty looks out the window. "That cop called to tell you I was lookin' for Ramon?"

That cop. Ty can barely stand to speak Coughlin's name. "He offered to go talk to the guys on the corner this morning. He found out you got there first."

"I've been so bugged about the cans, I couldn't even enjoy the concert last night. Soon as it was over, I came back to Jersey." Ty leans his head against the car window. "But there was no sign of Ramon or any of them guys, so I figured I'd get up early and come over to the hardware store. I knew I could find him there."

"But he wasn't there?"

Ty shakes his head. "The other guys were there, but no Ramon."

"That's a bad sign, right? If Ramon isn't out there looking for work, he must have discovered the money, don't you think?"

Ty removes his shades and rubs his eyes. "Probably. It ain't like Ramon to miss a day of work."

"Did you tell the other guys why you were looking for Ramon?"

"What kinda fool you take me for?" Ty cracks his knuckles. "A couple of them recognized me 'cause they know Ramon works with me sometimes. I said I needed to give him some money, so they told me where to find him."

"Good. So you don't think they called him to warn him?"

"Those guys can't know about the cans, or else they wouldn'ta told me nothin'."

That makes sense to me. So maybe we'll find Ramon, but how will we get the cans back? The lunacy of coming here without Coughlin is beginning to set in.

I find a parking spot right in front of the house, a two-story clapboard that's clearly been divided into several apartments since there are two front doors. In the bright light of Sunday morning, the neighborhood seems less threatening. Across the street a yellow and red Cozy Coupe is parked on the porch. Hand-cut paper snowflakes decorate the windows. But Ramon's house shows no such signs of cheerful family life.

Ty is opening the car door before I've even turned off the ignition. I grab his arm. "Wait. Let's just sit here and watch. As long as he's still in there, we can afford to wait for Coughlin."

"But we don't know—"

"Well, if he's gone, then we've lost him. Don't be impulsive. We'll just keep an eye on the house."

Think first, act later is not Ty's usual MO. He leaves the car door open, but doesn't move to get out. Yet. I feel like I'm sitting next to a cat watching a bird feeder.

My mind is churning with possibilities. The money might be right there, within our grasp. Or we might be walking into a nest of desperate men. And how can I keep Ty on a short enough leash that he doesn't make the situation worse?

I have no distractions as I think. The only movement on this quiet side street on Sunday morning is a squirrel scampering across a phone line. Then loud voices break the silence. We look around. The street is still empty.

"That's comin' from the house." Now Ty is out of the car and heading up the walk. He's done with thinking, so I guess I am too.

Once we're on the porch, the volume of the voices grows. They're speaking Spanish, but we don't have to understand the language to know they're arguing. One word is discernable over and over amid the frenetic flow: *dinero.*

Ty tries both doors. Locked. He's tall enough to be able to look through the fanlight windows at the top of the doors.

"This door opens to a hall that leads to the back apartment," Ty says. "I see people moving back there."

"Is it Ramon?"

"Can't tell." He spins around and bounds down to the yard in one leap. "I'm goin' around back."

"Wait!"

"They're fightin' over the money. They could duck out the back door."

This isn't good. Hasn't it been thirty minutes? Where the hell is Coughlin? I trail Ty down a narrow, rutted concrete walk that runs along the side of the house. He's already on the back porch by the time I come around the corner. Now the yelling has escalated to screaming, and we hear thuds and crashes through the house's flimsy wooden walls.

"Ty, watch out. There could be a gun!"

But Ty presses his face against the window, blocking the bright sunlight with his cupped hands.

"Is it Ramon?"

"Could be. One guy is short. They're across the room."

Now a piercing shriek.

"Shit. He's got a knife!"

"Who? Get away, Ty," I shout from the yard.

Dammit, where is Coughlin?

As Ty backs away from the window, the back door flies open and a man in a light gray sweatshirt charges out. His mouth forms a perfect O of surprise as he looks directly at me. But he keeps moving, leaping off the porch. That's when I see the bright red spray of blood across his shirt.

Ty springs into pursuit, but I fling myself in his path and wrap my arms around his neck. "No! The money isn't worth getting killed over."

Ty shakes me off, but the man is already at the back fence. In one fluid motion he scales it.

Ty moves to follow, but I hang on his arm like a panicked toddler. "Let him go!"

"Damm, Audge!" He pries my fingers away from his bicep. "I coulda' caught him."

"And then what? He had a knife." We glare at each other. "That wasn't Ramon, was it?"

Ty shakes his head.

"He had blood all over his sweatshirt," I say. Ty and I look toward the open back door and creep back up onto the porch.

"Hey, Ramon—you okay, man?" Ty shouts.

No answer.

We crowd the door and gaze into the dark interior. A stream of blood cuts across the faded yellow linoleum, inching toward us.

A man lies sprawled on his back, his right arm flung outward. I take one step closer. A black-handled knife sticks straight out of his chest.

I feel my stomach lurch and my hand comes up to my mouth.

Behind me I hear a crack, a moan, and a thump. When I turn, I see Ty crumpled on the porch.

"Ty! My god!" I run to him.

In the back yard, Coughlin stands with his gun drawn.

# CHAPTER 6

I hear a woman screaming hysterically. "You shot him! You shot him. Why, why, why?" She sounds like she's at the end of a long tunnel.

The woman is me.

Ty's mouth hangs open and his eyes have rolled back. My mind goes blank in panic. What should I do first? Check for a pulse? Start CPR? My hands shake so violently I can't even open Ty's coat to see where he's hurt.

A figure casts a shadow over us.

"Get away! Why did you shoot him?"

Sean charges past me and enters the house.

Ty's eyelids flicker. "What happened?" he murmurs.

"You were shot. I'll get an ambulance. Just stay focused on me. Are you in pain?"

He sits up. "Don't," I warn.

"I ain't hurt. I think I fainted. Can't stand seein' all that blood." Ty looks as green as it's possible for a black person to look.

Relief that Ty is unhurt washes over me. My joy doesn't last long.

Coughlin reappears. There's a flash of hurt in his eyes, that heartrending *why did you step on my paw* look—did I imagine it?—and then the familiar Coughlin is back. "What the hell are you playing at, Audrey? Didn't I tell you to call this punk off?"

Ty springs up. "I'm outta here."

Coughlin blocks his path. Sirens howl in the distance. "Too late for that, man. You're a witness to a crime. Come with me."

Ty's eyes widen. "I didn't touch nobody! Audge, tell him."

"Leave Ty alone, Sean! All he did is look through the window."

"So he's a witness. I need to talk to him." Coughlin puts his huge paw on Ty's shoulder and starts guiding him off the porch. "And to you," he adds without looking at me.

I scamper behind them. "Don't worry, Ty–I won't let anything bad happen." All Ty wants in life is to keep as far away from the cops as possible, but somehow, between me and his family, that never seems to happen.

Coughlin stops and glares at me. "Let's go around front. The crime scene team will be here soon."

I look over my shoulder. "Shouldn't we go in and try to help Ramon? The knife is sticking—"

Coughlin herds us in front of him, his face a block of stone. "He's dead."

When we turn the corner into the front yard, the narrow street is clogged with police cruisers, ambulances, and various dark unmarked cars and vans. Coughlin leads us to a cruiser with its engine running and a patrolman at the wheel. Without a word, he opens the back door and nods to me. A gust of warm air escapes and I realize I'm shivering. I'll be happy to sit with Ty and Coughlin in there.

Coughlin slams the door after me and starts walking off with Ty. I try to jump back out and realize the back doors of police cars don't open from the inside. I pound furiously on the window. Coughlin keeps walking, then reconsiders.

He comes back and opens the door, but extends his leg to prevent my exit. "You are also a witness,

Audrey. We interview witnesses separately."

I know that's true, but understanding and accepting are two different things. The echo of my promise to Ty rings in my ears. Can I protect him? The only reason Ty is here is because he wants to help me.

"What about Ty?" Do I sound belligerent, hostile, defiant? I'm trying for reasonable and inquisitive, but I'm no Meryl Streep. "Where are you taking him?"

Coughlin has that barely suppressed rage look most often associated with fathers dealing with tantrum-throwing toddlers. "We will be right over there. So when I pull out my stun gun, you'll be able to shoot video as evidence."

The sarcasm of that last remark is lost on Ty. He keeps looking back at me as Coughlin leads him to the back of a big black van marked Palmyrton Investigation Unit. I huddle in the back of the squad car. A friendlier person would try to chat with the young cop in the front seat, but frankly, I don't have the energy. Not two months after the violence surrounding my discovery of the true facts of my mother's disappearance, I'm once again face-to-face with murder. Poor Ramon is dead, dead because he had the misfortune to accept a donation of canned soup from Another Man's Treasure. I slump in the back seat, trying to block the image of that knife protruding from his chest. But Ramon—yesterday, smiling and helpful; today, lifeless—is all that fills my mind.

In about fifteen minutes, I see a red head bobbing above the crowd moving toward me and I feel a knot in my stomach. Coughlin's going to yell at me, that I know. Do I have a defense? Do I need one?

He opens the car door and slides in. "You couldn't wait?" No preamble. Typical Coughlin. "I told you to call off Griggs, not come over here with him."

"Everything would have happened the same whether or not Ty and I were here. The fight started while we were sitting in my car, waiting for you."

"And what did you think you were going to—" His voice reverberates in the small confines of the car. Coughlin takes a deep breath and starts over, asking me questions in a flat, emotionless tone, probably the same questions he asked Ty. I answer, recounting our every move from the moment Ty called me to the moment Coughlin arrived on the scene. Through the car window, I see a few neighbors standing on their front porches despite the cold. I get the sense that scores more are peeping through their curtains and blinds.

"Did anyone else see where the guy ran? He couldn't have gone far on foot. After all, he's covered with blood, and he doesn't even have a coat."

"My men are doing a house-to-house." Coughlin leans toward me. "You're sure you've never seen the guy before?"

He's already asked me this once, but I don't get testy. "It's possible I've *seen* him—on the street, in a store, sitting in the park. I don't *know* him." A young Hispanic guy in jeans and a sweatshirt. They're everywhere in Palmyrton. Their lives run parallel to mine but never intersect. It's like asking me if I can identify a particular leaf on a tree.

I look at the shabby apartment building. A showdown took place behind its nondescript walls. What desperation fueled that fight? "Is there anyone else in the house?"

"No."

I can no longer hold back. "What about the soup cans? Are they in there?"

"The tech guys are working the scene. I can't search 'til they're done."

I scan his face for more information. Impassive as always. But he seems too relaxed for my liking. "You don't think they're in there, do you? You'd be pacing outside the door if you thought you'd find them."

He looks out over my head. "If these guys fought

over the cans and someone got killed, they wouldn't leave the money behind."

Of course he's right. But then a hopeful thought occurs to me. "The guy who ran didn't have a bag with him. There were fifteen cans, each supposedly with a wad of cash. He couldn't have had that many bills stuffed in his pants pockets."

Before Coughlin can answer, another cop comes to get him and I go and sit with Ty.

He looks about as miserable as Ethel getting a bath. I pat his shoulder. "Don't worry. I'm not leaving until you can leave with me."

His big dark eyes hold mine for a long moment. Then he looks away. "Why you like that?"

"Like what?"

"Watchin' my back...you know..."

My heart swells with affection for Ty. This whole mess started because he could hardly wait to get to the Jeezy concert. Yet I can't be angry with him. He's twenty-two. Of course he wants to be with his friends on Saturday night. What does it say about me that I'm never in a rush to finish work on Saturday night? Sometimes I think I chose the estate sale business—in which Saturday is always the busiest workday— precisely because it provides great cover for Date Night. My math nerd friends understand. One of them sent me a T-shirt recently. "Introverts of the World Unite. We're Here. We're Uncomfortable. We Want to go Home."

I rest my head against Ty's puffy coat. "It will all work out," I say more to convince myself than him.

Before long, Coughlin emerges from the front door and walks straight towards us.

"I found the cans."

Ty and I both perk up.

"They're empty."

Of course they are. How could they not be? "Where were they?"

"In one of the bedrooms, near some letters addressed to Ramon Esevachia. Scattered around, all the lids popped off. Looks like someone left in a hurry. Couple dresser drawers empty, some stuff knocked over."

"Did they all have money in them?" Ty asks.

"I just said, they're empty," Coughlin snaps.

I feel Ty bristle and jump in. "He means, did any of the cans contain soup? We've never been sure if they all contained money."

For a split second, the curtain drops. Confusion. Embarrassment. Then right back to The Great and Powerful Oz. "I'll have to go back and check on that."

I inch forward. "Can I go look—"

"I'll handle it. Sit."

Coughlin turns to Ty. "Tell me about Ramon. How often have you worked with him?"

Ty jumps up. "Man, I already told you everything I know three times!"

I give Ty my best "behave yourself" look. He rolls his eyes and begins speaking with exaggerated clarity, as if Coughlin is an Alzheimer's patient. "Like I told you before, the first time I worked with Ramon was in the fall. I needed someone to help me move this giant roll-top desk." He turns to me. "Remember that, Audge? What sale was that?"

"Cornbluth." I can picture the desk: solid walnut, 1830s, original finish and hardware.

"You can check your records for the exact date?" Coughlin asks.

I nod.

"How did you happen to hire Ramon for that job?"

"I just pulled up to the corner by the hardware where all the Spanish dudes hang. Most a them so short and scrawny. I picked Ramon cause he was a little more ripped. Plus he kinda had a look in his eye...you know, like he really wanted to work." Ty continues to tell Coughlin how Ramon did a good job with the desk, so whenever he needed help, he'd look for Ramon.

"Did you always find him there?"

"No, sometimes he'd be out on another job. Yard work. Gutter cleaning. Roofing. See, mostly I need help at the end of the day. The contactors, they go get guys real early. But Ramon, he'd finish one job, then go hang at the corner hopin' to get another one. Like I said, he's a hard worker."

"He was sending money back home?"

Ty nods. "To Honduras. I know he's from Honduras, but don't ask me what town. It's some little shit village where they ain't got bathrooms or nuthin'. He's got a girlfriend and a bunch of brothers and sisters. That's all I know."

"You're sure he's illegal?"

"Yeah, he's always askin' me how can he get the *carta verde*. That's green card. I tell him I don't know." Ty shakes his head. "I understand why he took the money, but really he's a good guy, know what I'm sayin'? And he's real religious too. *Dios* this, and *Dios* that."

Coughlin straightens up. "He go to a church here in town?"

Ty shrugs. "I dunno. Why would I ask him that?"

"You ever hang out with him? Have some beers, smoke a little weed?"

Ty thrusts his face toward Coughlin's. "No! I told you already—he wasn't my friend."

I tug him back. "Calm down."

No sooner is that platitude out of my mouth than the scrum of cops bursts into motion. Two EMTs push a gurney along the sidewalk from the front door. A long black bag is strapped on top. Ty swallows hard and looks away. I reach out and squeeze his hand. He doesn't pull away.

They roll the gurney toward us on the way to the ambulance. Coughlin halts its progress. He unzips the body bag part way. "Griggs, come here."

Ty recoils and squeezes his eyes shut. I take a deep breath and step forward.

A face, once brown, now strangely pale, stares up at me. A young man, hoping for a better life, has died alone, painfully, thousands of miles from home. That much is certain, but....

"It's not Ramon."

I stagger backward and bump into Ty, who's trying to peer over my shoulder.

"Damn. You're right. That's not Ramon. That's just a kid."

"You're sure?" Coughlin asks.

"Face is too round. Lips too fat," Ty says. "And he looks like he's only fifteen or sixteen. Ramon is twenty-three, a year older than me."

Coughlin makes a note in a little pad he always carries. "Okay, Audrey—you can go. Ty, I need you to come down to the station with me."

"What! See, Audge—what did I tell ya? They tryin' to hang this on me somehow."

I plant myself in front of Coughlin. "Why does Ty need to go with you? He's already told you everything he knows."

Now he's the one to use the "behave yourself" look. "Witnesses have a tendency to remember more details...different details...over a period of time."

"Yeah—over a period when you're hammering at them, intimidating them, not letting them eat or sleep!"

"Oh, for Chrissakes, Audrey. I work for Palmyrton PD, not a Middle Eastern dictator. Your precious boy isn't going to be hurt."

"Boy" is not a word that goes over well with Ty. He looms larger behind me. I keep myself firmly planted between Ty and Coughlin. "Is Ty under arrest?"

"No, we just want to—"

"Then he's not obliged to go anywhere with you, is

he?"

"Innocent people are usually happy to cooperate with an investigation."

"This innocent person has been cooperating. If he thinks of anything else, he'll call you. If you need to talk to him again tomorrow, you can stop by the office. We'll both be there."

"Audrey—"

"This interview is over." I grab Ty's arm. "C'mon. I'll drive you home."

Ty keeps looking over his shoulder like he expects Coughlin now really will shoot him in the back.

"How come he's lettin' me leave?"

"You're not under arrest. You're not even a suspect." I walk faster and faster as my anger boils. "You're under no obligation to go anywhere with the police."

Ty trots to catch up, smiling for the first time today. "'You're under no obligation...' 'This interview is over'" He cackles. "You really know how to talk some trash, Audge."

Yes, I've managed to protect Ty, for now. But what about that young boy? Was anyone looking out for him? Why was he arguing with the other guy? Why did the man have to kill him if Ramon and the money were already gone? The Wainwrights and their damn soup cans are sowing destruction all across Palmyrton. Somehow four people who never would have encountered each other have come together because of me. One is royally pissed. Two are missing.

One is dead.

By the time I reach my Honda, the poor kid's body has been loaded into the ambulance. Coughlin speaks to the driver, then pivots and lopes toward my car. I'm tempted to peel out from the curb and blow past him, but I'm not naturally inclined to melodrama. I roll down my window and wait.

Coughlin crouches and his freckled face fills my window. "Protecting your employee from over-reaching cops is very noble, Audrey. Just remember this: a killer now knows you witnessed his crime."

# CHAPTER 7

Could my life possibly get any worse? An innocent
fifteen-year-old kid is dead. Ty and I have witnessed
his murder. The murderer has seen both of us. The
Wainwrights' money is still missing, either in the
possession of the killer or Ramon—who knows? I'm
dodging calls from Martha Wainwright, too terrified to
tell her the truth. And the one person who might be
willing to go out of his way to help me find the cash is
furious with me. And now, as the icing on the cake, I'm
shopping at New Jersey's most intimidating mall with
the man who knows he gave me good advice that I
refused to accept.

I was so rattled after dropping off Ty at his
grandma's place that I drove straight home,
desperately seeking love from the one creature who's
never angry at me. Only after I opened my door and
was greeted by creepy silence did I remember that
Ethel was still at my dad's place. So back I went,
straight into the maelstrom of Dad's disapproval.

News of the killing on Filmore traveled faster on the
Internet than my Honda moves on the streets of
Palmyrton. By the time I arrived, Dad had read all
about the police activity on PalmyrtonNow.com. I filled
him in on the details the reporters couldn't know: how
Ty was willing to fight an armed man to get the money
back, how terrified I was when I thought Ty had been
shot, how that poor kid looked with a knife sticking

out of his chest, how I refused to let Coughlin take Ty to the police station. The one thing I left out is the pain in Coughlin's eyes when I accused him of gunning down Ty.

Dad peppered me with questions and scolded me for recklessness. Question, scold. Question, scold.

With every "Audrey, you shouldn't have...", I felt my hackles rising. I know what Dad would have done in the same situation—retreat, withdraw, pull inside the turtle shell and hope the trouble goes away. But if I pointed out to him that his preferred approach hasn't always been effective, I'd only take the argument in a direction that will make us both unhappy. It was easier to escape his barrage by reminding him of his urgent need to visit the mall.

I once read an article about some Khmer refugees who were relocated from the jungle villages of Cambodia to Fargo, North Dakota. That's how Dad and I feel when we step through the doors of the Short Hills Mall. French perfume, lavender candles, cappuccino—the scents in the air are almost visible. Dreamy, quasi-classical music pulses on a subliminal level. A pale green orb generates a smooth sheen of water. How will I be able to help him buy a gift for some woman I don't even know? Where to begin?

"Do you have any idea what you want to get her?" I ask as hordes of highly motivated shoppers surge past us.

"I was thinking a scarf. Natalie often wears these colorful..." Dad flutters his fingers in the vicinity of his neck.

Okay, that's a start. It narrows the search down to roughly half the stores in the mall.

"Like that." Dad points to a stylish woman striding down the concourse, a fringy scarf draped artfully across her shoulders.

Leaving Dad, I sprint after her. "Excuse me, excuse me!" This is how desperate I am.

She pauses as I draw up next to her. From the way she clutches her designer bag, she expects me either to rob her or to ask her for change to get a cup of coffee. But when I point out poor old Dad leaning on his cane next to the fountain and tell her what we're after, she comes up with inspired advice: the Metropolitan Museum of Art gift store, just a few doors away. Once we're inside, Dad and I both start breathing easier. Gregorian chants play on the sound system and stacks of books share space with statues and paintings. Yes, it is a retail establishment, and yes, the art is all reproduction, but this is familiar turf for us.

Sure enough, there's a large selection of scarves. Too large. We're paralyzed by so much fashion. The salesclerk comes over and spreads two scarves across the counter. One is a swirl of blues and purples and pinks mimicking an Impressionist painting. The other is a precise repeating pattern inspired by Moorish tilework.

Dad doesn't ask my opinion. He doesn't need to; I know which one he'll pick.

His hand rests on the geometric blues and golds and reds. "I'll take this."

On the way home, we listen to *The Moth* on the radio, happy to let someone else's stories erase our own. When I pull up in front of his apartment building, Dad switches the radio off but keeps staring at the dashboard. "Thank you for helping me with this." He lifts the little Met shopping bag. "I'm afraid I may have been...abrasive...with my advice on how to handle the missing money." His Adam's apple bobbles. "I don't want you to come to any harm. Not now, not after—" He opens the door.

"Good night, Audrey."

I squeeze his hand. "Good-night, Dad."

As I stand outside the office door on Monday I can hear the low rumble of Ty's voice interspersed with

higher pitched notes. "Wow...no way...get out...no
*way.*" I know what I'll see when I walk in: Jill treating
her desk chair as an orchestra seat while Ty plays all
the roles in the drama of his Sunday. I pause with my
hand on the doorknob. I still can't hear Ty's words
clearly—I know he's standing across the room, near
the file cabinets—but I hear Jill's voice distinctly.

"Of course Audrey would back you up. Why would
you ever doubt that?"

*rumblemumblerumble*

"She doesn't care about that cop, Coughlin. He's too
big and Irish Catholic. Not her type."

How well Jill knows me!

*rumblemumble*

"Because she loves you, fool."

Do I? My eyes tear up a bit. Yes, I suppose I do.

I make a production out of blowing my nose and
rattling the doorknob. Their voices fall silent and I
enter.

"Good news, Audrey. It's only 9:30 and we already
have two new jobs."

My eyes light up at the two pink message slips Jill
waves in greeting. The month between Thanksgiving
and Christmas is always slow in the estate sale
business. Realtors don't like putting new listings on
the market then, so no one asks for their house's
contents to be sold. But over the holidays people still
retire and make plans to sell-up and move south. And
they still die. I keep meaning to check the stats on
this, but I think old people die more frequently in
December, their bodies drained by the effort to feign
enthusiasm for fruitcake and reindeer sweaters and
yet another scented candle in the Secret Santa
exchange. That's why January and February are the
months of pent-up demand for our services. But in
other years, I've spent the slow period networking and
trolling for business. This holiday season was
different. I was reeling from all that happened,

recovering from my hospitalization, depressed and dazed. I let new business prospecting fall by the wayside. Now bills are rolling in—my usual business expenses plus invoices from doctors and labs I never even knew I used. And the premium for my liability insurance. God knows, that will be increasing if they have to pay out for the loss of the Wainwrights' money.

Yes, I need clients.

"I have you scheduled to go out and look at the houses this afternoon," Jill says. One is over on Peyton Road."

I flop into my desk chair. "Hmmm. That won't yield much." Peyton is in a neighborhood of modest splits and bilevels. I know without even seeing the house that the probability of priceless heirlooms is low. But I can't afford to be picky if there's nothing better on the horizon.

I jolt upright. "Hey, is there a message from Elizabeth Haverford?"

"Is that the job where the house has a name, not a number?" Ty asks.

"Yes. Willowby," Jill says. "There was nothing on the voicemail. I'll check the email now."

While Jill is searching, I allow myself to fantasize. "You should see this house, guys. From the main road, you wouldn't even know it's there. You drive and drive down this private lane and boom! A Rennaisance Revival mansion. Columns, balconies, recessed archways, big tall chimneys." I sketch them in the air. "And the foyer has a *double* curving staircase."

Ty listens with his chin propped in his hands. "What do they got to sell?"

"All the important art and antiques have already been auctioned off. We would just handle what's left. But, oh. My. God." I close my eyes to conjure up a clearer mental picture. "Ten grand of china, crystal and artwork in the dining room, a cool two thou of high-end kitchenware, an easy fifteen in mirrors, lamps, and vases. And people will overpay just to say they own something from Willowby. Rugs, books, small furniture...." The numbers flash through my brain. "I figure a hundred twenty to a hundred fifty thousand. Easy." This one job could solve all my financial problems in one fell swoop.

Ty whistles. "When do we start?"

"We don't have the job yet. Elizabeth, the woman who's the property manager for the family who owns the house, said she'd call me with her answer in a week. She's also considering Jameson's Sales."

Ty snorts. "That guy's an asshole."

"I know. And Elizabeth and I had a great conversation about English creamware pottery and first edition books by mid-twentieth century authors. I feel like we really hit it off."

"Nothing in the email yet, Audrey," Jill reports.

"Guess she doesn't work over the weekend. Maybe we'll hear by the end of the day. So, what's the other job you said came in?"

Jill swivels in her desk chair and starts rooting through her file drawer. "Well, that one's not so....fancy. But it's for someone we know, so I knew you'd want to do it."

I wait. Nothing. Jill ducks her head and begins filing as if she were competing in some secretarial triathalon.

"And that someone is...?"

"Harold."

"Herald? Who are the Heralds? I'm drawing a blank."

"Not the Herald family," Ty explains. "Harold the Hoarder. Now we get to resell everything we ever sold to him."

"Absolutely not! Jill, what were you thinking?"

"We have to help him, Audrey." Jill looks like she does when she sees those ASPCA dog rescue commercials. "His niece called. The neighbors have been complaining to the health department that the house is a hazard. The town is going to condemn it and toss Harold out on the street if he doesn't clear out some of his junk."

"Harold doesn't need an estate sale organizer. He needs a trash hauler."

"Yeah," Ty chimes in. "Just call Palumbo's. They'll drop a Dumpster right in front of his door. They got guys in HazMat suits who'll drag everything outta there."

"No! His niece says Harold won't allow that. What they need is help separating the trash from what's valuable."

"Define valuable," I say. "I'm not spending days wading through his crap looking for some trinkets worth a few hundred bucks."

"But Audrey, he'll be homeless if we don't help him."

"I'm an estate sale organizer, Jill, not a social worker. We simply can't afford to take on jobs that use up more in labor than they produce in revenue."

Ty nods. "See, that's why Audge is the boss. We be belly up if you was runnin' this outfit."

"Shut up, Ty. No, I think he's got some seriously valuable stuff. Like maybe...well, I can't remember exactly what Nora said. Just talk to Harold's niece, Audrey. I told her you'd meet her around two, right after your appointment on Peyton Road."

Sometimes I suspect that Jill doesn't fully grasp that what we do here is not a giant game of playing store. "Look at me, Jill. The goal of Another Man's Treasure is to make money. Money to pay your salary, and Ty's and mine. I'm not going to Harold's house."

"But I pro-o-o-omised her!" Jill's wail ascends an entire octave.

"You should have cleared it with me first."

"But you're always telling me to just go ahead and make a decision. And now I did and you say I should have asked first."

She's got me there. I heave a big sigh. "All right. I'll talk to her. But I'm not committing to doing the sale."

While Jill is clapping her hands, the phone rings.

"Good morning. Another Man's *Trea*sure. How may I help you?"

Jill has been binge watching *Mad Men*, channeling the sexy receptionist character. All she needs is a tight skirt and bouffant hairdo.

She winces at what she hears. "Let me see if Ms. Nealon is available." I can practically see a cloud of frost coming out of her mouth. She puts the call on hold when normally she would just hold the receiver against her chest and yell.

"It's Martha Wainwright, Audrey. Should I tell her you're not here?"

"Don't be silly. Of course I'll talk to her."

As I reach for the phone I see Ty's face fade from warm brown to ashy gray. "I got shit to do," he says, and darts out the door.

# CHAPTER 8

I take a deep breath. The last time I traded texts with Martha was to assure her I was working on locating Ramon. The news about the murder on Filmore Street has broken, but the police reports have been low on details—she won't know that crime concerns her. Now I'm going to have to tell her that her money is either in the possession of a missing Honduran immigrant or a murderer on the lam.

"Hi, Martha," I begin. "I'm afraid some, er, complications have arisen. We've found the cans—"

"You have!"

"But not the money." Then I spit out the whole story in a rush, trying hard to be precise but entirely undramatic, as if witnessing a murder is just a minor speed bump in the process of recovering her cash. "So the police are investigating very intensively. I'm sure they'll have some answers for us soon."

Dead silence.

"Hello? Martha?"

The stream of profanity pouring into my ear makes me feel like I've stumbled into an NBA locker room after a big loss. This from a woman who teaches gym at a Catholic elementary school. I steady my nerves by mentally chanting "the customer is always right" as I wait for a break in the onslaught.

When she pauses for a breath, I continue. "Martha, I understand you're upset, but having the police on the trail of the money is a good thing. I'm sure they'll track these guys down quickly."

I'm whistling in the wind here.

"You were supposed to give the unsold goods to a registered charity. If you had done what our contract stated, none of this would have happened." Martha speaks with such steely precision that I almost wish she'd go back to cursing.

"I know that Martha. And I take full responsibility for my staff member's mistake. But please understand—Ty simply thought he was giving the soup to a poor person who could use it."

"I don't believe that for a minute." Martha's voice sinks to a low snarl. "You stole my family's money, and now your crooked accomplice has stolen it from you."

My hand tightens on the receiver. I swivel away from Jill's concerned face. "Martha, please—that's simply not true."

She doesn't bother to argue, just switches direction. "You said they found the cans. How many contained cash?"

Damn! Finding that out will require a call to Coughlin. "I'm not sure. I have to check back with the lead detective. I'll call you as soon as I know."

"Don't bother. I'll have my lawyer contact the police directly. You just remember one thing, Audrey Nealon. You stole my inheritance and I'm not letting you get away with that. You will *pay*."

I sit with my eyes closed and the dead receiver in my hand. How can I fix this? I can't simply wait around for the police. I need to take control and get this solved, fast.

"Is she, like, really mad?" Jill asks in a voice barely above a whisper.

"Like, furious."

"What are you gonna do?"

I speak with my eyes closed, taking deep breaths

between sentences. "Call Coughlin and find out how many cans held money. Call my lawyer. Call my insurance agent."

I learned in college to always tackle the most onerous homework first. Write the essay on the poetry of Keats before solving three pages of differential equations. So I prepare to call Sean Coughlin. I've noticed when I think of the controlling, know-it-all cop, I call him Coughlin. And when I think of the funny guy who likes my dog and talks antiques and blushes, I call him Sean. Who will the man be today?

He picks up on the first ring. "Calling about your cans?"

Coughlin, clearly. I feel my back go up even though that's exactly why I called. Typical Coughlin that he has to let me know he's one step ahead of me. But in an algebraic flash of clarity, it dawns on me that I don't have to respond to Coughlin. I could respond to Sean.

"Hey, guess where I went last night?"

Hesitation. Suspicion. "Where?"

"The Short Hills Mall. With my father. He wanted to buy a gift for this woman he met at the Parks Center. Natalie Renfrew. You know her?"

"Uhm, yeah." His voice softens. "She's a good person. The kids love her. Attractive, too. In a, you know, older woman kinda way."

"So you approve of them getting together? I don't want my dad chasing after some bimbo."

He chuckles. "No danger of that."

"Well, thanks for putting my fears to rest."

Now he's laughing. "You did not call just to ask me that."

"I called because we parted on bad terms. I want you to know that I've calmed down. I know you were doing your job, but I was doing my job too."

"I should know you didn't call to apologize, but I'll take what I can get. And by the way, ten of the cans were clean inside, with traces of solder on the lids. Five had soup residue."

So, a hundred thousand dollars—if each can had a wad of hundreds—not a hundred fifty thou. Not exactly a game changer for me.

"Thank you, Sean. I appreciate—" I hear loud voices in the background and someone shouting his name.

"Gotta go, Audrey."

I'm left with the dial tone. I never got to ask him what he's found out about the boy who died.

Next, I place a call to Emil Swenson. Mr. Swenson has been my lawyer since I picked his name out of the phone book to help me incorporate Another Man's Treasure ten years ago. Fussy, meticulous and an endless worrywart, he runs a solo practice out of a tiny office above a dry cleaners on Washington Street.

To Mr. Swenson, liability lurks everywhere. If it were up to him, I would have no employees, no van, no office. I dread troubling him with this news.

"Emil Swenson, attorney at law."

He always answers his own phone, always precisely in this way. I'm convinced that even when caller ID tells him it's his wife calling, he still says, "Emil Swenson, attorney at law."

I spit the whole sorry story out in one breathless rush. His only response is a sharp intake of breath. "You violated the terms of your contract."

I know he would prefer to hear that I robbed a liquor store at gunpoint. "I'm afraid I did, Mr. Swenson. Inadvertently."

"That's hardly relevant. And you say that ten of the cans were tampered with. But, of course, one cannot be certain that each altered can contained ten thousand dollars."

"No, but that's what my client believes. So, what's my liability? What should I tell my insurance company?"

"Don't notify them yet." I can hear him tsk-ing. "This is highly irregular. It necessitates some research. I will call you back later today." And he's gone. No "don't worry." No, "we can work this out."

By mid-afternoon, I've slipped further into a funk. The momentary rush I got from coaxing a laugh out of Sean has passed, and I'm back to worrying about money I've lost and money I haven't earned. I've gone to scope out the job at the house on Peyton Road. As I predicted, the proceeds from that sale won't put a dent into my problem. Everything in the house is too old to be in fashion, but not old enough to have come back into fashion.

Now, back in my car, I check my email and voicemail for a message from Elizabeth Haverford on the job at Willowby. I sent her a follow-up email, but I don't want to be too pushy.

Nothing yet. I remember what Elizabeth said to me as I left Willowby last week, *I've done my research. You come very highly recommended, Audrey. The Bulmers, The Fischmanns—they spoke glowingly of your work."* I'm sure I'll get the job. So why can't she call and put me out of my suspense?

I glance at the dashboard clock. I'm supposed to be meeting Harold's niece in ten minutes. I didn't want this appointment in the first place, and now I really want to blow it off. As if by telepathy, my phone rings: Jill. "Harold's niece just called, Audrey. She's waiting for you at the house. She's in the red Prius."

Handling the Willowby sale will require all our resources, plus some freelance assistance, but I know it's pointless to argue. Simpler to just meet the woman and tell her we can't take the job. "I'm on my way," I tell Jill. After I hang up, I wonder why she told me about the red Prius. It's 25 degrees out—why would she be in her car?"

Harold's house is across town in the Summit Oaks

neighborhood, a development built in the 1960s when Palmyrton was bursting with baby boom families. The houses are mostly four-bedroom colonials and expanded ranches. Nothing extraordinary, but the location—close to the train, but safe and secluded—has made the houses increase in value over the decades. I've done a few sales here—original owners clearing out to make way for a new generation of young families with kids. I never realized that Harold lived in such a respectable neighborhood.

I pull into the neighborhood on Pin Oak Drive, and follow my GPS through several labyrinthine turns. Every house I pass is nicely landscaped, with the requisite play structure in the back yard, and color-coordinated shutters on every window. I finally turn onto Acorn Lane—more very nice houses that scream upper-middle-class prosperity. Ahead, I see a red car parked at the curb—the only car parked out on the street. As I pull up, I see why.

Twelve Acorn Lane bears no resemblance to any other home in the neighborhood. It's as if the sky opened up and dropped a meteor of mess into the serene suburban landscape. In the front yard, rusting appliances share space with scores of birdfeeders, an entire flock of pink plastic flamingos, and several birdbaths and fountains filled with scummy green water. A nearly lifesize copy of Michaelangelo's David, executed in plaster, stands next to a plastic Mary and Joseph whose features have been scoured off by the weather. They kneel beside an empty manger, and across from a six-foot totem pole. The driveway holds three rusted cars, all with flat tires, all filled so full of papers, boxes, and clothing that there would be no room for a driver even if the cars would start. The house itself is a standard center hall colonial, once blue, but now a faded grey with the cedar shakes sprouting moss. The shutters dangle, the gutters droop, the roof sags.

But most extraordinary of all, the windows have no curtains and through every dirty pane I can see stuff: stuff in stacks and stuff in towers, stuff that must extend all the way to the ceiling.

I get out of my car just as a trim woman with short hair comes down the artistically curved front walk of the lovely house next to Harold's. She's headed to put a letter in her mailbox when she sees me and changes course. "Excuse me, excuse me," she waves and shouts as she comes closer. "You must be from the health department."

Before I can deny this, she rattles on, "Have you finalized the decision to condemn the house? When are you going to bulldoze it?"

Such lust for destruction coming from an otherwise kindly-looking soccer mom! I'm certainly not going to admit my reason for being there.

But I don't need to explain myself. She's more than willing to keep up both ends of the conversation. "All of us in the neighborhood are just praying for this eyesore to be gone."

"Uh-huh. Well, the final decision's not mine."

"Oh, I understand. You can't say anything yet." She winks. "Nice talking to you!"

Only after the nosey neighbor is gone does a woman emerge from the Prius. She's in her late thirties—just a little older than me—nicely but casually dressed. Despite the fact that Harold looks crazy and she looks perfectly normal, I can see a family resemblance: the same deep-set blue eyes, the same high cheekbones.

I walk toward her and she waves, turning her collar up against the wind as she gazes at the house. "I'm Harold's niece, Nora Phieffer, and this—" She turns and looks me in the eye. "This is my childhood home."

# CHAPTER 9

Before I can say a word, she starts talking. "We have to go around to the back. The front door doesn't open anymore." Nimble as a gymnast, she picks her way through the obstacle course of the front yard, challenging me to follow. I'm more certain than ever that I want no part of this job, but I have to admit to a perverse curiosity about what the inside of the house looks like. Rubbernecking a car crash has nothing on this.

Nora keeps up a steady monologue as she guides me to the back door. "My uncle was a petroleum engineer. He worked in the oil industry for years—overseas, mostly. Saudi Arabia, Kuwait."

"Really?"

She hears the surprise in my voice and pauses while I catch up. "Harold is quite brilliant. Everyone on my mother's side of the family is smart and crazy. I take after my dad—dumb and normal."

There's a statement with no good response.

Finally, we climb over the dilapidated grills (five—two gas, three charcoal) on the patio, and Nora yanks open the back door. Apparently, they don't keep the house locked.

As soon as the door swings open, I understand why. The stench emanating from the back hall deters thieves better than a pack of pit bulls.

I reel backward. "My God!"

"Sorry," Nora says. "I forget how bad it is the first time."

Towers of junk line the walls of the laundry room, but no wash is done here because the appliances are covered with stacked boxes and the sink is overflowing with shopping bags. Still, there's a narrow Sherpa's trail winding among the Himalayan peaks of rubble.

Nora steps up and begins edging her way along the path. A moment passes before she realizes I'm not following. There's not enough room to turn around, so she has to talk to me with her back turned.

"Just work your way through behind me. Harold comes in this way every day. It's okay."

In what universe could this possibly be okay? The towers of crap are perilously unstable. I'm beginning to think Nora is not as normal as I first assumed. The smell is overpowering: rotten food, urine, and the unmistakable aroma of something dead. All dead things smell the same—mice, rats, squirrels, groundhogs. The intensity depends on the size of the creature and the nearness of its passing. My nose says Harold's house is the tomb for something bigger than a mouse, smaller than what? A buffalo, maybe.

"Look, Nora—I'm not following you in there. This job is way beyond my scope. Way beyond."

Nora pauses and backs up a few steps, still speaking into the void. "Jill told me that you'd help us."

"I think she said I'd come out and look at the house. I'm sorry if she gave you the impression that I would definitely take it on."

There's a long silence. Then I see Nora's shoulder's shaking. Finally, I hear the sobs.

Now what am I going to do? I'm not good with tears under the best of circumstances. Whenever I cried as a child, my dad would leave the room. I soon learned that tears wouldn't get me what I wanted, and to this day I'm wary of criers.

"Please," Nora chokes out the word. "If you won't help us, we're going to lose the house. And then I don't know what I'll do with Harold. I can't let him into my home, or he'll destroy that too."

There's desperation in her voice. Even without seeing her face, I know her pain is real. "Can you come back out here for a minute? I have an idea."

I can't clear this house, but I do know plenty of trash haulers and clean-out crews who can help. I'll get Nora set up with some contacts and be on my way.

Nora backs toward me and jumps onto the patio.

I pull out my phone and start scrolling through my contacts. "Take down these numbers. Tell them I sent you and they'll move you to the top of their queues."

Nora lifts her tear-stained face, but she makes no effort to capture the names and numbers I'm rattling off. "Harold wants you. He trusts you."

"Well, that's very sweet, but you'll just have to explain to him—"

"Have you ever tried to explain anything to Harold?"

I think of our encounter on the front porch of the Wainwright house. "I know he can be a little...obstinate, but—"

Nora gazes out over the weed-choked wreckage of the back yard focused on a point in time, not in space. "Harold ruined my childhood. He ripped apart my family. He didn't mean to, but he did."

"Then why do you care what happens to this house? Let the town condemn it. Let Social Services deal with Harold."

Nora faces me, her eyes fierce. "That's what my brother says to do. But he lives in Connecticut. He's not the one who would have to see our uncle every day sleeping in the park, eating out of garbage cans."

Now I suspect that Nora is trying to manipulate me. "Surely it wouldn't come to that. Social Services would find him a new place to live, get him some help."

Nora begins to laugh. Not a pleasant sound as it

tilts toward hysteria. "There's no help for people like Harold. He's not"—She makes air quotes—"'a danger to himself or others'. Sometimes I wish he'd hold a knife to someone's throat. Then the doctors would commit him, make him take his meds. But Harold wouldn't hurt a fly, at least not intentionally. There's no help for gentle crazy people, only a life on the streets."

"Have you tried—"

"I've tried everything." She rattles off an acronym-studded list of government agencies and private charities. "No one will take him. He's not crazy enough. He has obsessive/compulsive disorder. And delusions brought on by post-traumatic stress. The closest I've come to getting him help is when the neighbors turned him in to the ASPCA for having twelve cats. A rescue group found new homes for the cats. Harold, they left behind."

Twelve cats! That explains some of the smell.

Out on the street, I hear a car door slam. "My only hope is to get the house cleaned up enough that the town won't condemn it," Nora says.

"Hi, how's it going?" a voice calls out somewhere between the pile of dismembered bicycles and the decaying redwood picnic table. A moment later, a Peruvian knit hat appears, followed by the rest of Jill's bundled figure. The little diamond stud above her nostril makes her nose look redder.

"Jill! What are you doing here?"

"Oh, I went out for lunch and thought I'd just drop by and see how you two are doing." She pokes at a family of ceramic turtles with the toe of her furry boot.

Jill is striving for guileless nonchalance but falling about half a football field short. She looks at the tunnel through the junk mountain. "So, have you been inside?"

"No, I—"

"Well, come on—let's check it out." Jill heads to the

back door.

I grab at the hood of her sweatshirt and haul her back. "No way are you going in there. It's not safe."

She jerks her clothing out of my grasp. "I want to see exactly what we're up against."

"*We* are not up against anything. We're not taking this job. The job at Willowby is huge. It's going to require all our effort."

Her eyes light up. "We got it?"

"Well, no—I still haven't heard. But I have a very good feeling about it. We'll know in a few days."

"So it can't hurt to just see what Harold's got in there."

Nora can see that Jill is giving her an opening and she chimes in. "It's not like you have to empty it totally. Just clear the kitchen and hallways. Then I'm going to check on him every week, and make sure that for every new thing that comes in, something else goes out. Once I get his housing situation stabilized, maybe I'll have better luck getting him into therapy."

Surely even a cock-eyed optimist like Jill can see that strategy will never work. I'm moved by Nora's plight, but this is not a project for Another Man's Treasure.

"Nora, I'm sorry, but I run estate sales. There's nothing here for me to sell. I simply can't afford—"

Her eyes light up. "You misunderstood. I'm not asking you to do this out of the goodness of your heart. Didn't Jill tell you? There's half a million dollars of Civil War memorabilia in there. Harold is willing to sell it to a museum."

I glance up at the sound of hammering and see a big woodpecker ferociously pounding a rotten cedar shake above my head. "You expect me to take Harold's word that he picked up priceless historical artifacts at a garage sale and stowed them away in the house?"

"Oh no—he bought them from a bona fide dealer. Fifteen years ago Harold had plenty of money and he bought these letters written between General Lee and Jefferson Davis. I've seen them with my own eyes. And there might be other Civil War memorabilia in there too."

Nora beams encouragement. "You just have to find them."

"See!" Jill chirps. "I told you there was valuable stuff in there. I just kinda forgot what." She heads toward to door. "Let's check it out and make a plan."

Often I get testy with Jill, more rarely I get irritated, but I'm headed toward full-throttle rage right now. Why is she defying me like this? It's hard enough saying no to poor Nora without Jill turning around and offering her false hope.

"Absolutely not." I actually stamp my foot. "We are not clearing out this house. Get back here, Jill!"

She pauses in the doorway and speaks to me in a tone she usually reserves for pushy telemarketers. "If I want to enter Harold's house, I am free to do so." Then she extends a hand to Nora. "Show me around. Apparently, Audrey isn't interested in this job. But I would be happy to do it for you on a freelance basis."

Then Jill and Nora disappear down the rabbit hole.

# CHAPTER 10

It's been a decade since I graduated UVA with a degree in math. My father continues to mourn the loss of my higher mathematical mind, and it's true that I am no longer clear on the law of biquadratic reciprocity. But one skill developed in my undergraduate days still comes in handy: I can tune out the world and focus intently on one problem. My anger at Jill hasn't dissipated, but there's nothing I can do right now to deter her insane determination to help Harold. And there's nothing more I can do to secure the job at Willowby. That leaves one problem to focus on: Ramon and the missing money.

I know finding my money isn't job one for the Palmyrton PD, but finding Ramon has to be important. He has the money, and that's why the other two were fighting. That's why that poor kid was killed. Maybe the killer is on his way to meet up with Ramon. Then I have a horrible thought—maybe Ramon is on his way to Honduras right now. Surely Sean has thought of that?

Do I have the chutzpah to call Sean again? I'm not sure I can pull off the charm offensive twice in one day. Finally I take the socially inept teenager's approach: I text him.

*Hey! How are you? Any news on Ramon?*

I stare at my phone, willing a response. Nothing. Maybe he's busy. Then words start to appear.

*Still trying to ID the victim.*

Wow, they still don't know who he is? Hasn't anyone missed him? Isn't his family looking for him? My eyes tear up as I picture that knife jutting out of his chest, his blood creeping across the floor. Doesn't anyone but me care? But his family is probably illegal too. They wouldn't call the police to report their son missing. I imagine them worried, searching. But not reaching out for help. That's not an option for them.

*Don't you need to question Ramon? He must know the boy. What if he's already flown off to Honduras?*

While I wait for the answer, I can't help picturing Ramon arriving back in his village like a conquering hero, swarmed by raggedy little children and embraced by the girl he left behind. Part of me wants him to make it back and build himself a little hacienda in the center of town. If it weren't for the damn Wainwrights, I'd actually be rooting for him.

*Can't fly. Watch placed on all airports*

See—I knew Sean was looking for Ramon. So if this hunted man wants to get back home, he'd have to drive, sneak across the Mexican border, make his way down to Central America, a risky journey that would take weeks and eat up a lot of the money. And we're still not sure how much there is. So maybe Ramon is nearby, hiding out with friends, but he's sent the money back to his country. I see all those storefronts on Webster Avenue offering wire transfers. I don't even know how that works.

*Have you tried those wire transfer places?*

The text message screen goes dark and my phone rings. "Audrey, I'm on it. You're not the only person on the planet who's competent. How about you let me do my job, and I'll let you do yours." Call ended.

Boom.

Of course finding Ramon and arresting the escaped killer is a job for the police. And I know Coughlin is competent. Mostly. But recovering the Wainwrights' money and keeping my business afloat is my job. And helping that boy's family is my job too. My father would say that's irrational, but it's not. If I had supervised Ty better, explained the importance of always abiding by our contracts, none of this would have happened. The buck stops with me.

Coughlin is a public servant. That's completely different than being an entrepreneur. I can't put the future of my company, and my conscience, in someone else's hands and just sit back and wait for results. I have to do something.

Then I think of the killer looking straight into my eyes as he jumped off the back porch on Filmore. I remember Coughlin's warning: I'm a witness to homicide. I don't want to cross paths with that guy, I really don't. But Ramon, Ramon is different. I know Ramon—he's a nice guy. Of course, I've been wrong about nice guys in the past, haven't I? But Ty agrees that Ramon is a good person.

In fact, Ty said Ramon was religious. What about some of the churches in town? I wonder if Coughlin has thought of that?

I can't call and ask, that's for sure.

I Google "churches in Palmyrton, NJ." Twenty-seven—no way! Who is the most church-going person I know who can help me whittle down this list? I pull out my phone and scroll through the contacts. Geez, I know a lot of sinners! I haven't darkened the door of a church since my grandmother's funeral. I haven't even heard a prayer since...since Thanksgiving. Since Ty's Grandma Betty led us in saying grace. Betty's definitely got to know her way around the churches in town. I have her number as the emergency contact in Ty's personnel file, so I dial.

"Hello, baby Audrey! How are you, girl?"

Grandma Betty is not the kind of woman you just hit up for a quick fact. So we chat: my health, her health, my dad's health. My dog, her grandchildren.

While this is going on, my brain is desperately spinning how I can explain why I called without getting her riled up about the murder. But I needn't have worried. Betty has her finger on the pulse of Palmyrton.

"Are you calling with news about that poor boy who got knifed? You know I'm worried sick about Ty seeing that. And that Spanish fella that helped Ty out—I think he's in trouble now, too."

"We need to find Ramon, Betty. The police are busy looking for the guy who stabbed Ramon's housemate. Meanwhile, Ramon's out there somewhere. Maybe he has the missing money and the other guy is out to get him. The police are looking for the killer, but I'm not so sure they're worried about Ramon."

"Huh. Police only worried about makin' an arrest. They don't care who gets hurt in the process."

"Ty says Ramon is religious. Maybe he'd go to his pastor for help."

"A church is a place of sanctuary, Audrey. No pastor is going to turn over a member of his flock.

"Don't you think I could persuade the pastor that I don't blame at Ramon?"

"Blame don't really enter into it. When you got a problem to be solved, you can't just be thinkin' about what's in it for you. See, I got a few years on you, and I know you gotta think, what's in it for the other guy, and how can I give him some of what he wants so I can get some of what I want."

I'm not entirely sure where this little excursion into behavioral psych from the school of Grandma Betty is leading. "Right. A-a-a-nd?"

"What's the one thing that boy Ramon wants more than anything?" Betty asks.

"To take all that money back to Honduras."

"Hmmm—I don't think so. From what Ty told me about him, what Ramon wants is opportunity. That's why he snuck into this country. That's why he works so hard. You offer that young man opportunity, maybe you'll get your money back."

I hear her take a breath and I jump in to divert the lecture. "You're absolutely right. I'll think about that. But which church in Palmyrton do you think Ramon might have attended?"

"If he's Catholic, he'd go to Our Mother of Sorrows, that homely little church over on Catalpa Avenue. It was ready to close down before all the Spanish folks moved to Palmyrton."

"And if he's not?"

"Then he'd go to the Church of Living Praise—that's the holy-roller church. They do some serious prayin' over there. Speaking in tongues and whatnot."

I don't even want to consider the whatnot. But at least now I have a place to start.

I'm trolling the Internet for information on those churches when I sneeze. And sneeze again. And again. I spin on my desk chair, groping for a tissue and see that Jill has slipped into the office unheard.

Neither of us speaks.

I grab a tissue and turn my back on her. And sneeze. Then I smell it. Dust and cat and that sickly-sweet death.

"Jill! What have you got on your clothes? You're stinking up the office and you're making me sneeze. You must be covered in mold spores. Get out!"

Jill backs away from me as if I'm a machete-wielding serial killer. "Alright, I'm sorry if I smell bad, but Audrey, the house is amazing—"

"Amazingly toxic, and you're polluting this office."

"Okay, okay—I'll change my clothes, but just listen to what I found. There are ten rooms and—"

"Ten rooms of filth! Enough rats to bring back the Plague. And the mold—you know that can make you seriously ill."

"Yeah, I know—I'll be more careful next time. But

the Civil War stuff–"

"No next time. Mold is a biohazard, not something you can just charge into with no training and expect to shift it all around and spread those spores and—"

"Audrey, will you please just let me speak!"

We glare at each other. Jill's maroon-tipped hair is frosted with gray dust. There's no room for dirt under her close-bitten nails, but the cuticles are grimy and the whites of her eyes are bright red. My own eyes burn just looking at her. But for all that, she doesn't appear miserable. Indeed, she's even more chipper than usual. Somehow, that infuriates me.

"Fine. Speak away."

Usually cowed by any signal of my disapproval, Jill today is undaunted. "The house is am-a-a-azing, Audrey. I know from the outside it just looks like a big pile of trash, but there's actually a method to Harold's madness. Every room is dedicated to a different category of—"

"Crap."

"You're interrupting." Jill conjures a look that makes her resemble Miss McGuiness, my third grade teacher, if Miss McGuiness had sported a pierced nose.

"Anyway, Harold has different collections in each room: tools, appliances, books, art, maps, and once a room is filled, he stops collecting that thing unless he finds something he really needs, in which case he'll take something out, but he won't throw it away. He always has to find a new home for it. He's like the ultimate recycler. But see, that's why the task isn't impossible. According to the health department, we just have to clear out enough stuff so that the kitchen and bathroom are accessible and the hallways are clear. And we have to promise Harold not to throw away anything that will end up in a landfill."

"What! How can you clear out that place if you can't throw anything away? It's—"

"Audrey, I'm not finished." She waits for my silence

with pursed lips, just as Miss McGuiness used to.

"So, I have a plan—I'll get to that later. The most important thing is, the Civil War stuff is in the master bathroom, but Harold hasn't been able to get back there for years because the master bedroom is filled to the ceiling with birds."

"Birds! Oh my god, that's so gross."

"Not real birds. Well, maybe some were real once. Bird-related items: bird cages, and bird houses, and bird pictures, and bird books. Birds are one of Harold's obsessions. So, as I was saying, I have to clear a path through the birds so I can reach the Civil War."

Jill does not even hear the absurdity of that statement. I need all the self-control I possess to let her talk until she runs out of steam.

"Nora has convinced Harold that a museum is the best place for the valuable memorabilia. So I'll sell all that, and take a cut. Harold gets enough money to pay his back taxes, and the town doesn't evict him." Jill spreads her arms like some game show hostess displaying her prizes. "Everyone wins!"

"Everyone loses." I duck my head and begin shifting file folders on my desk. I'm too angry to see straight, so I can't do anything productive—just move them from left to right. "Even if there's something valuable in that house—and you only have the word of a mentally ill person that there is—how are you going to clear a path through that solid wall of junk with Harold objecting every step of the way? It'll be like digging the Panama Canal with a spoon."

"That's what I keep trying to explain, Audrey. Harold *wants* to work with me. He specifically requested me." Jill stands taller, as if being sought out by a madman is some great honor. "I've promised him that I'm going to recycle or sell everything we get rid of. Did you know that paper and cardboard are selling for $20 a ton right now?"

"How much are recyclers offering for bird feathers?

And cat turds—what are those going for?"

"I have a plan for this job, Audrey, just like you taught me, but you keep shooting me down at every turn."

"You don't have a plan for safety. Think of the mold you're breathing in."

"Okay, oka-a-a-y. I'll wear a respirator next time I go in."

"There won't be a next time as long as you're working for me." I spin on my desk chair and turn my back to her.

"Why are you being so mean?"

All the shouting has made me feel a little lightheaded. I burrow into my chair. Why *am* I being so mean? Is it because Jill's hell-bent on doing something that I disapprove of? I can hardly fault her for that—it's the story of my own career. No, Harold's house makes me feel like Jill is sinking into a pit of quicksand, her hand just inches from my reach.

"I'm worried about you," I whisper.

"I said I'd be careful—wear the hazmat suit and everything."

"It's not just your physical safety. Harold and Nora—they're so unstable, their problems are so big and unmanageable.... Nora is desperate to keep her uncle from being evicted. They're both sinking and they're looking for something—anything—to grab onto. You're not strong enough to save them, honey. They'll pull you under, and then—"

Jill squints at me. "And then you think you'll have to jump in and rescue us all."

I shut my eyes and massage my temples. "I can't, Jill. Not after all I've been through since Halloween. I just want peace and quiet and nice, steady work. I don't have the strength for anything else."

Jill pats my hand. "I understand, Audrey. That's why I promise you I'll handle Harold's job all by myself. I'm really good at getting him to listen—even

Nora says so. There's only one thing I might need your help with." Jill stretches backward in a yoga move that puts her head below my desk. "When I break through to the Civil War stuff, you'll help me find the best price for it, won't you?"

The fight drains out of me. "Of course."

# CHAPTER 11

I expected to encounter a language barrier when I visited Mother of Sorrows Catholic Church later that afternoon to try to learn more about Ramon, but I didn't expect the language to be Polish. For some reason, even though the congregation is largely Hispanic, the Vatican's choice of pastor is Father Mikolaj, a meek man utterly baffled by New Jersey in general and the people who attend his church in particular. After ten minutes of fruitless miscommunication, I decide that even if Ramon did attend this church, he would never come to Father Mikolaj for help. I leave, knowing my next stop has to be the holy-roller church.

I was uneasy enough nosing around an unfamiliar Catholic church, but approaching the Church of Living Praise leaves me squirming. For one thing, I'm back in The Bottoms, the neighborhood of the murder. The building itself is totally nondescript: a squat rectangle of concrete blocks with no windows facing the street. It could be a small engine repair shop or a business that stuffs envelopes for mass mailings....or offers up small animal sacrifices. No! I can't think that way. I tug on the flat steel front door and find it locked, so I'm forced to prowl around back. The small windows are too high for me to peek into, but I keep my ears tuned for people speaking in tongues, whatever that might sound like.

Around back I find a wooden door with a doorbell beside it. I press it, and after a second I hear a click that indicates the door has been unlocked from within. I push it as if I'm entering a tiger's cage.

Once inside, I'm greeted by the reassuringly ordinary smell of coffee that's been sitting on a warming plate too long. The hallway I find myself in is brightly lighted and decorated with children's watercolor paintings of the three wise men bearing gifts. One appears to be bringing a PlayStation to baby Jesus. So much for being abducted into a cult.

Down the hallway, a man pops his head out of an office. "*Hola!* Welcome!"

I move forward, acutely aware that I've come blundering in here with no game plan. "Hi, uhm.. Do you work...er, are you the...?" Minister? Leader? Charlatan-in-Chief?

"Jorge Santiago." He smiles and offers his hand. Given his deep laugh lines, I'd guess he's in his forties, but his mop of dark hair and slightly overlapping front teeth give him a boyish appearance. "I'm the pastor here. How can I help you?" His English is entirely unaccented, and his eyes are so friendly that I blush at the negative thoughts I've had about this place, as if he can see straight into my soul.

"It's kind of complicated," I stammer. "I'm not sure where to begin."

He extends a hand to invite me into his office, then sweeps a pile of papers off a chair. "Start at the beginning, no?"

The office walls are covered with framed color photos of church life: a baby being baptized, a young couple getting married, the kids' Christmas pageant, the choir singing. All the faces look like Ramon's— brown skin, dark eyes, black hair. I know this is irrational, but there's something else about Jorge Santiago and the people in these pictures that reminds me of Ramon. Maybe it's energy, or desire, or faith. I can picture Ramon here; he would fit right in. I made the right decision coming here, I'm sure of it. Then Grandma Betty's advice comes back to me and now it makes a lot of sense. This is not all about me. If Jorge Santiago actually does know Ramon, why should he help me find him?

I begin slowly, telling Pastor Jorge—that's what he tells me to call him—about my business and how I sometimes hire the men looking for work in front of the hardware store.

"You know they are undocumented," he says. I can tell he's trying to assess where I stand. There are people in Palmyrton who complain about the men, think they should be arrested or deported, and others who insist their businesses would collapse without them.

I nod. "My business is unpredictable. Sometimes I need an extra set of strong arms. That's when I hire one of the men outside the hardware store. They're hard workers." Half an hour later, I wind up my story of soup cans and cash and lawsuits and murder. Pastor Jorge sits in silence with his dark eyes searching my face.

"Do you know these men—Ramon, the boy who was killed, the guy with the knife?" I ask softly. There's been no mention in the news that the victim has been identified, let alone the killer.

"People in my congregation have told me the boy had only been in this country a week or so. No one knows his name."

"What about his family?"

"He came here by himself. His family is back in Honduras."

My heart twists. The child died all alone on a floor in a house in New Jersey. Back in Honduras, his mother is probably going about her day full of hope, thinking about her son making a new start in America. And now the soup cans that I mishandled have changed the course of all their plans.

"He was just a kid," I whisper. "How could they expect him to survive here on his own? What was he doing in that house?"

"He was from the same village as Ramon."

"So you *do* know Ramon?"

His left eyebrow and left shoulder rise in tandem. "If I do...?"

Now I try to read his face as closely as he's trying to read mine. He hasn't denied all knowledge of these events; he's too smart for that. But if Ramon has sought his pastor's help, he's put Jorge in a difficult spot. They both need a way out, and maybe I can provide it. I take a deep breath—an idea has come to me via Grandma Betty as I've been sitting here. I can't make it work all by myself, but I think I know how to begin.

"Ramon is a good man, Pastor Jorge. He's a hard worker and he wants a better life for his family. He didn't steal the cash, but even so, it's not his to keep. I understand that it's a life-changing amount of money. But here's the thing: he'll never rest easy as long as he has it. He'll always be looking over his shoulder for the police, or the INS, or the Wainwrights, or me, or that guy with the knife. So here's what would make everyone happy: The Wainwrights get their money back, I get my business out from under a cloud, the police arrest the murderer, and Ramon....Ramon gets his green card."

Pastor Jorge purses his lips. "Maybe you are right, Audrey. A man such as Ramon might trade all that cash for the opportunity to stay in this country legally. But there's no way you can guarantee that for him."

"Not right here, not today. But just consider this. If I can put together a good offer, with a guarantee from the police and the support of a great immigration lawyer, will you bring the offer to Ramon?"

"Ramon worships here sometimes, but his location

right now...." He shrugs.

I sense that he is choosing his words to avoid an outright lie. *Right now.* But later.... Unlike Coughlin, I'm not interested in tripping him up to pry information out of him. I keep my eyes locked on his. "But if the offer was good enough, safe enough, Ramon would want to hear it, wouldn't he?"

Pastor Jorge rises from his chair, never dropping his gaze. He places his hand on my shoulder, warm and soothing. "I imagine he would."

I walk out of the building in a fog, my mind caught up in the next steps I'll need to take to pull off this plan. How can I approach Sean to get his cooperation? I hear my grandfather's voice in my ear, "You catch more flies with honey than vinegar, Audrey." But honey has always been hard for me. And I'm sure Grandpa didn't mean that I should use a man's romantic interest in me to achieve my goals. What's the line between being pleasantly persuasive and sexually manipulative?

My head hurts.

I get in my car and glance in the rearview mirror before backing out of my spot. There are no oncoming cars on the quiet street. But a short man in a knit hat stands in the alley beside the church, watching. When I twist to look over my shoulder, he slips away.

# CHAPTER 12

On the way back to the office I keep glancing in my rearview mirror. I see the usual mix of Palmyrton traffic. What did I expect—a tinted-window black sedan or a creepy unmarked white van that screams surveillance? But I can't shake the skeevy, pervey feeling of being watched. Was that man outside the church the killer who saw me in Ramon's backyard? Or was he just some innocent passerby? I wrack my brain trying to remember exactly what the killer looked like. In books, trauma always causes memories to be "seared" in the heroine's brain. "I'll never forget that face as long as I live," the victim always declares.

Bull.

All I can remember clearly is the bright red smear of blood across his sweatshirt. His face is generic. Eyes, nose, and mouth all in the right places, but more than that I can't recall. I take a deep breath and grip the steering wheel to calm my nerves. I can't go through my days suspicious of every Hispanic man I see. That's going to get old pretty fast here in New Jersey.

Still, when I pull up in front of the office, I look up and down the busy street. Two men approach with their collars up and their heads down. Suspicious, or just cold? I let them pass before I get out of my car. The office windows are dark. I had given Jill permission to spend the end of the day at Harold's house, but I expected Ty to be here when I returned.

My neck, already tight with anxiety, knots up a little more. I hope he hasn't gone out looking for Ramon. Of course, that's precisely what I've been doing, but I don't want Ty to follow my example. I unlock the office door and hesitate on the threshold. What's that murky tall shape to my left? I reach my hand inside and fumble along the wall until I find the light switch.

Ping! The cheery clutter of my desk and the kitschy knick-knacks that march across Jill's appear before me. The tall shape is not an intruder, just a set of golf clubs in a travel case waiting to be picked up.

My heart slows back down as I lock the door behind me and sit down to sort through my email. A few minutes later, the door-knob rattles.

I snap into high alert until I hear some muttering and swearing. Ty comes in.

"Why you got the door locked?"

"Where have you been?"

We stare at each other for a moment then Ty speaks. "I just came back from the recycling center. Harold had every issue of *National Geographic, Scientific American*, and *Petroleum News* from 1982 to 2013 in his back hall. You got any idea of how many magazines that is?"

"One thousand, one hundred and sixteen."

Ty narrows his eyes. "Chill with the *Rainman* shit, Audge. I can only take so much crazy talk in one day.

"Why were you helping Jill? I thought you wanted no part of the Harold job."

"I don't. But I got bored waitin' for you. Ain't enough to do around here."

I sigh. "Tell me about it."

Ty's forehead creases. "But we be all right by next month, right?"

I don't want him to take on my load of anxiety, so I smile brightly. "Of course we will. In fact, why don't you start getting the signs ready for that small sale we have coming up?"

Ty jumps on this task with relief, and I return to scrolling through my email. A subject line jumps out at me: COMPLAINT RECEIVED. The sender is the Better Business Bureau.

My stomach twists as I read the message. Martha has filed a complaint against me. I have two days to respond. I read what she has written: "The owner of the company violated the terms of her contract with me by giving away unsold items to a personal friend instead of donating them to a registered charity. This caused me to lose valuables that could otherwise have been recovered."

Well, I can't really argue with that, can I? I need to make this right for her. Why hasn't Mr. Swenson called me back about the liability insurance situation? But even as this thought pops into my mind, my eyes are scanning more email messages. There it is: Liability Insurance as a subject line. I open the email, which is many paragraphs long. Scanning through the legal rigmarole, I get to the bottom line: my violation of the terms of the contract has nullified my liability coverage.

With one exception. I perk up.

If I file criminal theft charges against my employee, I'll be covered.

I let my head sink into my hands.

My only hope is to find Ramon and the money. Fast.

At six, Jill reappears with an update on her work at Harold's. "I've almost made it through the kitchen. The counters, sink, table, and dishwasher are filled with dirty dishes because the water's been turned off for non-payment for several years now," she explains, dropping into her desk chair. "And Harold would just buy more plates at yard sales when he needed them.

Ty puts his hands over his ears. "Stop! I can't listen

to this no more."

"However," Jill continues, "I've found a company in south Jersey that makes mosaic flowerpots and they're interested in taking all the china. They break it up, so it doesn't matter that it's chipped."

"They're willing to take china with fried eggs and lasagna still stuck to it?"

"Actually, the soup kitchen has been so grateful for all the stuff I've sent their way that they're willing to let me run the plates through their industrial dishwasher. After hours, of course."

For about the two hundredth time, I have to suppress the urge to point out that all the time she'll have to spend at Harold's cannot possibly pay off. But my protests fall on deaf ears–Jill is relentless.

"Tell her about the fridge," Ty says, making gagging faces at me over Jill's head.

"Yes, that's a problem." Jill runs her hands through her crewcut. "The power has been turned off and back on several times over the years, but Harold has never thrown away any of the spoiled food. There have been some...explosions."

"Eeeeewww!" Ty doubles over clutching his gut.

"Surely you can throw the whole fridge away?" I ask.

Jill shakes her head. "We'll compost the food, recycle the containers–"

"Stop! He won't even let you throw out rotten food? You have to compost it? That's insane!"

"Actually, it's not." Jill stands up and addresses her audience of two as if she's giving a TED Talk. "See, Harold's hoarding is actually a byproduct of his creativity as an inventor. He can see the theoretical usefulness of just about anything, even rotten food. That's why he can't let anything go—he has to repurpose it."

I turn back to the spreadsheet I've just opened up. "That's a pretty generous analysis of Harold's problem,

Jill. I think he's just plain nuts."

"Any good quality taken to an extreme can become pathological," Jill says. "Take, for instance, the belief that numbers can justify every decision."

I continue running my cash flow analysis for a full thirty seconds before that barb sinks in. Did Jill, my sweet little scatterbrain Jill, really just say that to me?

I turn around slowly. "You think I'm a pathological number cruncher because I said taking on Harold's job wouldn't be financially worthwhile?"

Jill opens her big, black-mascaraed eyes wide. "I didn't say that. I meant, like, Wall Street types who close down companies and fire all the employees...you know."

I keep looking at her, trying to stare into her soul. She chatters on. "Anyway, the fridge actually still works. Nora said she'd handle cleaning it."

"How generous."

If Jill heard my sarcasm she ignores it. "I've really enjoyed getting to know Nora. She's told me a lot about her life. Listen to this: Harold graduated from MIT! Nora says he got a job in the oil fields of Kuwait and spent all this time living abroad in awful places. When the Middle East started getting really dangerous in the 80s, Harold came back to New Jersey. He had saved a ton of money, but he had no life—no girlfriends, no buddies, no home. So he moved in with Nora's family."

"Why not just get his own place near them?" Ty asks.

"Her dad had just lost his job and they were having a hard time making ends meet. Harold moved into the house and took over paying the mortgage. It was supposed to be temporary—Dad would get a new job, Harold would build a new life for himself here and move into his own place."

"But that didn't happen?" I'm trying hard to pretend I'm not paying attention, but it's like being in a room where *The Jersey Shore* is playing on TV. You can't help being pulled into the ridiculous drama.

Jill shakes her head. "Nora's mom and Harold would spend all day together while Nora and her brother were at school and their dad was out looking for work. Harold would take her shopping. At first it was for stuff they really needed. Nora said her mom had been pinching pennies for so long, she was thrilled to be able to buy her kids new clothes and get some stuff for the house. Then it became this hobby the two of them shared: finding bargains, scoring a deal. Her dad finally got a job, but by that time, Harold was totally settled in with them. He still had no friends— he was too smart for ordinary people. Nora's mom was the only person who understood him."

Jill's story has me hooked. "Harold didn't need to work? He must've been only in his forties in the 1980s."

"According to Nora, he held several patents for oil drilling technology, and he got royalties from that. He enjoyed inventing things. As his personality got stranger, he found it too hard to work in an office, interacting with other people. He was only comfortable spending time with his sister."

Now Ty and I are fully focused on Jill, like when I sit in the garage listening to the car radio for a while to hear the end of a really good story on NPR.

"That's when the trouble started." Jill starts milking her story for all its drama. "Slowly, the house started filling up. First it was the basement. Then the stuff started creeping upstairs. That's when Nora's dad left. He couldn't take it anymore."

"He left her and her brother behind?" I'm incredulous. There's nothing like hearing someone else's childhood horror story to make you feel better about your own dysfunctional family.

"Nora says he got a much better job in Connecticut. She and her brother could have gone with him, but

Nora was a junior in high school and couldn't imagine leaving Palmyrton High. You know how high school is—starting over seems terrifying. So she refused to leave, and her younger brother stayed too. Even though what her dad did seems reasonable, I think Nora feels like he abandoned them because after he left, things got really bad."

I'm not sure if Jill is fully conscious of her "pause at the cliffhanger" delivery, but Ty and I fall for it.

"Ah, shit—is that when the twelve cats moved in?"

"I think that came later. But all the rooms on the first floor got filled up, so naturally, Nora and her brother were ashamed to have friends over. And the kitchen became inaccessible, so they had to eat carry-out every night. Nora and her brother had to figure out strategies to take showers and wash their clothes at other people's houses, without letting anyone know the real reason why. Once when Nora went on a class trip for a few days, she came back to find them filling up her room."

"And they lived that way all throughout high school?"

"Until Nora left for college. Then George moved to Connecticut to be with his dad. Neither one of them has lived in the house since."

"That's crazy." Ty shakes his head. "Harold saved their family, then he wrecked it."

"So what happened to Nora's mother?" I ask. "It sounds like she was Harold's partner in crime."

"I'm not sure," Jill says. "Sometimes I ask Nora one little question and she spills out all kinds of information, but other times she clams up like I'm prying or something. She doesn't seem to like to talk about her mom. I figure she'll tell me if she's ready."

With her maroon crew-cut and her layered thrift-shop wardrobe, it's easy to write Jill off as some ditzy freak chick, but there's a keen brain between those multiple-pierced ears and a sensitive heart under that

morning glory tattoo. Jill went through some dark
times in high school because she didn't fit neatly into
anyone's clique. Then, just when she was hitting her
stride at the Rhode Island School of Design, her aunt,
who had helped raise her, died. Jill went off the rails a
little and dropped out of school to move back in with
her mom. That's when she started working for me.
She's slowly regained her confidence, but she's quick to
recognize pain in others. She makes me ashamed to be
as obtuse as I sometimes am.

"You're very kind, Jill."

"I like helping Harold and Nora. It makes me feel
good about myself. Like I finally have, I don't know, a
purpose in life, ya know?"

"My grandma always says doin' for others is good
for your soul. But that refrigerator." Ty shudders. "I
don't want my soul saved that bad."

# CHAPTER 13

Ethel welcomes me home with her usual fervor. No criticism of my judgment. No disapproval of my choices. Just pure unconditional joy that I am once again in her presence.

How does anyone survive life without a dog?

"C'mon Ethel, let's eat and then you can help me brainstorm." While I fix her dinner, I explain my problems. "I have a plan to lure Ramon out of hiding, but I can't possibly call Sean Coughlin three times in one day, so that will have to wait until tomorrow."

I set her bowl down, and she buries her face in it. I knew she wouldn't argue.

"And then I have to convince Martha Wainwright to withdraw her Better Business Bureau complaint. You know what I always tell you when you're chasing squirrels: know your enemy. Maybe if I understood Martha a little better, I'd be able to reason with her."

I get comfortable with a container of Stouffer's mac and cheese in front of my laptop. Where else to begin but by Googling her? Turns out Martha is all over social media: LinkedIn, Facebook, Twitter. I could have sworn Martha mentioned that she was an elementary school gym teacher, but her LinkedIn profile describes her as a "healthy lifestyle entrepreneur" and owner of a juice bar called Juiced Up in Palmyrton. Really? Where in Palmyrton? I can't picture it.

So I Google the juice bar and get several hits: two announcing the grand opening and one announcing the store closure. Juiced Up was only open for five months. Now that I know the address, I can just about picture the place. It was on a small side street near the county government office complex. No foot traffic from anyone but bureaucrats and they're probably not health nuts. So Martha must be in debt from the failure of her business. No wonder she's desperate for that cash. But if she had the passion to start a business, maybe I can get her to understand how important Another Man's Treasure is to me. Maybe I can convince her that I'd never knowingly hurt one of my customers. Calling her won't be easy, but I'm going to do it. But first let me see what else I can find out.

I switch over to Twitter and look at her most recent tweets.

*Has anyone had a bad experience with Another Man's Treasure? #theft #cheat*

*Too bad not all #localbusiness can be trusted. Avoid Another Man's Treasure. #Palmyrton*

Good lord—she's flaming me! Don't panic. She only has a few hundred followers on Twitter. No one has responded or retweeted. And the kind of people who hire me don't hang out on Twitter.

My hands tremble on the keyboard. But they do use Yelp. I click over there. My God—I've gone from a 4.5 star rating to a 2 star rating in just two days. There are five new reviews posted, all negative: *Dishonest. Don't use them for your sale. Can't be trusted.* Who are these people? They're not my customers. Martha must have rounded up people to post fake reviews.

I could post a response, but I know my reaction will only instigate a war that will draw more attention to the bad reviews. I'm trapped.

I lean back in my chair, massaging my temples. There's no point in calling Martha.

This is war.

Jill is not at her desk on when I arrive at the office the next morning. I find myself feeling irritated in a way I never would have before I was fighting a social media smear campaign and searching for six figures of missing money. "She must be trying to squeeze in some more time over at Harold's," I gripe to Ty. "Not cool. We have a lot to do to get ready for Friday's sale." This is not quite true: the house is small and the homeowners orderly.

"I already texted her 'cause I didn't know what to do about these boxes, but she didn't answer," Ty says.

When she doesn't answer my text either, I get anxious. Whatever Jill's faults, going incommunicado is not among them.

"We could swing by there on our way over to prep for the sale," Ty suggests.

When we pull up in front of Harold's house, Jill's Beetle is nowhere to be seen. Ty and I look at each other. "Maybe her mom dropped her off. Let's go in just to be sure," he says.

"Will the door be open?" I ask as we head around to the back.

"If it's not, won't take much to break in."

I take a deep breath of cold, fresh air and hold it. The doorknob turns in my hand and we walk in.

"Jill? Jill, are you here?"

I forget to listen for her response because I'm so stunned by how much the house has changed in just two days. Even though Jill has told us about her progress, I'm amazed to see scratched hardwood floors beneath my feet and faded Eighties floral wallpaper on the walls. She's cleared enough stuff that the house is now visible, at least in parts. There are still stacks around the perimeter of the laundry room, but they're modest in size. Cautiously, I allow myself to inhale. The smell has changed. The rottenness has dissipated; the mildew lessened. But the undertones of urine and decay are still here.

A sound from the hallway that leads to the kitchen draws me further into the house, and I come face to face with Harold. He jumps back like a squirrel darting away from an oncoming car.

"Hi, Harold. Where's Jill?"

He continues backing away as I advance. "No, no. There's no Jill here. No one here but me."

Ty points to wet boot tread marks on the dusty floor. "Those are too small to be your feet, Harold. Those are Jill's Doc Martens. Where is she?"

Harold shakes his head, his eyes open so wide that the whites are visible all around the pupils. "I don't know any Jill. This is my house. You can't come in. You have to go away now."

"Harold, of course you know Jill. She's helping you clean the house. Now where is she?" I plead.

Ty pushes past Harold into the kitchen.

I hear the stern tone of my own voice and I know I've made a serious mistake. Harold's eyes dart back and forth. He grabs my forearm, and his long dirty nails would sink into my flesh if it weren't for my thick sweatshirt. "You go now. Right now. My sister won't like this. The children are sleeping. You mustn't wake them up."

Whoa, this is new. Harold has dialed back a few decades. Maybe seeing the wallpaper is making him think he's still living in the house with Nora's whole family.

"Yo, Jill! Where are you?" Ty shouts. I slide right out of my hoodie leaving it in Harold's claw, and run through the house to the foyer. The theme here is music. A very narrow path has been cleared on the stairs, but each step is still stacked with sheet music. The stairway turns at a landing, but from here the path appears to dead-end in a solid wall of vinyl record albums. Above us, we hear a muffled sound.

"Jill?"

The sound repeats.

Ty begins kicking aside the stacks of music to make a broader path. Ripped sheets covered with notes flutter behind him.

Behind me I hear an anguished cry. A gray blur launches at Ty. Brought to his knees, Ty tumbles down five steps. In an instant he's on his feet, eyes blazing.

Harold takes a swing at Ty, a pathetic gesture given the size and age differential. But it triggers a visceral fight response in Ty that is better left dormant. He hauls his powerful right arm back. I see Harold's life and Ty's freedom dissolving.

"Stop!" I grab a big instrument case—trombone?–and use it as a battering ram to push Harold out of harm's way. He falls down, whimpering.

Ty starts back up the stairs and I'm right behind him. Now the sound of Jill's voice is recognizable. "Ty? Is that you? Oh, thank God!"

I feel a sharp jab on my right ankle and my leg goes out from under me. Harold is pulling me off the stairs. "No, no, no!" he shouts. "You can't bother the children."

The sheets of music slide from their piles and Ty slips, nearly falling back on me. He regains his footing and picks Harold right up, a quarterback recovering a fumble. He carries him kicking and clawing to the front door. The whole time, Harold is yelling, "Leave the children alone. They're sleeping!"

"You stay outta my way, man. Jill is in trouble upstairs, and I don't got time for your craziness."

I open the door and Ty tosses Harold out like a drunk at closing time. Then we throw the deadbolt and try once more to climb the stairs. Ty is in front, so I can't see a thing.

"Shit! How'd you get through here, Jill? I can't fit."

"Please, Ty—try. I need you."

I hear the quaver of fear in her voice. "Let me try, Ty." He and I do an awkward dance to switch places at the top of the stairs and now I see the challenge.

Record albums are stacked on either side of the hallway with a path less than a foot wide between them. At the end of the path, an album avalanche has entombed Jill.

"Are you hurt?"

"No, I'm just stuck. I heard my phone ringing but I can't even get my hands around to my pocket."

"Okay, honey—stay calm. We'll get you out." I pull out my phone. "We'd better get the rescue squad or the fire department or something. I don't see how we can move—"

"No-o-o-o!" Jill's howl sounds like it's coming from a dungeon.

"Jill, we have to shift these albums, but there's no place to move them to."

"No, Audrey! If the fire department sees this, the house will be condemned right away and everything I've been working for will be lost. Don't call them, I'm begging you."

Ty peers over my shoulder. "If you can squeeze down there, Audge, you can slide the records down the path to me, and I'll just toss 'em down the steps."

"Harold won't—" Jill's voice pipes a weak protest.

Ty kicks a mound of sheet music down the stairs. "I don't give a damn what Harold wants. He was willing to let you rot in there. You want out, or what?"

"Okay. Do it."

So we begin the slow process of disinterring Jill. I slide *4-Way Street, Blue,* and *Sticky Fingers* along to Ty and he pitches them into the foyer where they perish. At some point during the process, Harold has come around and re-entered the house through the back door. He stands below keening like a banshee at the loss of each record.

"These don't belong here!" he cries as each album comes sailing over the banister and crashes in the foyer.

After I shift the complete works of Frank Sinatra,

the purple spikes of Jill's hair appear. A few more Woody Guthries and I can see her entire face, streaked with dirt and tears, her respirator hanging forlornly.

This is not how I want to be spending my morning, rescuing Jill from a catastrophe that I predicted was bound to happen, but I don't have the heart to say I told you so. Not when she looks so pathetic. In silence, I move enough records to free her arms.

"I'm sorry, Audrey," she whispers.

I can't quite bring myself to say, "It's okay." I keep digging, and as I get closer to the bottom, I start sneezing. After warning Jill of the dangers of this place, here Ty and I are working without any protection. Anxiety made me forget about the stench, but now it intensifies, coating the back of my throat like a thick paste.

With her hands freed, Jill helps move the albums off her legs and I slide them out to Ty. Our hands meet on *The White Album* and we move it together.

And we scream together. Long and loud.

# CHAPTER 14

"BackupBackupBackup!"

Defying physics in his attempt to rescue us, Ty has managed to squeeze his big self into the narrow pathway in the upper hall, but all he's doing is blocking our escape, which we're desperate to make. Ty slides down the banister to get out of my way while Jill and I stagger down the steps and charge for the front door. I lean over the front porch railing and lose my breakfast into the bare shrubbery.

Jill is dancing around waving her hands over her head. "I touched it! Ohmigod, I touched it!"

"What? What" Ty shouts to be heard over Jill's shrieking.

"A cat. A dead orange and white cat, totally flattened, stiff as a board." Jill rubs her hands on her coverall trying to erase the sensation of hard feline.

"A tom." I wipe my mouth and sit on the stoop with my head in my hands. "I knew I smelled something big and dead in there. He must've been crushed months ago and he was mummified under all those records."

"This is messed up, big time," Ty says. "You gotta leave this place alone, Jill. That cat was buried alive, and Harold was willing to let the same thing happen to you. He kept telling us you weren't here."

I know it's unkind to pounce on Jill in this moment of distress, but I feel like I have to take advantage of this prime opportunity to persuade her to quit. "Jill, honey—this house is toxic. It's very kind of you to want to help Harold, but he's not just eccentric, he's dangerously ill. He let those poor cats live in terrible conditions, and look what happened. There are probably more dead ones in there."

Jill's face is pale and sweaty even in the cold air, and I see her swallow hard to fight down a wave of nausea. "I know," she whispers. "He keeps putting food out to attract more, to replace the ones the ASPCA took away. He knows he's not supposed to, but he does it anyway. Nora and I throw the food away whenever we catch him."

"Don't that prove he's nuts?" Ty spreads his hands. "You gonna do all this work cleaning out the house, and he be right back at fillin' it up as soon as you finish. It's like that story we read in English class once, 'bout a dude rollin' a rock up a hill, and it would roll right down again."

"Sisyphus."

Ty points a long finger at me. "That's the guy."

Jill finds a crumpled Dunkin' Donuts napkin in one of her pockets and blows her nose. "But what about the Civil War stuff?"

"You only got the word of a wack-job that it's even in there."

"No," Jill protests. "Nora has seen the documents. They're real."

"Maybe he had them at one point in his life, but you have no way of knowing they're still in the house. Nora hasn't seen this stuff in twenty years," I say.

"Maybe you're right." Her voice shakes. "I don't know how I'll break it to Nora that we're quitting."

"Shit, I'll tell her for you." Ty thumps his chest. " 'Jill is through with your crazy ass brother and his crazy ass'—"

"Shhh." She slaps Ty's arm and I look up to see a tall, lean man in running gear coming up the walk.

"Morning all." He extends his hand to Ty. "I'm Ed

Brandt. Live across the way at number fifteen. I've seen all the activity over here. Just thought I'd pop over and say hi."

We all stare at him like drunken teenagers trying to look sober. He's in great shape, but now that I'm looking at his face I can see that he's older than I first thought—in his sixties, judging by the laugh lines and hair that's cropped close to minimize the baldness.

He leans against a big oak and starts doing some stretches. "Who am I kidding? Everyone on the street has been dying of curiosity and they nominated me to come over and find out what's going on. Is poor old Harold finally going to move out?"

Ty looks from me to Jill. He's not sure who's handling this, but he knows it's not him.

Jill tries to muster some dignity, which is not easy given that she's covered in the dust of a hundred record collections and has only momentarily stopped crying. "Harold has no plans to move. We're just helping him, uhm, get the house in order."

"Hmmm." Ed rolls his neck and his vertebrae crack loudly. "I think it may be too late for that. Harold's made attempts to clean up before, but he can never make it last. The town says his time is up." Ed surveys the house and yard. "What we all want to know is, will they come in here with a bulldozer and just plow it under, or—"

"I can't listen to this!" Jill runs into the house, letting the door slam behind her.

"Say, I didn't mean to upset her." Ed looks from me to Ty and back again. "Is she...are you...Harold's relatives?"

"My family's crazy, but they ain't *that* crazy," Ty mutters.

I'm not so eager to reveal my professional identity to this guy. Thank goodness we came in my car, not the company van. "Her name is Jill. She's ...uh...taken an interest in Harold and Nora, in trying to help them out of this, uh..."

"Hell hole?" Ed offers cheerfully.

"Predicament. That's the word."

"If you say so. All I can tell you is, this predicament has been getting worse and worse for years, and the neighbors are really sick of it. Some of them chipped in to hire a lawyer to force the town to evict him."

"Not you?"

"Nah. Lawyers make everything worse. I've known poor old Harold for thirty years. He's a brilliant guy. I don't wish him ill—none of us do, really. But the house." Ed shakes his head. "The house is a health hazard."

Ty opens his mouth to chime in, but I shoot him a silencing look. I want Ed to move along so I can get back inside to Jill. "Thanks for dropping by. I've got to get going."

Ed offers a jaunty wave and trots down the walk. At the curb, he turns and shouts back to me. "Harold and his sister should tear the house down and sell the lot. A lot in this neighborhood is worth a lot of money. Tell Nora that's her best option."

Back in the house, Jill is nowhere to be seen. I hear a noise overhead–surely she hasn't gone back up into the cat tomb?

I start up the stairs following the faint sound of crying. "Where are you?"

At the end of the upstairs hall in the space we've cleared of records, I see Harold, not Jill. He's sitting cross-legged on the floor, one hand extended behind him, tears slipping from his eyes into his scruffy gray beard. I don't care to get too close.

"Harold, are you all right?"

"It's Petey," he says, coughing to clear his throat. The desiccated cat corpse is in his lap. "I knew he would never run away. I knew he was still here with me. Oh, Petey!"

"Harold, stop! You shouldn't touch that." My voice comes out harsher than I intended.

He turns his head toward me, his pale green-gold eyes open wide. "Don't wake the babies," he whispers. "Don't wake the babies."

I back away, seriously creeped out. "Jill! Come on, right now. We're leaving!"

"I'm down in the living room. I'll be out in a minute."

Her voice has lost its weepy tone. Down in the foyer, Ty notices that too, and his brow furrows. He picks his way along a channel of small appliances—the theme of the living room seems to be "items with cords." Soon I hear his voice. "Whoa! That's amazing."

Oh God, now what?

"Am I right?"

"I think so. Audge'll know."

"Know what?" I call from the landing.

The two of them appear at the door of the living room carrying something between them.

"It's a Tiffany lamp." Jill's face is flushed with triumph. "See for yourself!"

# CHAPTER 15

"Bring it over here. You know there are millions of reproduction Tiffany lamps floating around."

Jill lets Ty carry it, running ahead clearing a path so he won't trip and drop the precious load. "It says 'Tiffany Studios' on the base," she says.

"All that proves is that the reproducers did a good job," I answer. The Presbyterian Church in Palmyrton is famous for having a genuine Tiffany window. Last year, during the Palmyrton Pride Festival, the three of us were returning from a sale and got caught in festival traffic. Jill and I decided to take the church tour to kill time, and we dragged a protesting Ty with us. The lady giving the tour was a fount of Tiffany knowledge, and Ty ended up asking more questions than anyone. So now we're all Tiffany quasi-experts.

Ty sets the lamp on a table in the foyer and gently taps the leaded glass shade. "Hear that? It rattles because the lead is so old, it's loose. A new fake wouldn't do that."

He's right—that's exactly what the lady told us. I've never understood why Ty had problems in school because he's got an encyclopedic memory. Now he turns on the flashlight function on his cellphone and shines it up through the glass. Even through the thick layer of dust, the colors jump to vivid life. The shade features a garden of irises, their petals delicately drooping, their leaves standing tall.

"There it is," Ty shouts. "The confetti colors—the green in the leaves isn't solid green, it's all mixed with beige and yellow. The purple in the flowers has some gold and blue running through it."

I study the base—it's definitely bronze, not painted wood or plastic. The lamp is looking more and more genuine. Even without research, I know that if the lamp is a real Tiffany, we're looking at a six-figure sale.

"We'll have to take pictures and send them off to the Tiffany expert at Christie's. The fact that the lamp came from a hoarder's stash and has no provenance is a strike against it. Don't get your hopes up too high." But even as I say this I feel the familiar flush of joy that accompanies the discovery of unexpected treasure.

"Now we have proof there are valuable things in this house." Jill squeals. "This means we have to keep working."

"No!" Ty and I sound like the woofer and tweeter of a cheap car stereo.

"All this means is if the lamp is real, you'll actually get paid for all the work you've put in here so far." I turn my back on her pleading face. "And Harold will have enough money to find a small place to live."

"No, Audrey! This means there could be all sorts of priceless art and history in here. We can't let the town bulldoze the house! Think of what might be lost!"

Ty glances toward the living room. "Three hundred fifty-nine greasy toaster ovens."

"Jill, you agreed just ten minutes ago that working here isn't safe. That hasn't changed."

"But Audrey, that was before—"

My phone starts to ring and I'm eager for this interruption in the cascade of Jill's pleading. When I see the number on the screen, I'm even more eager. "Stop! This is Elizabeth Haverford, the property manager at Willowby. Once we get her job, I'm going to need both of you working full-time."

"Hello, Elizabeth. How are you today?" I hope I sound relaxed and casual, as if I'm sipping green tea in my sleek office, not sneezing out decomposing cat particles at Harold's. Ty and Jill are frozen in silence, trying to hear the conversation with their eyes.

I listen to her velvety voice with a smile on my face, so confident am I of what she is saying. A good thirty seconds pass before I process that the sentences flowing into my brain contain the words "regret" and "sorry" and "under the circumstances." She's seen the Better Business Bureau complaint. The Yelp reviews. I reach my hand back to find the support of the newel post. The green tendrils on the grimy wallpaper writhe before my eyes. My mind goes blank. Finally I stammer, "Really, the problem with the Wainwrights will have no impact—"

She cuts me off, her voice smooth but firm. "Willowby's owner has made his decision. The job is going to Jameson Sales."

The dead phone dangles from my weak fingers. We lost the Willowby job because my reputation has been ruined by the Wainwrights' missing money and my unsavory connection to a murdered immigrant. I can't bear to make eye contact with Ty or Jill.

My throat constricts. I wait for it to pass before I speak. "Let's get ourselves some good quality respirators, kids. We'd better hope the Gettysburg Address, Part Two is up in that bathroom."

# CHAPTER 16

I strip off my work clothes in my garage and dive into the shower as soon as I get home, but even after twenty minutes of scalding water and floral body wash, I still can smell piss and rot. It's not on my limbs; it's imprinted in the scent receptors of my brain. I may smell this in my grave.

So this is my life: the only person willing to hire me is a mentally ill hoarder, and even he is not enthusiastic about my services. I am clearing out his filthy home in a quest for uncertain treasure. My reputation is ruined—as the final kick delivered to a woman already on the mat, the family in the dinky split-level on Peyton Road called to cancel their sale. I owe an unknowable amount of money to a vengeful client. And I've looked directly into the eyes of a stone-cold killer who may, or may not, remember me more clearly than I remember him.

I feel a dangerous pressure in my chest, a prickling in my eyes.

I will *not* cry.

I look around my empty condo. I suppose I could cry. There's no one here but Ethel to see me.

And that thought makes a few tears spill over. Ethel climbs up on the sofa beside me and rests her head on my thigh. Deep in her throat she makes a sound that's a cross between a whine and a moan.

"Exactly." I stroke her silky ears. I wish I had

someone in my life who would just listen, not give me advice I don't want. Like my father—Close the business and go back to graduate school. Or Coughlin—Take a long vacation until all the arrests are made. Or Mr. Swenson—Follow the letter of the law and let your employee be prosecuted.

"Maybe we should wallow in a good tearjerker, Ethel."

Anxiety fills her big brown eyes.

"Don't worry. Not *Marley and Me*." I reach for my laptop. "*The Notebook? Titantic?*"

When my phone begins to vibrate sometime after Leo DeCaprio dances with Kate Winslet, I consider ignoring it. But Ethel digs frantically at the pocket of my flannel pants, so I relent.

When I see the name on the screen I bolt upright. Maura! "Hey! Where are you?" My best friend has been working in London for the past six months, and traveling to European hotspots between meetings and sales pitches.

"On West Carson Avenue. You've got exactly seven minutes to change out of your pajamas and put on some heels. We're going to that new jazz bar."

Is this divine intervention? "You're in Palmyrton? When did you get back?"

"Last night, but I've been asleep for twelve hours. Now I'm ready to rock. Are you up off your couch?"

How well she knows me! I shrug off my What's your Sine t-shirt as I head into my bedroom. Maura will not be amused. "I'm getting dressed, but we can't go to the jazz place—there's a line around the block every night."

"We'll get in. I know the doorman."

How can she know the doorman? How can she even know about the new jazz club if she's only been back in town for eighteen hours, and most of those asleep? But that's Maura.

I open my closet door. Every outing with Maura

involves a fashion crisis. As I flip through my sedate slacks and proper sweaters, I'm pretty sure I haven't bought a single new article of clothing since Maura dragged me to the mall before she left. I hear Ethel going crazy. Maura has the key to my condo and she's let herself in. I run to greet her.

The reunion is a big weepy, doggie, squealing lovefest.

"I've missed you so much!"

"I've missed you more," Maura says.

I don't know how that can be because Mara has never met a stranger. She makes friends wherever she goes. She's a classic extrovert, energized by her many social engagements. And I, I'm a classic math nerd. Slow to warm up, exhausted by parties. But we've been best friends since our freshman year at UVA. I tutored her through Intro to Statistics and held her hand when her first college boyfriend dumped her. She dragged me out of the library and introduced me to the kinds of people she knew I'd like, both male and female. We don't try to change each other. We know the very thing that drives us crazy about each other is actually the thing we love most about each other. She livens me up; I calm her down.

Maura steps back and sizes me up. "You're so skinny! Love the new haircut, but you need some product. Is that a training bra? Go put on something that gives you some lift."

As I knew she would, Maura heads to my closet. "Didn't I tell you to get rid of this awful gray sweater?" She tosses it on the floor where Ethel curls up on top of it. I guess my favorite cardigan is a dog bed now. "Are these the same– Hey, what's this?"

Maura holds a padded hanger in her hand. Suspended from it is a sleek black dress. THE black dress.

"Outstanding! Put this on."

I take a step backward. "I can't."

Maura cocks her head. "Now don't start that 'It's too sexy' thing. You own this. No tags—you must've worn it before."

Ridiculously, I feel my eyes well with tears.

"Honey, what's wrong?"

"It's the dress I wore on my first date with Cal. To Spencer Finneran's birthday party."

Maura opens her arms and I let her hold me and rock me. It feels good to cry with a woman who truly appreciates the healing properties of tears. Jill is frightened when I cry and my father is disgusted. And Coughlin, well, Coughlin would indulge my tears, just not tears shed over Cal. When I'm done, Maura wipes my face with a cold washcloth and shakes her head over the state of my red eyes and blotchy skin. She produces eye drops and concealer from her bag, and repairs the damage. Then she says, "Put on the dress."

"No! I can't."

"You can. You need to feel beautiful again."

Maura slides the dress over my head and zips it up, and she's right. The dead cats and dusty record albums and fraudulent soup cans drop away. For the next few hours, I'm going to be a different Audrey.

At 3:00 AM I push a snoring Ethel off my pillow and slide into bed. The room tilts precariously thanks to three apple-tinis. My calves ache from dancing a bastardized version of the cha-cha with a hilarious gay clarinetist in town for his cousin's wedding. Some stock analyst from Summit now has my phone number as a condition of calling a taxi for Maura and me. I'm going to have a colossal headache in the morning, but I'm happier than I have been for months.

Whenever I'm hung-over, I'm always tremendously hungry, so breakfast with Dad at the Athenian diner, which went so spectacularly awry on Sunday, is today looking pretty good.

But when I call him up to find out when he wants to go, he's got a different plan in mind.

"Kyle's basketball team made the quarterfinals at the Center. The game is at two this afternoon. They nearly lost their game on Thursday, but Kyle sank a three-pointer at the buzzer."

"'Sank a three-pointer at the buzzer'—who's writing your material, Dad?"

"I guess I've picked up some terminology from the other parents."

"How often do you go to the games?"

"I try to go to all Kyle's games. His mom can't get off work to go, and his dad's not in the picture. He doesn't have anyone to cheer for him."

I feel a ridiculous stab of envy. My father never came to any of my childhood recitals. He came of one of my high school chess matches once and made me so nervous I blew the game.

"So do you want to go today? Kyle would love to see you there."

I think of screaming fans and shrieking buzzers and thumping balls. My head throbs. Then I think of Kyle's bright, dark eyes and big lop-sided grin. Then I think of possibly running into Sean at the Parks Center and casually mentioning my plan to lure Ramon in from the cold.

"Yeah, sure—I'll pick you up at 3:30."

I content myself with egg, Taylor ham, and cheese on an everything bagel from Sol's and head over to Harold's house. By the time I pull into Summit Oaks, all the kids have left for school, the parents have left for work, and the stay-at-home moms are off to yoga or pottery or Suzuki violin with their toddlers. But as I follow the winding streets to Acorn Lane, I realize I'm not alone. In front of one house, three women emerge from a bright blue minivan carrying mops, and buckets and a vacuum. On the next block, two men cling to a steep roof, fixing a hanging gutter. Around the corner, a crew of window-washers takes advantage of the forty-degree weather to ply their trade.

They all have dark hair and brown skin. They all do the work most people won't touch. I want to shout out my window, "Do you know Ramon? Have you seen a man with blood on his sweatshirt?"

Would they tell me if they did?

When I arrive at Harold's house, the Another Man's Treasure van is parked at the curb, and a tow-truck is in the driveway hooked to one of the junked cars. Jill, Harold, and the driver are locked in an intense discussion. Jill told me yesterday that Harold had agreed to donate the three non-working cars to Habitat for Humanity. I can't hear the discussion, but I can guess at the problem. Harold is willing to part with the cars, but not the collections inside the cars.

I briefly consider getting involved, but decide this is Jill's show. My rationality is not particularly useful in dealing with Harold. As I get out of my car, I notice a man walking a small fluffy dog pause at the intersection of Acorn and Birch. He doesn't bother to conceal his curiosity at the scene. When he spots me, he strides over, dragging the reluctant pooch with him.

"Are they getting rid of the cars to make it easier to tear down the house?" he asks without introduction. He has a stocking cap pulled down over his ears and a scarf wrapped around his neck although it's not all that cold.

"There's no plan to tear down the house," I say. "We're doing some clearing out to make it more livable."

His eyes widen. "You're clearing the whole house? That will take months."

The thought of spending months here induces a wave of nausea. "Just selected rooms. We'll be done in two weeks."

I turn and walk away. I pulled that number out of

the air, but suddenly it becomes my goal. In two weeks we'll be done and I'll have those Civil War documents. A person can endure anything for two weeks.

I'm proud to say I made it through fours years at UVA without ever going to a Cavaliers game. So that means I haven't been in a gym since high school. The smell of sweat and floor wax and rubber mats takes me back to a miserable time in my life. Trying to negotiate the horrors of zits and PMS and braces and mean girls without a mother made me feel like the only girl on the planet who hated high school. Now that I'm safely on the other side I realize there's hardly a person on the planet who *didn't* hate high school.

Dad and I take our places on the bleachers and he nods to some of the other fans. My father is a regular at the basketball court! Dad is craning his neck looking for someone. Across the room I see a familiar splash of color. It's the scarf, the Moorish tile scarf from the Met Shop, wrapped around the neck of a slender woman with short, wavy silver hair.

I elbow Dad. "Is that who you're looking for?"

He stands up and waves. Good lord, he's blushing!

Natalie's face lights up when she sees us and she climbs up the bleachers, greeting people as she goes. Now she's in our row. "Hello, Roger." She pats his hand lightly, then turns to me. "And you must be Audrey. I've heard so much about you! Isn't this lovely that you've come to the game." She slides past Dad and sits down between us. "I want to hear all about your fascinating job."

This is promising. I guess Dad hasn't succeeded in convincing her that I've thrown my life away as an estate sale organizer. Still, despite her friendliness, I find her a little intimidating. Earrings, bracelets, scarf—all those accessories make me nervous. Although she's wearing khakis and flats, she projects a force field of elegance holding the stinky gym at bay. I suspect that if my mother were alive today, she'd look just like this.

"I hear you found what may be a Tiffany lamp at this house you're clearing out," Natalie says.

Now when did Dad have time to tell her that? Does he violate his self-imposed telephone ban to chat with her? "Possibly. I've sent photos off to the Tiffany expert at Christie's. We'll see what he has to say."

Before we discuss this further, the buzzer sounds and the teams run out onto the floor. As each Palmer Panther is announced, his family and friends cheer wildly in the stands. Kyle's best friend Jamal has a particularly large and boisterous crew. Then Kyle's name is called. Natalie and Dad look like they're clapping to welcome the concertmaster of the New Jersey Symphony to the stage. So although I have no experience in this, I feel compelled to stand up and scream. "Go Kyle!"

He looks up, startled, and a shy smile spreads across his face. It's not cool to wave, but I see his fingers flutter.

Then the two coaches cross the court and shake hands in the middle. One is a lean, balding man in glasses; the other is a tall and broad hulk with close-cropped red hair.

Coughlin.

I turn on my father. "You didn't tell me Sean Coughlin was Kyle's coach."

His eyebrows arch innocently. "Didn't I mention it? I thought I had."

At first I'm annoyed, but then I realize Dad is handing me the perfect opportunity. Now I can certainly "run into" Sean, do my best to be charming, and start to lay the groundwork for my plan to reel in Ramon. I settle in to watch the game.

Natalie is amazingly knowledgeable about basketball. She leans forward with her hands on her knees murmuring about zone defense and motion offense while my father pulls out a notebook to record the team's stats. When the ref calls a foul against Jamal, the man behind us loudly decries his eyesight and mental stability, but Natalie just purses her lips. Down on the court, Coughlin waves Jamal off the court and sends another kid in. The loudmouth behind us groans. I see Coughlin crouch to speak to Jamal eye-to-eye. The little guy's head droops.

"What did Jamal do wrong?" I ask, immediately sure the poor kid has been unjustly accused.

"Showboating again," Natalie says. "That pass was intended for Number 22. Jamal was so intent on getting it himself he fouled the guy guarding him."

Dad nods. "Jamal is the highest scorer. Sean spends a lot of time coaching him to work with his other team members. Sean puts him on the bench when he's a ball hog."

Huh. I would have pegged Coughlin as the "win at all costs" type.

With Jamal out of the game, the Summit Seekers soon pull ahead. I study Coughlin's reaction to the other team's successful shots, expecting anger or at least frustration. But Coughlin appears as serene as a Buddhist monk, his hands loosely clasped behind his back, his head slightly tilted. The guy behinds us screams, "Put Jamal back in!" but Coughlin doesn't react. The game continues with the Panthers slipping further behind. The quarter ends, and he gathers the team around him, speaking to them quietly but intently. On the far side of the court, the Summit coach is red-faced, jabbing his finger at his players. One kid is crying.

When the game starts up again, Jamal is back in but playing less aggressively.

"The kids really like Sean, don't they?"

"They respect him. They crave his approval." Natalie lays her hand on my father's knee. "Just as they seek Roger's approval."

Don't we all?

"Audrey is a champion chess-player," my father says, apropos of nothing.

What? Is he reading my mind?

"You should come to the center and help your father with chess club, Audrey," Natalie says.

Dad puts down his stat notebook and leans around Natalie. "Yes, you should. I'm getting more kids than I can handle."

How's that for double-teaming? "Uhm...Okay. I guess."

"Tuesday at four. Don't forget."

Before I can say more, Kyle steals the ball and flies down the court with it. The Panthers are back in the game. From that point on, the game is too exciting for conversation. When the buzzer sounds, the Panthers have won by two points. I find myself on my feet, screaming and cheering. As the kids swarm around him, Coughlin finally shows some emotion. A grin splits his face and he looks as young and carefree as the boys on the team. I notice him giving Kyle's shoulder a squeeze. I arch my back, knowing how Sean's warm hand feels. The two teams do their obligatory "good game" hand slap and Coughlin shepherds them off the court. Before he disappears into the locker room, he looks into the stands. His eyes meet mine and he nods.

There's an ice cream victory party upstairs in the lobby. I expect Dad will want to slip away—noisy mingling events are not his scene, nor mine–but he and Natalie are swarmed by kids and borne off to the sundae line. Coughlin is cornered by a crowd of fathers talking hoops strategy, and I'm stuck making some "Aren't those kids amazing?" chat with moms I don't know. Damn! I feel my plan for a casual Coughlin encounter slipping away.

Gradually, the energy in the room winds down. Families begin leaving for home and I find myself alone. Sean is still talking to one very intense father, so I retreat to a bench by the door and pull the partially finished Sunday *Times* crossword puzzle out of my bag, making sure I'm in Sean's sight-line. When I'm sure he's seen me, I duck my head and apply myself to the lower right quadrant of the puzzle. Soon enough Sean's huge feet appear before me.

"Did you do all that during the game?" he asks.

"I had most of it done before I got here. I promise I wasn't working the puzzle during Kyle's breakaway." I slide over, inviting Sean to sit. "You're terrific with the kids. They really enjoy playing for you."

He stretches out his long legs. "I try to keep 'em out of trouble. Makes my real job easier."

"I think you're more invested than that. It's pretty clear those kids adore you."

I expect a smart-aleck comeback, but Sean has a wistful look in his eye. "I get more from them than they get from me. When you spend all day with low-lifes and scumbags, you get a little cynical. A lot cynical. Before I started coaching, the person I was becoming, well, you wouldn't want to know that guy. I guess you still don't want to know me, but really, I used to be much worse. Those kids—their joy, their honesty—they turned me around."

How does Sean manage to do this? At the very moment when I had convinced myself that it would be permissible to manipulate him to suit my needs, he hands me his heart on a platter. Taking advantage of Bambi would be easier than this.

I take a deep breath. One of these days my fatal attraction to unvarnished honesty is going to get me killed, but right now, it's all I've got. "Sean, I want to apologize about the incident with Ty, about thinking you'd shot him." I start out looking into Sean's blue, blue eyes, but the intensity of his stare makes me shift my focus to my folded hands as I continue. "The whole scene was so surreal, and seeing Ty crumpled on the ground and you with your gun drawn—well, I leaped to a conclusion that wasn't irrational, but wasn't...uh...well thought-out." I glance at him from the corner of my eye. "I'm just trying to say, I'm...I'm sorry if I hurt your feelings."

Geez that was hard!

He watches me silently. Finally he speaks. "You're sorry *if* your thinking that I'm a cold-blooded, rogue cop assassin hurt my feelings?"

I try again, this time holding his gaze. "I know I hurt your feelings, Sean. I'm sorry. Please accept my apology."

Now it's Sean who looks away, studying the mural of Rosa Parks as if he's never seen it before. "Your good opinion matters to me, Audrey. I'm very impressed by your talents. Your knowledge of antiques, your business skills, all that math whiz stuff. I just wish you would give me a little credit for knowing how to do my job. I know I look like a big, dumb jock, but I do possess a brain."

"I've never questioned your intelligence, Sean. Only your conviction that you're always right."

"Unlike you." He plucks the crossword from my lap and scans it. "Thirty-eight across, common shape in cathedrals. You have 'arch'. Should be 'ogee'."

I snatch the puzzle back. "Oh my God—that changes everything! No wonder I was stuck."

"So you do believe I have a brain?"

"Of course I do."

He leans his forehead against mine and whispers, "Then try not to look so incredulous when I'm using it."

And that moment of weakness, when Sean has managed to make me feel guilty and flattered and bizarrely affectionate all at once, accounts for what happens next. Dad and Natalie appear and suggest we all go out to dinner at Fiorello's.

I say yes.

# CHAPTER 17

Sean and I face Dad and Natalie over a flickering candle. Puccini overtures play softly in the background. Bad reproductions of Italian masterpieces beam down at us as the waiter fills our glasses with red wine. I hold the big menu up in front of my face and pretend I'm not on a double date with my father.

Things get a little easier once the appetizers arrive and we've worked our way through half the wine. Natalie is an intrepid conversationalist, prying out details of all of our lives: Sean's college athletic triumphs, Dad's research on Diophantine equations, and my work at Harold's house.

"How tragic," Natalie says as I describe the conditions at Harold's house. "A brilliant mind run unraveled by all that junk."

"That's the incredible part. When I first started, I thought the house was just a big pit filled with garbage, but now I see the method to Harold's madness. He really does have a system in place for each section of the house although it's not always apparent to the untrained eye. Each room is like an archeological exploration of Harold's obsessions."

Dad purses his lips. "Are you making any headway? This sounds like a lot of work for no certain return."

Of course this is exactly what I've been complaining about to Jill, but I don't appreciate hearing it from my father. What's more, he doesn't know about the Better

Business Bureau complaint and the loss of the Willowby job, and that's the way I want it to stay.

"We *are* making progress. So far we've drilled through to the foyer. Jill has recycled fifty thousand paper road maps. Turns out Harold is a huge fan of Google Maps, so he let them go pretty easily. The mildewed atlases and broken globes seem to be causing him more trouble. Jill can't figure out how to recycle them, so we've just shoved them in a corner for now."

Dad opens his mouth to protest. I notice Natalie shoot him a warning look, and amazingly, he says nothing. Man, this woman really is a good influence.

"So the discovery of the lamp makes you believe there really might be more valuable stuff in there?" Sean drains his water glass and sets it on the table.

A busboy appears immediately to refill it as I continue my story. "According to Nora, there's Civil War memorabilia in the master bath. She remembered the name of the dealer who sold it to Harold, and Jill followed up with him—according to his records, in 1982 Harold bought a set of letters between Robert E. Lee and Jefferson Davis. We have to work our way through the Bird Room to get to the Civil War Room. Bird houses, bird feeders, bird books—I can hardly wait."

"Are you sure the letters are still there?" my father asks. But I have to admit, his tone is reasonable, not accusatory.

I shake my head. "The last time Nora saw them, they were in the master bath. She hasn't been up there for over fifteen years."

Natalie sets her silverware down and offers me a reassuring smile. "On the bright side, no one else has been up there either, right?"

The busboy clears the appetizers, the fettuccine and the veal saltimbocca arrive, and the conversation turns to anecdotes from Natalie's parenting class. We laugh and eat and drink more wine, and before I know it, the restaurant has emptied to two or three parties.

Natalie looks at her watch. "My goodness—nearly nine. Come on, Roger, I'll drive you home."

I open my mouth to insist that I can do it and someone, maybe Dad, maybe Sean, kicks me sharply under the table. I shut up, and the two of them wander off, arm-in-arm.

That leaves Sean and me to finish off the second bottle of Cabernet.

With Dad gone, I can finally ask the question that's been on my mind all night. "Any progress in finding Ramon?" I want to know what he knows, but I'm not quite ready to reveal what I've discovered.

The busboy comes by to refill our water again even though there's barely an inch of space in the glasses.

Sean shakes his head. "No one's talking. We can't even get a solid ID on the victim. I've been canvassing—" He pauses and waits until the busboy leaves.

"Man, that busboy is irritatingly attentive," I say

Sean watches him retreat to the kitchen. "I was thinking the same thing."

Our conversation dries up. "What's the matter?" I ask.

"Does that guy look familiar to you?"

"Who? The busboy? Why would I know him?"

"Could he be one of the guys we saw at that first house when we were looking for Ramon?"

I start to twist my head. Sean reaches across the table and grabs my hand. "Don't look at him. He's watching us."

"He is? Why?" Then I remember the guy I saw in my rear-view mirror as I was pulling away from the Church of Living Praise. I didn't see his face clearly, but he was short and stocky, just like the busboy. Uneasiness presses in on me and I feel like I can't get a full breath. I'm not up for more risk, more danger.

Part of me wants very badly for Sean to take care of the Ramon problem, take care of me. I want to immediately blurt out to Sean my conversation with Pastor Jorge, but I know I have to be more cautious. If I tell him I'm scared, he'll head right over there and start interrogating the poor man and ruin any chance of negotiating with Ramon. I look at his impassive face and know that behind that façade the wheels are spinning. If I withhold information from him now, he'll never forgive me, never trust me again.

I lean forward and speak in a low voice. "There's something I need to tell you."

The sandy eyebrows rise a quarter inch.

"Remember how Ty said Ramon was religious? Well, I discovered the church he attended, and I spoke to the pastor."

Sean's eyes narrow. He looks like he's practicing deep breathing to stay calm.

"It was only two days ago. But I think, maybe, that the busboy could be the same guy who watched me leave the church. Possibly. But—"

Sean flexes his right hand at the wrist. "Not here. Let's go."

Both Sean and I have our cars at the restaurant. He escorts me to mine, which is covered in a light dusting of snow that's started falling while we ate. "Drive straight to your condo. I'll be right behind you. Don't slide through any yellow lights."

"Sean, really, I'm not sure—"

"Do as I say. We'll discuss this at your place."

I know better than to protest. And truthfully, seeing his car illuminating the snowflakes right behind me every time I glance in my mirror is reassuring. Ten minutes later, we're sitting on my sofa. When Ethel sprawls across both of our laps, I don't shoo her away. How mad can Sean get with her furry tail brushing his arm?

"Talk."

"Okay, so when you told me that Ramon couldn't get out of the country with the money too easily, I just thought I'd ask around at the local churches to see if anyone knew anything."

Sean rubs his temples. "You're a regular Miss Marple, aren't you?"

"I didn't think it could hurt." I want to say, "You weren't doing it," but I bite my tongue.

"Go on. How many churches in Palmyrton know you're looking for Ramon?"

"I didn't just go door-to-door. I narrowed it down to the two most likely. The priest at the Catholic church was clueless, and then I went to the Spanish evangelical church, and that's where I got lucky. I think."

I try my best to recreate my entire conversation with Pastor Jorge, pausing to ask Sean occasional questions. "Did you know the dead boy had only been in Palmyrton for a week?"

Sean nods. "He had no I.D. Took us a while to find anyone who even recognized him. Some people said he called himself Jose. Others said Juan. No one knows his real name."

"Pastor Jorge says the boy and Ramon were from the same village."

"He was probably helping the kid, so the kid was trying to cover for Ramon. That loyalty got him killed."

Finally, I get to my offer to work some kind of amnesty deal to bring Ramon in from the lam. I finish with, "I got the impression the pastor doesn't know precisely where Ramon is, but maybe has a way to get a message to him."

To his credit, Sean listens without interrupting. Then he leans his head back on the sofa and shuts his eyes. He sits that way so long I think he may have dozed off.

"It might work." His eyes are still closed.

"Really?" I'm so excited I dump Ethel off my lap. She scrabbles to stay on the couch.

"I'll have to talk to my commander. And the DA. And he'll have to talk to the INS. They don't normally like to make deals with illegals. But we got nothing on this case."

I grab Sean's hand, infused with hope that he can work miracles. "That's fantastic!"

He straightens up and faces me. "It's not a done deal, Audrey. If Ramon has committed any crime, no matter how small, they'll never let him stay in this country."

"I understand. But he really didn't steal the money. Ty gave him soup and he accepted it. You have to make the DA and the INS understand that it was a case of mistaken identity. Mistaken Progresso identity."

Sean cradles my face in his hands so I can't look away from him. His hands are warm and hard but smooth. His touch is light. "You're going to let me handle this. Entirely. Your work here is done."

"Absolutely. I have enough to worry about at Harold's house."

"And if you want Italian food, don't go to Fiorello's. Not until I figure out who that busboy is." His thumb strokes my cheek.

A tingle of electricity passes through my core.

"I'll eat Chinese," I whisper.

Our lips meet so lightly that I register the sensation more in my chest than my mouth. Uh-oh.

Sean kisses me again, this time with full intent. I push Ethel out of the way. I want to be held. My hands slide under the collar of his shirt and I press him closer.

He needs no further encouragement.

What follows is a make-out session of such intensity that I lose track of time and place. There's only Sean's all-encompassing warmth and the steady, hard thump of his heart.

And then the snowplow goes by.

Ethel launches herself at the living room window barking loudly enough to register on the Richter scale.

Sean sits up and makes a vague effort to straighten his clothing. He runs his hand over my disheveled hair. "I have a lot to do tomorrow."

My heart is racing. That's because Ethel startled me, I'm sure. "Will you call me and let me know how it goes?"

"I won't have answers tomorrow." His eyes search mine. "But I'll call you."

# CHAPTER 18

I wake the next morning with a nose pressed against my ear.

A wet nose. Canine, not human. "Thank you," I say to her. "You saved me from a very big mistake."

Ethel cocks her head and begins a slow wag.

"Yes, this means a treat and an extra long walk."

She leaps out of bed and races to the kitchen cabinet where her Milk Bones are stored. I follow, which necessitates passing the scene of the crime. The couch cushions are still dented and tumbled. Dear lord, what was I thinking?

I flush at the thought of Sean's hands on my body and my all-too-enthusiastic response. If Ethel hadn't barked, I would have.... I shudder.

I toss Ethel a Milk Bone, and then, overwhelmed by gratitude, give her another. Astonished by her good fortune, she scoops them up and retreats to the laundry room before I can change my mind.

What got into me last night? I don't want Sean to think I was rewarding him for agreeing to try to set up a deal for Ramon. I jab my Frosted Mini-Wheats under their milk bath. I wasn't doing that, was I? No, I was genuinely enjoying myself.

A lot.

That's what's so terrifying. I can't do this right now. It's not what I want, not what I need. I laid my heart out for Cal and look what happened. Now, not two months later, I'm falling into the same snare with Sean. I need to stop and think.

Maura is back and what I need to do is hang out with her and all the lively people she attracts. Hang at parties, go to concerts, dance. I don't want to get tangled up with Sean Coughlin. Not now. Not yet. Maybe never.

Ethel staggers into the kitchen to remind me it's not a good idea to eat two Milk Bones before going out to pee. "I don't know how I'm going to fix this, Ethel."

She whimpers.

"C'mon. Your problems I can fix. Then I'm going to go tunnel my way into Harold's master bathroom. That's my punishment for being such a screw-up."

Ty has taken a long-arranged day off to help his cousin Marcus move to a new apartment, for which I'm grateful. Because of his legendary squeamishness, he's even less enthusiastic about working at Harold's than I am. Although Jill and I tease him about his weak stomach, we don't push too hard. We all have a tacit agreement never to mention Ty's brief stint in prison, and I suspect the thing he found most terrible about it was the lack of privacy and the exposure to strangers' bathroom functions. So I'm glad that on AMT's first official day of working the Harold Project, I'm solo with Jill.

I swing by the office to pick her up and we drive to Harold's house together. On the way, Jill bounces with happiness. "I'm so-o-o-o excited that we're doing this job together now, Audrey. I've tried to be really careful, but I've been worried that I might be accidentally getting rid of stuff that's valuable. Having you there to consult will be great!"

The putative Tiffany lamp notwithstanding, I'm still pretty convinced that 99 percent of the stuff in Harold's house deserves a one-way ticket to the dump. "Will Harold be there today? You know, I'm not going to have a lot of patience to negotiate with him about every little thing."

"Harold comes and goes. But don't worry—I'll handle him. You don't have to deal."

As much as I don't want Harold underfoot while we're working, the thought of what he might be up to if he's not at the house is equally worrisome. "He's not going out roaming Palmyrton on his bike, bringing more stuff back to his lair, is he?"

Jill twists her mouth into this funny little pucker, which I've come to know means she's about to tell me something she knows I won't want to hear. "He goes out on his bike every day. The need to be in motion is one of the symptoms of his illness. Garbage collection days are stressful for Harold because he sees all the useful things that people throw out. So I've devised a cycling route for him that takes him through each neighborhood only on non-garbage-collection days."

I glance over at her, not sure whether to be appalled or impressed.

"I don't know how you can be so forgiving, Jill. Harold tried to stop us from coming up to rescue you on Wednesday. And that whole flashback to the Eighties thing, ranting about George and Nora when they were little—has he ever done that before?"

Jill shrugs. "Sometimes. He has a few delusions that crop up now and then. See, some paranoid schizophrenics think the government has implanted chips in their brain or that they've ridden on alien space ships. But Harold's not like that, which is why I think he may not be a true schizophrenic. His delusions are more realistic, but they're still not true. Like once he told me in a perfectly calm voice that his entire family died in a plane crash. So maybe he's thinking about Nora and George, although they were older than babies when he lived with them. Or maybe he's got some totally different delusion playing in his brain."

She talks about his delusions the way someone else might say they have a few dandelions popping up in their lawn. "Doesn't that scare you? He would have happily left you walled up, like the girl in that Poe story."

"'The Cask of Amontillado'," right?" Jill waves her hand. "It wasn't *that* bad, Audrey. I was just stuck. I knew someone would find me eventually."

"The point is, Harold actually tried to prevent us from rescuing you. He may be delusional, but he knows what he wants and he'll act to get it. Doesn't that bother you?"

Jill shrugs. "He's mentally ill, Audrey. Sick. I wouldn't be mad if someone with Parkinson's Disease didn't help me get out."

"Someone with Parkinson's wouldn't deny you needed help."

Jill turns her whole body away from me. "Did you see that awful Mexican restaurant closed? I wonder what will go in that spot next? Palmyrton could use a good Indian place, don't you think?"

Mercifully, Harold is nowhere to be seen when we arrive, and once we strap on our respirators, the smell isn't too bad. Jill leads the way upstairs. Over the weekend she's found a vet willing to cremate Petey the cat for a minimal fee, and Harold now possesses his ashes. We're able to move past his tomb, and start in on the master bedroom.

As we work, Jill talks. She is my Scheherazade, spinning the fascinating tale of Harold's descent into madness. I'm dying to learn more about Nora's mother, a woman who abandoned her children without ever leaving home. I can't help but wonder what my own mother would make of her.

We're standing in front of a solid wall of one-pound coffee cans. "I thought this was the bird room," I say.

"Whatever's in the cans might be bird-related."

They're stacked so tight that pulling one out would certainly precipitate a fatal can-slide. Jill sets up the step-ladder and succeeds in prying one out from near the ceiling.

"Heavy," she says as she hands it down to me. "What's in it?"

I begin to pry the plastic lid up, then freeze. "You don't think it could be guano, do you?"

"Bird poop? Even Harold wouldn't save that."

"It's a very good fertilizer."

Jill's eyes widen. "Oh, gawd!"

I pull off the plastic lid like ripping off a Band-aid. Best to know the awful truth quickly. Jill's eyes are squeezed shut.

I look in cautiously and laugh. "Buttons."

"Whew, that's a relief. Not sure how that connects to birds," Jill says. "But believe me, there's definitely a pattern. Sometimes, it's a pattern only Harold can see, but it's always there."

I do some quick arithmetic. Twenty across, twelve up equals 240 cans of buttons. "What are your plans for these, Jill?"

"Etsy," she says. "Those crafters will eat these up."

So we begin to dismantle the wall. Jill stands on the ladder and hands cans down to me, chatting all the while. But the work is hard, and soon we both fall silent.

I reach my arms up for another can. "What's that noise?"

Jill cocks her head. Behind her is a faint but persistent scritch-scratch noise.

"I don't hear anything."

*Scritch, scratch. Scritch, scratch. Scratch.*

I set a can of buttons down and plant my hands on my hips. "Jill."

"Okay, okay. I hear it. But I think it's just a squirrel. I saw one pop in through a little hole near the roof the other day. The Bromley house had squirrels, remember?"

"In the attic, not the bedrooms."

Shaking my head, I carry a load of cans out to the van. The snow has entirely disappeared while we were inside working and the sun is beaming, giving us one of those freakishly warm New Jersey winter days. As I stack cans, a voice behind me causes me to jump.

"Good grief, what was Harold doing with all that coffee?"

I spin around to see the neighbor lady I encountered the day I first met Nora here, the one who mistook me as someone from the Board of Health. "Not coffee, they're all filled with buttons."

She crowds right up behind me and sticks her whole torso into the van. "Amazing. What else have you found in there?"

I pull off my work glove and extend my hand. "I don't believe we've formally met. Audrey Nealon."

She backs away and gives me a little Queen Elizabeth wave. Can't say I really blame her for not wanting to shake. "I'm Bernadette McMartin. I've lived next door for ten years. I'm chairwoman of the Summit Oaks Neighborhood Improvement Association."

*I bet you are.* I offer my best cheerleader smile, which doesn't amount to much. "How nice."

"I've heard that you people are trying to help Harold stay in this house." She blinks her eyes rapidly and squares her shoulders.

Despite my disgust with Harold, I take instant offense at being labeled "you people."

"We're helping Harold sell some of the more valuable items in the house. And recycle the rest."

"Value? There's nothing but trash in there." Her chin juts up in certitude. "Vermin-attracting, foul-smelling, eye-sore-producing trash."

I'm tempted to mention the Tiffany lamp just to wipe the know-it-all look off her face, but I still haven't heard back from the expert at Christie's. "There are some items that can be sold or recycled," I say.

"The people of Summit Oaks have had enough. Our lawyer has petitioned the town to have the house condemned." The eyelids are batting like wipers in a flash downpour. "This health hazard is coming down, once and for all."

As her voice gets louder and shriller, mine gets lower and quieter. "I don't think anything's been decided."

"It would be much easier for Harold and Nora to simply agree to sell the house as a tear-down. It would save them the public humiliation of having the house condemned."

"Seems like the bigger savings would be in lawyers' fees for your group." I'm not feeling particularly charitable about lawyers these days. "Now if you'll excuse me, I have some work to do."

When I get back inside, Jill has moved a second load of cans down to the front hall. I go upstairs to see how many more are left. The stack of cans has shrunk from a high rampart to a low partition. Now we can see most of what awaits us next: a neatly constructed fortress of boxes printed with the label, "Forgione Industrial Fasteners." Perhaps a theme is starting to emerge.

"I think because this room is big, it might have two themes," Jill says.

"Where's your respirator?" I scold.

"It was cutting into the back of my neck and giving me a headache. I had to take it off for a while. These cans aren't so dirty."

I'm in no mood to argue when we're so close to the end of this task. I pick up some sheets of yellowed newspaper and throw them in an open trash bag. Inside, I notice a tangle of what looks like pillow stuffing and purple Easter basket straw.

"Where did that come from?"

"Behind the last row of cans. Don't worry—nothing gross."

While Jill sweeps, I load the last of the cans into the van. Am I ever ready for lunch! Unfortunately, when I jump back out, a young mother holding a toddler has appeared in the driveway. Now what?

"Hi, I'm Phoebe Castleton."

She's slender with a cloud of softly wavy dark blond hair, wearing yoga pants and Birkenstocks with socks. The kid looks just like the mom, only her curly hair is white blond. Phoebe seems a little friendlier than Bernadette, so I smile at her and waggle my fingers at the kid. Immediately the little girl whimpers and buries her head in her mom's shoulder.

"Sorry," I say. "I'm better with dogs than kids."

"Oh, Tabby's just a little slow to warm up." Phoebe shifts the kid to her other shoulder. "I noticed that Bernadette was over here earlier. I live on the other side." She points to the expanded ranch to the left of Harold's house.

It's painted a golden taupe with cream trim and aubergine shutters and door. I would never have thought to put those colors together, but it works. "Nice house. I like the colors."

"Thanks. We've lived there six years, ever since Eunice, our oldest, was born."

Eunice? What a name! Phoebe reminds me of someone, but I can't think whom.

"I grew up in this neighborhood. It was a great place to be a kid. That's why once I had kids, I wanted to move back."

Her voice is wistful and sing-songy. Mia Farrow! A much younger Mia Farrow. I think I can see where this is headed. Harold's dump is destroying her dream. I decide to make a preemptive strike. "You're about the same age as Nora Phieffer. You must have known her, and this house, when you were growing up. Why did you buy right next to it?"

But Phoebe surprises me. "Sure, I know Nora, but we were never close. She was ahead of me in school. The house has been shabby almost as long as I can remember. But prices in this neighborhood have gotten really high. We never could have afforded a house in a better location. It's actually because of Harold's house that we were able to buy in Summit Oaks."*And now that you've got what you want, it's time to force him out.* I really want to say that, and if Phoebe were Bernadette, I think I would. But it's hard for me to be that mean to our little lost flower child here.

"I just wanted you to know," Phoebe quavers on. "Bernadette is a little, uhm, assertive sometimes. She seems to think she speaks for everyone in the neighborhood, but that's not true. My husband and I, we are…concerned…about the state of Harold's home, but only because it's not healthy for him. The cats and…." She trails off. "It would be nice if the place were cleaner, that's all."

"Look, Phoebe, I totally understand. We're helping Harold get the place under control."

"Are you going to clear out the entire house?" Her dreamy green eyes study the place, estimating the challenge.

"No, we can't afford to spend that much time here. We just need to make the main rooms inhabitable. We've cleared the kitchen, foyer, and stairs. Now we're working on the master bedroom. Once that's cleared, we'll be done."

She brightens. "That's all that really matters. Bernadette and her group want to have the house leveled, and then some developer will come in and build a McMansion here. That's not what's best for the neighborhood."

I raise my eyebrows. "You wouldn't rather have a three-story castle with columns here than…this?" To punctuate my point, a chunk of windowsill chooses that moment to detach from the second story and plunge into a scummy birdbath below.

Phoebe rubs her cheek against her daughter's downy head before she replies. "Summit Oaks is a special neighborhood. People care about one another here. The kids can roam and if they fall down, some mother somewhere in the neighborhood will bandage their knee and give them a hug. That's how it was when I was little and that's the way I want it to stay." Her voice gets louder. "If Bernadette's group succeeds in pushing Harold out, then the developers will start coming after every house that's small or hasn't been updated. There's already one new monstrosity up on Sycamore. Before long, I'll be surrounded by bond traders and investment bankers whose kids are being raised by nannies."

I think what Isabelle Trent, the real estate agent who sends me so much business, would say: Location, location, location. "Your place would go up in value if the neighborhood gets more upscale. You bought low; you could sell high."

"I'm not interested in making a killing on my house. I'm interested in raising my family in it." She kisses her daughter's head. "Safely."

Tabby has dozed off in her mother's arms as we talked. I feel a stab of envy for her trustful slumber, and I want to promise I'll create a safe environment for that little rug-rat, even though I know I can't deliver. Not for sure.

"I'll do my best to get the house under control, Phoebe. But we've got a formidable opponent in Bernadette over there."

Phoebe turns toward her own home, but pauses for one last word. "Bernadette never listens. She talks so loud and long that people agree just to get away from her. If you could get the house cleaned up a little, most of Bernadette's supporters would drift away."

"Sorry I was gone so long," I shout to Jill as I re-enter the house. "Two nosey neighbor encounters. I swear this house is under surveillance."

Before I take another step, my cell phone rings.

Coughlin. He told me he wouldn't have answers about Ramon today, but that he'd call me anyway. To find out how I feel? The screen trembles as I count the marimba trills—one, two, three, four, five and it rolls to voicemail.

I turn my phone off.

"Jill?" My voice is more urgent. I don't want to think about what I've just done. I want to work. Hard.

She doesn't answer me, but I hear a murmur of voices, sharp and then low, and follow the sound back to the kitchen. Jill and Nora are sitting at the recently unearthed kitchen table. I'm distinctly aware that the conversation has come to a halt upon my entrance. Jill's eyes look red. Has she been crying, or are they irritated from the bad air?

"Hi, Nora. Where did you come from? I didn't see your car outside."

"I can't park on Acorn Drive anymore. Bernadette recognizes my Prius and comes out to hound me. I have to park over on Aspen and cut through the backyards to get here."

"We saw Bernadette talking to you." Jill twists the bracelets on her wrist and refuses to make eye contact with me.

"She's a real piece of work. She seems outraged that you won't agree to have the house razed and the lot sold to a developer. That guy, Ed, who was over here earlier in the week, wants the same thing although he claims he's not part of Bernadette's Neighborhood Improvement group."

Jill and Nora exchange a glance.

"What's going on, you two?"

"My brother George is in town," Nora says. "He's pressuring me to have the house torn down and sell the lot."

Jill squeezes Nora's hand. "Nora feels like everyone's against her."

"Actually, the other neighbor, Phoebe Castleton," I gesture in the direction of the beige house with purple trim, "is totally on your side, Nora."

Why in God's name did I say that? Without realizing it, I seem to have joined forces with Nora and Jill.

"You've spoken to Phoebe?" Nora asks. "When?"

"Just now. After Bernadette chewed my ear off, Phoebe came over to tell me that Bernadette doesn't have as much support in the neighborhood as she thinks she does. Phoebe doesn't want a big McMansion built here."

I'm definitely not imagining the awkward silence that follows. Jill turns away and massages her neck. Nora picks at the bagel she'd been eating before I came in. I'd offer to go back upstairs and keep working, but I'm exhausted and there's an assortment of Sol's bagels on the table.

I sink into a chair. "Mind if I have one?"

"Of course not," they both answer. I peel off my work gloves and Jill squirts me with hand sanitizer.

I fix my bagel and wait as the silence grows more oppressive. Nora may be able to tolerate this, but I know damn well Jill will crack. Five, four, three, two...

"George wants money from the house soon," Jill blurts. "He thinks he deserves it."

With my mouth full of bagel, I raise my eyebrows. Nora picks up the story.

"My brother blames me for not getting him out of the house sooner when we were teenagers. It was the summer before my senior year and George's sophomore year when our dad got the new job in Connecticut and left. He wanted us to come with him, but I refused." Nora sighs. "Of course, looking back on it I can see that I was selfish, that my decision made life worse for George, but at the time—"

Jill squeezes her hand. "You were just a kid yourself. You weren't responsible."

"Why didn't George go with your dad? Did you force him to stay?" I ask.

Nora shakes her head. "Our father was always distant and sort of ineffective. George couldn't imagine living alone with Dad. He needed me to come with him. I wouldn't do that for him." Nora brushes at her eyes with the back of her hand. "Staying wasn't that bad for me. I passed my driver's test and Harold bought me an old used car. I had a job and a lot of friends. I stayed out of the house as much as possible. And during the summer, life wasn't so bad for George either. He spent his days at the pool and the park. But during the school year, he was trapped in the house."

Nora pauses and looks around the kitchen. Is she seeing it at a different point in time? A time when the slide toward destruction first began?

"George started falling apart. His grades tanked. He acted out in class. I think lots of people had to have noticed he was suffering, but none of us did anything to help him. And then, in the spring, I started getting my college acceptance letters. It finally dawned on George that he was going to be alone any way he sliced it—either alone with Dad or alone in this house with Mom and Harold. One afternoon, he stopped me in the hall at school. Told me when classes were over I had to drive him to the train station. He went to Connecticut with nothing but the clothes on his back."

"What did your mom and Harold say?"

"To be honest, I think a few days passed before they even noticed he was gone."

We sit in silence for a moment. The house seems to exhale around us, as if remembering with some satisfaction how it drove George out.

Now I simply have to ask what I've been longing to know. "Where is your mother now, Nora?" I say it gently, but Jill looks alarmed that I've ventured into forbidden territory.

Nora stiffens. "In the first year after George moved to Connecticut, my father talked to her a few times. Then the phone company disconnected the service. When I got a break from school, I came here to check on her and Harold. I found Harold all alone, scared and confused. She simply walked away one day. Told him she was going to the store and never came back. Abandoned him the way she abandoned us."

"You didn't try to track her down?"

Nora, normally so low-key, slams her fist on the table. "Why should I? So she can use me for what little money I have, just the way she used Harold? And then walk away again when the well runs dry?"

Whoa, I unleashed more anger than I anticipated. I know I should back off, but I can't let it go. I spent thirty years wondering about my mother. Doesn't Nora ever wonder about hers?

"It can't be that hard to find her. Aren't you...curious?"

Nora lifts her chin. "No. No, I am not the least bit curious. Wherever my mother is, I hope she stays put."

Eager to smooth that episode over, Jill starts straightening up the bagel leftovers. "So, where's Harold today?"

"Madison." Nora shuts her eyes like she's praying for strength. "It's their quarterly large item trash pick-up day. Since the weather's so nice, he was able to bike over."

"Uh-oh. Well, look on the bright side. He can't possibly bring large items back if all he has for transport is his bike."

Nora snorts. "Don't bet on it. He once convinced a NJ Transit conductor to let him bring a commercial-grade meat smoker on the train. Then the police called me and said they'd arrest him if I didn't come and get it off the platform in Palmyrton."

I set my bagel down. "Aren't you ever tempted to let

that happen? Let the police lock him up?" I've seen the ugly side of Harold, and I can understand the appeal.

Nora's eyes get shiny. "Harold could never survive in jail. He can't follow orders, and that would antagonize the guards. He can't keep his hands off anything that attracts him, so the inmates would beat him up for taking their stuff. Harold is impossible. But he doesn't deserve the death penalty."

Nora stands up and puts on her coat. "Thank you both for all you're doing here. And thanks for letting me vent."

"What about George?" Jill asks. "Will he shut us down?"

Nora yanks her hat down over her ears. "Let's hope when I bring him here and he sees all the progress, he'll have a little patience. I'll be in touch."

After Nora leaves, Jill stays sitting at the table, staring into space. "I wonder why George aims all his anger at Harold, while Nora aims all hers at their mother?"

"I don't know, my little armchair shrink. I think it's odd that Nora has no interest in finding her mother, even if it's just to tell her how much she hates her. Unless...."

Jill cocks her head. "Unless what?"

I gaze up at the cracked and stained kitchen ceiling. "Unless she knows it's too late to tell her mother anything. Because her mother is still right here."

# CHAPTER 19

That night, alone in my apartment, I make Ethel come into the bathroom with me while I take my shower. Not only have I freaked Jill out with my musings about Nora's mother, I've freaked myself out too. Jill insists that Harold isn't capable of having hurt his sister, and maybe she's right. But what if Sharon had tripped and fallen in that obstacle course of a house and Harold just left her there? When I suggested to Jill that might be why Nora tries so hard to protect Harold, Jill countered with her own good point: why would Nora let us clear the house if she knew we might encounter Sharon's body? Then we both said, "George!" at the same time. He's the one who doesn't want us there.

Once I have my jammies on, I pull Ethel into my lap for a snuggle. Breathing in her sweet, doggie smell, I murmur, "Oh, Ethel—I'd quit this job in a minute if I didn't need the money so badly."

She looks up at me with soulful brown eyes and arches her brows.

"You don't want to switch to WalMart brand dog food, do you?"

She sighs and lays her head on her outstretched paws. Of course she doesn't. She relies on me to bring home the bacon, and the Science Diet kibble, just as much as Jill and Ty do. I know that I'll go back to 12 Acorn Lane tomorrow and keep digging toward the master bath.

That's what's on my mind as I crawl into bed, so naturally my dreams are filled with bizarre permutations of "The Cask of Amontillado" meets the "I've fallen and I can't get up" infomercial. I toss and sleep and wake and toss some more. Finally, I sink into a dreamless sleep only to be roused by my ringing cellphone.

I fumble with the trilling contraption trying to get the noise to stop.

"Audge?"

Immediately my mind clears. "What's wrong?" Because a middle-of-the night phone call from Ty can't possibly be good news.

"Something happened and I don't know what to do."

"Where are you?" Already I'm thinking how I'll find cash for bail.

"At Marcus's place. Listen, after we got him moved in here, we went to a bar to watch the Knicks game. It was so loud in there, I didn't hear my phone ringing. Now I'm back at his place and I see a missed call from a number I don't know. I call it, and the guy who answers only speaks Spanish. We keep talkin' at each other, him in Spanish and me in English. I even tried a few words of Spanish, but he didn't understand. He hung up."

"Ramon."

"Well, I'm thinkin' it musta been Ramon who called me on someone else's phone. The guy who answered when I called back wasn't Ramon."

"Did you ask for Ramon?"

"Yeah. I said 'Yo. Necessito. Ramon.' Real clear like that, but he didn't put Ramon on. He hung up."

This is huge. Ramon has tried to reach out to us.

"Audge? What should I do?"

"Nothing. Nothing right now. Save that number in your contacts and text it to me too."

"You're not going to give it to the cops, are you? Cuz

I'm not down with that."

"No, I just don't want to lose that number. It'll be safer if we both have it. We'll try to reach him again tomorrow."

A moment later the number arrives and I save it to my contacts. A 973 area code—that means Ramon is still nearby. I feel bad that I've lied to Ty, but I've got to give this information to Coughlin. Eventually Ty will understand that I'm looking out for all of us.

I hope.

In the bright light of morning, the world looks a little different.

Harold's house doesn't seem so creepy.

Coughlin's help doesn't seem so essential. I still haven't talked to him since the make-out session. He hasn't tried calling again after I let his call go unanswered yesterday.

Maybe he's busy. Or maybe he has doubts too. Either way, I'm glad. And I'm not so eager to be the one to call him looking for a favor. Maybe I'll wait just until the end of the day to see if Ramon calls Ty again. The more I think about it, the more I suspect Ramon must have sneaked a call on someone's phone without permission. So tracking down the owner of the phone might not help. It might even hurt if it scares Ramon deeper underground.

Putting myself on hold instead of taking action doesn't come easy, but it seems right. At least until it doesn't. So I fling myself into work at Harold's house to curb my impulses.

By noon, we've tunneled another five feet into the master bedroom. Ty has hauled the industrial fasteners to a metal recycler and has returned to find us elbow deep in bird paraphernalia. Having Ty there proves a mixed blessing. He tirelessly hauls boxes downstairs and out of the house, but he never stops his running commentary of disbelief.

"This is bull! Why we gotta save this? Why can't it go straight to the dump? Who gonna want a busted parakeet cage?"

Normally Jill wouldn't show Ty the kind of patience she shows Harold, but I think she knows if she starts squabbling with him, I'll walk out. So she puts in her headphones and cranks up her tunes and simply smiles at Ty as she gives him the next box of duck decoys to put in the van to be offered up to a hunting club in Pennsylvania.

Ty comes back upstairs for his next load and pauses on the top step. "What's that sound?"

*Scritch, scratch. Scritch, scratch. Scratch.*

"A squirrel," Jill says before I can open my mouth.

"Aw, man—I bet it's rats. Listen to them! They sound like they're runnin' a race back there."

"Squirrels," Jill repeats, thrusting a box into Ty's arms. "I'll show you the hole where they got in."

Ty shudders and retreats with his burden.

"You know what's weird about this house, Jill?" I ask as we stack endless copies of *Peterson's Guide to Birds*.

She giggles. "Everything."

"Yeah, of course. What I meant is, every house we clear out tells a story about its owners. Like Mr. Wainwright's house was full of stuff for cooking and entertaining, so you could tell they'd had lots of parties there. And remember Mr. Reicker's house back in October?"

"He was the world traveler—all that pottery and carvings from foreign countries."

"And that lady whose son was a pro football player. She saved every trophy, every jersey, every ball he ever had."

Jill cocks her head, her respirator making her look like a quizzical giant insect. "And your point is...?"

"This house doesn't tell the story of the people who actually lived here. It just tells the story of Harold's bizarre obsessions. Do you think we'll ever reach the stuff that Nora, and George, and their mother left behind? I mean, if we clean out these bedrooms, will we eventually excavate deep enough to find Nora's stuffed animals and George's Matchbox cars and Sharon's, I don't know, 1980s leg warmers?"

"Geez, Audrey—you're making me sad."

But I'm on a roll and can't restrain myself. "Has Nora been upstairs since we've cleared a path to all the bedrooms?"

Jill shakes her head. "I don't think so. She doesn't seem to want to explore the house."

"Understandable, I guess. Not like she's taking a stroll down Happy Memory Lane here." I run my hands along the doorframe of the nearest bedroom. "Which bedroom was hers?"

"I dunno."

"I can guess," Ty says as he climbs the steps.

None of the bedroom doors can be closed because of all the stuff oozing out of the rooms, but Ty moves the door of the second bedroom on the left as far away from the wall as he can and points to something on the outside of the door. Jill and I come around to look.

Keep Out is scratched into the wood.

"Didn't do much good, did it? Jill says. "Harold and Sharon still invaded each kid's room. I guess George must've been in one of the rooms at the end of the hall, and Harold in the other."

I think about yesterday's debate with Jill. Clearing these other bedrooms is not on our agenda. Is that why Nora is comfortable with us working in the house? She knows the kitchen, foyer, hall, and master suite are safe to explore, and she's confident we're not looking for extra work in the other rooms.

"Do you think Harold has any interest in reclaiming his bed?" I ask, just to see what kind of reaction I'll get from Jill. "That flimsy cot Nora set up in the foyer for him can't be very comfortable."

Ty throws up his hands. "I am *not* clearing out his bedroom!"

Jill waves off the suggestion. "No one is asking you to. Nora doesn't expect us to clean the whole house. Anyway, the cot in foyer is better than sleeping wedged on top of boxes, the way he was before we got here."

It's hard to imagine a middle-class American, an MIT graduate no less, living in the kind of squalor Harold endured before our arrival. Had there been a memorable day when he realized he could no longer reach his bed? Or did he slip into sleeping like a possum in a tree, one inch at a time? On my way downstairs with a box I pause in front of Harold's cot. I guess this narrow, thin-mattressed bed represents a step in the right direction for him. Maybe that's the uncomplicated reason Nora doesn't care about reclaiming the other bedrooms.

As the afternoon progresses, Ty's scowl gets more and more ferocious. "This is bull, Audge. We bustin' our asses and all for nuthin'. I bet even that lamp we found is a fake. What'd the expert guy say?"

I pull up two chairs and hand Ty a soda from our cooler. Then I pull out my phone and call up an email I received early this morning to let Ty read it.

Ty leans forward and opens his eyes wider and wider as he reads. "He's coming out here to look at the lamp? He's gonna buy it? Jill!"

Jill skids up and grabs the phone. "Take it easy," I tell her. "He says the photos are very interesting and he needs to examine the lamp in person to make a determination of authenticity."

Jill's eyes light up. "But he thinks it's possible the lamp might be a real Tiffany?"

I nod. "He wouldn't come clear out here on a whim. He's got some other business in New Jersey, but he's making a detour for this lamp."

Jill starts jumping up and down. "I knew it! I knew

it! I knew we'd find something awesome in here. Why didn't you tell us right away?"

I point to her dancing with Ty. "Because I knew we had work that needed to get done before he arrives."

"You think the lamp is safe locked up at the office?" Ty asks me.

"No one knows it's there but us, right?" I ask.

"I don't have nobody to tell," Ty says. "If I told my friends about an old lamp worth six figures they'd think I was smokin' rock."

"Jill?"

"Uhm, I told Nora. But I said not to get her hopes up. When I told her where we found it, she said Harold must've gotten it recently at a garage sale. Her theory is that anything valuable has to be buried, dating to the time when Harold wasn't so crazy. She didn't seem too excited."

"Was she mad that you were exploring the living room?"

"Mad? Of course not. Why?"

I shrug and turn away. Later, when I pass through the foyer, I peer into the living room. Jill, attracted by light reflecting on the colorful shade, found the lamp only three or four feet into the room. Beyond that point is an impenetrable wall of mini-fridges, upright vacuums, humidifiers, and bread-making machines. I have no idea how someone as scrawny as Harold got it all packed in here, but whatever lies on the other side of that fortress is staying there. God knows, I'm not going in to explore.

Buoyed by the prospect of pulling down some green on the lamp, Ty returns to work cheerfully. He hauls out Audubon prints in warped frames and boxes of bird-watching binoculars without a complaint. Then I hear a shout.

"Augh! Get away! I'm gonna have nightmares all week."

"Oh come on—this one's kinda pretty."

Now what could that possibly be?

I run upstairs to look. From the depths of the room, sixteen bright golden eyes stare unblinkingly.

Eight stuffed owls. Ah, Harold.


Like relatives awaiting the doctor's verdict on the health of an ICU patient, we all gather around and watch as Carter Lemoine, 19th century decorative arts expert from Christies, examines what we've come to regard as "our" Tiffany lamp.

His brow furrows. He puts on his half-moon glasses. He squints. He takes off his half-moon glasses. He runs his long, exceptionally clean fingers over the shade, which Jill had been about to spritz with Windex before I yanked the blue bottle from her hands. Flamingo-like, he twists his long neck to stare up under the shade and emits a strange little grunt.

Finally, Ty cracks. "Whattup? Is it legit?"

Mr. Lemoine straightens. He pulls out a white handkerchief and methodically polishes his glasses. Finally he speaks. "Hard to say."

Ty is wearing his "don't mess with me" look, a look that makes men much, much larger than Mr. Lemoine scurry out of the way. Our expert, however, is not intimidated.

"I can say with reasonable certainty that the lamp does contain Tiffany glass." He picks up a pencil from my desk and with the eraser end points to purple iris petals and green leaves. "But I can't verify with confidence that this lamp was created by Tiffany Studios."

"Say what?"

Mr. Lemoine draws himself into a lecture pose. "As you know, there was a period in the 1930s when Tiffany glass fell out of fashion. Wealthy people would give the lamps to their servants. Entire windows ended up salvage yards." Mr. Lemoine shudders. "Then, when prices began to rise, artisans would use the glass from broken and damaged Tiffany pieces to create new pieces."

Ty nods. "Kinda like a rapper sampling old songs to make a new track. That's not illegal."

Mr. Lemoine arches his eyebrows. "A novel analogy, and quite apt. But when the rapper creates a new song, he puts his own name on it. He doesn't claim it's a piece by an old star."

Ty offers Mr. Lemoine his clenched fist for a bump to acknowledge a point well made. After a confused pause, the art expert gives him a tentative tap.

"Wait," Jill says. "There's gotta be a way you can determine if this is a reassembled Tiffany or a real one. Isn't there like...lab work, an art autopsy or something?"

Mr. Lemoine shakes his head. "That's why we must establish the provenance. If you could show that the lamp had been sold previously as an original, that would help. Or if the man who put it in his garage sale could say from whom he received it...."

"And if we can't," Jill's voice gets quavery, "this awesome lamp will be worthless?"

"Oh, not worthless. I agree, it's a lovely piece. But Tiffany lamps sold by Christie's have fetched between $700,000 and $1.2 million. A dealer who handles lesser pieces," he pauses as if it pains him to admit such creatures exist, "might be able to get you $5,000 for this with no verification."

"Hold up. You're sayin' even though it's all real Tiffany glass and it's just as pretty as a lamp that Tiffany made in his studio, if some no-name dude assembled the pieces it's only worth $5,000? That's messed up."

Mr. Lemoine arranges his Burberry scarf around his neck. "Scarcity and authenticity create value. That's the nature of the art business. So, speak to your eccentric friend and see if you can determine from whom he purchased the lamp. Even the family name of the previous owner could be helpful in verifying authenticity."

"Wow! Up to a million two if it's a real Tiffany." Jill sprawls in her desk chair fanning herself with a take-out menu. "And we get twenty percent of that. So that's twenty thousand dollars?"

"Two *hundred* thousand," Ty corrects. "And you went to college?"

"Shut up. I was an art major."

"Two hundred thou divided by three—that's $63,000 for each of us," I say. "If we can get Harold to remember where he found it. That's a big if. So no sports cars yet."

"You're splittin' the money even-up with us?" Ty sounds as incredulous as if a total stranger had offered to share his Lottery winnings.

"You two found it. I didn't want to take this job, remember?"

"Neither did I," Ty says. "If you goin' by that, Jill should get it all."

"You rescued me from the cat tomb—that's worth 63K." Jill stands and circles the lamp. "If only you could talk and tell us where you've been."

"What's your strategy for getting Harold to cooperate?" I ask.

"I think I'll bring him and Nora here to look at the lamp. Harold will need to see it to remember, but now that I know how valuable it is, I don't want to drag it back to the house."

"You honestly think he can remember where he got that one thing out of all the tons of junk he's collected?" I ask.

"It wasn't too far into the living room, so it must be a fairly recent acquisition. And Harold's got an incredible memory for facts. It's people and emotions that confuse him."

"You bring him back here." Ty stands up and

stretches his powerful arms. "If he won't say where he got this lamp, I'ma knock the dope right outta him."

# CHAPTER 20

At 3:00, my phone chimes a reminder: Rosa Parks Center at 4:00. That's right—I'm supposed to help Dad with the Chess Club today. Working at Harold's makes the prospect of teaching complex board games to restless third-graders look enticing. Before I leave, I pull Ty aside. "Maybe Ramon will try to call at the same time tonight. Can you swing by my place tonight so we can be together if he calls?"

Ty nods. "You got it."

Halfway to the Parks Center, I break into a cold sweat. Will I run into Sean there? If I do, will I keep the chatter light, pretend like nothing happened? Can I pull that off? More important, will I be tempted to tell him about Ramon's call?

At the Center, I find Dad in a room setting up chess boards in various stages of play. He hands me two diagrams. "This is Kyle's game, the other is Jamal's. I'm teaching them the Sicilian Defense. You do that and I'll work with the beginners."

"Really? I get the fun stuff?"

Dad keeps his eyes on the knights and pawns. "I want you to come back."

Before I can process this, Dad changes the subject. "By the way, Sean told me he's got a lead on the identity of the boy who was killed."

My head snaps up. "Really? Did he say anything about Ramon?"

"No. He's working nonstop on this case. He won't be here today."

"When did he tell you—" But before I can finish, a horde of kids tumbles into the room. Kyle and Jamal and their partners quickly catch on to the Sicilian defense, which allows me to watch my father from the corner of my eye. He's remarkably patient with the beginners, even the little girl playing house with the king and queen on her board. He succeeds in getting everyone going on a basic opening and referees a few squabbles about which pieces can move in which directions. The hour passes quickly and as abruptly as the kids exploded into the room, they're gone—off to Cooking with Marie or Homework Helpers.

"Wow, that's a whirlwind! No wonder you need help."

Dad sits in a kid-sized chair with his long legs stretched out. "If they had put me in a room with all those kids when I first came here, I wouldn't have lasted ten minutes. But I started with Kyle and Jamal, and every week a couple more players trickled in. Now it's—"

"A zoo!"

"A nice zoo, though. Don't you think?"

Could it be my father is seeking my approval? Talk about role reversal! "Definitely nice. But, all that noise—it doesn't bother you?" Growing up, our house had all the liveliness of the period rooms at the Metropolitan Museum of Art. One icy glance from my father silenced any visiting friends, and few cared to return.

He turns a rook over and over in his hands. "I know it's no excuse, Audrey, but I was terribly unhappy during your childhood. Other people's joy, no matter how innocent, grated on me. Your laughter, your silliness, only reminded me of all I'd lost." He sets the chess piece down. "I'm sorry, Audrey. I can't bring those years back."

My eyes itch with welling tears. Part of me wants to fling my arms around my father, but perched in that tiny chair as he is, I would flatten him. Besides, I don't recall ever sitting in my father's lap, or resting my head on his shoulder. How can I begin now?

I open my mouth, not sure what will come out. Before any words form, one of the girls from the class skids into the room. "Mr. Roger, Miss Audrey—Mrs. Dawn wants to know can you be chaperones on our trip to the Play-O-Rama?" Her braids bob up and down, pink plastic barrettes clacking. "Please say yes or else we can't go!"

I look to my dad for direction. If he's in, I'm in.

Dad struggles up from the low chair. "All right, Briana. Tell Mrs. Dawn we're coming."

I have no point of reference to comprehend Play-O-Rama. These giant indoor playgrounds didn't exist when I was a child, and even if they had, no one, not even my generous grandparents, would have brought me to one. We enter a cavernous room with the decibel level of the main runway at LaGuardia. Immediately, our twelve charges take off, heading for what looks like a huge hamster tunnel maze. Within it there are slides and ball pits and rope ladders and all sorts of obstacles to exhaust even the boundless energy of the Parks Center kids.

"We'll be right on this bench," Dawn shouts, her voice hopelessly lost in the cacophony. She plops onto the bench and flags us to join her. "Don't worry. We stay for ninety minutes. All we have to do is leave with as many kids as we brought."

Conversation is impossible, so Dad and I silently share the crossword puzzle while Dawn knits. As closing time draws nearer, the crowd thins and the din lessens a bit. One of our older charges runs up, flushed and panting. "Miz Dawn, Rosalia is stuck."

"What do you mean, stuck?"

The girl points to the top of the maze. "She's up there and she's too scared to come down. I tried to help her, but she keeps crying and she won't move. You gotta come get her."

Dad, Dawn, and I each look for a white knight. Climbing through a giant hamster maze is clearly not part of my father's stroke rehab plan. And Dawn, while perfectly healthy and not much older than me, has—to put it delicately—quite a bit of junk in her trunk. If she goes up, we'll have two people stuck. I guess that leaves me.

So I follow my guide. She points to the long yellow tunnel I must enter to reach Rosalia. "You go first," I say.

"Not enough room at the top." Someone calls to her and she scampers off, done with playing Good Samaritan.

I stick my head in the sloping tube and start to climb. At first it's not hard, although I try not to think of how many snotty little fingers have covered this terrain before me. But the longer I'm in it, the tighter the tunnel seems to get. This must be what cockroaches feel like when they squeeze under a baseboard. While I'm scooting forward I hear an announcement on the loudspeaker, "Play-O-Rama will close in five minutes. Please exit the climbing structure." Ascending faster, I reach a three-way intersection: to the left, a slide into a ball pit; to the right, a climbing wall; straight ahead, a mesh sleeve. The sleeve seems like the least of the evils—at least it's open–but it sags and pitches as I crawl through. I'm breathless by the time I reach a bouncy platform at the other end. Then I see what lies ahead.

The only way off the platform is straight up. I must insert myself into a vertical tube designed for someone a third my size, and pull myself up using hand and footholds on the sides. I begin to haul myself to the top, cursing how infrequently I use the upper body machines at the gym.

The lights go out. The yellow tube turns black.

Surely it hasn't been five minutes already? How can I get myself and Rosalia out of here in the pitch dark? Haven't Dad and Dawn told them where we are?

I drag myself one notch further up, opening my eyes wide for any glimmer of light above.

The lights come back on. A face is inches from mine, filling the exit hole above.

Not Rosalia. A man.

A Hispanic man.

The busboy.

# CHAPTER 21

He reaches down to grab my wrist.

I scream.

My voice is lost in the shouts of the kids scrambling to leave and the parents hollering to collect them. I realize now that the flickering lights were meant as a second warning to exit.

He leans further into the tube. Now the air smells like sweat, and onions, and anger. His front tooth has a gold cap.

"You stop lookin' around." He shakes me and my feet fly off the footholds. I'm dangling by my left arm. "You stop talkin' to the big cop."

I twist away and drop through the tube like a cue ball.

I land with a bounce–not hurt, but shaking. I think the busboy is too broad to come down the tube after me, but I'm not waiting to find out. I scramble through the mesh sleeve, my feet caught in the webbing. Stupid, stupid thing! Who could possibly have designed this as an amusement? I finally clear that obstacle and reach the intersection.

Up the wall that leads to a clear, open space? Or down the slide to the dim ball pit?

The man is up; Dad and Dawn are down. I slide.

I hit the balls hard, tumbling head over heels. Falling and floundering through the drifts of balls, I search for a break in the screened walls. The lights

blink off again, another signal to the stragglers.
Hardly anyone is left. I keep moving smooth, cool balls
as a swimmer moves water.

My hand touches something warm and solid.

Hairy.

The lights flick on.

I'm face to face with the busboy. I see his big pores
and the hairs in his nose. His breath is hot in my ear.
"Stay away or I hurt you. *Comprende?*"

"Yes." I'm too scared to answer above a whisper.

He throws me far into the ball pit. When I
resurface, he's gone.

"Are you crazy? You have to tell him. Call him right
now."

I'm sitting in Maura's apartment. It seemed the
safest place to go after I took my father home. When
I'd escaped from the Play-O-Rama maze, I found out
Rosalia had come down on her own when the lights
flashed. I guess the dark was scarier than the slide. In
the rush to get the kids loaded into the van, no one
had seemed to notice I was pale and trembling. No one
except my father.

He peered at me. "What's wrong?"

"I'm fine." I forced a smile. "It's just a
little...claustrophobia."

If he was suspicious of my answer, he didn't press
the point. I said my good-byes and headed to Maura's.
She lives in one of the few doorman buildings in
Palmyrton, so if the busboy was following me, he
wouldn't be able to get any further than her lobby.
Now I'm listening to her harangue me about calling
Coughlin.

"If you don't do it, I will," she says.

"But the guy told me he'd hurt me if I talked to
Sean."

Maura hurls a sofa pillow at me. "I'm going to hurt
you if you don't! You're talking like the heroine of a

teen slasher movie. TSTL."

"I'm not too stupid to live. I'm just," I feel my throat closing up, "scared."

"Oh, baby—I'm sorry." She wraps her arms around me.

Breathing in the scent of her hundreds of dollars' worth of lotions and potions and creams calms me a bit. "I need to figure out what really happened at that place." I sit up and start talking. "How could that guy have known I'd be at Play-O-Rama? How could he know I'd have to climb up to get some little girl?"

Maura rakes her mane of dark curls. Her eyes blink rapidly the way they used to when I'd try to pull her through some baffling calc problem. "Are you saying he set you up?"

"He must have. It can't be a coincidence that he ran into me there."

"Maybe he followed you to the Parks Center, then watched for you to leave and followed you to Play-O-Rama."

"The Center van was parked in their indoor garage. He couldn't have seen me get into it unless he was in the Center with me. And he wasn't."

"How did you end up going on this trip anyway?"

"Dad and I were asked to fill in for someone who cancelled."

"Who?"

"That's what I need to find out."

Maura hands me my phone. "Not you. Sean Coughlin. Let him figure it out."

"There's another reason I don't want to call him." While Maura listens with arched eyebrows, I tell her about the recent sofa incident.

When I finish, Maura prods me with her perfectly manicured foot. "For God's sake, Audrey. You drank some wine and necked with the guy a little. We're not in high school anymore—that doesn't mean you're going steady. And I'm sure he can separate the personal from the professional."

Can he? Can I? I try again. "But if he starts asking questions like that at the Center, the busboy will know I talked."

"Sean volunteers at the Center too. Don't you think he's smart enough to find out without interrogating people?"

Ogee.

I text "That busboy threatened me tonight. Call me."

Fifteen minutes later, Sean is in Maura's living room.

I'm flustered when he first walks in, but Maura was right (of course). Sean is all business, reassuring me that he traveled from the police garage to Maura's garage unseen. He asks me questions methodically and takes me through the incident moment-by-moment three times in a row.

That's what I want. I guess.

I answer patiently, trying hard to remember how all the little insignificant moments tied together into one big significant climax. The moment the first girl came to ask Dad and me to chaperone. The moment the other girl told us Rosalia was stuck. The moment it was decided I should go up to get her.

"Did Dawn encourage you to climb up?" Sean has asked this before, but I don't get testy. I'm starting to understand how he works.

"No. No, I'm sure she didn't say a word to me. We all looked at each other and it was pretty obvious I was the best choice."

"None of you thought to contact the playground staff?"

"The place is a madhouse, Sean. And the staff are minimum wage teenagers."

"What do you think Dawn would have done if you'd refused to go up?"

I shrug. "Maybe persuade the girl who came to get us to try again to help Rosalia. I asked her to—" I stop, thinking about that moment when the older girl scampered off.

Sean leans forward. "What?"

"Maybe it's nothing, but I asked the girl to go up ahead of me, to lead me to Rosalia, but she refused. She said there wasn't enough room at the top. She said that right away."

"As if she'd been coached?"

"Maybe. And then someone shouted, and she ran off."

"Someone called her name?" Sean's voice is low and intense.

"I don't know her name, so I don't know if someone called it. And it's so loud in there, with kids shouting non-stop, it's impossible for me to say if she was responding to someone calling her. I just assumed her friends were calling her back to their game. But maybe—"

"Maybe her handler called her off."

Maura has been listening quietly, but now she jumps in. "Wait, you think the girl was put up to this? And Rosalia as well? You think the busboy knows them?"

"His kids must know those kids."

"His kids? How do you know he has kids?"

"Unaccompanied men aren't allowed into Play-O-Rama," Sean says. "Adults can't come in unless they're accompanied by kids."

"They give you a bar-coded bracelet to match you to your kids," I explain.

"Wow, these are things you don't think of when you're not a parent," Maura says. "Otherwise, the place would be a pedophile's paradise, huh?"

"But, Sean—all this seems like so much work. If he wanted to warn me off, why didn't he just approach me outside my office or while I'm walking the dog?"

Sean crosses his arms and sits silently for a while. Quite a while. Finally I can't stand it any longer.

"Sean?"

"Because somehow he knows you. Knows what you're like—persistent, brave." He squints at me. "Reckless. He wanted to really rattle you."

"He succeeded."

"Wait," Maura says. "You're saying this Spanish guy...this busboy in a restaurant...knows Audrey well enough and is clever enough to dream all this up?"

Sean stands up. "No. I'm saying there's something larger at play here."

# CHAPTER 22

Ethel trots ahead of me, pausing occasionally to sniff for squirrels and cats who might be foolish enough to invade her turf. I'm aware of Sean waiting at the corner ahead in an unmarked car. We've agreed I should spend the night at Maura's, but first I had to collect Ethel and take her for a walk. When she and I reach the corner, I can see another unmarked car in front of my condo. Sean is taking no chances.

As I look down my block, I notice a tall man in a puffy coat loping along. I know that walk. Oh my God, it's Ty! In all the drama of this night, I totally forgot that I told him to meet me at my place tonight. And now he's probably seen Sean and thinks I set him up. I reach into my pocket for my phone, but remember Sean is watching me. It will have to wait.

On the way back to Maura's his car follows me into her parking garage and he watches as I signal that the elevator I'm about to get into is empty. Then he lopes across the parking area and gets in with me. On the ride up, I ask about his progress on the talks with the DA and the INS on a deal for Ramon, but he is tight-lipped. "There's interest" is all I can get him to say.

Now that we're outside Maura's door, I try again. "Have you found out any more about the boy who died?"

"Got the autopsy results. From looking at the teeth and the growth plates in the bones they can tell he was only fourteen or fifteen years old." Sean shakes his head. "Kid came all the way from Honduras by himself. My sister won't let her son ride the train to Penn Station alone."

"Why would his family send him off like that?"

"They're desperate, Audrey. Honduras has the highest murder rate in the world. People get killed going to work, going to shop for food. It's no wonder they want to get out."

"How did he travel all that way alone?"

Sean glances away as if he's struggling. Then he takes me by the shoulders and looks deep in my eyes. "I'm not supposed to talk about this, but it could affect your safety."

"What?"

"We think the kid was killed by coyotes. Smugglers who were paid to get him into the country."

"I don't understand. You think Ramon is a coyote?"

Sean shakes his head. "We're not sure how Ramon fits into this. People say he was looking out for the kid. Maybe he was supposed to make the final payment. Maybe it was supposed to come from somewhere else."

"So probably the killer didn't know about the money in the cans. That's a good thing for me, no?"

"We can't be sure what he knows. The point is, this wasn't two day-laborers having an argument that got out of hand. These coyotes are vicious. They don't hesitate to kill—not even a child."

My legs feel like rubber. If not for Sean's firm grasp, I think I might sink to the floor. "And what happened tonight. The busboy. You think he's one of them?"

"Has to be. What worries me is how they tracked you down so quickly. When the killer saw you in that back yard, he couldn't possibly have known who you were. Now, two days later, he knows how to find you in a place you didn't even plan on going to."

"My visit to Pastor Jorge," I whisper. "They followed me from there. They know where I work. Where I live.

They followed us from the Parks Center to Fiorello's."

All Sean does is raise one eyebrow slightly, but it feels like he's shaking me and yelling "I told you so."

"But wait. Is it just a coincidence that this guy works at Fiorello's and saw us together?"

Sean's lips compress. "I don't believe in coincidence. The undocumented community has a whole underground communication system that the rest of us don't know about. Tomorrow, I'll talk to the owner of Fiorello's and find out how long that guy has worked for him. Fiorello's is the closest restaurant to the Parks Center. Staff and volunteers eat there all the time. Maybe he thought that was a good place to wait and watch."

Now I know I have to tell him about Ramon's call to Ty. I take a deep breath. "There's something else."

His eyes widen. "Jesus, Mary and Joseph! Now what?"

"Last night Ty had a missed call from a number he didn't recognize. When he called back, the person who answered only spoke Spanish. Ty asked for Ramon, and the guy hung up."

"I need that number."

I pull out my phone and show him.

He shakes his head as he writes it down. "You couldn't have called me as soon as this happened?"

"It was the middle of the night."

"Or sometime today? Maybe returned my call?"

Eeew, there it is. The moment I thought I could escape. "I...I'm sorry. Today was hectic."

"Your day has twenty-four hours. My day has twenty-four hours."

The "I'm so busy" excuse has never sounded lamer. I take a deep breath and try again. "Wednesday night made me feel....confused."

Sean reaches for my hand. His thumb brushes the soft underside of my wrist. "Really?" His voice is low. The anger is gone. "I know us guys aren't great at guessing what's going on in a woman's mind, but I coulda sworn confusion was not the emotion you were feeling on Wednesday night."

Now my legs feel rubbery for a different reason. "Things felt different on Thursday morning."

He pulls me closer and whispers in my ear. "Why?"

My phone begins ringing. A second later, Maura flings open the door. "Audrey—there you are! I was getting wor—" She realizes what she's interrupted. "Oops. Sorry."

Before Maura can close the door, I push Ethel forward and follow her. "I'll check in periodically all day tomorrow, Sean. I promise."

According to veterinarians, a dog's nose can distinguish one hundred thousand different smells, so it's no wonder Ethel is beside herself with glee when she enters Harold's house. I can't leave her alone all day in Maura's unfamiliar apartment, so I've brought her to work with me, much to Jill and Ty's delight. Jill pirouettes around the kitchen with her, talking in high-pitched doggie talk, until Ethel breaks free to follow her nose into a corner stacked with boxes of decaying cookbooks. She begins scratching the floor, frantically trying to insert her whole muzzle into the pile.

"Yo, Ethel—you ever smelled anything that bad before? You be careful, girl. Most likely a big ol' rat behind there. You not a street dog. You don't wanna mess with that."

Ethel pauses and cocks her head.

"See that," Ty says. "She's listening to me. Dog's smarter than you, Jill."

Despite his jokey manner with Jill and the dog, I sense a coolness between Ty and me. I'm not sure how much I want to tell Jill about the Play-O-Rama incident; she's so excitable. I'll give her a quick run-down later. But I need to tell Ty everything. When

Jill's back is turned, I gesture for him to follow me out to the van. "Help me bring in that box, Ty."

Mercifully, he doesn't say, "What box?", and follows me out.

Once we're behind the van, I tell him about what happened last night. "So, it's not safe for me to stay in my apartment until we figure out what's going on. Sean followed me home last night so I could get Ethel and grab some clothes. I had to tell him about the call from Ramon, Ty."

Ty slaps the side of the van. "Why'd you do that?"

"Ty, listen to me. These coyotes work for human trafficking rings. We're talking organized crime here. We can't mess with this ourselves. We have to let the police handle it."

Ty says nothing. He stares into the back yard.

"Did Ramon call last night?"

Ty shakes his head. "Nuthin'"

I study him closely. "Ty, are you hearing what I'm saying? These guys know that we witnessed their crime. You're in danger too. Now, are you being completely truthful that Ramon didn't call again?"

Immediately his shoulders go back and his chin comes up. "My phone did not ring. You wanna check?" He holds the phone out.

I know if there is to be peace between us, my answer has to be no.

So we head back into the house, both a little edgy, walking in just as Ethel begins barking her unmistakable "stranger alert" bark. Following the sound, we find Harold sitting at a card table covered with paper, rulers, pencils and a calculator. He's utterly oblivious to the unfamiliar dog barking at him.

"Hi, Harold," Jill says. "Whatcha workin' on? Your toilet design?"

He looks up, roused from deep concentration. His bright blue eyes are calm, alert. "Yes, I've solved one of the constraints in quite a novel way, I believe."

Ty and I exchange a glance. Harold sounds so scholarly, so confident.

"Bill Gates has a contest for engineers to develop a cheap toilet to be used in poor countries where there's no running water. Harold's working on a design," Jill explains. "The winner gets $100,000."

Harold tsks at the mention of prize money and his eyebrows draw together. "Money doesn't matter. This is vital work. Life-changing."

I actually have heard of the Gates Foundation project. Could Harold seriously be working on it? I step closer. His papers are covered with drawings of squat, toilet-like objects with notes and mathematical formulae in the margins. "What are you calculating here, Harold?"

"The volume required to allow for a decomposition rate of at least eight percent per deciliter," he answers promptly.

I'm not an engineer, but the equations look plausible. Harold puts his head back down and returns to pounding his calculator.

"He seems so normal today," I whisper to Jill when we are all upstairs.

"I know. He has days when he's very lucid. He even makes jokes. He just said, 'I used to work getting minerals out of the ground. Now I'm working on putting them back in.'"

"You think he could actually win the competition?" It's the sort of fairy-tale ending that would really appeal to Jill.

She rolls her eyes. "There are entire teams from Stanford and Cal Tech working on the Gates contest, Audrey. Harold can't win, but focusing on engineering is really good for him. On days when he's designing, he doesn't collect, and he doesn't notice when I smuggle stuff into the trash."

Like a parent checking on a napping baby, Ty peeps over the banister at Harold working below. "How you know he's not just playin'? Pressin' the buttons on the calculator and scribbling numbers on the paper?"

"I'm not sure exactly what his goal is, but the equations I saw made sense mathematically," I say. "They weren't random numbers."

"Huh. What makes him stop designing and turn crazy? When he does that 'don't wake the babies' shit, he really freaks me out."

Jill sighs. "If anyone could figure that out, he'd be cured."

I drop a load of non-functioning flashlights. "Hey, since he's so coherent today, maybe it would be a good time to take Harold to see the lamp. See if he can remember where he got it."

Jill's face lights up. "Let's go at lunch!"

When we break for lunch, Harold is gone.

"Uh-oh, his bike's not here," Ty reports after looking into the back yard. "You think he's out collecting?"

"Since he's having a good day, he might be at the library," Jill says. "He does a lot of research for the toilet."

"Maybe after he invents it, he can get one right here," Ty says. "That way, next time his water gets shut off, he be all set."

Jill prods Ty with her foot. "Stop. Now that the water company has turned the water back on, I hope Harold will be able to keep at least one bathroom clear and open. He told me the other day it was nice to be able to pee indoors."

"Yeah, now that we got all the flower vases outta the tub, maybe he can take a shower. Mind tellin' me what that was all about?"

"Harold had a plan to bring garden flowers to shut-ins at the nursing home. Except there are no flowers in his garden any more, and the neighbors freaked when he tried to pick theirs, and the nursing home wouldn't let him in."

"Where did you take the vases?"

"That new florist in town. Told her she had to take all of them, and throw away the ugly ones herself. Harold won't know they didn't all get recycled."

Before Ty can make a smart comeback, we hear forceful pounding on the front door.

"That don't sound like Girl Scouts."

Ty and Jill look at me. Apparently answering aggressive knocking is in my job description.

Three more loud raps. "Health Department. Open up!"

Jill claps her hands to her cheeks, looking for all the world like the kid in *Home Alone*.

When I open the door, I meet a short balding guy who says he's from Palmyrton Building Code Enforcement and a thin, young man who's from the Board of Health. They are, they explain, looking for code violations.

Jill's face has drained of color so her ever-present black eye makeup stands out in ghoulish relief. "Do you have a search warrant?" Her voice quavers, undercutting her effort to sound tough.

The old guy snorts. "We ain't the cops, lady. We got several community complaints that this house is a health hazard. We have to investigate."

As they walk through the first floor, I hear the younger one dictating into his phone. "Front and back door accessible...kitchen functional....one bathroom and one powder room functional...furnace and hot water heater accessible and functioning...stairs clear....two rooms totally blocked. Some rodent traces. No signs of extreme infestation."

The men head upstairs, and Jill pushes me to follow them. "You've got to do something, Audrey!"

Like what? Prostrate myself in front of the master bedroom? Jill has ridiculous faith in my ability to work miracles. "All we can do is wait for them to finish. I don't even know what they're looking for." But surely they'll hear the scratch-scratch of scampering rodent feet. Will that count as a sign of infestation?

Given that the only part of the second floor that's passable is the hall, the men come back down quickly. The older one stands by the front door, brow furrowed, scribbling notes. As he turns to leave, he hands me a sheet of yellow paper with some incomprehensible scrawl on it.

"Wait—what does this mean?"

"The home does not meet the conditions to be condemned," the skinny young guy says.

Jill begins to squeal. "We're okay? We're okay? Ohmygod—we're okay!"

The older guy turns to face me before he steps out the door. "This place is still a firetrap, lady. The roof, the chimney, the floors, the air quality. I wouldn't spend another minute in here if I was you."

I stand on the porch watching them head back to their car. I wouldn't spend a minute more here either if only I had another job to go to. But with each day that passes, the house seems to exert more pressure on us to stay. For a fanciful moment, I imagine the head rodent upstairs holding up tiny paws to silence the others while the inspectors pass through.

Before they reach the curb, the front door of the house next door bangs open and Bernadette McMartin runs down her walk at a speed to rival a Kenyan sprinter. Her face is lit with joy as she approaches the men, but as they talk to her she stamps her foot and tugs her hair. "No! That's outrageous!"

She spins away from the inspectors. Joy twisted to rage, Bernadette points to me on the porch of Harold's house. "I hold you responsible."

# CHAPTER 23

As my work day winds down, Sean and I have been trading texts about where I'm to spend my evening. Home is out of the question; Maura has a meeting and won't be back to her apartment until eight; Ethel limits my options. Then I get a brainstorm. "How about Blue Monday? I can take Ethel, and the place is crawling with cops."

"Perfect. Get Griggs to ride over there with you. I'll have one of the guys follow you to Maura's when you're ready to leave."

I hate the feeling of being constantly supervised, but I hate the idea of encountering the busboy or the coyotes he works for even more. The cops have been watching Fiorellos and the Church of Living Praise all day with no sign of the busboy. Apparently he was working at the restaurant to fill in for the regular guy, who called in sick but supplied his own replacement. They both work off the books, so the owner has nothing more than a cell number to offer as a lead. These men seem able to appear and disappear at will, as if they populate a Harry Potter novel. Meanwhile, I live in 21st century Palmyrton, on display for all to see. My vulnerability makes me compliant. This is no time to resist Sean's plan.

Ty insists on following Sean's directions to the letter, escorting me all the way into the restaurant, looking around as if he expects armed gunmen to spring out from behind the bar, and leaving reluctantly when he's satisfied there's no one in the place but a few off-duty firemen and two elderly couples having the early-bird special. Ethel and I settle into a booth and I pull out my laptop to work on my accounts until our food arrives.

But first, I check my Yelp rating. Sure enough, three more negative reviews of Another Man's Treasure have cropped up. After trying one last time to reason with Martha and getting nothing but screaming threats for my efforts, I've blocked her number on my phone. So she's taken to bombarding me with email. One of yesterday's emails contained the threat of a lawsuit, so I forwarded it to Mr. Swenson. Now I read his reply. Never one to be consoling, he assures me that I'll know when this has actually happened when a process server hands me the papers.

Great. Another unsavory person to avoid.

I'm deeply absorbed in my accounts payable when someone speaks. "My goodness, you're always working, aren't you?"

A totally innocuous statement, but my heart rate kicks up. I look at the man speaking to me: tall, thin, a little younger than my dad, holding an Anchor Steam in one hand. Surely this isn't a process server? He looks vaguely familiar, but he's not a friend. How does he know my work habits?

"I'm meeting some buddies, but I guess I'm the first one here. Mind if I join you?"

He drops right into the booth before I can respond.

"You a regular here? 'Cause I thought when I met you the other day I might have seen you around before."

Who the hell is this guy, and why is he acting like my new best friend?

Then he unzips his coat, revealing a Princeton Half Marathon T-shirt. Of course—Harold's neighbor, the runner. Ed, Ed Brandt—that's his name.

"Uh—sure, make yourself comfortable. Ethel and I are waiting for our burgers. No, I'm not a regular. This is only my second time here."

He peers under the table and scratches Ethel's ears. "You look like a nice dog. Why in the world are you named Ethel?"

"That's what I asked the man at the shelter. He said, 'Lady, we get fifty dogs a week–they can't all be named Sparky.' Since she already answered to Ethel, I kept it."

"Well, better to give a dog a people name than give a kid a dog name." Ed stretches out on his side of the booth as if he owns the place. "Like our neighbor, Phoebe. Her kids' names are Eunice, Tabitha, and, get this, Zeus."

"Zeus?"

"Yeah, the week they moved in, I hear Phoebe outside calling, 'Zeus, Zeus.' I figured it was the dog, but then this little boy ran up." Ed shakes his head. "Whatever happened to naming kids Mary Beth, Cathy and Bob?"

Ed is undeniably funny, but I feel guilty laughing at Phoebe's expense. "She seems like a really good mother."

"She is, she is." Ed takes a swig of his beer. "Phoebe—our little organic, vegan, tree-hugging peace-nik. She's an amazing mom when you consider what she came from."

"What do you mean? All she does is talk about how idyllic her childhood was in Summit Oaks."

"Oh, it was. Until her mother flipped out. Went after her husband with a carving knife. Two hundred stitches and two pints of blood later, the family announces he cut himself slicing an onion. Right."

"You know better?"

"My golf partner's sister was the ER nurse who treated him."

"Why did she do it?"

Ed grins. "So far as I know, there's only one reason a woman goes after her husband with a knife."

Ed may only be able to think of sex as a reason, but I think if I were married to him, I could come up with a few more. But I want to keep him talking. "So did Phoebe's parents get divorced?"

Ed steeples his long, bony fingers. "Strangely enough, they didn't."

Despite his athleticism and a Harrison Ford, geezer-hot look, Ed has the personality of a gossipy haus-frau. So I figure as long as I'm stuck with his company, I may as well pump him for info on someone I'm actually curious about: Nora's mother.

"Speaking of crazy moms, what about Harold's sister, Nora's mom? Whatever happened to her?"

Ed takes a long pull from his beer bottle and waggles the empty at the waitress across the room. I guess telling this story is thirsty work. "Sharon. Oh my, Sharon! She was the life of the party, and let me tell you, back in the early eighties, Summit Oaks was one big party. In the summer we used to put our kids to bed and hold the party in the backyard. This was before baby monitors—we'd just open all the windows. Figured if the damn kids really needed something, they'd yell loud enough that we could hear."

I have a vision of drunken leisure-suited men and big-haired women dancing to Donna Summer while their nightmare-plagued toddlers cry in vain, but I smile encouragingly.

"Sharon was always the center of the action—organizing, decorating, cooking. That is, until her husband lost his job. What was his name?" Ed looks to the ceiling for inspiration. "Wow—I can't remember. I can barely picture what he looked like. Quiet guy, kind of a nothing personality. Not sure how Sharon ended up with him. Anyway, after he lost his job, Sharon had no money for Hawaiian outfits and tiki lights and rum. Our parties kinda lost their zip. Course it didn't help that little Frannie Ascher fell out her bedroom window during a clam bake."

"One of the kids fell out a second story window while her parents were at a party?"

Ed waves off my shock. "Landed in a rhododendron. Not a scratch on her. Anyway, that's around the time Harold moved in."

"Nora told me he helped her parents with their expenses, but then he and her mother started shopping compulsively and her dad left."

"That's the short version," Ed says. He has an arch expression on his face, urging me to beg for more. One part of me wants to know, but the other part finds Ed increasingly distasteful so that I can't bring myself to ask another question. We sit quietly for a moment. But Ed's desire to talk is bigger than both of us.

"During this period I was the North Jersey sales rep for Delta Pharmaceuticals. My territory included all of Palmer County, so many times I'd stop home in the middle of the day." Ed winks. "Kids in school, wife alone and bored."

Somehow I doubt Mrs. Ed was all that bored, but I keep a blank expression on my face in hopes we won't have to pursue Ed's amorous history.

"Anyway, Sharon probably did spend time shopping with Harold, but there were many times I'd see her drive off alone, dressed to the nines."

So in Ed's overheated imagination, Sharon was having an affair. Maybe.

"But where did Sharon end up?" I ask. "Her husband left, her kids left, and she remained on Acorn Lane with Harold. Nora says she came home from college and her mother was gone."

Ed leans across the table and lowers his voice, "Nora asked around at a few of the neighbors in the spring of 2005. The best anyone could recall, the last time we saw Sharon was fall of the previous year."

"No one reported her missing?"

Ed shrugs. "If a grown woman leaves home and none of her family looks for her, that's not the neighbors' problem, right?"

"I don't know. All the neighbors in Summit Oaks seem pretty wrapped up in one another's business. Did Bernadette tell you that Harold's house passed the Health Department's inspection? It's not going to be condemned."

Ed takes a long swig from his beer. "Oh, I heard about it all right. Bernadette got her jungle drums beating the moment she found out. She's called an emergency meeting of the troops to plan her next move."

I'd love to be a fly on the wall at that meeting. "Are you going?"

"Can't be bothered. I've got a ski weekend planned."

I want to ask him what he thinks Bernadette has up her sleeve, but just then the waitress arrives with my BlueBurger, and Ed spots his running friends at the door.

"Nice talkin' with you, Audrey. Keep an eye peeled in that house. Maybe Sharon never left!"

Ed's words echo as I pick up my burger. My appetite departs without a backward glance. Could the pervasive reek in Harold's house really be from a dead human body? One that's been there since 2005? Would the Health Department overlook that? Surely Nora wouldn't protect her uncle if she thought he'd killed her own mother. The shudder passing through me knocks a French fry onto the booth. Ethel's snout appears and snaps it up. No, I reassure myself, Ed was trying to be funny. He couldn't know about the cat, couldn't know how tone-deaf that joke was.

The prospect of eating the burger seems overwhelming, but the thought of explaining to the waitress why I'm leaving with it untouched is worse. I nibble. A little grease, a little cheese and my appetite stirs. Between the drama over Ramon and the stress of the busboy, I'm more sensitive than usual. As I eat, I feel stronger, and Ed's monologue sounds more like nonsense. Still, it couldn't hurt to ask Sean about Sharon Pheiffer. If there's any truth to *Law and Order*, with a few clicks of his computer Sean should be able to reassure me that Sharon is alive and kicking somewhere.

Harold's craziness probably drove her away.

I bet even his partner in collecting had her limit.

# CHAPTER 24

"I don't understand why you won't go out with him. I think he's hot."

Coughlin arranged for one of his colleagues at the Blue Monday to escort me to Maura's once she was home. Now she and I are curled up on her couch drinking sauvignon blanc. Given that her wine glasses are the size of fishbowls, I'm pretty relaxed.

"He's attractive in an oversized sorta way," I admit.

"He's not oversized. Everyone else you've ever dated has been undersized."

I open my mouth then close it again without speaking.

"Not Cal. That's what you were going to say, isn't it?"

It's hard for me to watch Maura rolling her eyes at the mention of Cal. She was only out of the country for a few months but she managed to miss the biggest thing that ever happened to me. Now I can't make her understand how Cal wasn't just one in a long line of date-from-hell types that she's counseled me through over the years. I'm still trying to unravel the threads of his love, his betrayal, his sacrifice.

"Sean's attractiveness is not the real issue. It's...he..., he makes me confused. The thing I like about him is the same thing that drives me crazy."

"And what thing is that?"

I put my head between my knees and wrap my arms

around myself. "I don't know, his, his..strength.. I can't explain it."

"When you were making out with him the other night, what was the part you liked the most?"

I heat up at the memory. Sean's strong hands, used so gently. The clean scent of him, unadorned by anything purchased in a mall. Without looking at Maura I mutter. "The way his heart beats."

She spits out her wine. "The way his heart beats? What, can you dance the salsa to it?"

"It's slow and steady. When my head was on his chest it felt so good to feel his heart going thump, thump, thump."

Maura takes my hand. "He makes you feel safe, honey," she whispers. "What's wrong with that?"

I lift my head and Maura looks a little hazy, maybe from wine or maybe from a film of tears. "Because when I let myself enjoy him protecting me, I start to feel out of control. Like I'm not in charge of my own life. Sean likes being in charge too much. I have to keep him at bay."

"Oh Audrey! You've been in charge of your own life since you were three years old. Go ahead and let someone else share the load."

Maura goes to bed early because she has a big meeting in the morning, and I lie awake on the sofa bed in her living room snuggling with Ethel. Should I listen to Maura even if her advice goes against my grain? Normal couples rely on each other, right? Giving up a little autonomy doesn't mean I'm turning into a Real Housewife of New Jersey.

Does it?

I bury my face in Ethel's soft fur. Maybe this control issue is a blind alley. Maybe I feel guilty for how quickly I've turned my affections from Cal to Sean. I want someone who's faithful and true, but how true have I been? Are any of us even capable of faithfulness, or are we all on a continual quest for the next big thing, like Sharon and Harold at a flea market?

Oh, this is too much for me. I wish I could put my emotions in a spreadsheet and assign them each a probability factor. "Statistical analysis of the heart. That's what we need, Ethel."

As if he can hear me thinking, Sean sets my phone vibrating with a text. I look at the screen.

*Make it home OK?*

*Yes. I'm at Maura's*

*Busy?*

My hand hesitates above the screen before I finally type. *No*

A second later, my phone is ringing.

I answer, hoping he's calling to give me the good news that they've arrested the busboy. But no such luck. He explains that the search will continue tomorrow and that the cellphone number that Ramon tried to contact Ty on was a pay-as-you go phone. Untraceable.

"You sound exhausted. Where are you?"

"Still at the office. I'm ducking calls from my family."

"Can't they just call you there?"

"Only my mother has my work cell number, and she's under strict orders not to call it unless someone dies. Otherwise I'd be dealing with their crazy crap all day long."

As a member of an uber-nuclear family of two, I'm perversely fascinated by Sean's big Irish clan. I'd love to have a sister to squabble with or a cousin to make my eyes roll. I wouldn't avoid them. I'd jump right in. "What crazy crap is going on now?"

"Planning a party for my parents' anniversary. Will it be at Brendan and Adrienne's or won't it? My sisters keep debating, but when it's too cold for a party to spread outside, Brendan's house is the only one big enough to hold us all. It's pointless to resist. So I'm not answering my phone until they get themselves settled. Anyway, why did you want to know where I am?"

I choose to ignore the hopefulness in Sean's voice, and start telling him about my encounter with Ed. "I know I'm being silly, but I'd feel better about working in the house if I knew Sharon was still alive somewhere. Is there a way you could you check her records?"

A beat of silence.

"I didn't mean right now. Go home and get some rest. Just...if it's possible...but if it's not, I totally under—"

"Audrey."

"Yes?"

"Wanna see my office?"

The answer comes to me without conscious thought. "As a matter of fact, I do. I want to be able to picture where you are when you call me."

A throaty chuckle comes over the line. I'm not sure I meant to please him so much. "I'll pick you up in ten."

Following Sean into the Palmyrton Municipal Complex, I see nothing but blank beige walls and unmarked metal doors. On TV, police stations are always dark and gritty, but here in Palmyrton crimes are investigated from a place no more grim than an insurance company's headquarters. My curiosity builds. Will Sean's office be as impersonal as this hallway, or does he have family photos and funny coffee mugs? Is his desk messy or neat? The need to know grips me with surprising force.

Sean leads me to a big room filled with computer terminals. "We need to search the records here."

I feel a twinge of disappointment, then remind myself this is what I came for. I watch as Sean calls up a database and taps in Sharon Pheiffer's name. More than forty files pop up.

"You know when she was born?"

"Late forties, early fifties, I guess."

That reduces the list by more than half.

"Maiden name?"

This stumps me until I realize that of course, it's the same as Harold's last name: Voss.

We're left with three possibilities. Sean reads them aloud: "Sharon V. Phieffer, born 1948, died 2010 in Phoenix; Sharon Voss, born 1951, currently living in Charleston, South Carolina, and S. Elizabeth Phieffer, born 1947, currently living in Saranac Lake, New York."

"That sounds promising." I crane my neck to see over his broad shoulder. "Can you tell if any of them ever lived in New Jersey?"

He tilts the screen away. "What are you planning to do with this information, Audrey? You have no reason to contact her, do you?"

"No. Of course not." *Other than being consumed by curiosity.* "I just wanted to be sure we weren't going to uncover her corpse in the house."

"Seems unlikely." Sean logs out of the database.

"Thank you, Sean. But hey, I still want to see your office."

He grins. "Right this way."

I follow him down a featureless corridor until he opens a door into a good-sized office with two desks. Every square inch of one is covered with files and papers and post-it notes. The other is entirely clear, with three neat stacks of color-coded folders in one corner.

"The neat one is yours," I say.

"Correct. I've worked with Pete Holzer for years. He can pull stuff out of that heap like he's got a divining rod. I can't operate that way. But we get along."

I circle around the desk. Next to his computer monitor are four framed school photos of gap-toothed, freckle-faced kids. "Your nieces and nephews?"

"Those are my sister's kids—Alyssa, Liam, Frankie, and Joe. I've got four more, but their parents aren't as good about supplying the pics."

I plop into his swivel chair. "This is where you sit to bark out the orders?"

He perches on the edge of his desk and spins me around. "The orders that fall on deaf ears when I press 'Nealon comma A'?"

"Try an order right now."

He opens his mouth, then hesitates. A flush spreads up from his neck.

"You're blushing! What kind of order are you thinking of?"

He pulls me towards him and whispers in my ear. "Come to my place. Don't you want to see where I live too?"

"I do. But I can't leave Ethel alone at Maura's for long."

He pulls away. "My building doesn't allow pets. And I've got to be in here at seven tomorrow."

We look at each other, and I can't deny there's just as much desire in my eyes as there is in his.

"Saturday?" I suggest.

He winces. "Saturday is my parents' anniversary."

"The big bash at Brendan and Adrienne's?"

"It's nothing fancy. Would you consider...? We wouldn't have to stay long. And then—"

He's surprisingly adorable when he's flustered. I twine my fingers through his. "Then what? You start issuing orders?"

He buries his face in my hair. "Yes."

"Okay," I whisper.

"You'll go? Really?"

I nod.

What have I done?

# CHAPTER 25

"Morning, Harold."

Harold looks up from tapping his calculator: good sign. But his eyes regard Jill as if she's some stranger approaching him on the subway: bad sign.

All the disruption surrounding the Play-O-Rama episode has distracted us from our mission to get Harold to say where he found the Tiffany lamp. This morning, Jill arrived at the house determined to bring Harold and the lamp together. But I'm not sure today is shaping up to be a "Good Harold" day.

Jill sits down across from him at his card table/desk. "Harold, would you like to take a ride today to look at a pretty lamp?" Her voice could cajole a skittish kitten out from under a couch. "On the way back, we could stop for ice cream at Friendly's."

Harold shakes his head. "Busy."

"I can see you're busy. What are you working on?"

"Capacity parameters."

"Hmmm. Do you think you might be able to take a break in a little bit to go see the lamp? It's such a useful lamp, and I'm trying to find the person who could use it the most." She tilts her head to make eye contact with Harold. "Could you help me with that, Harold? I'd be so grateful."

Harold exhales deeply. "Okay. But I have to finish this first."

I squeeze Jill's shoulder once we're upstairs at work.

"You're amazing."

"Not really. I've just learned how to play the usefulness card." She peeks over the railing. "We'd better keep a close eye on him so he doesn't slip away."

Jill doesn't wear her headphones so she can hear when Harold's calculator stops tapping. As soon as we detect silence, we go downstairs and gently herd Harold into my car, overcoming many objections that it would be more energy-efficient to ride bikes. Jill sits in the back chatting with Harold, while Ty sits up front with me, rolling his eyes.

Once we arrive, Ty gets the lamp out of the safe and sets it on a table. "Yo, Harold, you remember where you got this?"

Jill places herself between Harold and Ty, and I pull him into a chair next to me to watch as Jill works her magic.

"Harold, do you remember this lamp? It was in the living room of your house, the room with all the appliances, right near the door to the hall. Someone got rid of it just because it doesn't light up anymore. But I know a good electrician could fix the wiring and then it would be such a useful lamp again. But it's a special lamp, so we have to find the right electrician to fix it. Do you remember when you got it?"

Harold seems mesmerized by Jill's lilting voice. "Fall. There were leaves in the driveway."

"Ask him where—"

I squeeze Ty's forearm.

"Leaves. Good. Was the lamp outside in a sale in someone's driveway?"

Harold nods. "The man had a lot of useful things. But he wanted too much money. He wanted ten dollars for the lamp. But that was too much. Because it doesn't work. And the cord is frayed. That could start a fire."

"So you didn't give him ten dollars?"

"No, I said five. But he made me give seven. He

wasn't nice."

I'm astonished. Harold really does remember the transaction. And to think he bargained the owner down from ten bucks to seven on a lamp that might be worth a cool million!

"Well, I think you did the right thing getting the lamp for seven dollars," Jill coos. "It's going to be a very useful lamp once we get it fixed up. Now, the man who wasn't very nice—where did he live?"

Harold begins to squirm in his chair. He wrings his hands and stretches his neck. "He had glasses. Dark glasses so I couldn't see his eyes. I don't like that."

"No-o-o-o. I don't like those glasses either. Where was his house, Harold? Was it here in Palmyrton?"

Ty and I lean forward.

"Have to measure the thermal maturity," Harold murmurs. "Hydrocarbon production is suboptimal."

"Oh, no—not this shit again!"

Jill shoots Ty a look that would stop a moose. "Harold," she whispers, "look at the lamp. We want to fix it so someone can use it, but in order to do that, we need to know where you got it. It was a fall day, you were in a driveway with leaves, the man wasn't so nice...where was the house, Harold? Was it near your house?"

Harold sits frozen, his eyes staring at something only he can see: an oil field in Kuwait, a driveway in Palmyrton. Who knows? Time ticks by.

"Madison? Summit?" Ty's voice isn't loud, but Harold flinches.

He covers his head with his hands. "Don't wake the babies, don't wake the babies."

The ride back to the office is grim. While Jill walks Harold to the Friendly's take-out window for the promised ice cream, I pat Ty's arm. "Don't blame yourself. It was over the moment Harold started in on the geology. We just have to wait for a better day and try again."

"Sometimes I think he's just messin' with us. He knows what we're after and he switches on the rock talk and the baby nonsense to get us off his back."

"I don't think he's capable of that much strategy. He's mentally ill."

"Humpf. Crazy like a fox. He's takin' us for fools."

Ty slumps in the passenger seat until we arrive back at 12 Acorn Lane. Then he jumps in the van without another word to us, and drives off to recycle a load of bottles that happen to have birds on the labels.

"Ugh! We're out of trash bags." Jill stands with her hands on her hips surveying a pile of moldering bird seed. She had previously secured Harold's reluctant permission to discard this, but since the trauma of the lamp ID, he's been erratic and restless. Permission could be rescinded if we don't act quickly.

With Ty gone, Jill encourages me to take my car over to Wal-Mart to buy some bags.

I glance in Harold's direction. "I'm not leaving you here alone."

"Don't be silly. I'll be fine."

What I don't want to say is that I'm nervous to make the trip alone. If the busboy could threaten me in a playground, the rambling Wal-Mart parking lot seems entirely too perilous.

I fold my arms across my chest. "No way. We need to be more cautious. Harold is unpredictable. And he's stronger than he looks. All that bicycling has kept him in good shape."

Jill tugs on her respirator. "How about borrowing some from Phoebe? She'd help us out."

I peek into the foyer where Harold paces and frets. Jill pushes me toward the door.

"Just pop over and ask. You won't be gone more than a few minutes."

When I ring the bell, the door is answered not by Phoebe, but by a skinny, bouncy little girl. This must be Eunice. A sixty-ish woman with frizzy gray hair appears behind her.

"Grandma, it's the lady who's cleaning Harold's house," Eunice announces.

"Right you are." I smile at the kid and address the old lady. "Is Phoebe home?"

"No, she's at her yoga class. May I help you?"

I hesitate. It's awkward enough to be cadging a loan from someone I barely know, let alone someone I've never met.

Eunice grabs my hand and tugs. "I'm going to my first tennis lesson. Wanna see my new racket?"

There's a clatter from somewhere deep in the house and a male voice shouts, "Jean? Where are you?"

"Come in, dear. It's too cold to chat with the door open. Be right there, Chip!"

I step into a foyer filled with the detritus of childhood: snowboots, mittens, dozens of mismatched shoes, a one-eared stuffed bunny, a scattering of Legos.

A tall lean man with silver hair and a deep tan appears from the back of the house. He surveys the chaos before him and massages his temples. "Eunice, aren't you dressed yet? We have to leave in five minutes."

"I can't find my tennis skirt."

The other two kids tear through the hall, little Tabby unsuccessfully pursuing her brother, who's waving a doll by its hair just out of her reach.

"Now, Zeus honey, give that doll to her. Grammy will be right back to finish the Legos with you." She speaks with the same dreamy implacability as Phoebe, but she looks nothing like her pretty daughter. Physically Phoebe looks more like her dad—slender and fine-featured. This is the couple that Ed Brandt told me about. I try to picture these doting grandparents as a passionate younger couple fighting over infidelity. It's easy to imagine that Chip was once a ladies' man—he's still quite handsome. Harder to see the sweet, pillowy Jean as the woman scorned, wielding a knife.

Grandpa Chip taps his watch. "The tennis clothes, Jean."

"Oh, right. I'll find them." She runs her hand through her already disheveled hair, then remembers me. "I'm sorry...?"

"I just wondered if I could borrow a few garbage bags. But, never mind, I've come at a bad time."

"She's working on cleaning Harold's house, Chip."

He arches his eyebrows. "A cause we've got to support. Come with me while Jean gets Eunice ready. Garbage bags I'm capable of finding. Tennis skirts— that's beyond me."

I follow him down the hall. There's something familiar about his walk. Is this the neighbor I spoke to on the day the tow truck came for Harold's old cars? The guy walking the little white dog? But he doesn't mention having met me.

Despite the clutter, the house is full of striking details—two abstract water-colors that evoke the ocean on a cloudy day, some raku pottery, a large hand-woven rug. On the kitchen wall Phoebe has stenciled in the round: "Our family, a circle of strength and love forever unbroken."

"Your daughter has a lovely home," I say as Chip rummages beneath the sink for the garbage bags.

He emerges from the cabinet, kicking a bottle of Windex back in and slamming the door before anything else tumbles out. "Phoebe is long on creativity, short on organization." He brushes some lint from his cashmere sweater. "A product of both her parents."

He hands me the bags. "How much progress have you made?"

"We've made it to the upstairs hallway."

"You've cleared the entire first floor? My, you're quick!"

"We're not emptying every room. We just need to make the house livable. And locate some of the more worthwhile things Harold has collected over the years. He needs the money."

"Surely, there's nothing of value in that junk heap?"

I'm not about to share the news on the Tiffany lamp, so I ramble vaguely. "Oh, here and there we find a few things."

"Are you looking for something in particular, or just hoping to stumble upon a prize?" He studies me with bemused interest. Probably he's just making chit-chat, but I'm still reluctant to talk about the Civil War documents we hope to find in the master bath.

"Nora's given us some guidelines. So," I turn the conversation, "do you and your wife still live in the neighborhood? I thought maybe I've seen you walking your dog."

"I don't have a dog. But, yes, we live a few streets away. I'd love to get a condo downtown, but Jean won't hear of it. Not while the grandkids are little and we're on call as babysitters. Justin, our-son-in law, is in sales. Always on the road."

"Did you know, Sharon, Harold's sister?" The question spurts out of me, an embarrassing belch at a dinner party.

If Sharon was Chip's long-ago lover, there's certainly no trace of fondness or interest now. He purses his lips. "She was a nut. When Jean and I first met her, Sharon was nutty in a fun way—impulsive, up for anything, you know. But as time went on, she got crazy-nutty. The shopping, the hoarding—she and her brother brought out the worst in each other."

"What happened to her?"

Chip shrugs. "No one seems to know. No one in Summit Oaks really cares." Then he narrows his keen blue eyes. "Haven't you asked Nora?"

Before I can respond, Eunice's voice pipes from the foyer. "Ready, Grandpa!" Chip pats his pockets and glances around the kitchen.

I spot a cigar and a lighter on the counter amidst a clutter of crayons and paper. Surely not Phoebe's husband's. "This what you're looking for?"

He winks at me and tucks them in his shirt pocket, under the sweater. "My little indulgence."

I follow Chip to the front door.

Eunice stands ready with her racket and pleated tennis skirt. Jean is plopped on the floor with Tabby and Zeus building a Lego creature with multiple appendages.

"I want him to have a horn," Zeus says.

"And a tail," squeals his sister.

"Excellent ideas." Jean scoops up Legos from the pile and offers them around like canapés.

"Back in an hour, dear." Chip steps around them and holds the front door open for me and Eunice. His sleeve hikes up and his tanned, long-fingered hand rests on the dark purple wood.

From the wrist to the first knuckle stretches a jagged white scar.

# CHAPTER 26

After a long day at Harold's, Ty has accompanied me back to the office so I can pick up some papers, then he will drop me off at Maura's and take my car to his house. Even though I chafe at my restraints, I've agreed to not drive anywhere alone. Jill is still at Harold's house. The girl is unstoppable.

As she works on the house, I notice a change in Jill. She seems calmer, more in control. It's as if being needed by Harold and Nora has made her less needy. I thought I'd have to help her find outlets for all the stuff she's disposing of, but instead, she's turned up some great new resources that I never knew about. Every day her back gets a little straighter, her nails get a little less chewed. On the day that she finds a place that will accept 275 broken umbrellas and turn them into components for hydroponic gardening, I know we've turned a corner. Jill is not my goofy little assistant; she's become my colleague.

This is what I've always claimed to want, but I want it in the same way that Ethel wants the UPS truck. It's safe to want things that you know are unattainable. What would Ethel do if she actually sunk her teeth into the bumper of that big brown behemoth? What will I do when Jill no longer needs my guidance?

Ty slips up behind my desk chair.

"What is that—all those colors. Some kinda game?"

"No, I'm doing a cash-flow analysis. You know how we're busiest in spring and fall, and really slow right before Christmas? And last year was worse than usual with me being in the hospital twice."

"We're in trouble, aren't we?" Ty's eyebrows draw down. He may not know cash-flow analysis, but he knows "If we pay the rent, we can't pay the electricity." I'd love to share my troubles with someone, but I can't burden Ty that way. He depends on me.

"Oh, we're okay, but I still have to be able to pay your salary and our other bills even in the slow times. So I need to figure out how to manage our money so we always have enough cash on hand."

Ty watches the colors pulse across the screen. "You learn to do that in college?"

"Not really. I studied math, not accounting."

"So what was the point of going to college if you didn't learn nuthin' you need to run this business?"

I stop what I'm doing to look at him directly. "It's true I don't use differential calculus here in the office. But in college I learned skills I use every day. I learned how to solve problems, how to analyze and research. I learned how to *think*."

"I know how to think."

"Why did you have trouble in high school, Ty?" I ask softly. We've never treaded close to this topic. "You're very smart."

"I liked school when I was real little. But high school was all about rules, and work sheets, and doing shit just to do it. I didn't see the point. So I stopped going."

And dropped out. And got tangled up with some losers. And drove the car when they robbed a store. He passed the GED while he was in jail.

"You're right—high school can be pretty bad. But college is different. You ever think of going?"

He blows air out through his lips. "You gotta take a three-hour test to go to college. I can't sit still that long."

"Not every college requires the SAT. You could take a class or two at the community college, just to try it out."

"I got no money for that."

"You could afford it if the money from Harold's lamp comes through."

Ty's face brightens. I can see I've piqued his interest and I forge ahead. "You could still keep working here. Just take a class that interests you."

Ty points at my computer screen. "I wanna learn to do that. I like numbers if I can see the purpose for them."

"You could take Intro to Statistics. And maybe Art History."

He tilts his head. "You mean learn about the kinda stuff we find in the houses sometimes?"

"I'll warn you right now—you'll learn more than you'll ever need to know in this business. We're unlikely to find any Michelangelos in New Jersey. But it's interesting. I bet you'd like it."

Ty folds his pay stub into ever-smaller squares. "I dunno. I'm not so good at studying and stuff."

"I'd help you." I'm too eager, pushing too hard. I can sense Ty pulling away.

"Maybe." He jumps up. "Whattya want me to do with this delivery from Staples? Unpack it or leave it for Jill?"

"Go ahead and unpack it." I turn back to my computer. No matter how I massage the numbers, I can't produce enough cash to pay our next insurance bill and my quarterly income tax.

That lamp has to be real.

For Ty's sake. And for mine.


The next morning, 8:30 comes and goes with no sign of Ty. I text him and get no answer. He must be driving over to get me. At 9:00, Jill calls. "Where are you guys?"

"I'm still waiting for Ty to pick me up. He hasn't answered my texts."

Silence.

"Jill?"

Silence.

"Jill! What do you know that I don't? Tell me!"

"I can't," she whines. "I promised."

"Does this have to do with Ramon? Dear God, please don't tell me Ty went to meet with him alone!"

"He went last night," Jill says in a small voice.

"You knew and you let him go? You didn't try to stop him?"

"How could I stop him? He never listens to me."

"You could have told me," I yell into the phone.

"Ty said not to. He said he'd have the money back this morning. We both know how worried you've been, Audrey. The cancelled jobs. The bad Yelp reviews. Ty blames himself. He said he lost the money, so it was on him to get it back. I told him you didn't blame him, but that's not how he sees it."

I pace up and down my living room as Jill talks. I should have known that Ty would never be able to ignore his sense of street honor. When I remember that terrible moment when I thought Ty had been shot, my head swims. He can't come to harm because of me. He can't.

"Where did he go to meet Ramon? Do you have any idea?"

"Ty wouldn't say. But I know Ramon called him again from a different phone. He told Ty he wants to give back the money because it's *mal suerte*. Bad luck. He thinks it's cursed or something. So we figured if Ramon wanted to give it back, how dangerous could it be for Ty to go get it?"

"My God, Jill—it could be a trap. These people that Ramon is mixed up with are dangerous criminals. Ty witnessed one of them committing murder. They want to—"

*Get rid of him. And me.* Everyone's been so concerned with protecting me. Just because Ty is young and tough and strong, doesn't mean he's not in danger too. How could I have let this happen?

"Do you have any clue where he was meeting Ramon?"

"No," Jill says. "But I know he drove your car."

"I have to call Coughlin."

"No!" Jill's screech makes my ear drums vibrate. "Ty specifically said that if anything happened and you found out, you were not supposed to call the cops. He made a promise to Ramon. He said it could be risky if Ramon and his friends thought Ty broke his word."

"But Jill—"

"I'm coming to get you. Don't call until I get there."

While I wait, I wrack my brains to figure out what to do. If Ty had been successful in his encounter with Ramon, then surely he would have answered our increasingly frantic calls by now. Silence means trouble. I know I have to tell Coughlin. He can put out an APB on the car. If they find the car, then at least they'll have some idea where…

The bitter taste of my morning coffee heaves up in the back of my throat. Do I honestly think the cops will find my car parked in front of a house full of Hispanic mean, and knock politely on the door, and find Ty unharmed, eating a plate of rice and beans with Ramon and his friends?

Or what if Ty actually did get the money back and is driving home right now? What if the cops see that my car is wanted and pull him over? A young black man driving a car not registered to him. What if Ty asks them why they stopped him and they pull their guns?

Every scenario ends with Ty on the ground, bleeding, his eyes blank and lifeless.

Jill enters my condo talking.

"Grandma Betty just called me," she announces. "She heard Ty's phone ringing in his bedroom. It's full of unanswered texts and missed calls from his friends, starting at 10:00 last night."

I rub my temples. "Oh, that poor woman. She must be worried sick. What are we going to tell her?"

"I took care of that. Told her Ty is out on a job and left his phone home because he's avoiding some girl. Didn't want to be tempted to answer."

"Jill! How could you tell such an outrageous lie?"

"She fell for it, so now she won't worry for a while. But don't you see Audrey? This is good news."

"It is?"

"Ty would never forget his phone. So he intentionally left it behind when he went to meet Ramon. That explains why he hasn't called."

"Maybe. But why leave it?"

"It must be part of the deal he made with Ramon. So no one could follow him."

"Yeah, no one can rescue him either."

Jill grabs my hand. "Don't call the police yet, Audrey. I think Ty doesn't need rescuing. I think he has a plan."

I jerk away from her. "A plan to get himself killed."


"Where's Ethel?"

Unable to sit still in my condo, Ethel and I have joined Jill at Harold's house. We're making a vague pretense of work, but not accomplishing much. Ethel has been underfoot all morning, but now I realize I haven't seen her for at least half an hour. My stomach clenches. What else can go wrong today? "Jill, you didn't leave the front door open, did you?"

"No, it's too cold."

"Ethel? Ethel?" My voice rises in panic. The memory of the night she got lost trying to protect me is too raw. Does everyone who wants to keep me safe get hurt in the process?

Jill runs upstairs. "Ethel—where are you? Ethel?" On the way through the foyer, she turns to ask Harold what he's seen, but Harold is in a trance. I approach the still densely packed living room. Could she have wormed her way in there? The vision of flattened Petey the cat looms large. Jill stays upstairs.

"I hear her," Jill says and I run back up. Sure enough the sound of scrabbling dog nails, much louder than the usual scratch-scratch we hear—is audible through a solid wall of toys in one of the smaller bedrooms.

"She's inside that! She's burrowed into it." I hear my voice spiraling toward hysteria. I brought her here because she enjoyed having our company all day. Now this damn house is going to crush her.

Jill falls to her knees. "We gotta get her out. How're we going to get her out?"

"Go get some turkey from yesterday's lunch leftovers."

When Jill returns, she reaches one arm under the pile with the turkey between her fingers while I call to my dog. "Ethel. Come. Come get a treat."

"She's sniffing my fingers."

"Grab her collar."

"I got it, but she's digging in her claws. She doesn't want to come."

Despite my coaxing, Ethel continues to resist Jill mightily. Some boxes of wooden train tracks shift.

"She's got something in her mouth and she won't let it go." Jill says.

"Oh, god, it's not a rat, is it?"

"No, it's hard."

I move some still unopened science sets—the kind every adult buys and no kid wants—from the top of the tunnel Ethel has disappeared into. The maneuver allows Jill to squirm a few inches closer and get a better grip. She pulls and now we can see Ethel clearly.

In her mouth is a bone.

We finally get her out into the hall. I stick my finger into her mouth. "Ethel, release!"

True to her obedience school dropout temperament, she twists her head out of my grasp and her powerful jaws crunch down on the small bone.

Jill peeps at Ethel through splayed fingers. "It's not a cat bone is it? Please tell me it's not a cat bone."

I'm not sure why Jill is objecting to a cat bone. Honestly, I can't think of any alternatives that would be better. It's not like Ethel could have found a fresh-grilled pork chop bone under all the trash in bedroom.

When I finally pry her mouth open, all that's left of the bone are a few dried splinters.

"Eeeew." Jill squinches her eyes shut.

Ethel is unfazed. In fact, she's squirming away from me, ready to go right back into the tunnel we just pulled her out of. Behind us there's a creak. Then a crash.

I pull Ethel into my arms as the balance in the toy room shifts and a load falls forward and spills out the door.

"Whoa, another avalanche, like with the records," Jill says. When the dust clears, she stands on tip-toe to look into the room. "Look, I think this was definitely Nora's room."

I peer over her shoulder. Mounted on the far wall is a pink shelf painted with now-faded rainbows. Sitting on the shelf in an orderly row are stiff-legged Barbies, their hair matted with dust, and homely Cabbage Patch Kids, and a realistic infant-sized doll in a flowered onesie.

"Those look like they could actually be the dolls Nora played with," I say. "I had a Cabbage Patch Kid when I was little."

We stand silently, joined in a little requiem for the mundane lives once lived here. Mundane until

Harold's arrival turned them to the gothic. "Hmmm," I say. " Maybe that's why Harold's always saying 'don't wake the babies.' Maybe he's remembering this."

"Hey, way to psychoanalyze, Audrey. I think you may be right."

Or maybe the babies are just another of Harold's sad delusions.

The Ethel incident has given us a little respite from worrying about Ty, but the minute the dog is safe, our anxiety comes crashing back in on us. As Jill silently picks up the toys that have spilled into the hall, I notice a big tear sliding down her cheek. She sees me watching her.

"I thought he'd be back by now," she whispers. "What's taking so long?"

I sit staring at the wall. I'm trying to think like Ty. And think like Ramon. Grandma Betty's words come back to me. What Ramon wants more than anything is to stay in this country. My effort to work a deal for him hasn't amounted to anything. So maybe he's turned to Ty to get what he wants. Finally, I speak.

"Ty didn't just impulsively chase after Ramon. Ty left the phone because he worried I'd tell Coughlin when I realized what he'd done. He knew the cops could use it to trace his movements." I look up at Jill. "And what other thing could the cops use to find him?"

"Your car?"

"There are a million Honda Civics on the road, Jill. But only one with my license plates." I jump up and run downstairs. Harold doesn't even lift his head as I rush out to the driveway. There sits the last of Harold's three junked cars. Jill couldn't persuade Harold to give this one up because it's filled with "valuable" garden implements. So here it sits. Last time I looked, it had plates.

Now it doesn't.

Jill and I quickly find my plates slipped under a box

of hand trowels on the front seat of the car. I stand staring at the familiar numbers. "I think Ty knew he would be driving further than just to some nearby town in New Jersey. He knew if he was going to be spending some time on the road, it needed to be in an untraceable car."

Jill's brow furrows. "But I thought everyone said Ramon still had to be nearby."

"I think he was nearby when he called Ty. I think Ty took him somewhere."

Jill's face lights up and she grabs my hand. "You know what I couldn't find today? Our cooler! I thought Harold took it, but it must've been Ty. He's helping Ramon get away in exchange for the money! Wow!" Then Jill's smile fades. "Are you going to tell Coughlin?"

I press my hands into my eyes. "Good lord, no."

# CHAPTER 27

That evening I tell Maura I have a splitting headache and pull the covers over my head before she tries to make small talk. I can't tell her anything about what happened today. It's bad enough that Jill knows what Ty has done. The crushing fear that Ty has been killed by the coyotes has been replaced by a dread of a fate that is almost worse—that he'll be arrested for harboring a fugitive or hindering an investigation and wind up back in jail.

I know Ty would rather die than go back to jail. That he would risk this for me leaves me breathless. And that he planned it, that his act is not even an impulsive act of bravado, is more than I can get my head around.

The more I think, the more I writhe. Ty did this not to save me personally, but to save Another Man's Treasure for me. Have I given him and Jill the idea that the business means more to me than they do? I would give up estate sales forever and cheerfully work as an insurance actuary just to have Ty back home safely. What if I never get to tell him that?

In the midst of my agony, my cell chirps the arrival of a text. I grab my phone eagerly.

Sean, not Ty.

*Arrested the man who threatened you at Play-O-Rama. Need you to come ID him. Sending a uniform to pick you up.*

*Now? Why aren't you coming?* I text back.
*You're a witness. I can't talk to you before the ID.*

Inside the station it's just like on TV. I'm behind a big glass window and five Hispanic men walk in. There are several cops there—detectives and uniforms. Sean stands off in a corner. I can't ask him anything about Ramon or the coyotes. As I look at the men in the line-up in profile, I panic—they're all short, they all have dark hair, they all have brown skin. What if I can't pick him out? What if I make a mistake and the wrong man gets in trouble? But as soon as they turn to face me, my anxiety evaporates.

"Number three," I say without hesitation. That's the face that breathed on me in the play structure. Those are the eyes that stared into mine with no compassion. That's the man who threatened me. Has he also threatened Ramon? Are there other guys in his gang who are on Ramon and Ty's trail? Does this guy know anything about that?

The two other cops with Sean ask me a few questions, and when I answer with certainty they exchange glances and smile as they file out. Sean and I are left alone.

"What's next?"

"With your ID, we have enough to arrest and hold him. They'll interrogate him tomorrow morning. They've called in a state police specialist to assist."

"This guy's that big a deal?

"He's our best shot at finding the boy's killer. And finding Ramon. And your money."

I glance away. Whatever they get from this guy, I'm almost positive it won't be the money, unless they get to Ty before Ty gets to me. "Why aren't you interrogating him, Sean?"

"We need a native speaker of Spanish and an expert interrogator so we don't blow our chance."

"You're an expert."

A smile twitches his lips. "Yes, but I have a relation– I know the person he threatened. I can't be part of the interrogation team."

"If, if this guy provides information that leads you to the coyotes, will you still look for Ramon?" I'm afraid to look into Sean's eyes. Afraid that he'll see I'm hiding information from him again.

Sean shifts his weight and flexes his fingers. "We still don't know Ramon's role. We don't know if he's a victim or if he's aiding—"

"He's not!" The objection leaps from my mouth unbidden.

"Ah, Audrey—defender of the downtrodden." Sean places his index finger gently against my lips. "You'd better get some rest. I believe you have a party to attend tomorrow."

I'm happy to accept the change of subject before I say something else stupid. "Yeah, I don't want to meet your family with bags under my eyes."

He squeezes my shoulder. "I'll pick you up at five-thirty."

"At my condo, okay? I'm tired of staying at Maura's."

He hesitates, then nods. "Should be fine."

A normal girl with a big date on Saturday night would spend the day primping, but I'm such a nervous wreck about Ty that I can't stand to be alone. I head over to meet Jill at Harold's house for a few hours.

As soon as I walk in, Jill grabs my arm and pushes her phone under my nose. I read a text that came in late last night.

*Everything chill See you soon.*

"See you soon. He must be on his way home." Jill's face is beaming. "He's okay."

The message unwinds one tendril of anxiety, but the knot is still pretty big. Once Ty is back, how will I be able to return the money to Martha without Coughlin knowing how I got it back? If Coughlin even suspects that Ty was in contact with Ramon, he and the other cops will be on him like white on rice. How will I protect him?

Jill is oblivious to my worry. Ty's message has put her in a good mood. She's got her earbuds in and she's hauling boxes of bird paraphernalia at a brisk clip.

I hear the distant clang of a cowbell, followed by shouting.

"What's that noise?" I ask, setting down a box of little fake birds, the kind that florists put in wreathes.

She bobs her head to her music. I might as well be talking to myself.

I stop dragging boxes and strain to hear. Sounds like chanting, or a football cheer.

I tug on Jill's arm, and point to my ears.

"Huh?" she asks as she pulls out her earbuds.

"Listen."

Jill wrinkles her nose. She hears it too, but doesn't understand. Of course, all the windows upstairs are covered—we haven't worked our way to an exterior wall yet, so we head downstairs.

In the dining room, the sound of voices is much clearer. "Hey, ho—he must go. Hey, ho—he must go."

Jill lifts a tattered curtain. "Ohmygawd. There's, like, fifty people marching down the street."

I nudge her aside so I can see. Coming down the cul-de-sac is Bernadette leading a parade of people—gray-haired men, little kids, moms pushing strollers, a man in a track-suit, women in jeans, women in skirts and heels. Some of them are waving signs, but I can't read the writing from here. Then the cowbell rings again, and a little boy blasts one of those annoying horns people blow on New Year's Eve. The chanting begins again. "Two, four, six, eight—rats we don't appreciate."

As they march along, more people come out of their houses, and some join in the protest.

"Bernadette's such a looney-tune," Jill says. "What

does she think she's going to get from this? The Health Department already cleared us."

"Publicity." The *Daily Wretched* news van is following the protesters.

"Big deal," Jill says. "Nobody reads that rag. And it's not like they can embarrass Harold into leaving." She glances into the foyer where Harold is pounding away on his calculator. "He's oblivious."

Jill thinks the whole scene is funny, but I'm not so sure. As the marchers get closer, I can see their faces. Not pretty. Now I can see the messages on their signs: SAVE OUR KIDS. RAZE THE TOXIC HOUSE. PROTECT OUR NEIGHBORHOOD.

They've reached the house and they form a line down the sidewalk.

"I don't like this," I say.

"It's street theater," Jill reassures me. "Like the time we marched on the Admin Building dressed as members of a chain gang to protest low wages for the service workers."

As if to prove her point, Bernadette's minions struggle with a big gray bundle. Then, before our eyes, a giant rat starts inflating.

"I love it!" Jill claps her hands. "Unions always have those things to protest when scabs are crossing their picket lines."

"Hey, ho—he must go!" "Two, four, six, eight—rats we don't appreciate." The crowd keeps shouting as the ten-foot rat sways in the breeze.

Once she's sure she has everyone's attention, Bernadette pulls out a bullhorn and starts making a speech.

"The Palmyrton Board of Health has blatantly disregarded unsafe conditions in this house. Their refusal to condemn the property is creating a dangerous situation that will only get worse when the spring rains arrive. We are prepared to take action to protect our lives and the lives of our children!"

The crowd cheers.

By now, all the noise has finally roused Harold. He comes into the dining room and peers out the small clear space in other window, showing about as much interest in the protesters as a man watching tropical fish circle a tank.

The crowd gathers around waiting expectantly for their leader's next move. "This is an act of civil disobedience," she proclaims. With her down jacket flapping open, Bernadette and another woman unfurl a large green square. Now what?

I hear a sharp intake a breath from Jill. "Oh, no— they wouldn't dare."

"Ummm—yes they would," I say. "They've got themselves a Dumpster in a Bag."

Talk about irony. Usually, Jill, Ty, and I love using these things. Three thousand pounds of crap can be loaded into what amounts to a gargantuan, performance-fiber tote bag. They're portable and much cheaper than a standard metal dumpster.

The protesters break ranks and a free-for-all commences. They grab birdbaths and flower pots and garden tools and pink flamingos. In a mad frenzy of cleaning, everything is pitched into the bag.

A high keening sound fills the dining room.

Before either of us can catch him, Harold runs out the door.

# CHAPTER 28

We watch in horror as Harold disappears into the crowd of protesters. All I can see of him is occasional flashes of his gray pony-tail bobbing among the tossing, heaving arms and legs of the neighbors. Then the crowd shifts and I see Harold latched onto one side of a rusty lawn chair. A young mother determined to toss it is connected to the other side.

"No. That's useful. I need that." Harold tugs so hard, the young woman pitches forward on her knees.

The crowd rushes forward.

"Lisa! Did you see that? He pushed Lisa down."

As a swarm of sympathetic women scoops up their fallen comrade, the burly man in the tracksuit comes after Harold.

"Audrey, do something!" Jill pushes me toward the door. "They're going to kill Harold."

I hesitate on the threshold.

The big guy picks Harold up by the collar. Harold's feet start flying and land a solid kick.

"Call 911, Jill," I take one step onto the front porch.

"There she is!" Bernadette yells and points and every head in the crowd turns toward me. Suddenly I can sympathize with Lindsay Lohan being swarmed by paparazzi. The mob doesn't look like individual human beings, each with two eyes, a nose, and a mouth. It's a seething mass of bristling anger.

"*She's* responsible for keeping this house from being

condemned," Bernadette says through her bullhorn, her index finger thrusting in my direction. "*She* cleared away just enough so that it would pass inspection. As soon as she leaves, Harold will fill it up again." Bernadette turns to the crowd and raises her arms as if to conduct a symphony. "There's only one solution." Her arms drop.

I reach for Jill, my only protection. Does Bernadette's solution involve dragging me off?

"Tear down the house, tear down the house," the crowd chants.

The kids get into it, jumping up and down and screaming at the top of their lungs. "Tear Down the House! Tear Down the House!"

Their parents catch fire. The chant crescendos. "Tear Down the House, Tear Down the House!"

This isn't street theater anymore. This could tip out of control. Kent State. Watts. Ferguson. Ordinary people gone crazy.

Although Harold has stopped struggling, flabby tracksuit-guy still has him collared. Like a child being bullied on the playground, Harold has covered his head with his arms. The shouts rain down on him like shrapnel.

A heavy curtain of rage hangs before us. I set down one uncertain foot, holding my arm out before me. A bratty little kid darts toward me and shakes his sign in my face. "Tear down the *house*."

The taunt galvanizes Jill. Side-stepping the brat, she strides toward Harold, the glower on her face clearing a path. I'm gathering courage to follow when we get some unexpected help. A curly blonde-haired woman streaks across the yard from the right. Phoebe Castleton runs straight up to an unprepared Bernadette, plucks the bullhorn from her hand, and tosses it into the Dumpster in a Bag.

The crowd falls silent.

"What's the matter with you people? You're

terrifying an elderly man in his own front yard. You ought to be ashamed of yourselves." Phoebe's voice has lost its breathless quality. Even without the bullhorn, she projects to the back row, transformed from Mia Farrow to Liza Minelli. "This is Summit Oaks. We look out for one another here. Why are you following Bernadette like a bunch of sheep? Go home!"

In the distance we hear the wail of police sirens. People on the edges of the crowd scuttle away.

Jill glares at tracksuit-guy. "You need to get yourself a life. Come on inside, Harold."

But Bernadette isn't throwing in the towel. If anything, Phoebe's appearance has ignited a fanatic gleam in her eyes. She turns on her neighbor. "You, you... Breastfeeding kids who are old enough to read. Sleeping all in one bed. Eating vegan hot dogs. You think you have friends here? You don't belong. Everyone thinks you and your kids are *freaks*."

Jill jumps back as Phoebe lunges at Bernadette. "Shut up, bitch!" The two women go down in a swirl of thrashing legs and clawing hands.

Jill, Harold, and I make it back inside as two burly cops stride up to the fight. They need all their strength to separate the women. The cop holding Phoebe struggles to drag her slender body away. Scratched and bleeding, with long strands of Bernadette's dark hair streaming from her fingers, she turns to spit out one last threat.

"No one hurts my children, Bernadette. No one."

# CHAPTER 29

There's no working after that.

Jill sits at the kitchen table with a catatonic Harold. His eyes, pupils hugely dilated, stare at nothing. That weird high-pitched hum thrums from his diaphragm. When he's not humming, he's muttering, "Don't wake the babies." Jill tries to coax him to drink a cup of tea.

Jill's anxious face peers at me. "We can't leave him here. It's not safe. What if those rioters break in and hurt him?"

"Well, we can't take him home with us, now can we? His own niece won't have him in her house."

"What're we going to do-o-o?"

As if in answer, my phone rings. Coughlin.

"What the hell's going on over there? I gotta report of a riot."

"Hello to you too."

"Audrey," he warns.

Even though I don't care for his tone, I have to admit I'm glad to hear from him. I tell him about the insanity that just unfolded. "And I want you to know, I did nothing to provoke this. The lady next door is furious that Harold's house escaped being condemned. We want to get out of here, but we're afraid to leave Harold here alone. He's not," I glance at his blank, trembling form, "uhm, feeling well."

"Never mind Harold. Are you all right?"

"Sure, I'm fine." But I'm not. "I'm fine" is the official

Audrey Nealon knee-jerk response. The truth is, I'm scared.

That crowd, that fight—where did all the rage come from? I could dismiss Bernadette when I thought she was simply one of those perpetually disgruntled busybodies who makes a career from complaining. But what I witnessed today goes way beyond an over-zealous Neighborhood Watch captain. I saw true hatred in Bernadette's face. And in Phoebe's, too. The crowd fed on that, turning normal soccer moms and lawn-mowing dads into zealots.

And what's really scary—a lot of that rage was directed at me.

But I don't say any of that to Sean. I don't need him joining my dad and Maura telling me to quit this job.

"We're all fine," I repeat. "We just need some help protecting Harold. And the house. God only knows what these lunatics will do after we go home."

"Are the uniforms still outside?" Sean asks.

"Yes."

"I'll talk to them. Let them in when they come to the door." And the line goes dead.

While we wait, Jill goes back to fixing Harold tea, and I go back to worrying. The level of neighborhood anger seems way out of proportion to news that Another Man's Treasure has rescued Harold's house from condemnation. After all, we *are* cleaning it up. You'd think they could be satisfied with that. Why are they hell-bent on evicting poor Harold?

What's come over me! Did I just refer to Harold as "poor Harold"? I look at his trembling hands sloshing hot tea onto the table. Am I growing more fond of him? No, *fond* certainly overstates the case. But I guess I am getting more sympathetic to his plight. He's sick, and he can't cure himself. The neighbors deserve to have the house cleaned up, but Harold deserves a home. He shouldn't be forced into a life on the streets because of his illness.

My God, I sound just like Jill!

I watch her patting Harold's shoulder and murmuring reassurances. No, I'm nowhere near that nice. But Bernadette's actions have definitely shifted me onto Team Harold. I think Bernadette brings out the fight in me for the same reason that my father and Coughlin do—she's always so damn sure she's right.

Of course, Sean and Dad say that about me.

Well, I think I am right about Bernadette. There's something fishy about her sudden escalation, and I'm going to get to the bottom of it.

I think about a house I pass every day on my way through Summit Oaks, a house being offered for sale by Trent Fine Properties. If anyone has an insight into what's going on in this neighborhood, it's Isabelle Trent.

I take a moment to mentally compose my questions. Isabelle will always take my call, but she never has time for idle chat. I hit her number and prepare to start talking.

"Audrey, darling—how are you?"

I know that question is purely rhetorical so I don't bother to answer. "Hi, Isabelle. I'm calling about Summit Oaks."

"Marvelous neighborhood. Didn't I see your van there recently?"

I give her the Spark Notes version of the Harold Project and the riot. "Do you know anything about this Neighborhood Improvement Committee? It's led by a Bernadette McMartin."

"Ah, Bernadette. She once called me in to give her an appraisal on her house. Wasn't happy with my numbers. She's a little quirky."

"Quirky" is Isabelle-speak for bat-shit crazy. "Yeah, I noticed. She wanted you to list her house? Why is she leading the Improvement Committee if she's planning to move?"

"She's been trying to move for over a year. Her

husband took a job in Silicon Valley. She and the kids can't follow until she sells the house."

This explains some of Bernadette's anger. "But it won't sell because it's next to Harold's?"

"Darling, I've never met a house I couldn't sell. It's all a matter of price. The McMartins have a lovely home: excellent maintenance, recent updates, neutral décor. But they can't fix the view from all their east-facing windows. The other two houses in the neighborhood I've listed at close to seven hundred thousand. If I were to list Bernadette's house, I wouldn't be able to get more than five."

"Ouch. But why is she so mad at me? She should be happy I'm cleaning the place up."

"She'd get even more with a new custom home next door. She needs every penny she can get to be able to afford a comparable home in California. Silicon Valley is pricey."

"But what if the developer built a monstrosity like that pink villa up on Sycamore?'

"Possible. Although someone on the Zoning Board got fired after that creation got approved."

So that explains why Bernadette and Phoebe are enemies. Harold's house is the reason one got into the neighborhood. And the reason the other can't get out.

"Okay, but why is she working so hard to get the rest of the neighbors riled up?"

"Darling, think. A house is the average person's biggest asset. Ever since the real estate bubble burst in '08, people are desperate to protect their investment. It can make them a little..."

"Quirky."

Just as I finish talking to Isabelle, the cops arrive. On the way from the front door to the kitchen, the patrolmen assure me they'll be cruising the neighborhood all night long. But they take one look at Harold, blankly staring and totally unresponsive, and announce they're taking him to the hospital.

"The hospital?" Jill says. "For what?"

"Psych eval," the older cop answers as he calls for an ambulance.

"Really? You can get him psychiatric help?" Jill asks, her eyes brightening. "His niece always says no hospital will take him."

"Lady, he's catatonic. Believe me, they'll take him."

"I'd better call Nora," Jill says, but Nora doesn't answer, and the ambulance arrives quickly. Together the cops and EMTs try to get Harold to lie on the gurney. But Harold's having none of it. He snaps out of his trance, thrashing wildly, biting and kicking, his eyes huge in his pale face.

"Get the restraints," one EMT orders.

Jill gulps when she sees the medic pull out a white cloth thing that looks like a big dress with no sleeves. Another produces thick leather straps with buckles.

"No! What's that?" Jill clutches my arm.

It takes four powerful men to force Harold into the straight jacket and bind him to the gurney. Still he twists and fights.

"Stop! Let him go!" Jill cries. "Audrey, make them stop. They're hurting him! Look how scared he is." She clings to my arm. "Ohmygod, this is awful. I made a terrible mistake."

I pull her into a hug. "He'll be better once he's at the hospital. Those guys know what they're doing."

We stand in the doorway and watch as the flashing ambulance carries Harold away from his home.

We did the right thing.

Didn't we?

# CHAPTER 30

After Harold is hauled off, I barely have time to make it home and shower and dress for the Coughlin family party. Sean's brother and Adrienne, the sister-in-law that Sean claims is so high-maintenance, live in Mendham, a good twenty-minute ride from Palmyrton. Sean is chatty as we start off, talking about the Parks Center kids and the next basketball game in the tournament, but he grows quieter and quieter as we come closer to our destination. I'm nervous too. I don't dare ask him about the interrogation of the busboy. I have to assume that if the busboy revealed something vital about Ramon, Sean wouldn't be here with me. Then I worry that he will find it fishy that I'm *not* asking about it. But silence is safer than talk. One thing is certain—if the topic of the missing money were to come up, I would never be able to successfully lie to Sean.

Rather than force conversation, I content myself with looking out the window. In our snowless January, the countryside is bleak, but I know that April through October this part of New Jersey is glorious: rolling hills, grassy meadows, blooming gardens, brilliant foliage. All along Route 24, charming old stone farmhouses renovated to suit the needs of the 21st century call out to me. We pass through Mendham's quaint little main street and drive even further into the countryside, now passing new developments of center hall colonials on steroids. I expect Brendan to live in one of these, but I'm wrong. His house is at the end of a lane of beautifully constructed custom homes. Sean pulls into a long driveway that ends in front of a rambling fieldstone and cedar shake house with Craftsman influences.

I'm pretty sure I'm not supposed to gush about how nice the house is, but honestly, it is pretty spectacular: big without being ostentatious, luxurious but not flashy. The result of a career in finance, not criminal justice.

Sean parks behind a long line-up of cars in the driveway and we walk up to the walnut front door. When no one answers the doorbell, Sean tries the door and walks in. The foyer is big enough to hold a flock of grazing sheep. To the left is the unoccupied living-room; the right, the unoccupied dining-room. Both look like model rooms in a high-end furniture emporium. But we can hear the sound of laugher and conversation in the back of the house and head in that direction.

The kitchen, family room and breakfast nook (if you can call a 20' x 20' room a nook) are filled with Sean's relatives. Immediately I can pick out his brothers: Brendan is as tall as Sean but leaner. Where Sean's hair is strawberry blond, Brendan's is deep auburn. Across the room is a shorter, paunchy version of Sean. This must be his younger brother, Terry. There are several women, one of them hugely pregnant, and it's not immediately apparent who is a sister and who a sister-in-law. But then I spot a very thin woman. Her jeans are not Levis, her hair is not SuperCuts, her face is not freckled. This has to be Adrienne.

There's a noticeable drop in the buzz as everyone pauses to check me out. Then Brendan steps forward. "Sean! Now the party can really start. And you must be Audrey." He engulfs me in a bear hug. "Welcome to the Coughlin family circus."

Sean takes me around the room, where I'm hugged

by his older sister, his younger sister, his other brother, his sister-in-law, his dad—geez, haven't these people ever heard of handshakes? But by the third hug, I start to enjoy the attention. After all, this is the kind of big, loving family I've always longed for. Finally, I arrive before his mother. A heavy-set woman with gray frizzy hair, she doesn't stand to greet me, just looks me up and down from her easy-chair throne in the family room. Her pale complexion hasn't aged well, or maybe it's the trials of raising five kids that have etched her face with lines. She hasn't bothered with make-up and her clothes are frumpy. But she's got the same clear blue, all-knowing eyes as Sean. I'm under her microscope for what feels like a full ten minutes but probably isn't even three seconds. Then a beaming smile lights her face. "Well, hello there, luv. Sean's told me all about you. I think he's right—you do look like the sensible sort."

I have a hard enough time accepting compliments like, "Your hair looks good." I'm really stumped on how to respond to this.

Sean winces and pivots me around. "Let's get you a drink, Audrey. You're going to need it."

With a beer in my hand, I feel a little braver, but the din of the party scrambles my mind. A wide screen TV in the family room blares a football game where most of the guys are gathered screaming advice to the coaches and refs. Clustered around an iPad, several of the ladies send up squees of approval or dismay over someone's wedding photos. Sean gets pulled into some highly opinionated cop shop talk with his dad and younger brother. The kitchen's various high-end appliances beep and trill, and Adrienne flies around slamming pots and baking sheets on the counters. I consider offering to help her, but I can tell from her look of fierce concentration that I'd only get in her way.

"Kinda crazy, your first time."

I turn to locate the source of the voice. A wiry young man with jet black hair and olive skin has appeared beside me.

"You're obviously an in-law."

"Soon." He extends his hand to shake. "Anthony— I'm engaged to Colleen. I was out in the garage bringing in more beer when you arrived."

"Are the parties always this loud? I'm starting to understand why the Army blasts Aerosmith to disorient terrorist targets."

"This? This isn't loud. Wait'll someone starts crying." He offers me a platter of spinach and cheese puffs. "Eat up. When the party is at anyone else's house, all you get is boiled corned beef and cabbage."

"So, you survived your first Coughlin party and came back for more?"

"Yeah. They were all distracted by someone else's drama at that time, so I flew in under the radar."

"I have the feeling everyone already knew about me when I walked in."

Anthony acknowledges the truth of this with the tilt of his Harp bottle. "It's not that they've been discussing you in particular. There's just a lot of talk about what Sean needs this time around. And the consensus is, he needs a woman who's not high-maintenance but one who can stand up to him." He scans me head to toe. "You look to fill the bill."

This time around? How many women has Sean brought home to be inspected? Anthony registers what must be a look of horror on my face. Sean and I have only been on two dates and his family has us paired off for life. He squeezes my shoulder. "Just messin' with you. But honestly, you do seem pretty calm, and this family could use some non-excitable DNA in the mix."

Sean returns to my side and I observe him for signs that my accompanying him to this party is more than the favor he billed it as. But he is relaxed and casual— no PDA, no pride of possession. Before long I'm having a good time chatting with Anthony and Colleen about the house they're buying and with Mr. Coughlin about his travels in Ireland. I tell Adrienne how good the food is—which is true—and she loosens up a bit. We move on to discuss the value and utility of copper-clad cookware, and I promise to keep an eye peeled for a vintage copper sauté pan. Despite the dull roar of the football game, which interests me not at all, I'm starting to feel like one of the gang.

Then Sean opens a door that leads to the basement. "Hey, your favorite uncle is here!"

A whoop sounds from the depths. In an instant, little children start pouring through the door. One, two, three, four, five....the basement is a circus stunt car disgorging clowns...six, seven, eight. Wow!

The kids clamber on Sean, the littlest ones begging to be picked up, the older ones high-fiving and hugging. One little guy climbs up on a chair, then launches himself onto Sean's shoulders. The noise becomes a whole order of magnitude louder.

Adrienne's lips tighten. "I prefer for the kids to stay in the playroom."

"Hey, Spartacus done freed the galley slaves!" Terry shouts as the kids tumble through the kitchen and into the family room.

One kid stuffs an hors d'oeuvres into his mouth, then chokes and spits a black blob directly into his grandmother's hand. "I thought it was chocolate," he gasps.

"Nah, those're olives, pet. Nasty things."

A little red-haired girl grabs the remote and switches the TV to Cartoon Network just as the Jets receiver is heading for the end zone. The men scream in unison, "Alyssa!"

The terrified culprit springs backward and drops the remote.

It lands with a crash on the coffee table, knocking over a full bottle of Guinness.

A chestnut stream of beer splashes over Adrienne's cream Berber rug.

The explosion of sound makes me feel like I'm in the stadium at the World Cup when Germany defeats Argentina.

"I told you not to let those kids—"

"It was an accident—"

"Aieee!"

"Now, now, darlin', don't cry."

"For Chrissakes, Adrienne, it's just a fuckin' rug."

"Language! Oh, now you've gone and woke the baby!"

An infant's squall joins the cacophony, and I realize I haven't noticed a tiny baby who's been sleeping in an infant seat in a corner of the family room. While the screaming continues, I slip into the kitchen, find a bottle of seltzer in the fridge and some white vinegar in the pantry, and quietly return to the scene of the crime.

While I'm down on my knees with a dish towel and the tools of my trade, the battle rages on above.

"Don't you *ever* talk to my child like that—"

"Why can't we simply have a civilized—"

"Civilized? Is that what you call having a stick up your—"

"Easy for you to get the kids wound up. You get to go home to your bachelor pad."

Working systematically from the center of the stain out to the edges, I blot, rinse, repeat.

Amid the sniper fire, a bomb falls. "No wonder your marriage didn't last, Sean."

My hand hangs suspended over the carpet. Marriage? Sean has never mentioned a wife, ex or otherwise. I lower my unsteady hand and blot one more time. No shadow of brown remains. When I rock back on my heels to study my work, I feel Sean's mother's eyes fixed on me. She gives me a quick nod and hoists herself from her chair. One sharp clap of her hands and the clamor pipes down.

"Looks like Sean's lass has fixed up your rug just fine, Brendan. Come along, Francis. It's time for us to go." And with a tug of her flowered rayon blouse, she marches out.

# CHAPTER 31

The ride home is excruciating.

Sean can't speak. He sits behind the wheel, his hands clenched at ten and two, his profile immobile. He could be the fifth face on Mt. Rushmore.

I know he's mortified and I want to reassure him, but I honestly don't know what to say. "These things happen to my family all the time" clearly won't play. The truth is, I'm appalled. Such noise, such anger, such name-calling—all over a spilled beer! Nealon-style repression looks pretty good to me right now.

And what about the big reveal at the end? Sean was married and he's never seen fit to mention it to me. How can he justify that?

The longer we ride in silence, the more impossible it becomes for either of us to break it.

When he pulls up to the curb in front of my condo, Sean finally turns to face me. "I'm sorry to put you in the middle of that, Audrey. My family, well, they tend to over-react. Your response...." He looks away and even in the dim light I can see the flush that's spread to the roots of his hair. "You did what I should have done. But instead, my siblings always manage to yank my chain."

*And you know how to yank theirs.* Why did Sean urge all the kids up out of the basement when he easily could have gone downstairs to play with them? It seems to me he was intentionally flouting

Adrienne's rule. Control. We always come back to that.

"I don't know anything about brothers and sisters. I do know about stain removal. Doing something useful helps me cope when I'm in over my head." I say this intending to be light-hearted, but it comes off a little prim.

We sit in silence.

He shifts in his seat. "Look, I wasn't trying to conceal the fact that I'm divorced. The break-up of my marriage was very difficult. It's not something I care to revisit often." The muscle in his jaw that twitches when he's upset is going overtime.

"How long ago..."

"Two years. We were only married for four. It was very tumultuous. We started fighting on our wedding night and didn't stop until about a year after the divorce was finalized."

"What did you fight about?" The moment those words are out of my mouth I want to pull them back in. What business is it of mine why they fought? I don't care. I'm not adding a JEALOUSY column to my spreadsheet of emotions.

"How much I worked. How much she partied. How possessive I was. How inconsiderate she was. Our values were different."

"Values?"

"Look, we made a mistake. We were both young. We should've just had fun with each other and moved on. Instead, we got married."

I nod. A youthful mistake—everyone is entitled to one of those. Still, I can't shake the feeling that Sean is leaving something out of the story. I think of the way his mom sized me up. The remark Anthony made about getting calm DNA into the family mix. Most of all, the way all those little nieces and nephews pounced on Sean as if Santa himself had arrived.

"You wanted to have kids and she didn't." I phrase it as a statement, not a question.

His gaze slides away from mine. "I see now that it was best we didn't have kids. We weren't solid as a couple. She understood that better than I did."

"But you're ready now."

The car seems too small to contain two adults and all our combined anxiety. Surely the doors will blow right off.

Sean stares straight ahead. "I won't lie to you—I want to have kids someday. But there's no rush. You and me—we don't need to even be thinking about that."

We certainly don't. I feel overheated and queasy as I reach for the car door latch. "Right. Well, goodnight, Sean."

My body is three-quarters out the door when he grabs my arm. "Audrey, please—let's forgot this day ever happened."

Forget? Does he think I'm a computer who can be unplugged and rebooted? But I won't say that. I won't prolong this episode. I want to be in my house. Alone. Now.

"Sure." I deliver a dry peck on his cheek. "No worries."

# CHAPTER 32

Ethel nearly knocks me down when I open my front door.

"Believe me, baby, I'm glad to see you too." While I was gone, she apparently crashed into the hall table because a week's worth of mail is scattered across the hall floor. I try to make my way into the living room as Ethel runs in circles around me. "Geez, Ethel. I'm not that late. I'll take you out in a minute."

The light on my answering machine is flashing. Could Ty possibly have called while I was gone?

I press play and hear the querulous voice of Mrs. Simchak, my next-door neighbor. "Audrey? Are you all right? I saw you go out earlier, and then about seven I heard the dog barking like crazy and I looked out my window and saw someone on your front porch. And then the person tried to look in your window. So I called the police. I hope you don't think I'm a nosey old woman, but after what happened in the fall..." The machine runs out of space and cuts her off.

I feel the hairs on the back of my neck rise. "Is that why you're so wound up, Ethel? Was someone here?"

She gazes up at me, eyebrows cocked in concern.

I check my watch: 10:00 PM, too late to call Mrs. Simchak for more information.

I'm sure as hell not calling Coughlin.

I take a deep breath. "We'll be all right, Ethel. These are all new locks. We've got the alarm system now." She trots behind me as I double-check each door and window. How I wish Ethel could talk, tell me who was here looking for me.

I settle for pulling her into my bed.

I wake up late on Sunday feeling like I haven't slept at all. I need to talk to someone about what happened at the party. Not Maura. Not Jill. Someone rational. Logical. Impartial.

I pick up my phone and dial.

"Dad. You wanna take a walk?"

Ethel trots ahead of us on her retractable leash as Dad and I walk toward the duck pond at Loantaka Park. I give him a blow-by-blow description of the party culminating in the Ghastly Guinness Gaffe.

"And while I was cleaning up the beer and all of them were arguing, Adrienne said, 'No wonder your marriage didn't last.' To Sean."

"That's rather harsh. Sean's quite sensitive about his divorce."

I stop walking. "Wait. You knew he was divorced? Why didn't you tell me?"

"I assumed you knew."

"When did he tell you?"

"I don't remember. It just came up in passing, maybe when we were talking after basketball practice."

"You see—he doesn't hide it from other people, only from me."

Dad makes the batting away gnats gesture that he uses to dismiss any sort of nonsense unworthy of his consideration. "I'm sure he wasn't intentionally hiding information."

"Tell me exactly what he said when he told you."

Dad gazes into the woods where a doe stands immobile, waiting for us to pass. Finally, he sighs and speaks. "Actually, I don't think Sean himself told me. I think I must've heard it from Natalie. She teaches

Lamaze at Overlook Hospital. She mentioned that Sean's sister-in-law and his ex-wife ended up in the same class together. It was awkward."

"Whoa, whoa—back up. Lamaze...as in natural childbirth? You're saying Sean's ex is pregnant?"

"Apparently she just gave birth to twins."

"Oh my God! Don't you see? That's why he feels under pressure. He wants to one-up her. Get married quickly and start producing offspring. He's falling behind—all his siblings have kids and his baby sister is getting married in a few weeks. Sean's very competitive."

I know if I said this to Maura she'd tell me I'm being ridiculous. But my father gives patient consideration to my words before speaking. "Sean genuinely likes children, Audrey. However, he is certainly competitive. But then, so are you."

"Not about having babies."

"What's really at issue here, Audrey? You and Sean have only had a few dates. It's far too soon to be thinking about having babies together."

I mull his words. Silently, we cross a footbridge, pass a park bench. Then I speak. "Do you know what my favorite TV show was when I was a kid?"

"I would hope it was *Nova*, but I suspect I'm about to be disillusioned."

"*Full House*. Grandma and Grandpa let me watch every single episode. It was about a man who was a widower, and he had three daughters who got along great and never seemed to be bothered by the fact that they had no mom. And his best friend and his brother-in-law lived with them, and then the brother-in-law got married and had twins and they all still lived together as one big, happy family."

Dad grimaces. "Sounds preposterous."

"It was. But it was my fantasy to have a family like that. To live in a big house where there was always someone home. To have sisters who watched out for one another. To have funny misunderstandings that always got patched up."

"A total fairy tale."

"I know, Dad. But I've never been able to let it go. I've always envied people with big extended families, people who have to haul out mismatched folding chairs for every holiday dinner. Spencer and Anne Finneran had that kind of family. That's why I was attracted to them."

"Huh! You saw the rot that lay beneath the surface there."

"I did. I think that's what's scaring me about Sean's family."

"The Coughlins are certainly not murderous, Audrey."

"I didn't mean to imply that." I turn my head, focus on the papery leaves clinging stubbornly to the beech trees. "The Coughlins terrify me. I thought I wanted what they have, but now I see I could never endure their never-ending storm of emotions."

"Don't be hasty, Audrey. If you allow yourself to love Sean, you'll learn to accept his family."

I swing around to face my father. "Don't tell me what to do! Not when I know I could never survive as part of that family."

Dad shakes his head. "Ah, my dear—there's no way of knowing what your heart can endure until you're faced with the unendurable and find yourself surviving."

As darkness settles over my condo complex, I hear a sharp rap on my front door. Ethel's ears perk up. My heart goes into overdrive.

Ethel runs to the front door, but she doesn't bark. Instead, she jumps up and starts scratching, her tail wagging furiously.

I peer through the cloudy peep-hole. A tall man dressed in black, looking away from me over his shoulder at a car parked at the curb.

Could it be? I flick on the porch light.

"Ty!" I scream as I open the door.

He steps in. The grin on his face is so wide it must hurt. He drops a small duffel bag at my feet. "$98,372. You can take the rest outta my paycheck, twenty bucks a week. Car's out front."

"Shut up!" I throw my arms around him, then step back and punch his arm"

"Ow! What's that for?"

"You had me worried sick. I'm still worried sick." I drag him into the living room and point him to the sofa. "Sit. Talk."

So Ty begins, right from the moment when Ramon received the soup. As we suspected, Ramon honestly thought Ty was giving him the box of cans to keep. So he took it home, and popped some open for his dinner. Then he popped another can for the kid staying with him, Horacio, from his home village. That's when they discovered the cash. They opened all the cans, and it truly seemed like a miracle because Horacio was in big trouble with the coyotes who brought him to the U.S. His parents had paid them a down payment back in Honduras. Now the final payment was due, and they didn't have the money. So Ramon thought he'd use some of this windfall to help Horacio, and send the rest to his own family. He took the cash to a wire transfer place, but they started asking a lot of questions about why he had so much to send. Ramon got nervous and left. Thought he would ask some friends the best way to send it. And on his way back to the house, he heard what happened to Horacio. He panicked and ran. Some friends drove him to Dover, and he'd been hiding there ever since. But he couldn't work, and the friends weren't going to keep him forever.

Ty leans forward on the sofa. "Ramon called me because he heard you came lookin' for him at the church. He told me nothing but bad has been happening to him since he found the money. He thinks there's a curse on it. So he wants to give it back. In exchange, he wants me to tell the cops about the coyotes who killed Horacio. He's afraid to get mixed up in it, afraid he'll get deported. All he wants is to start over in a new town where no one knows him. So we made a deal."

"He gave you the money. And where did you drive him to?"

Ty shakes his head. "I gotta keep that on the down-low, Audge. Let's just say, I seen some states I never been to before. I needed to use some of the money for gas and stuff. And I gave Ramon some cash to get him started in the new town. But like I said, I'll pay you back."

"Ty, stop! Of course I don't want money back from you." Tears slip from my eyes. "I'm so glad you're all right. I never blamed you for the money getting lost. I never would have wanted you to take this risk to get it back."

Ty straightens up. "I lost it. I'ma get it back. That's the way I roll."

I run my fingers through my hair. "But, Ty—you're going to be in trouble with the police now. I'm not sure if I can get you out of this."

He leans back with his hands locked behind his head. "Don't sweat it, Audge. I'm a man with a plan."

"Oh yeah? What's that?"

"Ramon gave me the 411 on the coyote who killed Horacio. I know where the cops can find him. Nobody else gonna tell them that. I give them the info and agree to testify that I saw the guy stab Horacio. Deal and done."

"I got news for you. They arrested the guy who threatened me at Play-O-Rama. They've been questioning him for two days. For all I know, they already have all this information. Now how will you deal?"

For the first time tonight, Ty's cocky smile fades a bit. "They still got nothing on me. I didn't steal your car, right? I didn't steal the money."

"You transported across state lines an undocumented alien who's wanted for questioning. I'm pretty sure that's a crime."

"They can't prove that. No one saw us together. I was real careful. They'll never find Ramon." Ty stands up and pulls on his jacket. "Prison fulla talkers. Street's fulla guys who keep their mouths shut."

I wrap my arms around him and we stand swaying in front of the door for a long minute. When he lets me go, he nudges the bag of money with his foot. "Let's go find Martha and give it back right now."

I shake my head. "We have to wait until we see what's happening with the murder investigation. If I give this money back right now, Martha will start talking and Coughlin will find out. I need to think of some explanation for how I got the money back that doesn't get you in trouble."

"You gonna leave the money here?"

I think of the man creeping around my condo last night. Has he already seen Ty arrive here with the bag? "Let's take it over to the office and lock it in the safe."

Ty picks up the bag and reaches for the front door knob.

"No." I call a taxi and tell him to wait at the entrance to my development. Then Ty and I put Ethel on her leash and slip out the garage door, walk through the cul de sac, and meet the taxi. We don't see a soul.

Rarely have I been so happy to see Monday morning arrive. I need the distraction of work, and with Harold in the hospital, we ought to be able to pitch a lot of junk and really make some progress.

I open the front door and bump directly into a man.

Harold.

Cleaner. More alert. But definitely Harold.

"Good morning," he says pleasantly. "I believe Jill is waiting for you in the kitchen. I have some work to catch up on." He sits down at his card table and pulls out his calculator.

I dash into the kitchen where Jill is nursing a cup of coffee. "Where did he come from?"

She shrugs. "He was here when I arrived. I finally got through to Nora last night. She said the hospital never called her. They must have just held Harold overnight for observation. When I told Nora how good he looked, she said they must've done what they've done in the past when he freaks out: clean him up, gave him some meds, and release him."

I'm stunned. "The doctors didn't notice he needs more than a bath and a few pills?"

Jill shakes her head. "Nora says this is what always happens. They won't hold him. They say they can't because he's not a danger—"

"—to himself or others. Right."

Ty pops into the kitchen. "Hey, Audge. Yo, Jill—I don't see that box you want me to take to recycling."

Jill rolls her eyes. After squealing for ten minutes straight last night upon hearing the news of Ty's safe return, I see that this morning she has fallen right back into her usual bossy attitude. "It's right at the top of the stairs. The big box with red lettering. It's full of *American Birding* magazines."

Ty plants his hands on his hips. "And I'm tellin' you, there is no box full of magazines at the top of the stairs. Look for yourself."

Jill gets up and flounces off to prove Ty wrong. A minute later I hear her plaintive call, "Audrey...Audrey come here, quick."

How can a box of ancient magazines be a problem? But I'm so grateful for the return of Ty and the cash, I go upstairs cheerfully.

Jill stands in the middle of the hall looking perplexed. There is, indeed, no box of magazines at the top of the stairs. "Things have been moved," she says.

The hall looks as topsy-turvy as ever. Toys are still spilling out of Nora's old bedroom. The master bedroom still has a wide tunnel lined with boxes. "How can you tell?"

"The box of magazines is all the way at the back of the tunnel. These decorated Russian eggs were off to the side because I was going to sell them on eBay, and now they're right in front. And these puzzles that were from Nora's room were put back in the master bedroom."

"Toys in the bird room. You know Harold didn't do that," Ty says.

"Someone was in here last night." Jill says. "Snooping."

I roll my shoulders as if someone is literally breathing down my neck. First a person creeping around my condo. Now this. "Is anything missing?" I ask.

Ty leans against the wall. "Huh. We should be so lucky."

"Did they make it any closer to the master bath?" I follow our tunnel to its furthest reach. There are still massive barriers between us and our goal.

"I think Bernadette and her crew were in here looking for evidence she could use to get us condemned," Jill says.

"That's whack," Ty says. "You're getting as crazy as Harold."

"It's not! You weren't here for the riot." Jill relates the story in breathless detail. I fill him in on what Isabelle said about Bernadette's need to sell.

"Call the police, Audrey. Tell them we've had a break-in," Jill pleads.

I shake my head. "The police aren't going to care that a few boxes of junk were moved around in here.

They've got bigger problems."

"Well, I'm going to let Bernadette know that we're on to her." Jill stomps downstairs. Before long she's made two signs that she posts on the doors, front and back:

PRIVATE PROPERTY

VIOLATORS WILL BE PROSECUTED

THIS MEANS YOU, BERNADETTE

While Jill bustles around with the signs, Ty gazes out the window. Bernadette's house is in his line of sight, but he seems to be seeing something much further away.

"What are you thinking? I ask.

Ty shoves his hands in his pockets and keeps his face turned away from me. "When I was in prison I met a guy my same age. Worked at Burger King, saved up to buy a North Face. Nice blue color. Size large. One night he went to a house party. Got hot and took the coat off and somebody stole it. On the way home, he sees a dude walkin' down the street in his blue coat. He goes to get it back and the dude won't give it up. So he pulls out a knife and stabs him." Ty kicks at a pile of mildewed atlases beneath the window. "Dude's coat was a size medium. Murder two, twenty-five to life."

"For a coat."

Ty turns toward me. "People work hard to get something nice, they gonna fight to keep it. Someone try to take it away, they gonna get nasty."

He swings his foot harder. *Travelers Guide to South America* sails across the kitchen.

"Real nasty."

# CHAPTER 33

As we work, several texts from Sean have arrived, but I haven't answered. Finally he texts:

*You can't keep avoiding me. Pick up.*

Then my phone rings. I take a deep breath and answer. As usual, no preamble.

"You've been on my mind. We need to talk."

On his mind because of the party? Or on his mind because somehow he knows about Ty and Ramon and the money? I dread a conversation about the first. I'm terrified by a conversation about the second. All I can manage in response is a weak "Oh?"

"We can't talk about this in a restaurant. Come to my place tonight. I'll make you dinner."

I'm reluctant to go to his apartment, especially after what happened when he came to mine. But he's right—we need a resolution and we can't have this conversation in a restaurant. And the advantage of being on his turf is that I can leave at any time. It will be harder to boot him out of my place.

"Let's just say drinks. I'll meet you there at six."

When I step off the elevator in Coughlin's building, I smell food cooking. Maybe it's a neighbor. No, as I get closer to his door, the smell gets stronger. Typical cocky Coughlin. So sure he'll win me over. There's still time to turn around and leave. I hesitate with my hand raised to knock.

The door opens.

"Hey, c'mon in. I heard the elevator." He takes my coat and looks me up and down. Why did I wear this blouse? The top button always pops open. I chose my leggings because they're comfortable. I forgot they're clingy.

I back away and look around.

Apart from the fact that it's very neat, the apartment is nowhere close to what I imagined. No recliner. No wide-screen TV. No sports paraphernalia. Instead there's a Mission-style sofa and easy chair with William Morris-inspired upholstery, a nice bookcase with leaded glass doors, and an oriental rug. There are potted herbs—herbs!—on the windowsill. A sad-sounding woman singer—Nina Simone? Billie Holiday?—croons in the background.

Sean watches me, pathetically eager for my approval. I can't be so cruel as to withhold it. Besides, the apartment really is nice.

"This is great place, Sean. Very distinctive. I love that bookcase."

We make awkward chit-chat about furniture as he pours me a glass of wine. Then we fall silent and stare at each other.

Sean takes a deep breath. "I feel like I've been stumbling around in the dark these past few days, Audrey. And that's not an experience I enjoy."

That doesn't seem to require a response, so I sit waiting with an expanding lump in my stomach.

His blue eyes search my face and I force myself not to look away. "They're keeping me out of the loop on the interrogation of the busboy for now. They're going to want to talk to you. Expect a call tomorrow."

I take a slug of my wine. "All right."

Sean takes my hand. "It's very important that you tell them the complete truth, Audrey."

I clench my fingers. "You think I would lie?"

"I think you might omit some details to protect Ty

and Ramon. It's been days since you asked me about the search for Ramon or the deal you want us to offer him. I find your lack of urgency a little—"

I shake off his hand and stand up. "Suspicious? I'm a suspect now?"

"Uncharacteristic."

The truth gnaws inside me like a tapeworm. I have a strong urge to blurt out everything to Sean. But fear holds me back. I'll have to admit how much information I've already withheld. And no matter how much I beg him to protect Ty, Sean's first obligation is to his job. As it should be.

But my first obligation is to Ty.

"I didn't want to pressure you," I say. "But since you brought it up, has the deal moved forward?"

Sean shakes his head. "I think they're waiting to see what information the busboy, Ramirez, can offer."

"Well then, I guess we'll know something tomorrow." I keep my tone light as I study the books on his shelves, but Sean is not convinced.

He speaks to my back. "I'm not going to ask you a direct question about whether Ty has been in touch with Ramon. Because I don't want you to tell me a lie. But don't mess with these guys tomorrow. It won't end well."

A buzzer sounds from the kitchen. I jump as if I've been shot.

Sean rises and goes to check on his meal. As he fiddles with something on the stove, he speaks to me over the counter separating us.

"So. Let's do what we said we'd do, huh? Tell me why the party at Brendan's upset you so much."

I take a deep breath and another gulp of wine. "You're the one who talked about values. I don't think we have the same values, Sean. You're so committed to your family. You're all so involved in one another's lives...making decisions...making judgments."

Sean adjusts the heat on the stove. Covers the pot.

Wipes a splash off the counter. Then he walks back into the living room and sits down beside me.

"I guess we are. But they mean well, Audrey. I know the argument sounded loud and angry, but it was like a summer thunderstorm. A big blowup, and the next thing you know, the sun is shining. No hard feelings."

I look away. There's a pretty little carving of a porcupine on his end table. I stroke its quizzical face. "I wouldn't be able to live like that Sean. If anyone spoke to me the way you and Adrienne spoke to each other, I wouldn't be able to come back with no hard feelings."

Sean looks baffled. "That's just the way families are."

My hands grip the carving. "I wouldn't know."

He leans forward with his hands on his knees. "Is that what's bothering you? That you don't have an equally noisy family to back you up?"

I don't meet his eyes. "Maybe. I have no experience with extended family dynamics. I can't embrace what I don't know."

"Audrey, Audrey—you think everyone's childhood was perfect except yours. Yeah, my family is close, but it's not like we didn't have our struggles. We were always short on cash. My dad moonlighted so much he never had time for our games or concerts or class plays. My mom could barely control the chaos at home. My childhood wasn't all bedtime stories and home-baked cookies. Neither was yours."

*Get over it.*

He doesn't have to speak the words for me to hear them. I set the little porcupine down carefully. "I can't erase my past to turn into the woman you want me to be."

His voice takes on a slight edge. "I'm not asking you to erase anything. To be anyone but yourself."

I meet him and raise him. "When I'm myself, we fight. And your family doesn't need any more of that."

"You're using this whole family thing as an excuse, Audrey." Sean jumps up and towers over me. "You lead me on, then push me away. You use me when you need help, then turn your back when things are going your way. I think you enjoy toying with me. Catch the mouse. Let it go. Catch it again."

Toying? Me! I don't even know how to flirt, let alone toy. "If that's what you think, why do you even want me?"

We glare at each other. Sean drops his gaze first. The muscle in his clenched jaw jumps. "Who can explain attraction, Audrey?" he whispers. "I know what I want."

"You need to find another woman, Sean. A woman who can give you the life you have planned. A woman who can follow orders."

I stride to the door. Step out, then turn.

"It's not me."

# CHAPTER 34

Tuesday morning after the world's worst Monday and I'm staring into the coal-dark eyes of the state police interrogator. He's introduced himself, but I'm too wound up to retain his name. Although he leans back in his chair with his legs crossed, he radiates intensity. Sean is a ginger tabby compared to this panther. I'm certain he must've turned that busboy inside out and scraped every morsel of truth right out of him.

What will he do to me?

Ty and I have agreed that he will wait to talk to the police until I find out how much they know. I've told him to make himself scarce today. If no one knows where he is, including me, the cops can't come for him until we're prepared. But on one point Ty is adamant: he will talk. Part of his deal with Ramon is to provide the information the cops need to bring Horacio's killer to justice.

The interrogator taps the eraser end of a pencil on the arm of his chair. "Tell me exactly what the man said to you when you were in the play structure together."

I repeat the busboy's words: Stop looking around. Stop talking to the big cop.

"Did he ever mention Ramon?"

"Not by name, no." The interrogator speaks flawless English, but when he says Ramon he trills the R.

"Did he mention the money specifically?"

"No, but he said to stop looking. What else could he mean?"

One dark eyebrow ascends toward his close-cropped hair. He glances at the other cop in the room, a guy standing silently with his arms crossed. "The man we arrested has no knowledge of Ramon or the murder on Filmore Street. As we questioned him, it became apparent we were barking up the wrong tree. This guy is Salvadoran, not Honduran. He lives in Dover. He's not one of the regulars in front of the hardware store looking for work—he has a full-time job working for a landscaping contractor, and moonlights occasionally at Fiorello's. He's a naturalized citizen."

Dover is the town where Ramon had been hiding out, but of course I'm not going to mention that. "What difference does that make? He could still know Ramon if they go to the same church. Remember, I saw him first outside the Church of Living Praise."

"Did you? He worships at a Catholic church in Dover. The priest there knows him."

I'm struck with a queasy uncertainty. I know the man they arrested is the man who threatened me—we were nose-to-nose in Play-O-Rama. But is he the same man I thought was watching me outside the church? I only saw that man in my rearview mirror. Did Sean put that idea in my head?

"I, I'm not sure. He, they...."

"All those Spanish dudes look alike, huh?"

I feel myself flush hot red. "No, that's a terrible thing to say."

"Relax, Ms. Nealon. Cross-racial identification is notoriously difficult. If it's any consolation, all you gringos look the same to us, too." He begins to gather his papers.

"Wait. Where are you going? You don't believe me?" My voice shrills in indignation. "You think I'm lying that this guy threatened me?"

He stands and looks down at me. "No one saw him with you at Play-O-Rama."

"Of course not! I told you, we were inside the play structure and the lights were flashing."

"You never mentioned you had been threatened when you got out of the structure. Never even told your own father."

I don't like him towering over me, so I jump up to level the field. "My dad sensed something was wrong, but I didn't want to upset him. All I wanted was to get out of there."

"And let the culprit get away."

"He said he'd hurt me if I talked! Why would I make something like that up?"

He perches on the edge of the desk, one long leg swinging. "How long have you been having a relationship with Sean Coughlin?"

What kind of non sequitur is that? "I'm not having a relationship with him. I've known him for a couple of months."

"How did you meet him?"

"You must know how we met. He investigated the attack on me last October."

"You were quite a celebrity in New Jersey, Ms. Nealon. Must be hard to go back to being just a regular old working woman."

I look in confusion from one cop to the other.

"You think I made this up to get attention? From a guy?" Have I been transported back to middle-school? This is so ludicrous that I have to laugh. Taking a deep breath, I speak slowly to the interrogator. "Does this man deny being in Play-O-Rama that evening?"

"No, he admits he took his kids there. But he denies attacking a grown woman in the ball pit."

The state police interrogator has a look of studied indifference on his face. I know he's playing me like a fish on a line, but like that fish, I feel powerless to let go of the bait.

"Does he admit he recognizes me from Fiorello's restaurant, when he was eavesdropping on my conversation?"

"He tells the story a little differently. Says you were watching him as he did his job. He thinks when you spotted him again at Play-O-Rama, you got this idea to accuse him of threatening you."

"And you believe that?"

"Frankly, Ms. Nealon, it's no more improbable than your version of events."

I'm so thunderstruck I can barely find the words I need to object. "You think I would pick out a random Hispanic man to accuse of a crime for no reason?"

"Oh, no, Ms. Nealon. Everyone has reasons for what they do. Sometimes a little twisted, but always there. Maybe you thought inventing this threat would keep the police on the job looking for your missing money."

"I did not invent this attack to get my money back!"

He shrugs. "Maybe now you have your money back. Has Ramon contacted you again?"

"No." I can say that without lying. Ramon never contacted me.

"Do you have the money back?" His voice is level, calm.

There it is—the question Sean wouldn't ask me. I can answer it today even though I don't want to. The busboy has given the cops nothing. They're no further along in solving Horacio's murder. They need the information that Ty can provide. Maybe we really can strike a deal.

I speak slowly. "Yes, I have the money back. My assistant, Ty Griggs, got it back from Ramon. He went without my knowledge. All I know is that Ramon thought the money brought him bad luck, and he has some information about the boy's killer that he wants to pass along to you."

This bombshell produces quite a reaction. The cops pound me with questions, but I stick to the party line.

I don't know where Ty picked up the money: true. I don't know what Ramon told Ty about the killer: true. I don't know where Ramon is now: true.

I don't know if Ty and Ramon were together: *not true.*

I have done it. I have lied to the police. As the words leave my mouth, I think of all the famous liars of the past who have ended up in a deeper hole than they started in. Nixon and Watergate. Clinton and Monica Lewinsky. Mark Sanford and the Appalachian Trail.

But I lie not to protect myself, but to protect Ty. He took a terrible risk for me. Now I must take this risk for him.

And it seems to work. After two hours of endless repetition, the cops finally give up on me.

"You can go, Ms. Nealon. We're bringing your assistant in right away to talk to us."

"He's not talking to you without a lawyer. He'll be here tomorrow morning."

"You talked to us without a lawyer."

"I'm not a twenty-two-year-old black man with an arrest record." I switch direction. "What about Juan Ramirez?" I look from the interrogator to the other cops in the room. Every face is wooden.

The interrogator raises one eyebrow. "You have your money back, Ms. Nealon. Time to end the charade."

"You're letting my attacker go?" My voice cracks with outrage.

"We have no reason to hold him. It's your word against his." He leans across the table until his face is inches from mine. "We have a murder to investigate. Mr. Ramirez had nothing to do with it."

"But wait—there was someone else. While I was out on Saturday night, my neighbor saw someone prowling around my condo, looking in my windows. She called the police. Check your records."

"Yes, we know all about your neighbor." He checks his notes. "Mrs. Simchak, is it? She doesn't seem to recall exactly what she saw—a medium sized person in a hat and ski jacket. Maybe black, maybe white, maybe Hispanic. Not even sure if it was a man or a woman." He smirks. "You didn't coach her very well."

When Sean was trying to date me, my word was as good as gold. Now, a day after our break-up, it's worthless. I think of all the women who have ever accused men of assault and haven't been believed—the battered wives, the date-raped co-eds. Suddenly, I'm one of them.

I jump up. "So now I have to look out for this man and his friends around every corner?"

He gathers his notes and slides them in a folder. "You'll be just fine. We'll see Mr. Griggs tomorrow at nine."

Now I'm scared.

For me. And for Ty.

# CHAPTER 35

I spend the next hour on the phone with Emil
Swenson trying to find a lawyer who will go with Ty
when he talks with the police.

"I need a crackerjack criminal defense lawyer, Mr.
Swenson. Someone who knows how to cut a deal with
the police."

"Hmmm. Martin Levine is the best criminal
attorney in Palmer County."

"The name sounds familiar. Is he the one who got
that woman who poisoned her husband off by
convincing the jury the weed killer blew into the
potato salad at a windy picnic?"

"That is he."

He sounds like an awful person, but just who I need
to protect Ty. "Great. How do I reach him?"

"Ms. Nealon, you should know that Mr. Levine
charges upwards of $600 per hour. And I rather doubt
he can be procured on such short notice."

Six hundred dollars times an all-day interrogation—
I don't need my math skills to know my empty
checking account can't support this. "Well, who can I
get on short notice who's reasonable?"

Mr. Swenson clears his throat. "There are some
criminal attorneys who hang around the bail-
bondsmen looking for work."

"Not an ambulance-chaser! Someone good."

After a long pause, Mr. Swenson speaks. "There is a

young attorney who used to be a prosecutor. He knows the police. He's just started his own criminal practice."

Perfect. Surely someone like that can work the deal Ty needs. Mr. Swenson promises to have the guy contact me. While I'm waiting, I call Ty. All I know is he's not in Palmyrton. I don't want to know more.

"The police want to talk to you tomorrow at nine. I'm getting you a good lawyer."

"I don't need no lawyer."

"My God, Ty—have you never seen an episode of *Law and Order*? That's what the suspects always say, and in ten minutes, Lenny and the other guy have a confession."

"I'm not confessing nothin'. My mistake when I was arrested before was trying to make the cops understand how it went down. Now I know better. I got three facts I'm going to tell them: Ramon called me to give back the money 'cause it was *mal suerte*; I picked up the money at the closed rest stop on Route 287; I don't know where Ramon is now. I say those three things over and over and nothing else. If they want to know what he told me about the coyote who killed Horacio, they're gonna have to let me walk."

"Ty, half of that isn't true. You can't lie to them. They'll keep picking at you until they trip you up. I won't let you take the chance of being arrested. You're not going in there alone."

"A lawyer is expensive. We don't have the money."

It's not Ty's job to worry about money. He's in the jam because I let him know too much about my finances. "We will when we sell the lamp. And find the Civil War papers."

"But we need that money for—"

"Shut up, Ty. We're hiring a lawyer."

After an hour, Mr. Swenson still hasn't called me back, so I decide to seek comfort at Maura's.

"What you need is some retail therapy."

Shopping is Maura's answer to all of life's problems. And all of life's joys, for that matter.

"You seem to forget that I hate shopping. It doesn't cheer me up," I protest from my fetal curl on her sofa. "Plus, I'm broke."

"Nonsense. You look good, you feel good. All your pants are too baggy. If I was walking around looking like I had a load in my diaper, I'd feel depressed too."

"Maura, I have a legit reason to be depressed—the police think I'm a hysterical liar and they released the guy who wants to hurt me and now they're after Ty and I just broke up with the man who might know how to help me."

"So call him."

"I will not! Don't you understand? I broke up with him. I told him we couldn't see each other anymore. I can't turn around a day later and beg him to come to my rescue. For all I know, he's the one who put this crazy idea in their heads."

"What do you mean by that?"

"His feelings are hurt. He seems to think I've been stringing him along—pulling him closer, then pushing him away. Maybe he told the other cops to let the busboy go to get back at me."

"Oh, Audrey—surely you don't believe that of Sean?"

"I don't know what I believe." I pause to blow my nose. "I know that Sean is a good cop, an ethical man. But he's wounded. And wounded people don't always act rationally. My father is living proof of that."

Before Maura can respond, my phone rings. Mr. Swenson at last. I sit up eagerly to hear what he has to say. But as he talks, I sink back into the sofa. By the time he's done, I've curled up with Maura's arty shawl pulled over my head.

She lifts up the corner and peers in. "What did he say?"

"The lawyer he had in mind isn't free to represent

Ty. But Mr. Swenson has called the police and arranged for one more day before Ty has to go in. Mr. Swenson is going to represent him. He says he'll use the extra time to do a little research on the crimes Ty may have committed."

"So, that's a plan. Why do you look green?"

"Maura, everything about Emil Swenson is sort of grayish-beige. His office. His hair. His suits. Even his voice. He's not a criminal defense lawyer. He's not a wheeler-dealer. He has to do research because he doesn't know how to handle this. Ty needs Alan Dershowitz and I'm giving him Mr. Rogers."

Maura ponders this for a moment. Then she springs to her feet. "C'mon. We won't go to the mall. Just stop in a few little shops here in town. The fresh air will help us think of something."

I can see it's pointless to protest. Maura hauls me out of her apartment building and heads to Palmyrton Square, chatting away about some store that sells miracle pants that make every woman look ten pounds thinner. I let my problems drift into my subconscious for a while, hoping that if I give them a rest, some solution will reveal itself.

After fighting a brisk breeze for three blocks, we stop in front of a big window filled with headless mannequins wearing very short, wildly printed dresses. The sign over the door reads "Chloe, Chloe" as if the customers are shaking their heads over what the owner has to offer.

"I hope we're stopping here for you," I say, "because this doesn't look like my kinda place."

"Just you wait," Maura answers as she shoves me through the door.

Inside, she immediately strikes up a conversation with the salesgirl instead of shooing her away with a muttered "just looking" the way I always do. Before long, Maura has an armful of outfits in the fitting room and she begins dressing and undressing me like

I'm a giant Barbie doll. She's right about the miracle pants—they do make me look good, but I put my foot down at an orange and green geometric print blouse.

"No way—it looks like something road workers wear to be visible to drivers."

The mini-skirted salesgirl, who looks all of nineteen, teeters over in her six inch platforms holding a drape-y taupe thing. "It doesn't look like much on the hanger, but it's fabulous on. People have been snapping it up."

Although the girl's own wardrobe choices don't inspire confidence, I try the top on and sure enough, she's right. I look at myself in the mirror and see a confident, classy woman looking back. Score one for retail therapy.

"I'll take it," I say. "I can wear this to my perjury trial. Now, can we stop shopping?"

"A neutral outfit like that cries out for accessories," Maura says. "You need a scarf." She unwinds a brightly colored silk oblong from a display, but I check the price before I let her wrap it around my neck. "Seventy-five dollars! No way."

"Never mind. I know a better place for scarves."

So the shopping expedition continues. I trudge along in Maura's wake, holding piles of items she wants to try on while my mind is a million miles away, replaying the interview with the state cop.

Maura holds up two necklaces. "Which do you like better?"

I squint. "Aren't they exactly the same?"

She shakes her head and goes back to picking through the racks of the funky Indian imports shop we've landed in.

"What if the cops and I are both right?" I ask.

Maura stops admiring herself in a strand of spangly beads and frowns at her reflection. "You're not sure if the guy really did threaten you?"

"Oh, he threatened me all right. But what if he wasn't threatening me about Ramon? The cop kept asking me exactly what the busboy said. I realize now he never mentioned Ramon by name, but I leaped to the conclusion that a Hispanic man's threats had to concern the other Hispanic man who's causing me grief. Subliminal racism."

Maura offers a big smile to the woman in the sari behind the counter, and nudges me deeper into the store. "So you think he didn't mean stop looking for Ramon?"

"Yeah, and when he said stop talking to the big cop, maybe he didn't mean stop talking to him about Ramon."

Maura holds a fuchsia and black scarf next to my face. "Then what *did* he mean?"

"It has to be Harold's house. What else am I involved in? Stop looking around Harold's house. Stop telling the cop what you're doing there. Most of the neighbors don't want the house to be cleaned up; they want it torn down. And I was telling Sean about that when the busboy was hovering around at Fiorello's."

"But why would this busboy threaten you about Harold's place? He couldn't possibly have an interest in that house."

"He works full-time as a landscaper and picks up extra money working at Fiorello's. Maybe there are other odd jobs he's willing to do for pay."

Maura tilts her head. "Like, he's a hired enforcer? For whom?"

"Bernadette and her Neighborhood Improvement Group. Maybe they hired him."

"This is a little far-fetched, girl."

"You didn't see the riot outside Harold's house. Those people are ruthless."

"But how would the Summit Oaks nosey neighbor brigade know this busboy dude?"

"Are you kidding? No one in Summit Oaks does their own yard work or their own housecleaning." I pick up a pair of paisley harem pants with an elastic waist. They look comfy. "Every time I'm at Harold's place, I see work crews trolling through the neighborhood—cleaners, landscapers, snowplowers. They're all Hispanic."

Maura removes the pants from my hand and replaces them with a fringy shawl. "Accessories only here. So what's your next move? Bang on Bernadette's door and demand that she call off her hit man?"

"Perhaps a more indirect approach. I need to infiltrate the neighborhood inner circle somehow."

Maura moves toward the cash register laden with beads and scarves. "You've got the perfect undercover agent at home."

"What do you mean?"

"Ethel. I took her for a walk one day when you were staying with me and I met two cute guys, a young mother, and a bag lady in one trip around the block. Start walking her in Summit Oaks."

# CHAPTER 36

Overnight, five inches of snow has fallen, wrapping the houses, trees and streets in a cleansing blanket of white. Even Harold's house looks clean. Despite the fact that all the main roads have been cleared since dawn, we arrive to find the neighbors in Summit Oaks behaving like the Donner Party. Everyone is outside digging and shaking their heads and wondering if they'll ever get out, as if it never snows in New Jersey. They haven't started eating one another yet, but I'm watching my back.

Ethel is delighted by the snow, so it seems the perfect opportunity to use her for a little undercover work. I haven't been alone on the street since the busboy was released, but it's broad daylight and lots of people are outside and I have the dog to guard me. Still, I look around at every intersection, alert to every movement.

As usual, Ethel walks me. I've allowed her to follow her nose and now we are heading up a steep hill. This street makes the outer ring of the Summit Oaks neighborhood—I've never been up here.

Ethel sets off at a trot. Apparently there are some great-smelling mailbox posts over on this side of the neighborhood. Not to mention some juicy squirrels. A moving van is parked in front of 27 Elm; two burly men carry a sofa down the snowy walk. Isabelle Trent's bright green TRENT FINE PROPERTIES sign is still in the yard with SOLD plastered across it.

We round a corner, and stop short.

"Holy crap! Where did that come from?" Ethel and I stare at a monumental Italian villa sandwiched between two modest ranch houses. Every other house in the neighborhood is sided in cedar shakes or clapboard. This one is stucco. Pink stucco. It's got columns and two-story windows and a giant stone staircase leading to a massive front door that could keep Attila the Hun at bay. It stands out in Summit Oaks like a flamingo in a flock of ducks.

Ethel gives the house three sharp barks and turns tail on it. "I agree, baby. That's one ugly McMansion. No wonder Phoebe's worried."

We trudge a little further and encounter a crowd of kids sledding. Their moms stand at the bottom of the hill to keep them from overshooting the yard and landing in the street. A little boy spins down the hill in a red saucer and slides to a stop at our feet. When the kid tumbles off into the snow, Ethel promptly joins him rolling through the drifts.

"Can I take your dog for a ride on my sled?"

"I don't think that would work too well. She wouldn't be able to hold on."

He studies her paws, registers the absence of opposable thumbs, and scampers off.

"Danny loves dogs," his mom tells me. "I promised him we could get one this summer."

The other ladies chime in, offering advice and asking me about Ethel. Shelter or breeder, big or small? Maura is right. Ethel is the ideal secret agent. If any of these chatty ladies were part of Bernadette's riot, they're showing no sign of recognizing me, bundled up as the Michelin man. Our conversation continues above the background noise of shrieks and laughter from the kids.

"Isn't this great?" a lady in a blue parka gushes. "After four years in Atlanta, Timmy doesn't remember what real snow looks like."

"The first big snow of the season is fun, but if school is closed all week, I'll kill myself!"

"Yeah—my house already looks like a bomb went off in the family room."

"Speaking of mess," the lady who moved from Atlanta asks, "can anyone recommend a reliable house cleaner?"

Two ladies answer at once. "Estrella Camion."

"She's great," another lady chimes in. "She cleans for lots of people in the neighborhood. You'll see her van everywhere: SuperStar Cleaning."

"Is that the blue van with the yellow stars?" I ask. I've seen it in the neighborhood almost every day. On Friday is was parked on Acorn Lane all day—Bernadette, Phoebe, and Ed all seem to use the same service.

"That's the one." One of the first recommenders continues, "Not only does she do a great job cleaning, but she also knows people to do any other job you need done: lawn work, gutter cleaning, snow removal. You name it, she's got a friend or a relative who will do it."

My ears perk up. Does she know men who will do dirty work, like threatening women in Play-O-Rama? Estrella Camion. I file the name away for future research.

"All I know is, if I don't get some help with my cleaning, Bernadette will be sending the Health Department to condemn my house!"

The ladies all laugh. The one who wants to get a dog continues in a lowered voice. "I heard the reason the Health Department refused to condemn the house is that Harold's niece paid them off with some of the cash and jewels they've found in there."

"That can't be true," another mom objects.

"How else can you explain how the house managed to pass inspection? There had to be a payoff."

Just then, two of the sledders crash. Amid shouts

and tears, Ethel and I slip away.

Interesting theory about the bribe. I'd believe it myself if I didn't know that we haven't yet found any cash and jewels. Ethel barks at the mail truck making his rounds. The carrier passes us with a wave.

Finally we reach the crest of the hill. The mail truck is about five houses ahead of us. At the house to our right, a blonde woman on crutches with a cast on her foot stands on her porch eyeing the long, icy pathway from her door to her mailbox. I see more broken bones in her immediate future.

I wave to her. "Don't try to come down here. I'll bring your mail up to you."

"Aren't you an angel!"

I wouldn't go that far, but with so many things going wrong, it feels good to make one thing go right. I open her mailbox and take out the usual collection of catalogs and solicitations. On top are two bills and some brightly colored, hand-addressed envelopes. Mrs. Claire Dean, they all say.

Ethel and I pick our way up the slippery sidewalk to Claire Dean and hand over her mail.

"Thanks so much. I knew I shouldn't try to go down to the mailbox." She has kind eyes with laugh lines in the corners "But today is my birthday. I thought there might be some cards for me."

"Looks like you've got quite a few."

She looks over her haul. "None from my nieces and nephews. They all send me my greetings on Facebook and Twitter. I've got twenty-five so far today."

Again, my antennae wave. Claire seems to be plugged into social media.

She bends down to pat Ethel, who's displaying remarkable restraint in not bowling her over. "Where in the neighborhood do you and your sweet dog live?"

"I just moved in to 27 Elm." The lie pops out with disturbing ease. But I figure by the time she meets the real owners, I'll be long gone. "I want to get involved in the community. My Realtor told me there's some kind of neighborhood association with a chat group. Do you know how I'd get information on that?"

Claire waggles her hands. "Steer clear. It used to be a nice group, organizing the Fourth of July picnic, planting flowers. Now all they do is argue endlessly and spread silly rumors about that messy house on Acorn Lane."

To keep her talking, I arch my eyebrows and murmur, "Rumors?" Ethel pitches in by fixing her with a soulful gaze.

"Oh, for years, people have been speculating about that house, asking what could possibly be in there. But once Bernadette McMartin started her campaign to have it torn down, the rumors seemed to escalate. All of a sudden, some people are claiming there are tremendously valuable items in the house."

"Like what?"

She shakes her head. "Jewels, antiques, cash—the story changes depending on whom you're talking to. I teach school. Believe me, I know something about gossip. Once someone launches an idea, it takes off with a life of its own."

*But who launched this idea? And why?*

"Does anyone really know what's in the house?" I ask, working hard to keep my tone casual.

"Ha! People claim they're going to find out." Claire pulls her coat tighter and turns to go inside. "If you ask me, all they'll find is trouble."

After Ethel and I are back on the street, I think about what Claire Dean said. Did someone intentionally launch the idea that Harold's house is full of treasure? Or are people just reacting to the presence of the AMT van parked outside every day? And the astonishing decision of the health inspectors? Nora is the only person who knows for sure what we've found and what we're after. But whom would she have told? She seems to be alienated from everyone in the neighborhood.

Ethel and I trudge down the hill on the final leg of our loop through Summit Oaks. The neighborhood looks like a twenty-first century rendering of a Currier & Ives print. If I could peek behind those frosted windows and snow-draped porches, what would I see? Moms serving hot cocoa and cookies? Gentle souls knitting scarves and listening to Mozart?

Or zealots hunched over their laptops planning their next assault?

As Ethel and I turn the corner at the bottom of the hill, Harold's house comes into view. The Dumpster in a Bag filled by the rioters is still there, a misshapen mound softened by a blanket of snow. I see a bright speck of color on the front door—Jill's warning note to Bernadette to keep out. But what if it wasn't Bernadette nosing around in the house? Maybe there's another faction in the neighborhood just as determined as we are to find a pot of gold.

Gold that's nowhere near a rainbow.

"I stopped by the office on my way here," Jill says when Ethel and I return from our walk. "There was a voicemail from Emil Swenson."

I freeze. "Did he get that other lawyer to take care of Ty?"

"No. The message said, 'Mr. Griggs and I are meeting at an undisclosed location to prepare for tomorrow's interview with the police. We will be unavailable for the rest of the day.'"

I look down at the snow dripping off my boots onto Harold's dusty floor. "I'm worried, Jill."

"I know." She coughs, a raw hacking cough. When she resumes speaking, her voice is cracked and wavery. "But Ty is smart. And so is Mr. Swenson. We have to trust they know what they're doing."

Trust. Jill's got boundless quantities of it. Me, not so much.

"And there's this," she says in a tiny voice, handing me a letter from the pile of mail she's brought here from the office. The heavy paper and five-name return address warn me that this must be from a lawyer.

"What?" Jill asks, watching my face anxiously.

"Martha's lawyers know the money has been recovered. They want 'a plan for immediate restitution.'" I hand the letter back to Jill. "You call the guy and work out a way for them to move all that cash from the office safe to Martha's bank. Maybe that will bring the end of all our *mal suerte*."

She takes the letter and exchanges it for a small cream square that she's pulled out from the remaining tangle of bills and advertisements. "This looks like something personal for you, Audrey."

Too small to be a wedding invitation. Maybe a shower. But why would a friend send it to my office? The handwriting is loopy and dramatic, not familiar at all. I turn it over. The deep blue monogram is a big C flanked by a smaller A and V. The printed return address reads Mendham.

Adrienne Coughlin.

Please God, don't let her be inviting me to a baby shower! Clearly she doesn't know Sean and I are over. I slit open the envelope like I'm disarming a bomb.

Inside, the monogram is repeated on a notecard. I open it up and find not a party invite, but a handwritten message:

*Dear Audrey,*

*I'm writing to apologize for the terrible scene at my home last weekend. There is so much to explain—much you do not know–and it's best done in person. Please meet me for lunch in Palmyrton one day this week. I look forward to hearing from you.*

She ends with a flowery Adrienne and her cell number.

"No way."

"No way what? What is it?" Jill asks.

I wasn't aware I'd spoken aloud. "It a note from Sean Coughlin's sister-in-law. She wants to meet me for lunch to talk about the argument at her house. No way am I meeting her for lunch. No way am I calling her."

"Well, you have to respond to her note. It would be very rude to ignore it," Jill says.

"Who are you? Emily Post with a nose ring?"

"Good manners transcend fashion," Jill sniffs.

"Fine. I'll text her." I fire off my regrets and assurance that no further discussion is necessary. Seconds later, my cell phone is ringing.

"Sonofabitch! You see what politeness has got me?" I stare at the trilling phone, paralyzed.

"Answer it. She knows you're there."

I hold the phone to my head as I watch Jill watching me. A torrent of words pours into my ear. The whole family is mad at her. They blame her for the break-up. She has to talk to me.

"It's not your fault. Don't worry about it." I will not allow myself to be intimidated by a woman who possesses monogrammed note cards.

More pleading. She wants me to meet her for lunch at L'apogée. As if I have time to screw around for two hours in the middle of the day eating fois gras! "That's really not necessary, Adrienne. Sean and I are too different. We simply weren't meant to be."

Adrienne's tone changes. I suspect she realizes the lunch won't happen, so she's going for the full-court press on the phone. "Don't be so hasty, Audrey. There's a lot you don't understand about Sean."

Is there? My hand tightens on the phone. "Did he put you up to this?"

"No, no! Please don't think that. Oh, God—this call is going to backfire on me. I'm going to become one of them."

"One of whom?"

"A busybody Coughlin. They're all in each other's

faces, up each other's butts all the time. It drives me crazy. It drives Sean crazy too. That's why he's so mad, mad at himself. He knows he should never have brought you to a family party so soon."

Despite myself, I'm curious. "If you admit the family's so awful, why are you so eager to drag me into it?"

She laughs. "Because I want company. Besides, you're clearly a calming influence. You take care of business instead of yelling. That's what we all need."

"Look, Sean's and my argument really wasn't about the party. It's more about control. At work, Sean's always in charge. He seems to think he should run his personal life the same way. I don't like feeling controlled."

Adrienne's voice comes through the line, low and urgent. "What Sean wants is a partner. He's watched his siblings pair off and the husbands all go out and work and the wives all stay home and crank out kids. That's not what Sean wants. He really admires you for running your own business. He couldn't stop talking about it at Thanksgiving and Christmas."

He's been talking about me that long? I ponder this tidbit, not wanting to be touched.

"I know what you're thinking. Where does she get off criticizing? She's home cranking out babies like the rest of them, right?"

I cough. She said it.

Adrienne continues in a gush. "When Jimmy was born, Brendan and I still lived in the city. I went right back to my job in marketing at Estee Lauder after a three-month maternity leave. We hired a nanny. Brendan's mom and sisters were horrified, but I didn't care. Then when he was starting to walk, Jimmy pulled a lamp down on top of himself while he was with the nanny and needed ten stitches. They all acted like I'd left my son with an ax murderer. Brendan convinced me to stay at home until Jimmy was in school. We moved out here—the house was my consolation prize. Then I had Larissa and the countdown clock got reset. This September she starts kindergarten, and I am definitely going back to work. Brendan agrees the time is right."

"At Estee Lauder?"

"No, that job is long gone. And I can't imagine commuting into the city every day. But I'll find something. I just don't know what." She falls quiet, lost in her own thoughts, then speaks again. "Sean and I kinda have a love/hate relationship."

I snort. "That's easy to do with Sean."

"Brendan is only eleven months older than Sean. Irish twins. They've always been super-competitive: sports, school, career. And love. When Sean's marriage broke up, his pride was wounded, not only by his ex, but because he lost face with Brendan. He reacted by sniping at me, and I stopped speaking to him for months. Finally, I figured out what was going on, and we patched things up." Adrienne pauses. "Now this! We all want Sean to be happy, Audrey. Give him another chance. Please?"

Her voice is so earnest. I wish I had known some of this before the fateful non-dinner at Sean's apartment. But I can't let Adrienne get in the middle of the situation. And I certainly don't want her reporting back to Sean that I'm wavering.

I take a deep breath. "Look, Adrienne, I appreciate your concern. I really do. But you need to step away. Sean and I are..." I choke on the word "over." "...both tangled up in other pressing matters right now."

"I understand. Maybe you just need a little break."

Her voice sounds ridiculously optimistic. No, no, no. This isn't the impression I want her taking back to the Coughlin clan. Then Sean will think I'm jerking him around some more. "Adrienne, I'm begging you. Please let Sean and me handle this ourselves. Don't breathe a word to Sean or Brendan or any of them."

A beat of silence.

"Adrienne," I warn. "You said you didn't want to be a busybody Coughlin."

She sighs. "Right. But remember this. Sean is incredibly loyal. He would never let you down. That's not a quality that's easy to come by in a man.

# CHAPTER 37

Keep working.

That's the only way to keep all my anxiety at bay. Coughlin, Ty, the busboy, Bernadette—I feel like a planet bombarded by asteroids of uncertainty. If I could vaporize just one of the rocks heading toward me, I'd feel a whole lot better. While Jill continues excavating above, I settle in for a little detective work. First, I call Fiorello's Restaurant. The busboy who threatened me was a substitute. I wonder if there could be any connection between the restaurant and SuperStar Cleaning.

Luckily, I'm calling in the lull between lunch and dinner, and Mr. Bonini, the owner, is willing to talk to me. I know that when Coughlin first talked to him about the busboy, Mr. Bonini was pretty vague about how the guy happened to be filling in there. I take a shot in the dark.

"Hi, I'm checking the references of a cleaning service I'm considering hiring. SuperStar Cleaners, Estrella Camion—have you had experience with them?"

"Estrella! Oh, yes, she's been cleaning for me for years. Started out cleaning house for my wife, and now her ladies clean the restaurant too. Wonderful woman. You can't go wrong with her."

"Thanks, that's good to know. I hear she can find you workers to do other jobs too."

Mr. Bonini chuckles. "That's kind of an informal sideline. You'll have to ask her directly. But I'll tell you, she's eager to please. Once I was complaining about having to have my mother-in-law over for Thanksgiving. Estrella said she'd find a family who would take her." Now he's laughing so hard, I can barely understand him. "I told my wife, 'Your mother better watch her step or she'll be eating beans and rice for Thanksgiving!'"

Mr. Bonini is still chortling as he hangs up.

Jill shuffles into the kitchen and collapses in the chair opposite me, coughing that barking, raw cough again. "I think people were in here again last night. I took pictures of how I left things at the end of yesterday, and when I started today, they were moved."

"That does it," I say. "We're getting out of here." I stand and begin tossing the personal items that have accumulated in Harold's kitchen into my tote bag. "I'm more and more certain that someone in this crazy neighborhood is responsible for the guy who threatened me. They're breaking into the house looking for treasure. I bet one of them was the person my neighbor saw trying to break into my condo. And on top of everything else, this place is making you sick. It's crazy to keep working here. We've got to quit."

"No-o-o-o! I'm very close to breaking through to the master bath. I think we can do it tomorrow. There's a big metal thing I can't budge—I think it might be a chick incubator."

"We don't even have Ty to help us. We've got to stop. You're exhausted. Let me make you some tea."

Jill rotates her neck and drops into a gravity-defying yoga pose. "I just have a headache. My qi is out of whack."

"Maybe it's the flu. You should go to the doctor."

"I'm meeting the lawyer at our office in half an hour to hand over the money, then I'm going to see my acupuncturist." She switches yoga positions. "Should I say anything about the bad on-line reviews?"

"No. I figure I'll give Martha some time to be cheered up by all that cash. Then I'll contact her about taking them down. But I'll take care of the money. You'd better go home and rest."

Jill staggers as she gets up from her yoga and leans against the table in a paroxysm of coughing. "No, I can do it. It's on my way to the wellness center."

"This house is making you sick, Jill. We need to get out of here."

"I'm fine, really. We're so close to breaking through upstairs, Audrey. We can't quit now."

"We can if the lamp sells for a million bucks."

Jill shakes her head so vigorously that dust flies out of her hair. "Finding out where Harold bought the lamp is just the first step in proving its provenance. You know that money is not a sure thing at all. And Harold needs every penny we can find to fix this house up enough that the neighbors leave him alone." She spreads her arms wide. "This is his ho-o-o-me, the only place he feels safe."

"What about your safety? I'm worried about you, Jill. You never get sick. You're the healthiest person I know."

"I just have a little cold." She sips the tea. "It can't be related to the house. After all, you and Ty aren't sick." She shivers.

"Do you want me to shut this window?" The kitchen is the only room where we can take off our respirators. I've been keeping a window open for fresh air despite the cold.

"No, leave it."

I sit down across from Jill. Her eyes are bloodshot, her face pale. But I've never seen her look more determined. I reach for her hand. "Why is saving Harold so important to you?"

"Why was finding out what happened to your

mother so important to you?" she counters.

"You're comparing Harold—who's an acquaintance, a customer—to my mother?"

"Harold means more to me than an acquaintance." She squirms in her chair, but keeps holding my hand. "I've never told you much about my father, right?"

"Just that your parents got divorced when you were a little girl, and you only saw him a few times after that, and now he's passed away."

Jill lifts her head and locks her eyes with mine. "My Dad had schizophrenia, Audrey. At first, he thought people at his job were sabotaging his work, so he quit. Then he thought the government was pursuing him. Finally," Jill's voice cracks, "he thought my mom and I were trying to kill him."

"You? How old were you?"

"Eight," Jill whispers. "He would disappear for weeks at a time. One day, I was staying with a neighbor after school until my mom got home from work. We were playing in the yard when my dad showed up, and I ran to him because I was so happy to see him. He offered to take me for ice cream, and the neighbor let me go. My mom had never told her what was going on with my dad—she was embarrassed, I guess."

Jill—who tells me more than I want to know about her love life, her finances, her tattoos and piercings— has never mentioned any of this. I feel a sick dread anticipating what's coming next.

"I don't remember everything that happened," Jill continues. "I guess I blocked it out. But somehow we ended up in Paterson. As young as I was, I knew this wasn't good. There was definitely no ice cream in this bombed-out neighborhood."

"Then what happened?"

"He started screaming. I couldn't even understand him. He parked the car," she looks down, "and he ran away."

"And left you alone in Paterson?"

Jill nods. "I sat there for hours. It was nine o'clock before the police found me."

I try to picture an eight-year-old Jill with pigtails and a gap-toothed smile, huddled all alone in a car in the dark in a run-down neighborhood. Time passes so slowly when you're a kid. She must have felt utterly abandoned. "Did they arrest your father?"

Jill shakes her head. "The cops couldn't find him. That's when my mom and I moved in with my aunt in Palmyrton. I never saw my dad again. When I was sixteen, we got word from someone who worked with homeless people in Florida. They found his body in a liquor store parking lot. The only thing in his pockets was a picture of my mom and me with our names written on the back. Cause of death—alcohol poisoning and heat prostration. He was forty-three."

I come around to her side of the table and squeeze onto the same chair so I can wrap my arms around her. She feels hot and her breathing is ragged. "I'm so sorry," I whisper into her hair. "Why did you never tell me this before?"

"I've thought about that a lot," she says with her head still buried on my shoulder. "Watching George and Nora with Harold has made me realize something about myself. I've been ashamed, ashamed and scared. Ashamed that my dad had schizophrenia and scared that I might get it too. It can be hereditary. Every time someone calls me crazy—" Her voice breaks.

I stroke her back and she continues softly.

"My dad was very creative, very funny. My mom met him at the ad agency where they both worked. She was in the art department; he was a copywriter. They had a whirlwind romance, and my mom was already pregnant when they got married. Things were only good for a few years. Then he started acting strange. He refused to believe he was sick. My mom finally got him to see a doctor, but he wouldn't take his meds because they had terrible side-effects. She got so tried of struggling with him." Jill lifts her teary face. "I don't blame my mom, Audrey. It's really hard to help people with mental illness. But," she squeezes both my hands, "we've got to *try*."

# CHAPTER 38

Now that I understand why helping Harold has become such a crusade for Jill, I feel differently about the house. Up until now, I just wanted to get to the master bath, find the papers, and get the hell out. I really didn't care if the house came down after we were gone. But Jill is convinced that she and Nora will be able to persuade Harold to accept psychiatric help once all the disruption surrounding the house has ended. That means money available, us gone, repairs made, neighbors mollified. Only when his home life is stabilized will Harold be calm enough to coax into a doctor's care.

That's Jill's mission. I can't stop her.

And when I hear her wheezing, tear-choked voice in my head, I know I have to help her keep fighting to preserve Harold's house. So after Jill leaves, I decide to take Ethel and cruise past the address I found for Estrella Camion's SuperStar Cleaning (ten Yelp Reviews, all five-star). If I can get to the bottom of these neighborhood factions, maybe we can finish our work on Acorn Lane in peace.

Her address is in The Bottoms, near where Coughlin and I searched for Ramon. Finding the place is easy: two bright blue minivans painted with yellow stars are parked in front of a small storefront. As I pull up, one van disgorges a crew of chattering ladies. They head inside, I guess to report on their day and collect their wages. I haven't really thought through a plan, but now that I'm here, I feel an overwhelming desire to go inside and get some answers.

I look around as dusk settles over the neighborhood. I guess it would be crazy to go in there all alone when no one knows I'm here.

Ethel whines.

"Oh, all right. I'll call for back up." Who is closest? Dad.

His apartment is only a few blocks away. I call and tell him I need his help with something.

He sounds pleased.

By the time I park and get up to the front door, the last group of cleaning ladies are on their way out. They hold the door open with smiles, and walk off to their homes in the neighborhood. Dad is sitting in the car, watching my every move. I waited until I had him captive before I told him exactly what I intended to do. He has been protesting loudly that an elderly stroke patient is not a suitable bodyguard, but I tell him anyone can dial 911. He just needs to be alert.

I enter the building, greeted by a nose-twitching combination of lemon, pine, and chlorine. To my right is a store room lined with shelves of cleaning supplies and racks of brooms, mops and vacuums. To my left, a small office with one desk.

A woman in her fifties with bright pink lipstick and gold-streaked hair lifts her head. Her face lights up with such delight that I glance over my shoulder to see if someone else is behind me.

"*Hola*! Hello! Come in. I am Estrella." She stands and extends her hand in greeting. I'm embarrassed to touch my grubby mitt to her well-manicured fingers. Clearly Estrella is no longer on the front lines of the cleaning operation.

"Have a seat." She beams at me. "You need some help with cleaning? How can I make your life easier?"

Ha! She could restore my ruined reputation. Blast a hole through to the master bath at 12 Acorn Lane. Restore Harold's memory of where he got the Tiffany lamp. But for starters, she can just tell me if she set the busboy on my trail.

I must say, Estrella strikes me as an unlikely organizer of goons. The warmth in her eyes is genuine. I hesitate about giving her my real name, but let's see how she reacts. "Hi, my name is Audrey Nealon. I own an estate sale organizing service called Another Man's Treasure."

I watch her face closely for a sign of recognition, but there's nothing. Instead, her eyes light up with the good businesswoman's delight at a promising prospect.

"You need some cleaners to help at these sales?"

"No, not cleaners. But I've heard you can help with other workers as well. I think you helped Mr. Bonini find a quick replacement busboy?"

"Oh, yes. Mr. Bonini is a very nice man. I know his wife a lotta years." She stretches her arms wide as if to embrace the entire neighborhood. "I know a lotta people. I bring people together—ones who want to work, ones who need help. I help you. What do you need?"

"It's not a steady job," I explain. "I need someone occasionally who can help with heavy lifting. I used to just go over to the hardware store and hire one of those—"

Estrella wags a red-tipped finger. "No, no, no— that's not good. You never know who you're going to get. Some of those guys are hard workers, some not." She tips an imaginary bottle. "And you're a woman, you gotta be careful. I find you the best guys. Nice family men. Good, strong workers."

"That would be great. How much advance notice do you need?"

"You call me when you need a guy." She snaps her fingers. "I send him—fifteen minutes, half-an-hour, tops." While she's talking, she's pulling out a form and a pen. "You fill this out and we're all set."

As I write, I keep chatting with her. One or two questions and I get her whole life story: how she arrived penniless from Columbia twenty-five years ago. How her no-good husband left her and she cleaned houses to support her kids. Oh, how people love to talk about themselves! And now she owns a house, a business, and her three kids have college degrees. And once she was successful, the worthless husband showed up again making trouble, but she sent him packing. She ends by putting her hand over her heart. "Ten years ago I became an American citizen. Happiest day of my life."

Geez, the woman should be doing tours at the Statue of Liberty. I want to like her, but I keep a solid wall around my heart. I need to stay tough for what comes next.

I smile and slide the completed form across the desk. "You're a remarkable woman, Estrella. Even though I've just met you, I feel like I've known you forever. You understand how hard it is for a woman to build up her own business."

She cradles my right hand in both of hers. "We are *hermanas*—sisters—and we have to stick together, eh?"

"Exactly. So that's why I'm wondering...there's something else...maybe you can give me advice—" I cast my eyes down and feel the warmth of her hands holding mine. Am I a good enough actress to pull this off?

"You need help with something else? I tell you, I know all kinds of people. Lawyers, accountants, doctors. You pregnant? Guy left you?"

Ah, what an opening she's handed me. "I'm not pregnant, but the problem is with a guy." I look into her motherly brown eyes. "A few months ago, I went out with this guy a few times. At first, he seemed nice.

Then I started to get a bad vibe. He lied to me about having a job. He was real possessive. I told him I didn't want to see him anymore, but now—"

"He won't leave you alone."

I nod, hoping I look scared. "And the police say there's nothing they can do."

"Police," Estrella dismisses them with a huff. "You don't have any brothers to help you out?" She's still holding my hand across the desk.

I shake my head. "I'm an only child."

"What you need is someone to do what any brother would do for his sister. Talk to this guy and tell him to go away." She squeezes my hand. "Or else."

"You know someone like that?"

She nods. "Of course, he doesn't work cheap."

I straighten my shoulders and increase the pressure on her hand. "Frankly, Estrella, I believe I've already met him. A short, strong guy with one chipped tooth. Lives in Dover. Mostly works as a landscaper, except when he's helping Mr. Bonini. And threatening me."

Estrella's eyes widen and she tries to pull away.

I increase my grip. "I want to know who hired him. Who paid him to threaten me?"

"I don't know what you're talking about. You have misunderstood me."

"No I haven't. One of your housecleaning customers needed a man to warn me off a job I'm doing. You set it up."

Her hand is sweating. Her eyes dart back and forth.

"It's someone who lives in Summit Oaks." I squeeze her hand harder. "Who?"

She yanks her hand away. "Get out of here." She reaches for her phone. I shove it away.

"You think you know a lot of people, Estrella? Well, so do I. You know who I'm really dating? An IRS agent. Maybe he would be interested in checking your books. I hope you've been paying taxes on all those people who work for you now and then. And I hope you haven't knowingly hired anyone who's an illegal alien. Perhaps my other friend at the INS would be interested in coming here to look into that."

Behind the pink lipstick and purple eye shadow, her face grows pale. I didn't think I had it in me to be this ruthless, but I'm determined to find out who's trying to hurt me.

"My business," she whispers.

"That's right. You have a business you've worked hard for and so do I. I don't want you to lose your business, but someone is trying to hurt me, trying to stop me from making a living. All I want is to know who it is. Then I'll leave you alone."

"Please—I didn't know the man was told to threaten you. My customer, he said he needed help getting a drug addict to move out of a rental property he owns." She puts her hand to her chest. "I, myself, have had this problem. So naturally, I said I would help."

Ah, Estrella—you're all heart. "Tell me who your customer is, Estrella. I won't tell him how I know. I won't tell the police. I won't tell the IRS. I just need to know who's trying to hurt me."

She swallows hard. Her lips part. I sit tensed, waiting for Bernadette McMartin's name to emerge from her mouth.

"Mr. Marchand."

"Who?"

"Mr. Walter Marchand. He lives in Summit Oaks."

"What's the address?"

From the back of the building, we hear a voice. "Mom, are you done? What's for dinner?"

Estrella nods to the door. "Go. You got what you came for."

I return to the car bursting with the information I've uncovered.

"Wait'll you hear how brilliant I was, Dad!" I put the car in gear and begin pulling out of my parking spot. "I tricked her into telling me who sent that thug to Play-

O-Rama, so now I can figure out what the hell is going on in Summit Oaks. Apparently it wasn't Bernadette after all. It was this other faction who's been sneaking around in Harold's house and..."

Dad's lips are pressed in a thin line. He's staring out the window at the dark street with the fixed interest of a tourist in Yellowstone.

"What are you mad about? I'm back in twenty minutes, all in one piece. We can get some nice carryout from Whole Foods and celebrate at my place."

"Take me home." There's more ice dripping from his voice than from Harold's gutters.

"Fine." Two can play that game.

We drive in silence until my father snaps. "What you did was completely irresponsible, Audrey. You had no idea what you'd find in there. You could've been killed. And now you plan to antagonize some other violent lunatic."

"Stop exaggerating. I simply plan to ask this Walter Marchand person why he paid the busboy to threaten me. I'll embarrass him, put him on the spot, and he'll have to back down."

"You need to tell the police everything that you know and let them handle it."

I jolt to a halt at a stop sign and twist to face him. "The police think I'm a liar. What don't you understand about that?"

"If you calmly present them with the facts, I'm sure—"

My foot falls hard on the accelerator. "You're sure, you're sure. You're always sure that logic will win the day, right Dad? Always sure that you're right."

We ride the final block in silence. I've barely pulled up to the curb before he's opening the door. "Certainty must be genetically linked. Good-night, Audrey."

Still fuming from my tangle with Dad, I head to the new Whole Foods to pick up dinner. As usual, the parking lot is packed.

Two months ago, an exhausted old A&P full of wilted iceberg and green-tinged hamburger patties was replaced by a gleaming emporium of grass-fed beef and line-caught tuna. People flock to the store. Even though the grand opening novelty has dissipated, it seems like three-quarters of Palmyrton's population is trolling the aisles at any given point in the day. It's like they've never seen an organic gooseberry before.

I'm the worst offender. At least twice a week I weave my little Civic through the parking lot, cutting off BMWs and Land Rovers for the last available parking space. I'm paying through the nose for food that's beautifully presented, but speaking as someone who's eaten far too much lo mein straight out of the white cardboard box while standing over the kitchen sink, I think I deserve the illusion of elegance in the food I carry out. Besides, after a long day at Harold's and an argument with my father, I need beauty wherever I can find it.

Now that I know Walter Marchand hired the busboy, I feel bolder about traveling around Palmyrton unescorted. Walter's got to be a little unhinged, but at least he's not a murderous coyote. "I'll only be inside for fifteen minutes, Ethel. You bark at anyone who comes near the car, okay?"

She sits up straight in the passenger seat and slobbers on the window as I look back and wave. No one will car-jack me with Ethel on board.

I'm barely into Produce before I run into a girl I graduated from high school with, and, down by the greens I wouldn't know how to prepare, I meet a man whose father's house I cleared out last year. After I visit the salad bar, I head for the prepared food, where short ribs and butternut squash are calling my name. As is Ethel's vet, who's right behind me in line.

Before heading to the checkout, I make a final detour into Beverages for a box of insanely delicious green tea with lemongrass. I turn at the end of the aisle and pull up short. On the other side of a tower of organic quinoa I spot a familiar red head. Why wouldn't he be here? Everyone else is.

I duck behind the display, but I needn't have bothered. Coughlin is looking straight ahead at a woman–tall, smartly bobbed, incredibly fit. He comes up to her and shows her a jar of something and they confer over it, their heads nearly touching. He's wearing sweatpants and a tight Dri-Fit shirt that strains over his biceps. Even though it's twenty-five degrees outside, she's wearing running shorts that reveal every muscle in her perfectly toned legs. This is the kind of girl who scared the crap out of me in high school. He places his hand on the small of her back. Apparently they're making a gourmet meal together after a workout session.

And presumably before another workout session.

I turn quickly, nearly mowing down a little kid trailing after her mom. I can't risk apologizing out loud, so I nod rudely and scurry away. Adrienne's words mock me. *Sean is incredibly loyal.* Clearly, she doesn't know him as well as she thinks she does.

My sweaty hands stick to the handle of my cart. I told Coughlin to find someone else, and he did. That's good. I no longer have to feel guilty for rejecting him.

Then why are the letters on the aisle signs swimming?

# CHAPTER 39

The morning after my fact-finding mission to SuperStar Cleaners, I pull up in front of Walter Marchand's house, 35 Birch Lane, which is only a few streets away from Harold's. Last night I discovered Walter has a pretty low-key Internet presence: no Facebook, Twitter, or Linked In, so I couldn't find a picture. He must be old. Good—easier for me to intimidate. I'm stoked for this encounter. At this very moment, Ty and Mr. Swenson are facing the police. There's nothing I can do to fight that battle, but I can enforce a little justice right here.

The house is a perfectly maintained colonial: driveway plowed, walk shoveled, bird-feeder filled, cheery red and pink Valentine's Day flag blowing in the breeze. It's hard to be frightened by someone who decorates for minor holidays, but I remind myself that Bernadette's house is straight out of HGTV and still contains a lot of rage.

I take a deep breath and ring the bell. Inside I hear the Westminster chimes and the sound of a small dog yapping. I wait with my heart pounding.

And wait.

I ring again. Nothing.

I step back to see if anyone's peeping through the curtains. The house seems empty.

I'll have to come back later. But now my adrenaline is pumping. I've got to do something with all this energy. Tie up some loose ends.

Resolve...*something*.

I think of what sits in my office safe now that the cash is gone: the Tiffany lamp. A big lump of potential help for Ty. College tuition. His own car.

A defense lawyer.

I shiver and get back in my car to head for my office. Today is the day we will make Harold tell us where he got the lamp. Jill keeps wanting to wait for him to have one of his good toilet-engineering days, but the effects of the meds he got at the hospital have worn off, and Harold seems to be getting worse, not better. Today may be as good as he ever gets.

A plan forms as I drive. I will bring the lamp to the house so Harold can see it in a familiar setting. I'll get Nora to meet us there so Jill has some extra support.

I will make this happen.

"Harold, remember the lamp you bought from the man with the sunglasses?" Jill coos.

Nora has slipped away from work for an hour, and she Jill and I are gathered around the kitchen table with Harold. The lamp glitters before us.

He shakes his head. "That lamp was lost in the fire. Very sad." He turns and wanders back to his card table in the foyer.

Nora rubs her temples. "This will never work. My brother George is back in town. He's softened recently on wanting to tear down the house. I told him to meet us here so he can see the lamp and see how much progress you've made clearing out. But if Uncle Harold acts like this, George might change his mind again."

Jill doubles over, wheezing so hard she can't catch her breath. Just then, a cold breeze sweeps through the kitchen. A younger, much better groomed version of Harold steps into the kitchen.

"George!" Nora turns on an upbeat voice. "You made it. Meet Jill and Audrey. This is the Tiffany lamp they found. Isn't it gorgeous?"

Nora's brother puts one reluctant foot in front of the other like he's walking the plank. He circles the lamp with a dubious expression on his face. "Looks like all the other dusty old crap Harold collects."

I shine my flashlight under the shade and the colors jump to life. The purple irises, the yellow lilies—it really is a magnificent creation. The more I see it, the more convinced I am that it must be real.

"Humpf." George jams his hands in the pockets of his jacket and glances around the kitchen. "This house is like a freakin' time capsule of the eighties. Look at that wallpaper."

Cheerful fat geese—once white, now a dingy gray— waddle around the border near the ceiling carrying baskets of flowers in their beaks.

Nora smiles. "Remember when Mom put it up? She was so pleased—it was the height of fashion."

George turns his back on his sister. "You seem to forget you're four years older. I have no memory of things ever being happy and normal in this house." He studies the lamp again. "If Harold has managed to acquire something of artistic value, it's pure chance. He has no eye for beauty."

I switch my flashlight off and the lamp returns to obscurity. Is it my longing for it to be real that makes it more beautiful?

Harold wanders back into the kitchen. He takes one look at George and freezes.

George's eyes widen. "My God, he looks awful," he blurts, as if Harold were in a coma.

Nora elbows her brother into silence. "Look who's here, Uncle Harold." Nora speaks in that high-pitched, sing-song that parents use to convince toddlers they should be happy to see the dentist. "It's George. You haven't been together in a while."

Harold blinks his eyes a few times then looks away.

Nora crosses the room to him and puts her arm

around his shoulders. "Come over here, Uncle Harold. Let's look at this lamp. Remember? You got it at a garage sale, I think."

Harold steps closer and his face stiffens. I've come to know that look, and it's not good. It usually appears when Harold's about to dig in his heels on something.

"It shouldn't be in the kitchen," he says. "It belongs in the living room. Lamps and appliances go in the living room."

"You're right, Harold," Jill says. "We just moved it temporarily so we could see it a little better."

Harold takes a step forward. "It needs to go back."

"Okay, no problem. We can put it where you want it." Nora moves to pick up the lamp, but George grabs her arm and jerks her back.

"Stop indulging his craziness! I'm sick of catering to his ridiculous whims."

Harold covers his ears. "Don't wake the babies."

"Shut up!" George roars. "Never say that again!"

Jill and I exchange glances. "Harold says that a lot," I say. "What does it mean?"

"How the hell should I know?" George is still irritated, but he's lowered his voice. "He was always muttering some incantations. The kids in the neighborhood thought he was a witch doctor."

Harold's breathing gets more labored. He sidles closer to the table. "We have to put this where it belongs. It shouldn't be here."

"Okay, okay," Jill murmurs. She moves to pick up the lamp.

"No!" Without warning, Harold lunges at Jill. He sinks his fingernails into her arm. "You're the one who took it away. I don't want you to touch it."

Jill gasps and winces, but never loses patience. "Okay, it's all right."

Not so George. He grabs Harold by the collar. "Take your hands off her. She's trying to help you, and this is how you act?"

Harold squirms to escape his nephew's grasp. His grimy sweatshirt comes halfway over his head. George is younger, but Harold is taller. They struggle until Harold's right arm pulls out of his shirt. Unexpectedly, he's free and lurches backward.

One skinny hip catches the edge of the table.

In slow motion the lamp tips.

I dive.

Shattering glass echoes.

Emerald. Ruby, Amethyst. Gold.

The colors are all that's left.

# CHAPTER 40

I pick up a shard of green from the floor and study the many shades: turquoise, emerald, sea foam, cream. Even without form, it's beautiful.

The destruction of the lamp triggered a huge screaming match between Nora and George. Harold bolted like a skittish horse. Nora eventually returned to her office, while George seemed to vaporize while our backs were turned. I expected Jill to dissolve in despair, but she didn't shed a tear. Instead, the catastrophe seems to have hardened her resolve.

Now she and I are alone at the scene of the crime. I step around the tragic pile of glass on the floor, strap on my respirator, and prepare to head upstairs. Jill reaches for hers and triggers a coughing fit.

"Honey, please—stay down here. Now that we got the chicken incubator out of the way, I just need to sift through the collection until I find the valuable papers. You ride herd on Harold in case he comes back, and keep him out of my hair."

Jill lets her respirator slip from her fingers and clatter to the floor. Too out-of-breath to speak, she nods and sinks into a kitchen chair.

Now I know she's really sick. She's staying only to make sure I stick with the plan. I've got to find those papers today and get Jill home to bed.

The trudge up the stairs feels like the final assault on Mt. Everest. Like the doomed climbers in *Into Thin*

*Air*, the only thing that keeps me putting one miserable foot in front of the other is the dread of having come so far for nothing. At the door of the master bedroom I shut my eyes and give myself a pep talk. *You can do this. The papers exist. Think like Harold and find them.*

Then I squeeze past the pantheon of stuffed birds in the bedroom and wriggle into the bath. The en suite bathroom was still a luxury when this house was built, and the bath doesn't have the square footage of today's master baths. There's barely enough room for me to turn around. Through the murky glass door of the shower stall I see hundreds of Civil War books. Floor to ceiling, Bruce Catton to Jeff Shara, wedged so tightly I probably can't even pry one loose. Harold could have slipped the papers between any two volumes, but somehow I doubt it. Books are books and letters are letters, and in Harold's OCD mind, the twain don't meet.

I move to the bathtub: Civil War uniforms, hats, capes, disintegrating shoes. The trove has spilled over onto the floor. Under the blue wool of a soldier's jacket I see the corner of a once-fluffy pink bathmat. Some of this might go for fifty or a hundred bucks on eBay, but I'm not here to screw with collectibles. The toilet must be in that little alcove, but it's completely buried in weapons—swords, scabbards, rusty bayonets, rifles, revolvers, and a lead cannonball. Once I find the papers, it might be worthwhile to come back for a few of those guns. Right now, eyes on the prize. The his-and-her vanity is neatly divided between bullets in sink one and medals in sink two.

Gingerly, I open the vanity drawers. Eighties era tubes of dried out Maybelline lip gloss and compacts of blue and purple eye shadow are nestled together with maps of the Gettysburg battlefield and walking tour brochures of Civil War sites in Richmond. This seems promising.

Next drawer: Sharon's electric curlers and a museum guide to Appomattox Courthouse.

Final drawer: Brut aftershave, Gillette shaving cream and brochures on Andersonville Prison.

I yank open the cabinet under the sink: flinging aside evaporated cleaning supplies, I see a narrow box in the back. Yes!

No. Guides to every Civil War site in North Carolina.

Only one place left to look. I put my fingers on the latch of the mirrored medicine cabinet door. My exhausted masked face peers back at me in the spotted glass. *Please, God...*

I open the door to narrow shelves jammed with packets of Bayer aspirin and bottles of Robitussin and tubes of Neosporin. I sweep the long-expired medications aside.

And there, jammed behind the removable shelves is a thick manila envelope. I claw the shelves out. Printed on the upper left hand corner: William C. VanderMere, Historical Artifacts.

Inside is another envelope, acid free to protect fragile documents. I peek inside and see the spidery handwriting of 150 years ago.

*"Dear General Lee,"*

"Jill, I found it!" I clatter downstairs, clutching the manila envelope in my hand. Harold, back at his card table as if nothing has happened, looks up briefly as I tear past him into the kitchen. "Look!"

Jill's head rests on her arms flat on the kitchen table. She must have dozed off. I squeeze her shoulder to urge her up, but she doesn't move.

"Jill, look. I found the papers." I shake her, and her left arm falls limply to her side.

Her face is gray, her lips blue.

"Jill!" I pull her upright in the chair. Her body is dead weight.

She's not breathing.

I scream, but there's no one but Harold to hear me. Frantically, I scrabble through my tote bag to find my phone. Why, today of all days, is it in my bag instead of my pocket? My shaking fingers release the envelope into the tangle of junk in the bag. Finally, they close over the familiar rectangle of the phone.

I dial 9-1-1 and shout at a maddeningly calm woman that I need an ambulance. "She's blue. She's not breathing. What should I do?"

The woman drones calm instructions in my ear about stretching Jill out and checking her pulse. I do as she says, but how can this help? Oh, God—why don't I know CPR?

I stare into Jill's slack, blue face and a wave of terror overtakes me. She can't die. I can't let her die.

Crazed, I run to the always-open kitchen window and scream. "Help!" Maybe Bernadette will hear me. "Help, please someone help me."

I dart back to Jill and try to find a pulse in her cold arm. Hopeless. My own hands are shaking too hard. Tears blur my vision.

How could I have let this happen? Why did I let her work in this house? George is right. This place radiates evil.

"Helo-o-o-o? Is everyone all right here?" A male voice calls from the foyer. Definitely not Harold.

"Help! In here, in the kitchen."

A moment later, Ed Brandt appears in the doorway. "I heard shouting as I ran by. You okay?"

I've never been so happy to see Ed's busybody face. "Jill's not breathing. I need someone who can do CPR."

He nudges me aside and drops to his knees. "I learned after a buddy dropped dead during a race."

I have to give Ed credit. He performs CPR ceaselessly, falling into a rhythm of chest compressions and rescue breathing. I'm too hysterical to provide much help, but as Jill's face gradually pinks up, I dare to hope that she will recover.

I sense a presence above me.

I glance up to see Harold frowning. How long has he been in the kitchen? I'm always unnerved by Harold's ability to pop up or slip away so soundlessly. "That man shouldn't be here. He's a stranger."

"He's a neighbor, Harold. Jill's sick. He's helping her."

"What he's doing doesn't work." Harold stretches out his hand to stop Ed. His long filthy nails revolt me.

I've had all I can take. Something snaps.

"Get out. Get out of this kitchen, do you hear me?" I spring up, stamping my foot and waving my hands like I'm shooing a feral cat.

Harold backs off to a corner, and I turn my attention back to Ed.

It feels like hours have passed since I dialed 9-1-1. Where is that damn ambulance?

Then I hear sirens growing closer.

"The ambulance is coming, Ed." I run to the front door to let them in. No Harold. I hope he's gone for the day.

Uniformed men fill the house with barked orders and medical jargon. I answer their questions and call Jill's mom. Ed sits in the corner recovering from his efforts. The EMTs load Jill on a stretcher, her face covered with an oxygen mask. Her eyelids flicker. She's regaining consciousness, isn't she?

*She'll be okay. She will. She has to be.*

As they wheel the gurney through the foyer, Harold appears on the stairs. His eyes are glazed and his lips move as he watches the commotion. No one but me even notices him.

One of the gurney's wheels topples Harold's card table.

Harold snaps out of his trance. In an instant, he's off the stairs. With a choked scream, he pounces on the EMT in the lead, sinking his long nails into the man's exposed neck.

"What the–? Get offa me!" But Harold hangs on, a furious cat.

The cop who's come along on the call finally pries Harold loose and twists his arm behind his back.

"Please, let him go," I plead, knowing that's what Jill would want. "He's sick, and scared. He didn't mean any harm."

The EMT holds gauze to his neck. "Freakin' lunatic. Good thing I'm up to date on my tetanus."

"He drew blood," the cop says. "That's assault." He handcuffs Harold and drags him toward the door.

Harold twists to look at me, eyes wide with fear.

I turn my back. Harold's on his own this time. I'm riding to the hospital with Jill.


"Have you encountered rats in this house?"

After huddling together for an hour in the ICU waiting room, Jill's mother and I are finally talking to a doctor.

"The neighbors keep complaining there are rats, but I haven't seen any myself. But we hear sounds of animals scurrying. Jill kept insisting they were squirrels. She worked at the house for a day by herself when it was really bad. And then...."

My mind streams back to the day I first met Phoebe, the day we were dismantling the wall of coffee cans filled with buttons. I picture the scene when I saw the tangle of stuffing and straw that Jill had swept up behind that barricade of Maxwell House and Folgers.

"And then what?"

I pull out my phone and call up Google images.

"Everyone uses the term rat's nest when they talk about someone with tangled hair, or a really messy desk. But have you ever literally seen a rat's nest? I haven't." I type the words and a string of images fills the screen: big piles of shredded paper, strips of cloth, puffs of insulation. I show the doctor. "We found a pile just like this at the house. And Jill swept it up."

He grabs his phone and barks out incomprehensible orders for tests. Then he tells someone to call the Department of Public Health.

"What are you testing for?" Jill's mother asks.

"Hanta virus. It's rare in New Jersey, but there have been a few cases. If that's what she has, the house will have to be sealed off. Hanta is spread by inhaling particles carried in rat feces. It causes high fever and respiratory distress."

I search his face. "But once you know what it is, you can cure it, right?"

"There's no time to waste. Once the lungs fill with fluid, it can be fatal."

That evening the TV news is filled with reporters standing in front of Harold's house talking in apocalyptic tones about the arrival of Hanta virus in New Jersey. Bernadette looms in front of the cameras, saying "I told you so" for every station. When I picture Jill lying in her hospital bed, I have to admit Bernadette was right. But that doesn't stop me from throwing my shoe at her smirking face on the screen.

Jill's mother is allowed to sit by her bedside in the ICU, but I'm not. I long for Ty to comfort me, but he's still not answering my texts. I only have Mr. Swenson's office number, so he's unreachable too. Could they still be in the interrogation? Surely Mr. Swenson would let me know if Ty had been arrested.

Finally around 8:00, I get a cryptic text from Ty: *All done. Worn out. Catch you tomorrow.*

I guess that's good news. If he's got his phone, he's not in jail. I want to call him and demand details. Is he totally clear? But if I do, I'll have to tell him about Jill. And since Ty won't be able to visit her, there's no point in his knowing how sick she is. I'm still twisted with worry about both of them. And powerless to help.

The TV blares on as I pace around my condo. I open my tote bag to look at the Civil War documents. Maybe

I can start researching prices to occupy my mind. A jumble of papers greets me: a flier for the upcoming blues festival, a carryout menu for the Taj Mahal, a receipt for my last oil change. I don't know how this bag can swallow up so much stuff, but it does.

The reporters are announcing that the condemnation procedures for 12 Acorn Lane have been reinstated.

I dig deeper.

A catalog with some funky skirts I liked...a copy of my last set of dental x-rays to give to my new dentist...a coupon for a sale at Lord & Taylor that ended two weeks ago.

My heart rate kicks up a notch. Where is that manila envelope with the Civil War letters?

I dump the entire bag out on my dining room table. Loose change and dried-up lipsticks and lint-covered cough drops roll across the room. I sort all the papers into piles.

No manila envelope.

I do what I always do when I've lost something—try to retrace my steps and envision every place I've been since the last time I saw the lost item.

I picture myself finding the papers. I let out of whoop of joy. What did I do next?

I took them downstairs to show Jill and passed Harold in the foyer

I relive the moment of discovering her limp body and my throat constricts. I take a deep breath. *Don't start crying or you'll never stop.*

I had to call 9-1-1. My phone was in my bag on the kitchen table. While I dug for my phone, I slipped the envelope inside my bag.

I took the bag back and forth from the hospital to my house twice, but I never looked for the envelope again until now.

A horrible sinking feeling grips me. While I was preoccupied with helping Jill, Harold could have gone into my bag and taken the envelope back out. He knew I'd found the papers.

Where would he have put it?

I hear his nasal whine. *'This doesn't belong here.'* I rest my head in my hands. He has to have put it back into the master bathroom.

A flash of yellow on the TV screen catches my eye. A backhoe is being unloaded in front of Harold's house. The reporter intones, "Tear-down will begin tomorrow morning."

Without the Civil War letters, these last horrible weeks have all been for naught. The loss of the Tiffany lamp, Jill's illness, Harold's arrest, the condemnation of the house—one catastrophe after another. The letters are all we have to show for that filthy, exhausting work. Their sale is the only thing that can get Harold the help he needs. Not to mention pay Jill and Ty for their work.

And pay the company health insurance premium. Who knows how long Jill will be in the hospital?

And pay Mr. Swenson, or someone better, for defending Ty. He may not be in the clear yet.

And now the letters are right back where they started out. The police line is set up. The demo equipment is poised for the kill. First thing tomorrow morning, Harold's house is dust.

Oh, Harold, Harold, what have you done?

I never want to go back to 12 Acorn Lane. But what else can I do? The police won't stop the demo for this. The Heath Department won't let me go in after some papers. I'm going to have to sneak back in to get them.

I don't relish running into Bernadette or any of the neighborhood wackos—they'll call the cops on me for sure–but if I park on another street and slip through the backyards, I should be able to make it in and out unseen. As for the virus, I've been working in that environment for weeks. What's one more hour? I assure myself it's no big deal.

So why am I rooted to my chair?

Ethel looks at me from under wrinkled eyebrows.

"Yeah, I know. I'm confused too. It's just, I'm a little scared, ya know? The busboy dude, the protesters, the break-ins, the rats."

Ethel whines.

"I know you'd go with me, but I can't trust you not to bark. There are raccoons at night. You know how you get around them."

She hangs her head, knowing I'm right.

Who can I get to go with me? Jill's in the hospital. I won't ask Ty to do anything illegal. If we get caught, I'll be let off with a warning and he'll get sent back to jail. Maura is in Chicago on business. My father has made it clear he wants no part of my escapades. And I'm sure as hell not calling Coughlin.

I scroll through the contacts on my phone looking for inspiration. When I hit the halfway mark, I find it.

Natalie.

No, I can't make my father's sixty year old girlfriend go into that toxic house with me. But she can spot me. I dial.

I give her the background, then ask my favor. "I'm going over there, Natalie. But I want you to be my back-up. I'm going to call you once I have the papers. If you don't hear from me by midnight, I want you to call 9-1-1. Okay?"

"Audrey, I don't think this is a good idea. Surely there's another way. Let's think—"

"I'm going, Natalie. I'm ninety-nine percent sure nothing will happen. Just be my one percent back-up— please."

She sighs. "All right. But I'm not waiting one second past twelve."

"Deal."

I'm about to hang up when I put the phone back to my ear. "Oh, and Natalie, don't breathe a word of this to my father. Promise."

"But, Audrey—"

"Natalie, please. I can't deal with weeks of disapproval from him right now. Promise."

"All right. I promise."

The streets of Summit Oaks are not laid out in a grid—that would be too straightforward. Instead they twist and twine and double back on each other to create charming lanes and quiet cul-de-sacs...not to mention opportunities for back-stabbing. Now, what is the street whose houses back up to Harold's? The one Nora always parks on? Birch? Beech? Damn these tree names. I pull down Birch, trying to remember the color of the house that I can see from Harold's back yard. Taupe. Every other freakin' house is taupe. I drive at a snail's pace squinting to peer through the thick trees that fill every yard. A man walking his dog stops and stares at me. I speed up.

Next I try Beech, but that road twists sharply at the midpoint, taking me away from the direction of Harold's house. I think.

Up ahead I see a sign. Aspen Drive. Aspen, I'm pretty sure that's where Nora parks. Sure enough, when I get halfway down the street I can see the top of the bright yellow backhoe parked in Harold's backyard. I park and study the houses that back up to Harold's. One is lit up like a Christmas tree, curtains all open, people moving from room to room. Too risky to cut through that yard. I set off down the edge of the driveway of the dark house next door. I've got my respirator stowed in a small backpack. At the end of the pavement I set my foot down and screech.

I'm ankle-deep in a freezing puddle of slush. In the house next door, I can see the woman in her kitchen lift her head and listen. I duck behind a prickly bush. When she goes back to her work, I head deeper into the yard, choosing to cut across a large flagstone patio to avoid any more slush.

Suddenly I'm bathed in light. I freeze. A dog begins barking, giving a pretty convincing impression of the Hound of the Baskervilles. Shit, these people are home. I run straight back, my heart rattling the cage of my ribs.

A ten-foot stockade fence stands before me.

It takes a moment for me to realize that no ferocious dog is tearing my legs off. He's charging up and down a dog run in the yard on the other side of this one. And the lights seem to have been triggered by a motion detector. Why are these people so damn paranoid?

Finally, I can see Harold's property through the trees at the back of the brightly lighted house, and I slip over there to make my crossing. Of course, Harold's yard hasn't had maintenance for twenty years. I thrash through brambles and chest-high stalks of dead weeds before finally breaking through. Orange plastic temporary fencing encircles the yard. Signs are posted at intervals: "Biohazard—Keep Out." What's a plastic fence at this point? Lewis and Clark weren't stopped by the Rockies. I push it down in a low spot and clamber over.

I slip from tree to tree being sure to stay out of view of Bernadette's house. The backhoe looms over me, its claw a bright yellow T-Rex poised to kill. This house will be laid open, disemboweled. Tomorrow morning, jail is probably the best place Harold can be.

I shake myself. No time to be maudlin. Just get in and get out.

I reach the back door. The police have hammered a piece of plywood over it and posted another Biohazard sign. Shit! I never expected this.

But the police don't know 12 Acorn Lane like I do. There's another door that leads directly into the room that holds the furnace and water heater, a door concealed by a giant overgrown bush. Sure enough, the cops have missed it. I jiggle the doorknob. It opens right up.

Inside, the house is pitch dark. The utilities have been shut off to prepare for the demo. I figure my cell phone flashlight is dim enough for me to use safely. Even eagle-eyed Bernadette won't notice if I keep it focused low to the ground.

I stumble into the kitchen, dodging piles of blenders and food processors. I'm conscious of every breath I take. Is the respirator filtering out those Hanta virus particles? A vision of Jill chained by wires and tubes to her ICU bed fills my brain. I can't allow myself to think about that. I've survived this house for two weeks—what's one more hour?

Get in. Get out.

I shine my light around the kitchen floor. Could I possibly be so lucky as to find the envelope here? Maybe it slipped out of my bag. Maybe Harold didn't take it back to the master bath.

But the kitchen looks just as we left it. A few take-out containers on the table. Corralled clutter in the corners. Broken Tiffany glass on the floor. No envelope.

I've got to go upstairs, leaving the air that might be toxic for the air I know is toxic. Upstairs where I know we found a rat's nest. Upstairs where I'm sure Jill got sick.

I wend my way through the foyer. Unlike in the kitchen, here the windows are still totally covered by Harold's collections, so I don't have to worry about my flashlight. At the foot of the stairs I take a deep breath as if I could possibly finish my mission on one lungful of air like some tropical pearl diver.

I'm about four steps up when I hear a noise.

Rustling. Movement.

I pause. My heart sends so much blood through my veins I feel like I might explode.

*No rats. No rats. Please no rats.*

I take another step up.

More rustling.

And a voice.

I freeze. Is that what I heard? Or is my imagination so overheated that I'm having auditory hallucinations? Every fiber of my being is attuned to sounds from above. I stop breathing to listen.

*"Careful."*

One word. Whispered, but distinct.

Not a rat.

Someone else is in here. For a moment I'm scared, but then rage pushes fear aside.

Those freakin' neighbors! Those greedy cannibals are in here trying to score some loot for themselves before the wrecking ball strikes. I grip my phone ready to call for help if I need it and charge up the steps.

At the top, the beam of my flashlight meets the beam of theirs.

A high-pitched scream.

A woman. If it's Bernadette, I swear I'll gouge her beady eyes out.

I step out of her beam and squint into the darkness. A cloud of wavy hair is caught in my flashlight beam.

Phoebe. And behind her stands a man.

George.

# CHAPTER 41

For a moment we are all too bewildered to speak. Then we all start at once. "Why are you—" What is going–" "But wait—" "How did you—" I'm wearing a respirator and the two of them are wearing simple dust masks, so all our words are garbled.

In the midst of the commotion, Phoebe sinks to her knees and begins to sob.

Her shoulders shake as she says something over and over that I can't quite discern.

George rakes his fingers through his hair. "Phoebe, stop!"

Typical guy. When has barking at a hysterical woman ever produced calming results? I crouch down beside her and rub her back. Gradually my ear unscrambles Phoebe's words. "I can't leave her here. I can't leave her here."

I look up at George. "Can't leave who here? What's she taking about?"

"Never mind. Whatever you're here for, get it and go. I'll take care of Phoebe."

Take care of her? I didn't even know these two were friends. "It's not safe for you to be in here with just those dust masks," I warn. "This is where we found the rat's nest."

Mention of the rats makes Phoebe cry even harder. "We have to find her. I can't leave her here. She doesn't deserve this."

"Who is she talking about?"

George's eyes meet mine over our masks. What the hell is going on here? My mind grinds like an ancient adding machine when what I need is a high-end Mac. Now George is looking back over his shoulder at the bedroom that used to be his. The bedroom where—

A queasy dread churns my stomach.

"That bedroom," I whisper. "My dog, she found a bone—"

I can see George evaluating.

"The bone wasn't from a cat, was it?" The horror of this house engulfs me. My God, Sharon is entombed here. Ed was right—she never left. The other Sharons I found on Coughlin's database weren't her.

But I'm still confused. Why is Phoebe the one who's so upset? My hand still rests on her back. "Were you and Sharon close, Phoebe?"

"Gabriella!" Phoebe moans.

Huh?

"Stop saying that name." George's voice is harsh and raw. "It doesn't have a name."

"Don't you call our daughter *it*. Don't you ever call her *it*. She was a beautiful little creature of God, and I won't let them scrape her up and throw her in a landfill."

My eyes search George's for answers. "You and Phoebe had a baby?"

We face each other in the hall. George's gaze darts toward the banister. I edge away. One lunge and he could throw me over to the foyer below.

"We were sophomores in high school." Phoebe's voice is flat. She recites the facts like a kid forced to give an oral report on the chief exports of Uruguay. "Both of our families were falling apart. George and I started spending time together. I got pregnant."

The bare facts release a flood in George. He takes over the story. "Her parents were so caught up in their own drama that they didn't even notice. Phoebe was in denial. I was clueless. One night, she had a terrible stomachache. We came here."

George covers his face. He can't go on.

The opportunity to tell her story seems to bring Phoebe some strength. "My labor was quick. I didn't even know what was happening to me. Sharon was useless. But Harold did what he could. He delivered our daughter. George was there."

"The baby came out all blue," George says. "The cord was wrapped around its...her...neck. Harold tried to get her to breathe, but—"

I feel my eyes opening wider and wider as the two of them speak. "The baby...your baby...is in here?"

Phoebe chokes out sentences between sobs. "This is why I came back to Summit Oaks, why I bought the house next to Harold's. For years, I pushed Gabriella's birth out of my mind. I pretended it never happened and went on with my life. But after Eunice was born—" She shakes her head. "Everything was different. Suddenly I was a mother, a real mother, and I couldn't stop thinking about the baby I lost. I had to come back to her."

I'm so creeped out. I feel like I'm having an out of body experience, looking down on myself and Ethel...commanding her to release the shattered bone crushed between her teeth.

"For the past five years, it's been enough knowing that I was next to her, nearby. My husband knows nothing about what happened when I was fifteen." Phoebe sits cross-legged on the floor, her eyes slightly out of focus. "Everything would have been fine if it hadn't been for Bernadette. I can't let them tear down the house and load it into trucks headed for a landfill. I've been coming in here looking for her. I have to get Gabriella out and give her a decent burial."

While Phoebe talks, George has been pacing in the crowded hallway. "Phoebe and I have families now. I'm a professor, I just got tenure, I'm engaged. I can't let my whole life blow up because of something that happened twenty years ago. Something that could have been resolved if both of us had normal, responsible parents."

Phoebe begins to rock. "It's my fault. I didn't take care of her when she was inside me. I let them take her away from me. All my fault."

"It's not your fault!" George's face is taut with anger. "You're a good mother. If Eunice turned up pregnant would you tell her to give birth at home without a doctor? Would you wrap the dead baby up in one of your seven hundred collectible blankets? Would you tell your crazy brother to squirrel it away in this hell-hole? Would you?"

George whirls to face me. "My mother and Harold are to blame for this. Everything they ever touched turns to poison."

George struggles to get his breathing under control, his voice lowered. "You can see how distraught all this is making Phoebe. We need to find the baby and get the body out of here. Then we'll decide what to do."

Phoebe distraught? It seems to me George is the one coming unglued. I assess my situation: I'm all alone in this toxic house with two desperate, unstable people. Phoebe is smaller than I am, but I've seen her fight ferociously. George might have a weapon, or might not. Either way, he's a thirty-ish man in very good shape. Now is not the time to announce that I'm calling the cops or plead with them to do it. I'd better just humor them until I can make it out of here. After all, poor baby Gabriella is long past needing help.

I try to summon the same calm, soothing voice that Jill uses with Harold. "Right, you do what you need to do, and I'll do what I need to do. I'm going into the master bath here to get the Civil War papers that

Harold has hidden there." I start to explain further, but I can see the two of them couldn't care less about Harold and his needs. Edging backward toward the bathroom, I use my flashlight beam to point to the little tunnel Ethel burrowed into when she found the bone. "If you want my advice, I'd look under there for–"

*Your daughter's bones* doesn't seem like the best way to end that sentence.

George focuses on the phone in my hand, then raises his gaze to meet mine. "You stay right here and keep your light shining on us. Once we find her, we'll all go look for the papers."

Okay, he may be panicked but he's not irrational. So much for Plan B: texting for help once I'm out of their sight. I train my light on the little hollow space in what was once Nora's bedroom and is now the Island of Lost Toys.

George begins to systematically move the toys. Vehicles first: Dump trucks, Matchbox cars, model trains, backhoes. Although I can't see them, I know the dolls are watching from above, glassy-eyed and judgmental.

Dazed and trembling, Phoebe tries to help, but only manages to push a few items out into the hall. She's mesmerized by the slowly enlarging opening. So am I. I really, really don't want to be here for the final reveal, yet I can't look away.

As I train my cellphone flashlight beam on the excavation, it dawns on me that I could text Natalie for help now. In the dim light, I scroll to her number without George noticing. Phoebe is beyond noticing anything. I start to type, but just at that moment George looks straight up at me and I still my fingers. When returns to work, I squint to read what I've managed to type.

XSKL 812

Brilliant. Even if Natalie figures out that means CALL 911, I still have to warn her to not call me back.

And to tell the police not to use sirens. I'll never be able to type all that.

George curses as he lifts a stack of jigsaw puzzles and the bottom drops out, scattering millions of tiny pieces everywhere. He kicks them away in a fury. Phoebe lunges at his foot. "Stop! Be careful. You're getting close."

I fight my instinctive impulse to be helpful and pitch in. The thought of what lies beneath the final layer of toys keeps me pinned to the wall outside the bedroom door.

Finally, George shifts a pile of board games, and the edge of a tattered pink and yellow blanket appears. Phoebe's left hand goes up to her mouth. I draw back, but there's no place further for me to retreat.

Gagging, George pulls it forward out from under the remaining boxes. If there's still a stench of death after twenty years, my respirator is screening it. The blanket is wrapped into an unraveling bundle, the center stained black. George backs away, staring at what remains of his daughter.

Phoebe springs forward and rips the decaying blanket open.

Inside is a skull—so tiny!—and a collection of disjointed bones, some broken and gnawed. Only the head looks human.

"Gabriella." The hysteria is gone from Phoebe's voice. She croons tenderly, soothing her poor lost child.

George staggers away from the grotesque reunion and retches in a corner.

This is my chance. I lower my flashlight beam and neither one notices, so caught up are they in their own pain. Slowly, I edge sideways toward the master bath, keeping one eye on Phoebe and George, and one eye on the narrow path I have to navigate.

I'm fully out of their sight now. I can send the text to Natalie. As I shift the phone in my hands, the flashlight beams into the bathroom.

There is the large manila envelope right where I expected it to be—on the vanity in the memorabilia pile, sandwiched between Civil War books and Civil War art. God bless Harold's compulsion.

I start to text.

"Audrey? Audrey!" George's voice holds a panicky edge.

My fingers fumble across the touchscreen.

"Audrey, ple-e-e-ease." That's Phoebe wailing.

I dart into the bathroom and grab the envelope just as George enters the room. "What are you doing?"

"Finding what I came for." I hold the envelope up. "Let's get out of here."

He grabs my wrist. His face is pale and his hand damp with sweat, but his grasp is powerful enough to drain the strength from my fingers. Even in the darkness, I can see the fear flaming in his eyes. My phone clatters to the floor.

George snatches it up. I watch him check the sent messages. The sent calls.

The three of us consider one another, each trying to determine how far the others will go.

"Why didn't you call for help?" George asks.

*Because I knew you'd check. Because I'm getting pretty good at dealing with crazy people.*

"I don't need help. I just want to get out of this dreadful house. After everything that's happened here, it really does deserve to be torn down." I raise the envelope. "I'm going to use the money from this to help your uncle as best I can. I'm not going to say a word about tonight. There's no one to hold responsible for what happened to the baby. You take her bones."

I have no idea what they intend to do with them, and frankly I don't want to know.

"See, I told you Audrey was a good person," Phoebe says. She tugs on his arm. George doesn't move.

Would he kill me? Surely not. I've done nothing wrong. And he's a philosophy professor, so squeamish he threw up at the sight of the skeleton. Then I think of Ty's prison friend, who killed a man over a coat. What did Ty say? People get ugly when something they worked for is taken away.

"I have a lot to lose too, George." I spread my hands pleading for understanding. "All the negative publicity surrounding this house has been bad for my business. I don't want to be caught up in more controversy. Let's go our separate ways."

A long moment ticks by. Then George nods. I guess he found the appeal to my own self- interest convincing.

George gives me back my phone and leads the way out to the hallway. Phoebe picks up the bundle of bones without hesitation, while George averts his head and holds open a wide canvas tote bag that they had left outside the bedroom door. I put the envelope and my respirator in my backpack. Silently, we walk downstairs.

At the back door, Phoebe touches my arm. "Good-bye, Audrey. Thank you."

I watch through the big bush as Phoebe and George slip back into her dark yard carrying their burden between them.

My phone chirps an alert. It's five minutes to midnight.

I dial Natalie, who answers on the first ring.

"I've got the papers. Everything is fine."

"I've been so worried! You're sure you're all right? You sound shaky."

"I'm just a little...drained. Thanks so much for your help."

"Are you out of that house."

I squeeze from behind the bush covering the utility room door so I can answer truthfully. "I'm on my way home. You can go to bed."

"Good-night, Audrey."

I put the phone in my pocket and step out into the

yard.

Searing pain slashes across my shoulders.

# CHAPTER 42

I'm not sure if I'm awake or asleep.

Or maybe dead.

I touch my eyes. They're open, yet I'm engulfed in blackness.

Something sharp is digging into my back. I move, and bright lightening bolts of pain ricochet through my head.

Good news: I'm alive.

Where am I? Gingerly, I extend my arms and feel around with my fingertips. Underneath me, a smooth floor. Behind me: stacks of boxes. To my right: cans. A familiar, pissy scent fills my nose. Oh, God, I'm back in the house.

How did I get here? And what room is this?

My mind turns and chews like a rusty meat grinder as I try to process fragments of memory into some coherent whole. I drove here...cut through the yard. Why? Oh, right—the envelope. I remember finding it, having it in my hand. Wait, something else happened... The baby! I jolt upright, setting off a Milky Way of stars in my head. But George and Phoebe left. The last memory I have is of them walking away from me into Phoebe's back yard.

Then what?

Pain. Someone hit me from behind. But it couldn't have been George. Who?

That question is entirely too abstract for my current

mental processing ability. I put it aside for more tangible concerns. Where am I in the house?

I slide my hands along the floor. Not wood, linoleum. Linoleum plus cans equals pantry. I'm in the walk-in pantry off the kitchen, a room we haven't cleared. That explains why there's barely room for me to stand up.

But stand I do, pulling myself upright. It's the respirator in my backpack that's been jabbing me. I take off the pack—the envelope is still inside. So I wasn't robbed. Encouraged, I feel for my phone.

Gone.

As my brain clears, my anxiety rises. The pitch black brings back memories of the fire in my father's house months ago, of having my eyes wide open but not being able to see. My throat tightens, my heart races. I take a steadying inhalation. I can breathe. Yes. Unlike in the fire, I can breathe here.

But I mustn't breathe here. Every breath is poison. I fumble to put the respirator on in the dark.

If I'm going to get out, I need to orient myself. I reach my hands out and work my way around the small space until I find the doorknob. I rattle it.

Locked.

I hear every breath that I take, every beat of my heart. I'm trapped in here in the dark house in the middle the night. And something else pops into my mind: Natalie. I remember calling her. Calling her to tell her I was okay. Now no one is looking for me.

Choking back a sob, I shake the doorknob harder. Then I grab a can from the shelf and pound the knob with all the force I can muster.

Nothing.

This whole damn house is ready to fall down. Why is the door so solid, so firmly locked?

My panic builds as I picture the giant claw poised above the house. At dawn it will take its first bite, crushing the house on top of me, scooping me up and hauling me off to the dump with the rest of the debris. Phoebe saved Gabriella from that fate. No one will save me.

I cry out loud in frustration and rage. And I hear my father's disapproving voice, "Crying will get you nowhere," he would say as my tears plopped on the chess board or on a page of equations. "Think."

Right. Think. Things could be worse. I'm not in a bare concrete cell. I'm in Harold's house, and God knows finding something utterly unexpected is always a possibility here.

Like what? A hack saw? A small explosive device?

Whatever, I'll know it when I find it.

By touch.

I grope in the dark for the nearest box and run my fingers over its contents: spoons and whisks and melon-ballers and egg beaters. A greasy-feeling pastry brush. A sieve with a hole in it. A garlic press.

Nothing useful in that box, but kitchen gadgets are a good category. Hope flutters in my chest. A thin knife would probably do the trick. The next box contains cookbooks. Hope dive bombs. If all the rest of the boxes in here contain books, I'm screwed. I struggle to shift the topmost heavy box to get to the next one in the pile. More books.

I kick the bottom box in the pile. It's solid, no rattling from within. I feel tears welling again.

I will die alone, forgotten. No one will miss me. Days will go by before they even notice I'm gone. This is what prisoners of war must feel like knowing that even the most loyal lover will eventually give up and move on. A sob shakes me. I don't even have that hope. My lover has already moved on.

*You shoved him out.*

Well, he recovered pretty quickly, didn't he? I tell that nagging voice. I think of that tall brunette in Whole Foods. And the clammy hands of the many jerks I've dated on my arm. I think of the flawed family I've got—just Dad and me staying afloat by clinging to the same little hunk of driftwood. And I think of the family I walked away from—the Coughlins—to preserve my own sanity. And Ty, and Jill—I tried to protect them and only brought them harm.

Oh, God, how did it all go so wrong? I sink to my knees and cry for everything I've found and everything I've lost.

My head throbs.

Snot is smeared across my face.

My eyelids scrape open. No tears remain.

Now that the fit of hysteria has passed, I actually feel a little better. Dad may think crying solves nothing, but Maura always says crying releases endorphins, and I think those natural high chemicals are stimulating my brain. I can pop this lock. After all, it's simply an old interior door with a push-in lock. I could jimmy it with a credit card. Except my purse is locked in my car. And I was traveling light with my backpack—respirator, keys and the envelope. There's got to be something in this pantry that would work as well. It's just a matter of finding it.

I think of the many kitchen items I've sold Harold over the years. There have to be more boxes of knives and tools in here somewhere. I grope on the shelves looking for a break in the cans. My hand sinks into something soft and powdery: flour or cornstarch. Something moves beneath my fingertips: pantry moth larvae. I sneeze and keep searching.

Finally I find another box that rattles with promise. Eagerly, I sink my hands in and immediately scream.

It's full of knives all right—sharp ones.

Gingerly, I select one and test its thickness. Too big. I set it aside and find another. This feels like a boning knife. It might work. I go to work sliding the knife up to the lock mechanism and trying to press it back. On TV, this works like a charm. In real life, not so much.

The knife is too stiff.

Despite the fact that the heat has been turned off, I'm sweating. This has to work! I give the knife a sharp thrust.

The tip breaks off. I fling the knife down with a scream of frustration.

I return to the box, trying to touch handles, not blades. I feel plastic connected to metal. The item feels light. I touch it carefully. Not sharp. I run my fingers over it. A long, thin, flexible spatula. My grandma used one of these to frost my birthday cake every year.

I hear something, and hold my breath to listen.

A rumble. They're warming up the heavy equipment. Morning–I must have been passed out for hours.

I run the cake spatula up to the lock and bend it. It slips up higher than the knife did. I wiggle it further, turn the knob as I press the tongue back. A little further...

The knob turns. I've unlocked it.

I'm free! Not.

Something heavy blocks the door.

For the first time in my math-nerd life, I understand the term "adrenaline rush." I rear back and hurl my body at the door. It opens another inch.

A few more body slams and I'm out.

The roar of heavy equipment is much louder now. The back hall is still pitch black, but I know which way the kitchen is. I trip forward, stumbling over the mini-fridge my captor pushed in front of the pantry door. Once I round the corner, the dim glimmer of dawn seeps in through the grimy window over the kitchen sink. All the other windows are blocked. I need to let them know I'm in here. I run to the open window, and hear shouting, but my frantic brain can only pick out a few words. "Back it up." "No." "Stand aside." The window faces Bernadette's house, not the backyard. I can only detect shadowy movements through the grime.

I scream. "Help! I'm in here!"

The men continue directing the roaring heavy equipment. Pointless.

An ancient Osterizer sits on the counter. I pick it up and throw it through the window. Glass shatters everywhere.

For a long moment, the voices outside stop.

"What the hell...?" I hear from the back yard.

Now the backhoe won't start digging. I turn and run to the utility room door. I slip out from behind the bush.

Before me in the gray light of the January morning I see a huge crowd of people: the neighbors lined up outside the orange security fence, waiting for the show to begin; the cops, enforcing order; ten or twelve guys in hardhats, ready to run the machines.

And a thin man with gray hair sitting in the mud in front of the backhoe.

# CHAPTER 43

"Dad!"

I run to him, heart exploding.

He catches me in his arms and we cling to each other.

"I was so scared," I whisper. "I thought I would die all alone."

"I knew something was wrong when you didn't answer your phone. Natalie told me you came here last night. I was determined not to let them start the demo until I figured out where you were."

The cop in charge and the hardhat in charge are striding toward us. I look over my father's shoulder and see Phoebe's stricken face framed by the fluttery curtains of her family- room French door.

A possible concussion earns me a brief reprieve on interrogation. Dad refuses to leave my side at the hospital as the doctors come in and out, checking my head, my eyes, my lungs. The interminable nature of health care offers us plenty of time to review the facts. In the privacy of my exam room, I confide George and Phoebe's secret to my father.

"But you're sure it couldn't have been either of them who hit you?"

"Definitely. I was watching them walk away from me when I got whacked from behind."

"So the attacker came from the direction of

Bernadette's house?"

"Yes, but for the life of me, I can't imagine why she'd want to hurt me now. After all, she's finally getting her dream: Harold's house was coming down. She'd be able to sell her place for a good price and finally move. All of the neighbors should be thrilled, even Walter Marchand, who hired the busboy to threaten me."

Dad's eyes narrow. "Did you confront that man?"

"I went to talk to him, but he wasn't home."

Dad contemplates this with his eyes half-closed. "None of the neighbors has a good reason to hurt you now that the house was scheduled for demolition. George and Phoebe have a stronger motive. They could have an accomplice. While you were collecting the papers in the master bath, George could have called for back-up."

"Possible. But both of them were keeping the baby a secret from their spouses. Even Nora didn't know about it. That's why she and George were arguing about the house. Harold is the only other person alive who knew, and he's in jail. So who–"

A nurse comes in to draw some blood and we fall silent. Once she's safely gone, I twist around on the hard examining table and pull the flimsy gown around me in a futile bid for warmth and modesty. "I'm worried about Phoebe, Dad. I saw her looking at me during the rescue. She's terrified that I'll give up her secret. I don't know how to protect her. Do you think I can—"

Dad jumps out of his chair. "No!" He points a finger at me. "Don't you even think of lying to the police about what happened."

I feel my body freeze. There's the old Dad I know so well. Disapproving. Authoritarian.

Before I can speak, he shoves the offending finger in his pocket. "I'm sorry. I didn't mean to sound like that. I'm simply concerned for your safety."

He's right, of course. I can't go through life looking

over my shoulder, wondering if someone is out to get me. Still, ratting out Phoebe feels like drowning a kitten. She's so vulnerable, yet so fierce in her love for her kids. What if they accuse her of harming the baby because she didn't seek medical help? How can prosecuting her for a twenty-year-old mistake possibly be in anyone's best interests?

My father is watching me so intently he can practically see the flow of thoughts through my mind. "Phoebe and George won't go to jail for this, Audrey. They were children when it happened. They've led exemplary lives since. And I doubt the police can prove exactly how the baby died. Phoebe and George may not realize it at first, but everything that happened last night may be for the best."

Dad steps closer and puts his hands on my shoulders. "Keeping secrets is dangerous, Audrey. Surely we've both learned that."

The police arrive after I'm cleared to get dressed and eat a meager dinner from the hospital cafeteria. All day I've been dreading the possibility of answering questions from Coughlin, but when the police enter, he is not in the group. Of course, everyone is aware we've been involved. I should have known they'd hand off my case to other cops.

I'm relieved.

Or am I disappointed?

Dad has no choice but to leave, so I'm left with two cops: one young, muscular, and buzz-cut; the other middle-aged, paunchy, and shaggy. I immediately dub them Bad Cop and Good Cop, which drives their real names right out of my head.

Bad Cop starts off, puffing out his chest and droning a long series of questions to establish the basic timeline of last night's events. Good Cop appears barely to be listening as he occasionally makes some squiggles on a dog-eared notepad. When I get to the part about Phoebe and George and the baby, Bad Cop finally registers some emotion. His eyes widen at the mention of the tiny skeleton. Good Cop writes a little faster.

Then Good Cop leans forward. In that one motion, the whole tone of the interview changes. Bad Cop retreats to the note-taker role. Good Cop leads me through the encounter with Phoebe and George. Over and over he asks questions with just a shade of difference in meaning. I notice the shrewdness in his heavy-lidded eyes.

On my third description of my blow to the head, I pause and blurt, "Do you share an office with Sean Coughlin?"

"Yes. Why do you ask?"

I feel myself flushing. "Just curious."

He doesn't smile—nothing that obvious—yet his expression changes. Maybe he's amused by Sean's and my drama. Or maybe he's thinking *Sean is better off without this one.*

"Curiosity seems to run deep in you, Ms. Nealon. So tell me—do you have any idea who could have hit you and locked you in that house?"

I shake my head. Geez, that hurts! I'm right back to where I left off with my father. "I know Phoebe and George seem to have the only motive. But I don't think it was them. They were both so horrified by baby Gabriella's death. I don't think either one of them is capable of hurting me. More than that—they're not capable of letting that house claim another life."

Bad Cop snorts.

Good Cop listens. "What if Phoebe and George didn't knowingly call an accomplice? Could there be someone else with a vested interest in keeping the baby's death a secret? Someone watching the house?"

"Sharon, George and Nora's mother. But no one has heard from her in years. Harold is in custody. Phoebe's parents never knew she was pregnant. They were so preoccupied with their own troub—"

"What?"

Random facts are clicking into place. I'm afraid if I speak too soon, I'll disturb them. Good Cop waits.

"Someone had to be watching Phoebe's kids last night. Her husband is away on business. She would never have left them alone in the house."

"She waited until they were asleep and sneaked next door," Bad Cop says.

"No, she wouldn't have done that. Her parents used to leave her alone at night. Her dad was having an affair. Her mom drank at parties at the neighbors' houses. Phoebe remembers waking up alone and terrified. No, someone was with the kids last night."

"And you think the babysitter attacked you?" Bad Cop can't keep the scorn out of his voice.

"Not some random teenage sitter..." Can I risk thinking aloud? What if I'm totally off-base?

Good Cop is watching me closely. I think he suspects what I'm going to say, but he would never put words in my mouth. I think of the afternoon I visited Phoebe at her house. Grandpa was taking Eunice to her tennis lesson. Grandma was staying with the other two while Phoebe went out. Clearly, they were regular babysitters. With a sinking heart, I remember something else. I glance up. Good Cop's weary brown eyes have magnetic power.

"The grandparents are regular babysitters," I stammer. "When I met them recently, Phoebe and her daughter were scolding Grandpa for smoking cigars." I pause. "I smelled cigar smoke last night when I was sneaking through Harold's yard."

"You never mentioned that before," Bad Cop snaps.

"It didn't seem significant. I heard a dog barking too, but I didn't mention that either."

"Tell us everything. We'll decide what's important." Good Cop's tone is mild. I sit up straighter. I bet he's the kind of dad who never raises his voice but has very

S. W. HUBBARD

well behaved kids.

"You say you met Phoebe's parents," he continues. "Tell us about that."

"They seemed like the typical doting grandparents. Although they are an odd match."

Phoebe's parents loom in my mind's eye. The mom— plump, dowdy, down on her knees playing with the two younger kids, her flyaway gray hair tucked behind her ears, her plain, round face crinkled with delight at the kids' antics. And the dad—trim, handsome, dressed in his immaculate sweater and slacks, archly amused as he waited to take Eunice to her lesson. His whole body was tanned except for the glaring white scar on his hand. I'm positive now that he was the dog-walking man who asked me about our work on the house when we first began even though he later denied it. His wife called him Chip. That's a nickname. He must have a real name, maybe one he doesn't like.

Could it be Walter?

I glance up to see Good Cop's expectant eyes, unblinking in their patience. "Phoebe grew up in Summit Oaks. Her parents still live a few streets away. One of the other neighbors told me some gossip about them from years ago." So I tell them all I know about the affair, the knife attack, the way the parents' misery made them oblivious to Phoebe's pregnancy. I tell them about Estrella and how she hooked up a man in the neighborhood named Walter Marchand with a guy willing to do some dirty work.

Bad Cop frowns. "I think we established that there's no basis for your claim that Juan Ramirez threatened you."

And Dad wonders why I didn't take the information on Walter to the cops. "You can check and see what Phoebe's maiden name is."

Good Cop says, "Sounds like the grandmother is the violent, unstable one."

I direct my attention to Good Cop. "I get the

impression that the affair unhinged her at the time. Now she seems like a sweet, fun grandma—the kind who doesn't care if the kids spill glitter or eat cookies on the couch."

I hesitate.

"You said they seemed like an odd match," Good Cop prompts.

"Look, I could be totally off-base here, but Phoebe's father is not only quite handsome, but also very fashionable. And her mom, well she strikes me as the kind of woman who was never particularly concerned about her appearance. She's plump and plain now and I bet she always has been."

"So that's why he had the other woman," Bad Cop says.

Good Cop's brow is furrowed. "Thirty years ago, why would a very attractive man marry a very plain woman? What would make a gentle woman so crazed she'd stab her husband?"

Our eyes meet. "There wasn't another woman," I whisper. "There was another man."

# CHAPTER 44

*I'm right outside your door. Don't freak out when I knock.*

I set down my phone and nudge Ethel snoozing peacefully at my feet. "Hello? Isn't it your job to alert me to the presence of strangers at the door?"

She raises her head and sniffs, then yawns and closes her eyes again. *That's no stranger, that's Sean.*

Briefly, I consider pretending I'm not home. But that's ridiculous. We can't go on ignoring each other like two middle-schoolers in a snit. I head to the front door, pausing for a moment before the mirror in the foyer. I fluff up my bangs.

What the hell's wrong with me?

I yank open the door in mid-knock. Sean practically falls into my condo.

"I came by to tell you what's happening. You may have reporters calling you tomorrow. I figured you'd need a heads-up."

"Thanks."

We stare at each other. My heart is pounding, and I suspect he knows that. I check his jaw. The little muscle is twitching. Then I remember my manners. "Come in. You want a cup of coffee?"

"Not at ten-thirty."

"Oh, right. Well, wine then?"

He takes a deep breath to prepare for a speech. Changes his mind. "Sure. Wine."

I pour us each a glass while Ethel slobbers over him as if he were a giant Milk Bone. Her ability to remain aloof is notably underdeveloped.

I set the glasses down on the coffee table. We do not toast.

"Pete Holzer took the information you provided and interviewed Phoebe Castelton's parents, Jean and Walter Marchand."

"Separately?"

"Of course. At first the father was adamant that he never went outside. Didn't know where Phoebe went. Didn't see or hear a thing. But the old lady reported that he went outside to smoke. From that point on, it was simply a matter of playing the two of them off against each other. The old lady got so pissed reliving the gay boyfriend business, she really went after her husband."

"So it really was Phoebe's dad who tried to kill me? He confessed?"

Sean nods. "If he'd kept his mouth shut and got a lawyer like the guy you got for Griggs, we might not have had enough evidence to bring charges. Of course, the fact that he hired a thug to go after you was pretty incriminating. But guys like Walter always think they're smart enough to outwit Holzer. They're wrong."

"I liked him."

"He liked you."

I take a gulp of wine and look away. "Did Phoebe's parents know about the baby at the time of the birth, or not?"

"The mother never knew. All those years ago when she suspected her husband was having an affair, she started drinking. When she discovered he was cheating on her with a guy, she actually had a psychotic break. She totally overlooked the changes in her daughter. The father noticed, but he was in denial, just like Phoebe. Then one day he saw the baby bump was gone. Even he couldn't deny that. He talked to

Sharon. She told him where the baby's body was. He decided the patch things up with his wife. Keep his sins and his daughter's quiet."

So they all decided to live a lie for the next twenty years. Because what would the neighbors say if they found out Walter Marchand was gay and his wife committed assault and his daughter gave birth to a baby at fifteen and the baby's other grandmother buried it in her house? What else could they do but lie? Until last night.

"He was waiting for me when I came out of the house. How did he know what Phoebe and George were up to?"

"Apparently he overheard Phoebe on the phone planning with George. He was watching their progress from Phoebe's back porch. When he saw you go into the house after they were in there, he grabbed his grandson's baseball bat and waited. When he realized you knew about the baby, he took action. He's not as trusting as his daughter."

I rub my head. "He hit me with a baseball bat?"

"Little League size. You're lucky the kid just graduated from T-ball."

"He didn't have to hit me. I would have kept Phoebe's secret."

"I'm sure you would have." Sean takes a sip of wine and his eyes meet mine over the rim of the glass. "Unfortunately, Mr. Marchand doesn't know you as well as I do."

"You think that's wrong?" My voice goes up a decibel. "Phoebe and George were victims. They needed guidance and the adults in their lives who should've given it to them were totally AWOL."

"Relax, crusader. I don't think Phoebe's a murderer."

"What will happen to them, Sean?" My voice drops to a murmur. "I feel terrible that I had to give up Phoebe's secret."

He reaches out a comforting hand then lets it drop. "Honestly, when I saw Phoebe, she seemed sort of relieved it was all out in the open. The medical examiner has to do an autopsy on what's left of the skeleton. I don't think he'll find much. As long as there's no overt sign of foul play, I doubt they'll try to prosecute. Clearly the adults were more at fault, and Harold isn't competent to stand trial."

"What about the house?"

"We had to search it again to make sure there were no more lunatic women stuck inside. There are four patrolmen stationed outside overnight. The demo starts tomorrow at dawn."

"Jill was so sure that Harold needed the house to get better. But now that we know what happened there, I've gotta believe Harold will be better off somewhere else. Good riddance."

"How is Jill feeling?"

"Better. The fever broke. Her lungs are clearing."

We sit quietly for a moment. Then something else dawns on me. "You said Walter Marchand needed a lawyer like Emil Swenson. Did he actually do a good job negotiating for Ty?"

Sean grimaces. "Griggs sat there silent as a stone. Swenson did all the talking. We needed the information, so we had to cut a deal. What he gave us was good. We arrested Horacio's killer."

"What about Ramon? Are you still looking for him?"

He shakes his head. "The DA thinks we have enough evidence against this scumbag coyote as long as you and Ty are willing to testify."

Sean knocks back the last of his wine in one gulp and stands. "So, as of January 24, no one's trying to kill you. Try to keep it that way for a few months, eh?"

"I'll try. Thanks for coming by with the news."

Sean makes no move to leave. The silence is deafening. Ethel begins to whine.

"Look, Audrey, there's one more thing I have to say

and then I'll go and I won't bother you again. I know you saw me in Whole Foods. That woman, we're just old friends."

"She didn't look—" Then I catch myself. That was a trap. "You're free to go shopping with whomever you please, Sean. It's no concern of mine."

A little smile twitches the corner of his mouth. "You were going to say 'She didn't look like a friend to me.' You're jealous."

"I am not. I simply thought it would be awkward to encounter you with a woman you were clearly trying to seduce, so I left."

"I wasn't trying to seduce her."

"Perhaps you had already succeeded. You seemed to be planning a long evening together."

Now why did I say that? Why am I so determined to prove him a liar when one-upping him like this only gives him reason to hope I care?

"So how come you didn't just say hi instead of spying on me from behind the organic quinoa?"

I feel my face burning. "I wasn't spying. I simply didn't want to intrude on a tender moment. But I assure you, next time I bump into you two, I'll ask for an introduction."

"All right, what can I say? Liza is sort of a friend with benefits. I met her at the gym. Kickboxing."

Figures.

"But I was hurt, Audrey. Drowning my sorrows."

"Hmph—nice for her."

"It was mutual. She's getting over someone too."

"Perfect." I feel my eyes well with tears. "Marry her. Have babies with her."

He grabs my arm. "I don't want Liza. She's hard, inside and out. I want you. When I saw Walter Marchand in the police station I wanted to pound his face to a pulp. If you had died in that house—" He shudders. His grip on my arm turns into a caress. "Holzer told me how you got out. Always resourceful."

He kisses the top of my head.

I let him.

"I thought about you when I was trapped in there, Sean." I speak looking down at my cats-chasing-dogs socks. "I thought about how much I regretted hurting you. But then I remembered that other woman and I figured you couldn't have cared that much if you were dating again. And then I thought about how I've always fantasized about having a perfect family, but every time I find one that I think is perfect, it turns out to be crazy, or damaged, or evil."

I lift my head up. "And then I cried hysterically over how everything I wanted to make right turned out wrong."

He pulls me into his arms. "All families are crazy, Audrey. They're crazy with love, and wherever there's a lot of love, there's the possibility of pain. Your family's no better or worse than anyone else's."

I burrow my head against his chest until I hear it. Thump. Thump. Thump. "I'm not as brave as you, Sean," I whisper.

He tilts my head back, forcing me to meet his eye. "Untrue, Audrey. You're the bravest woman I know."

My arms slide under his shirt and I topple him onto the sofa.

Ethel leaps, narrowly escaping with her life.

As I disappear into Sean's embrace, I see Ethel head towards my bedroom. Then she stops, looks over her shoulder, and changes direction.

Good choice, Ethel. Doggy bed in the laundry room is your best bet for a peaceful night's sleep tonight.

# EPILOGUE

"I love, love, love, LOVE weddings!" Jill twirls around Ty.

"You love 'em so much, how come you're not dressed better?" Ty straightens his tie and squares his shoulders in his new charcoal suit.

Jill's dress, an odd shade of lavender with multiple tiers and ties and one missing sleeve, must have required an instruction manual to get into. "I bought this especially for the occasion," she protests. "What's wrong—"

"Nuthin', nuthin'," Ty quickly backtracks. Ever since Jill announced that she is leaving us to go to NYU to get her degree in clinical social work, the two of them have been treating each other with unusual tenderness. It's as if Jill is going off to do her patriotic duty while Ty bravely keeps the home fires burning.

My eyes get misty thinking about how our lives are about to change. Jill cried so hard trying to tell me she needed to quit, I thought someone near and dear must have an inoperable brain tumor. But I know she's found her true calling working with the mentally ill. And Ty, as much as he'll miss her, is excited to be taking over part of her job and enrolling for classes at Palmer County College. He'll be second-in-command at Another Man's Treasure, and he can boss around our new part-timer, Adrienne. I could sell tickets to that bout.

"You both look fabulous." I herd them along, too nervous to care what anyone looks like, even myself. For weeks I've been alternating between escalating happiness and crushing fear.

Can something this good actually be pulled off?

Then I see the groom.

He, too, wears a snazzy new suit, his face suffused with joy. The ceremony is scheduled to start in ten minutes. Nothing can go wrong now.

I slide into place beside him. "You look lovely," he says, squeezing my hand.

"Thanks. It's not every day a girl gets to be best woman at her father's wedding."

As I wait for the bride to make her entrance, I look out at the assembled crowd sitting in delicate silver chairs on the lawn at the Old Mill Inn. Natalie's side is crammed with guests. Dad's is a little sparser: in one row, Jill and her mom, Ty, Grandma Betty, Maura; behind them, a few colleagues from Dad's teaching days at Rutgers; in the third row Sean sits with Brendan and Adrienne. He gives me a big grin and a thumbs-up. Ethel lies beside him, her leash wrapped firmly around his powerful forearm. Occasionally, she lifts her rear paw in a futile effort to scratch off the humiliating pink bow Jill has tied around her neck.

In the back row sits Nora. We've all grown closer to her in the six months since the house came down. The first few months were rocky. The assault charges against Harold were eventually dropped, but his stint in jail undermined his fragile grip on reality. He endured a period of homelessness, roaming the streets on his bike and sleeping in the cemetery or on the porch of the library. Finally, after weeks of tireless badgering and pleading, Jill managed to find Harold a spot in Palmer County's only supportive housing community for the mentally ill. Regular therapy and a low dose of meds to control his OCD have made a big difference. He still collects, but he only brings back things other residents in his group home can use. Still, the possibility of backsliding always exists. Nora will never be totally free of worry for her uncle.

This is my tribe.

Pastor Jorge enters stage left. He nods to the trumpeter, who begins playing Stanley's Trumpet Voluntary. Natalie appears at the doorway of the Inn, her hand resting lightly on her son's arm.

She glides serenely down the aisle, her cream lace dress fluttering in the late summer breeze, each step bringing her face into sharper focus. Such peace, such confidence! She knows she's making the right decision. I steal a glance at Dad. Same there. No doubts.

I move my left hand behind my back. The ring on my finger slips and slides, the weight of the diamond still unfamiliar to me. It's only resided there for two weeks.

The bride arrives.

She and Dad step together and clasp hands. Pastor Jorge begins the vows, his lilting voice covering familiar terrain. "Do you, Natalie...."

When Natalie says, "I do," her voice is firm but low. Only Dad, Jorge and I can hear.

Then the pastor turns to Dad. "Do you, Roger..." When he gets to, "for all the days of your lives," Dad's "I do" is so loud it startles a little flock of goldfinches in the garden. A ripple of laughter passes through the crowd.

Dad and Natalie kiss. I look away.

My gaze locks with Sean's.

He raises his eyebrows. *Are you ready?*

My lips move silently.

*Yes.*

THE END

# READ THESE OTHER EXCITING MYSTERIES BY S.W. HUBBARD

Another Man's Treasure

Dead Drift

Take the Bait

Swallow the Hook

Blood Knot

*All Available at Amazon.com*

# ABOUT THE AUTHOR

S.W. Hubbard is the author of the Audrey Nealon estate sale mysteries, *Another Man's Treasure* and *Treasure of Darkness*. She is also is the author of three Police Chief Frank Bennett mystery novels set in the Adirondack Mountains: *Take the Bait, Swallow the Hook,* and *Blood Knot,* as well as a short story collection featuring Frank Bennett, *Dead Drift.* Her short stories have appeared in *Alfred Hitchcock's Mystery Magazine* and the anthologies *Crimes by Moonlight, The Mystery Box,* and *Adirondack Mysteries.* She lives in Morristown, NJ, where she teaches creative writing to enthusiastic teens and adults, and expository writing to reluctant college freshmen. To contact her or read the first chapter of any of her books, visit: **http://www.swhubbard.net**. Follow her on Twitter @swhubbardauthor or like her Facebook author page, SW Hubbard author. Look for S.W. Hubbard on Pinterest and Goodreads too.

Printed in Great Britain
by Amazon

44444371R00194